PEARL HARBOR

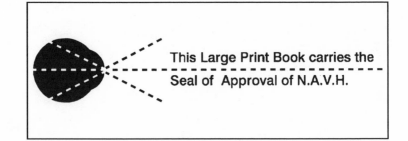

This Large Print Book carries the
Seal of Approval of N.A.V.H.

THE PACIFIC WAR SERIES: BOOK 1

PEARL HARBOR

A NOVEL OF DECEMBER 8TH

NEWT GINGRICH, WILLIAM R. FORSTCHEN, AND ALBERT S. HANSER, CONTRIBUTING EDITOR

THORNDIKE PRESS

An imprint of Thomson Gale, a part of The Thomson Corporation

THOMSON

™

GALE

Detroit • New York • San Francisco • New Haven, Conn. • Waterville, Maine • London

THOMSON
★ ™
GALE

LIBRARY OF CONGRESS CATALOGING-IN-PUBLICATION DATA

Gingrich, Newt.
  Pearl Harbor : a novel of December 8th. Book one, The Pacific War series / by Newt Gingrich and William R. Forstchen, and Albert S. Hansen, contributing editor.
    p. cm. — (Thorndike press large print basic)
  ISBN-13: 978-0-7862-9719-1 (hardcover : alk. paper)
  ISBN-10: 0-7862-9719-0 (hardcover : alk. paper)
  1. Pearl Harbor (Hawaii), Attack on, 1941 — Fiction. 2. World War, 1939–1945 — Hawaii — Fiction. 3. Large type books. I. Forstchen, William R. II. Hansen, Albert S. III. Title.
PS3557.I4945P43 2007b
813'.54—dc22   2007015441

Published in 2007 by arrangement with St. Martin's Press, LLC.

Printed in the United States of America on permanent paper
10 9 8 7 6 5 4 3 2 1

To those who gave the last full measure of devotion in the Pacific War, and, as well, to the often forgotten victims of all such wars . . . the parents, spouses, and children who gave so much when their loved ones fell, and for whom final victory would always be shadowed by profound loss.

ACKNOWLEDGMENTS

Acknowledgments for a book such as this can be a bit of a daunting task . . . because so many people were involved in helping to bring this story to life.

After the successful completion of our "Active History" series set around the Battle of Gettysburg, it was our editor, Pete Wolverton, who urged us to consider a story about Pearl Harbor. We dug into the research and found a plethora of works on the American perspective, but very few that took an in-depth and balanced look at the Japanese perspective that led them to the fateful decision to seek war at what they knew would be daunting odds. In particular, we must point out the historian John Toland's efforts, not only for his superb writing style and research, but also for his highly accurate footnoting that led us to dozens of additional sources for our own research. From that research our thesis about what might have happened at Pearl Harbor emerged and thus our subtitle of *A Novel of December 8th,* since but one change in the Japanese plans could have wrought a profoundly different outcome.

Early in 2006, Bill spent a week in Hawaii and we wish to extend our compliments to the incredible staff at the USS *Arizona* Memorial and the Battleship *Missouri* Memorial museum. Bill received a special opportunity, which anybody can request, for a detailed tour of the *Missouri* that provided tremendous insights for our work, particularly what it must have been like aboard the USS *Oklahoma* during its final terrible moments. Ironically the *Missouri* is moored where the *Oklahoma* met its end. Bill also had an opportunity to fly around Pearl Harbor in a World War II vintage aircraft to gain a better perspective from the Japanese side of the battle, and his own piloting experiences have come into play as well since he owns an original plane from the period. If ever you should go to Hawaii, plan at least a day to visit the "hallowed ground and sea" of Pearl Harbor and the profoundly moving National Military Cemetery located in the "Punch Bowl," and if possible, try to take an air tour as well to see it from "the other side."

A special thanks and salute to the men and women of CVN 71, USS *Theodore Roosevelt,* and a special thanks to the head engineer of that proud carrier, Commander Larry Scruggs, who provided a top-to-bottom tour of "his" carrier while operations were under way off the North Carolina coast, explaining the intricacies of damage control, relating how it is done now to how it was done in 1941. Though the technology has changed, the methods and procedures to "keep 'em flying" at sea is not much different now than in 1941. If any should doubt the ability and intellect of the young men and women who stand on the forward line of our defense, spend a day on the "T.R." and you will come away profoundly moved by their spirit, maturity, discipline, and patriotism. They are indeed worthy descendants of the "greatest generation."

Numerous others should be mentioned here as well. Our researcher for work at the Naval Historical Center, Batchimeg Sambalaibat, who did a superb job digging up obscure facts and photo research; Liz Dwyer, the computer genius who repaired a major formatting glitch in our "final" manuscript; the staff of the Patriots Point Naval & Maritime Museum in Charleston, South Carolina, where the USS *Yorktown* can be toured; Bill Butterworth IV for many a late-night conversation; and so many friends who took a special interest in this project and encouraged us to move forward.

We've been blessed with a great team at Thomas Dunne Books. We'd like to thank our editor, Pete Wolverton, whose editorial instincts were on the mark. Pete is blessed as well by an incredible assistant, Kathleen Gilligan, who is a joy to work with. We'd also like to thank what Bill and I call our "home team" of Kathy Lubbers, our wonderful agent, and advisors like Scott Cotter, Randy Evans, Joe DeSantis, and Stefan Passantino, who were invaluable with the creation of this work.

Also we extend our thanks to Callista Gingrich for her unflagging love and support in all things, Jackie Sue, Jimmy, Maggie, Robert, and Paul for their support as well, and Meghan Forstchen, who endured without complaint the long disappearances of her dad to his office. Thanks as well to Christine Inauen and Ron "Weasel" Weisbrook, who provided some excellent technical review points regarding World War II aviation.

Unlike our novels about the Civil War, some of our readers will indeed remember that "date which will live in infamy," and some were present on Oahu on that day. We hope our work does justice to the experience you endured and pays proper respect as well. Some historians now claim that the famed statement, attributed to Admiral Yamamoto, that the attack of December 7th had "awakened the sleeping giant" was actually not said by him. Regardless of who said it, it was indeed true. When faced with a crisis, America can indeed stand united, and for potential enemies to assume otherwise is folly. As we found in our research, the war in the Pacific could have been avoided if wiser heads had prevailed . . . but they did not and a terrible price was paid by both sides. Let us ensure that all the lessons from that day will always be remembered. For Bill and me, the connections between 1941 and today are clearly evident.

TECHNICAL NOTE

It has become standard practice in Western accounts of the Pacific War to reverse the usage of Japanese names from family name followed by given name, to the Western usage of given name and then family name. On a cultural level we found this to be an interesting point and yet again, a nuance of the cultural differences between Japanese and Western society. We hope that the continuation of the Western practice in this book is understood by all as a means of providing a clearer narrative for all readers.

In addition, the Japanese names for military ranks and also for equipment, especially airplanes, would create a most difficult hurdle except for the truly serious students of this conflict. Therefore we have adopted the Western equivalents for all ranks both military and political. One usage that is slightly off from the "time line" of history is the Western naming of Japanese military aircraft, the Zero/Zeke, Val, and Kate. All three of these aircraft, though already in use in China, came as a complete surprise to Western forces in the Pacific. It was not until 1942 that a standardized code name was given to different Japanese planes. For the sake of clarity and narrative flow we felt it acceptable to use these 1942 code names for aircraft in our narrative as, indeed, do nearly all historical accounts of that battle.

Spelling of Oriental place-names has always proven to be a difficult affair. In general, however, we opted to use the 1941 spellings, such as Nanking and Peking, rather than the currently accepted Nanjing and Beijing.

Honorific titles and the subtle nuances of the Japanese language, for example the difference in methods of address when an inferior and superior or a father and his son are talking to each other, tends to fail in translation, therefore in dialogue between our characters, a somewhat more Western style of twentieth-century speech is used as well.

We hope you go along with our "tweaking" of history and cultural differences for the sake of clarity in our story in order to bring a clearer picture of the Japanese perspective on events leading up to December 8, 1941.

The forward magazine of USS Shaw (DD-373) explodes during the second Japanese attack wave. To the left of the explosion, Shaw's stern is visible, at the end of floating dry dock YFD-2. At right is the bow of USS Nevada (BB-36), with a tug alongside fighting fires. Photographed from Ford Island, with a dredging line in the foreground. **Naval Historical Center**

Prologue

8 December 1941
Midnight Tokyo Time

The clock was ticking.

Admiral Isoroku Yamamoto looked up at the large, brass-mounted, nautical clock that hung on the bulkhead before him. All was silent, except for that clock, and the background noises of a ship laboring through heavy seas.

His staff stood respectfully, no one stirring, no one seated except the architect of this day, this day that all knew would be the most fateful in the history of their people, their race, their island nation, and their sacred Emperor.

Yamamoto took another cigarette from the silver case laid on the table by his side and reaching into his pocket pulled out a lighter, an American lighter, lit the cigarette, and then looked back at the clock.

It ticked through another minute to midnight, Tokyo time, 8 December 1941.

"It has begun," Yamamoto, the most successful noted gambler in the Japanese navy, whispered to himself.

On the Malayan Coast
8 December 1941
12:03 a.m. Local Time

Captain Cecil Stanford, eyes red-rimmed with exhaustion, lowered the heavy Zeiss night binoculars. The night was sticky, hot, and he rubbed the sweat from his face with a soiled handkerchief.

Though technically a captain of the Royal Navy, his duties leading to this night had led him far from the deck of any ship . . . he had been a teacher at a foreign naval academy, an alleged reporter, intelligence agent, advisor to a prime minister, and now, this night, an observer whom few had listened to and who had motored north over treacherous jungle roads the length of this peninsula colony.

His driver, Marine Sergeant Harris, leaned against the fender of their old Bentley sedan, sipping his tea, which was well fortified from Cecil's flask, and with cupped hands nursed a cigarette.

The only sound was that of tropical waves,

gently lapping onto a tropical beach. If his mind had been of a different cast, it would have perhaps stirred a fantasy of romance, but he had stilled his heart to that. There had been only one real love, and both she and their child were gone.

To the north several miles away a small port town, close on to the border with Thailand, glowed, the last of the cafés closing for the night, the town quiet. Everyone was asleep, or soon would be, or at least planned to be.

A flicker of light disturbed him, and he looked over his shoulder. Harris was lighting another cigarette, trying unsuccessfully to keep light discipline, hands cupped around the Zippo, but still it was almost blinding.

"How the hell did you survive the trenches at Gallipoli?" Cecil grumbled.

Harris grinned, took a second cigarette and lit it off the end of the first, handing it to Cecil.

"Now, sir. If I thought Johnnie Turk was out there and m' head was sticking above a trench, that would be a different story now, wouldn't it?"

And at that instant the world turned to brilliant daylight.

In that frozen instant he could see Har-

18

ris's face, eyes wide, then squinting, looking up in amazement. There was a flash thought of almost comic quality to it, as if Harris might think that somehow his small Zippo had suddenly illuminated the world.

Cecil turned, looked over his shoulder. The brilliant flashes just as quickly winked out.

"Bloody hell" was all Harris could get out when again the brilliant light appeared. Half a dozen star shells, high above the port town, the lurid light from the burning magnesium flares, even from several miles away, cast long shadows across the beach. Harris stood out in stark relief by his side and then long seconds later the distant, echoing boom of the guns that had fired them, several miles out to sea.

Then more flashes, dozens of them, flickering, bursts of light rippling along the ocean's surface.

Cecil raised his field glasses, squinting as he focused, the flash of the guns ruining his night vision, momentarily catching the silhouettes of the ships' cruisers, maybe even battleships. Nearly half a minute passed, and then the continual rumble of noise washed over them and from the town to the north, flashes as well, shells detonating along the waterfront, silent from this distance, noise yet to reach them.

Captain Cecil Stanford looked back at Marine Sergeant Harris.

"It's begun, sir," Harris whispered.

Pearl Harbor, Oahu
Hawaiian Territories
5:50 a.m. Local Time

The damn cigarettes were killing him. He had already crumpled up one pack of Lucky Strikes and pulled out the second one, the reserve, hidden inside his breast pocket. He had long ago mastered how to do it with one hand, "the claw" as he called it, grasping the pack as he fished out a cigarette, putting it to his lips with his "real" hand.

Pacing back and forth in front of the main administrative office, Commander James Watson kept a steady eye on the gate, waiting for Admiral Kimmel to arrive. He had hounded the night desk repeatedly to put a call through to Kimmel's home and had repeatedly been told that the admiral would arrive shortly. Though he was jumping far above the chain of command, at some risk to himself, he felt five minutes with Kimmel might finally generate some proper response, at least get more of the reconnaissance PBYs up earlier than usual.

Goddamn! Kimmel was most likely still asleep.

It was early twilight, the sky to the east, glowing bright, stars still shining to the west, visible through the scattered broken clouds, typical of a tropical dawn.

The air was rich with the scent of the ocean, mixed in with the smells anyone in the navy was familiar with: diesel oil, some fumes from a tug heading down the main channel, its engine rumbling. The base was quiet except for the chatter of morning birds and nearby the muffled yawn of a shore patrolman, as he shifted back and forth on his feet, waiting out the last few minutes before his relief came out and he could hit the rack.

And yet Commander Watson was wide awake, his nerves jittery from the cigarettes chain-smoked through the night, the half-dozen cups of coffee, and the silence, the overbearing silence down in the basement office of Naval Intelligence.

Silence because the genuine Japanese signal traffic had dried up. Dried up for days now. The vast ocean of noise of the technology of radio, audible to those who had the tools to listen, was usually a ceaseless cacophony. Ship-to-ship communications, idle messages tapped out at three in the

21

morning between bored men on radio watch, sometimes even playing chess by telegraphy, weather reports, even the false traffic put out to confuse. Other ships were "talking," but the Japanese had gone completely silent. It reminded him of the bad line from many a Western, that it was "too quiet" out there. A flight of B-17s had signaled in an hour ago, announcing their approach by eight in the morning. The usual traffic of commercial steamers traversing the vast distances of the Pacific. A few radio checks from cargo ships, tramp steamers, an echo from the Indian Ocean of a British destroyer, but silence where it counted the most.

Everyone in the basement of Naval Intelligence knew, felt certain, something was coming; the warnings of the last few days from Washington, his own coded signal to his friend in Singapore, who confirmed the report that Japanese transports had been sighted near the coast of French Indochina and that his friend was leaving Singapore to go up the coast to look around.

But of the main battle fleet of the Japanese, their vaunted battleships and carriers, silence, other than a clatter of traffic from bases in the Sea of Japan. But that clatter, it just didn't have the feel, the right feel. The traffic was fake, false signals sent to delude a listener into thinking the main fleet was still in home waters. Though he and his team had yet to break the new code, several times the sequencing of numbers had been identical, though spaced a day or so apart. His suspicion: the signalers were reading off a well-prepared script and had gotten a bit lazy, repeating supposed messages from a day or two earlier.

Also, his best "listeners" claimed, and he believed them, that they knew the "fist" of various operators, each telegrapher having slight idiosyncrasies that a well-trained ear could instantly recognize, as distinct as the difference between a Brooklyn versus a Louisiana accent. They even had nicknames for them, "Long A," "Too Fast," "Sloppy Ending." And his listeners claimed that all those men on the other side, whom they knew so well, had stopped sending more than a week ago, replaced by others. Over coffee, the whispered agreement was that the Jap carriers were all at sea. With each passing day, he had, on a small folding map kept in his desk, drawn a wider circle, ranging outward another four hundred miles as to where they might be.

That circle, this morning, lapped far beyond the Marshalls, down to the coast of

New Guinea, and arced up to within less than three hundred miles of here, the Hawaiian Islands.

Somewhere out there the main striking force of the Japanese Fleet must be moving, and when they moved they would move to strike and not dally about; therefore they were at the forward edge of the circle on his map. He could not shake from his mind the comment of a friend, who in a day or two might be his enemy, about what Japan had learned from its war with Russia of forty years past. The first strike must be the fatal blow to their enemy if ever they had a hope of winning.

He stopped his pacing and looked back across the narrow harbor. Eight battleships of the line were tied off, a ninth in dry dock. They were what most considered to be the strength, the backbone of America's presence in the Pacific. If I were to make a fatal blow, it would be against them.

He stubbed out the cigarette on the pavement, ignoring the slightly perturbed look of the marine guard stationed outside the administrative headquarters of base. To hell with looking for a bucket to snub out the butt. He fished another cigarette out of the pack and lit it.

Looking back to the main gate he saw a

taxi pull up, and absurd as it was, he started toward it. Kimmel always arrived in his own chauffeured staff car, never a taxi, but maybe it might be carrying someone who could shake things loose.

He slowed. Five sailors piled out, all of them obviously drunk to the point of collapse. Laughing, shouting, cursing, they started to argue with the driver.

The security at the barred gate came out of their small office, wearily shaking their heads.

Something compelled Watson, at least it would be a diversion for the moment, and he walked the hundred yards up to the gate.

"Damn cabbie is robbing us blind!" one of the sailors was moaning as he fumbled in his pockets.

The marine guard at the gate stood silent, obviously annoyed at this disturbance of the peace of a Sunday morning.

Watson stepped around the gate, not even sure why he was doing so, and the marines, seeing his approach, came to attention and saluted, though they looked at him with a bit of a jaundiced eye. He had long ago acquired some of the idiosyncrasies of those buried down in the basement office of Naval Intelligence: rumpled uniform; in his case, the replacement hand, his claw as he called

25

it; a coffee stain or two on his jacket; unshaven for two days; he looked not much better than the drunken sailors, but nevertheless they came to weary attention and saluted.

"Problem here?" Watson asked.

At the sight of him the drunken sailors came to pantomimes of attention, several offering exaggerated salutes, though a chief petty officer, still holding a touch of sobriety, saluted formally.

"Sorry, sir," he said, swaying slightly.

"Two dollars," the cabbie snapped, leaning out his open window.

"Like hell," one of the drunks replied, "you said a buck for back to the base."

"That's before one of you got sick in my cab. Now I got to clean it!"

"We ain't got the money," the sailor who had obviously gotten sick replied, barely able to stand.

The petty officer looked at Watson and shrugged.

"We're broke, sir," he said thickly.

"I'll take care of it," Watson said, and in fact he was glad for the momentary distraction. He could well remember more than one similar night in his own life.

Watson pulled out his wallet, found two bucks, and went up to the cab, wrinkling his nose slightly at the smell wafting out of it. It was a mess inside and he pulled out an extra dollar.

"I'm sorry about this," Watson said softly, and handed him the money.

The cabbie nodded, taking the money.

"Thank you, sir," the petty officer announced, and the others chorused their profound and eternal gratitude.

"When you're clean and sober, come back and pay me. I'm Watson, Naval Intelligence."

The petty officer nodded, as if taking deep and profound note of this information.

"Now go down and find your Liberty Boat and get the hell back on board your ships," James snapped.

"Come on, boys," the chief petty officer slurred. One of the men started to collapse, his comrades held him up, and they started to pass through the gate.

The petty officer turned and saluted again.

"You are a gentleman, sir. I know I'm drunk, sir. Stinking drunk. But when I'm sober, I'd like to buy you a drink. Just look me up. O'Reilly sir, Quentin O'Reilly, thirty years," and he pointed to the hash marks on his sleeve.

"I'm retiring next week; that's why me and my boys got drunk. So, look me up."

"Fine, I'll do that," James said with a smile. He had been a midshipman at Annapolis when this man was already at sea.

"Promise?"

Watson nodded.

"Ask for me on my ship, sir. Everyone knows me," and he proudly pointed out across the channel.

"There she is sir, the *Arizona,* finest battle-wagon afloat."

They staggered down toward the dock where the weary crew of the overnight Liberty Boat waited to haul in the last of the drunks staggering back from Honolulu.

James shook his head, his anxieties of the moment forgotten, glad actually for the diversion.

"Thank you, sir."

It was the cabbie, standing now outside his vehicle, lighting a cigarette.

"Sorry about the problem."

The cabbie chuckled softly and shook his head.

"Darn stupid kids, most of them. Usually I can spot the ones who are about to get sick and drive past them. Now I got to clean that mess," and he gestured to the backseat, "before calling it a night."

"Again, I'm sorry."

The cabbie actually smiled.

"Deal with it all the time, sir. It won't kill me. Besides, like I said, most of them are just kids acting stupid."

Nothing was said for a moment. James looked over at the man. He looked to be in his early thirties, Nisei, Japanese.

There had been so many warnings, reports, spies everywhere. General Stark had decided that a war warning meant to look out for sabotage and thus he had ordered all planes at the air bases to be parked wing tip to wing tip so they could be more easily guarded.

Was this a spy? James wondered.

The cabbie noticed his gaze.

"Looks like you've had a long night yourself, sir," the cabbie said.

James rubbed the stubble of his beard with his good hand and chuckled softly.

"An all-nighter, you could say."

The cabbie dropped his cigarette on the pavement and stubbed it out.

"Hope all these war rumors are just hot air," the cabbie said softly.

A bit surprised, James looked at him.

"Imagine the fix it puts me in? I was born in Japan, but now I'm an American. My kids were born here; my wife was born here. Yeah, I heard the rumors; bet you did too. I hope it doesn't come, that's for sure."

The cabbie smiled.

"Well, sir, got to clean this rig out and call it a night."

He hesitated and then extended his hand, and James took it warmly.

"Luck to you."

The cabbie smiled sadly and got into the cab.

"Good luck to all of us," he sighed, "I think we're going to need it soon."

The cabbie made an exaggerated gesture of exhaling due to the smell and, shifting gears, he drove off.

James turned away, sighed, and looked down at his watch. Five fifty a.m. Damn all, Kimmel should be up by now. Surely he must be up and on his way in.

The Liberty Boat with the drunks on board was slowly motoring over to the *Arizona,* clearly visible in the light of dawn.

The battleship row was now clearly illuminated by the morning light, a few men stirring on the decks, lights shining from open hatches and portholes, smoke curling up from galley stoves preparing to serve out the traditional Sunday morning breakfast of bacon and eggs.

It was all so peaceful.

Admiral Halsey was frustrated and annoyed.

He was supposed to be pulling into Pearl in another two and a half hours so his men could go ashore for Sunday.

They were simply not going to make it.

Head winds and heavy seas had made refueling the destroyers really difficult. The tin cans were always the ships that ran out of fuel first, and you simply had to slow down to refuel them when they got too thirsty. The result was a significant delay in getting home.

Still, he thought to himself as he looked out from the bridge of the *Enterprise* toward the destroyers and cruisers surrounding his flagship, we have had a good run out to Wake Island and we are trained to fighting trim. Besides, it was damn good just to be out of Pearl and out at sea. For the last month, anytime they were anchored in port, it set his skin to crawling, the thought of just how damn vulnerable they were.

It was almost light enough to launch the carrier air patrol and forward on a flight of planes back to base. With the off-load of

31

marine aircraft at Wake Island, and the launch in a few hours of a flight back to Pearl Harbor, he'd be down to less than sixty aircraft on board, but still it was enough to protect the carrier task force and throw a pretty good punch if he had to.

Sitting back in his chair, he looked down on the flight deck in the early morning twilight. Crew chiefs were already at their planes, waiting for enough light to give them a final going over. Up forward, the "sweep down" crew would soon line up to walk the deck, checking every inch of the launch area for anything that might be swept up into an engine. Even a dropped penny blown up into a whirling prop could definitely ruin somebody's day. His crew was damn good, nearly all of them kids, but damn good kids, proud of their ship and their jobs. All of them had taken from him the sense that a crisis was close at hand. They were ready for it.

If trouble does come, we will ensure America can be proud of the big *E,* he thought to himself. He took another long sip of coffee, his gaze focused eastward, taking in the beauty of an approaching dawn over the Pacific, the moment, a peaceful one.

The Imperial Japanese Navy carrier *Akagi* turned eastward into the wind. Standing in the cockpit of his "Kate" three-seater torpedo bomber, Commander Fuchida braced his hands to either side of the open canopy, fearful that his trembling would be visible.

Akagi heeled over as it turned, pounded by towering forty-foot waves that, as their heading shifted from south to southeast and now to east, became a stomach-lurching sea, from the crests of waves, spray scudding over the bow with each downward plunge of the 34,000-ton aircraft carrier.

With each plunge a shudder ran through the ship, deck crews bracing themselves, more than one doubling over, the sickness of the sea overtaking them. Yet the excitement of the moment drove them on, and even retching they would continue with their efforts.

The quartering wind was now head-on, and he could feel the vibration coursing up from the steam turbines in the engine room, through the flight deck, up the struts of the landing gear of his plane, striking the soles of his feet, the trembling of the ship matching his own trembling of excitement. They were racing up to flank speed, 133,000 horsepower, from the nineteen steam boilers turning the four drive shafts, the roar of the exhaust screaming out of the starboard side stack heard even above the howling of the wind. She was alive, her 850 feet of deck swarming with life, the nearly fifty aircraft of the first strike wave. The Zeroes were forward, the lightweight fighters needing the least room to launch, followed by the Kates and Vals, all ladened with torpedoes or bombs for the total strike force to be launched from six carriers; over fifty of those bombs were actually sixteen-inch naval artillery shells, a ton in weight, mounted with stabilizing fins. The specially picked pilots of those planes would have a tough time on rollout, their planes launching with half a ton of weight over their design limits.

Deck crews raced about, the chief mechanic of each plane standing to one side, watching intently, listening, eyes scanning back and forth. The engines had been running now for over twenty minutes, were warmed up, the shifting of the wind forcing more air through the cowling intakes. Over the shoulder of his pilot in the forward seat, he could see the temperature gauges for oil and manifold dropping slightly, good, there was always the danger of overheating. The fourteen-cylinder Sakae air-cooled engine, rated at just over one thousand horsepower for takeoff, was running smooth.

All checks had been run, magneto switches thrown, crew chief listening carefully to the slight drop in rpms with each magneto check, able to tell without even looking at a

Japanese naval aircraft prepare to take off from an aircraft carrier (reportedly Shokaku) *to attack Pearl Harbor during the morning of 7 December 1941. Plane in the foreground is a "Zero" fighter. This is probably the launch of the second attack wave. The original photograph was captured on Attu in 1943.*
Naval Historical Center

gauge that all was well. Carb deicer was cleared and off, oil pressure good, fuel pressure good, artificial horizon and turn-bank indicator swaying back and forth with the rocking of the ship.

He caught the eye of his chief and nodded; the chief had given him the traditional headband that he now sported like a samurai of old, grinned, and gave a thumbs-up signal that all was well.

Assistants knelt under either wing, hands wrapped taut around the ropes that would pull the wheel chokes clear. In this mad, rolling sea, there'd be a disaster in the making if they were removed too early. A plane rolling back or forward into another, since they were spaced but a few feet apart, could set off a chain-reaction explosion that would sweep the deck and in an instant shatter the entire plan.

He faced into the more than fifty-knot blow sweeping the deck. It was refreshing, bracing. Three days ago, as they steamed down from the northern waters, it had been bitter, freezing, ice forming on the deck. But in the last day and a half they had shifted into more tropical waters and now, in his heavy flight suit, padded with rabbit fur, the heavy boots, kapok life vest, revolver in shoulder holster, padded leather flight helmet, he was sweating profusely and knew that once at altitude that sweat could be dangerous.

The wind was a cooling blessing.

He checked his chronometer, it was just after 6:00 a.m. local time.

He shifted his gaze to the bridge and made eye contact with his friend, the intellectual architect of this moment, Commander Genda.

Years ago it was Genda who first postulated this type of plan. He was met with such violent reaction that his lectures had to be curtailed, and yet he had persevered, citing every source from the German Clauswitz and the concept of the Schwerpunkt, to the teachings of the American strategist Mahan. For any hope of victory, Japan must effectively end its naval war on the first day, with the first crippling strike that would shatter enemy morale and cripple his ability to respond. We did so at Port Arthur in 1904, he said, the decisive blow as the opening move, the true tradition of the samurai who in one blinding sweep ends the duel before it has really started. It was Genda who had finally risen to the inner circle of naval advisors, and his words had reached Yamamoto when the government finally made its choice to turn "south" rather than "north," meaning a naval war to seize the rich colonies of the collapsing European powers rather than confront the beleaguered Soviet Union for control of Siberia, rich in resources yes, but a nightmare to organize and make productive for an industrial nation. Besides, the army had bungled its probing attacks in Mongolia the year before, crushed by the power of Soviet armor and artillery.

Fuchida caught Genda's eye, salutes were exchanged between two old friends, and he knew Genda was in agony, wishing to go with them and not tied to the deck command bridge.

The shuddering of the engines leveled out into a steady pulsing, drumming rumble. The bow of the great ship rose up on the waves, paused, and crashed down. Even in this, the most rigorous of services, if this was an exercise, the operation would be canceled. But not now, not today. A typhoon could be blowing, and yet still they would struggle to launch.

It was a few minutes after six local time. The tropical twilight was brightening to the east, arcing under low, scudding clouds, the trailing wisps of the storm front that had covered their advance across four thousand miles of northern seas breaking apart in the morning light.

A bosun's pipe shrieked over the ship's public address system. He went rigid, eyes focused to just aft of the bridge to the string of signal flags, heart pounding. And there it was, the legendary Z flag, the flag that had been reverently brought out from its honored place aboard the old flagship *Mikusa* and with full honors brought aboard this ship, to be used for this moment.

The very flag that Admiral Togo had raised in 1905 to signal the commencement of action against the Russians at the Battle of Tsushima.

Another shriek of the bosun's pipe and the flag that was at half-mast ever so sharply rose to the top of the signal mast. At the sight of it thus, a wild shout went up. The years of training now came to the fore. Within seconds he could see the first Zero begin to roll forward into the near sixty-knot wind, its rollout timed so that the deck would be level and dropping away.

It lifted easily, fifty feet shy of the bow. Already behind it rolled a second Zero, then the third. To meet the plan a plane had to clear every fifteen seconds. If the pilot lost an engine now, he was ordered to press over, go into the towering seas, and thus meet his fate. There was no time now for delay.

Ten of the Zeroes were clear. A last look over at his crew chief who, with right hand raised, was twirling it in a tight circle, signal to the pilot of his plane to rev up.

The plane shuddered with its pent-up fury, massive radial engine thundering, exhaust whipping back. Fuchida was actually tempted to remain standing, but knew

A Japanese Navy Type 97 carrier attack plane ("Kate") takes off from a carrier as the second-wave attack is launched. Ship's crewmen are cheering "Banzai!" This ship is either Zuikaku *or* Shokaku. *Note light tripod mast at the rear of the carrier's island, with Japanese naval ensign.* **Naval Historical Center**

that was foolish bravado.

He slipped down into the cockpit, quickly buckling his harness on, pulling the shoulder straps tight, slapping his pilot, directly in front of him, on the shoulder.

Now seated, he could not see ahead and could only catch a glimpse of the wingtip of the Kate in front and to their port side.

The crew chief continued to circle his fist, faster and tighter, the plane shuddering as the engine roared to at full throttle, only the chocks and the pilot with both feet locked to the toe brakes keeping it from leaping forward. Unlike a ground takeoff, there was no room to zigzag into place, observing ahead, the massive bulk of the engine forward blocked the view.

With a dramatic gesture the crew chief pointed down with his left hand, signaling the crews holding the lines to the chokes to pull clear. At the same instant he looked back up at the pilot, saluted, and then pointed directly forward.

The heavy Kate began to roll forward, the launch chief, up on the bridge, timing the moment so that the deck was pitching up, thus by the time they reached the end of the deck, it would be pitching back down.

"Wind speed seventy," the pilot shouted, "seventy-five." They were past the bridge.

Though indicated speed was seventy-five, in fact they were just barely moving at little more than twenty-five knots. The pilot already had his stick slightly forward to raise the tail up, the big rudder aft biting into the wind with plenty of right rudder by the pilot to counteract the tremendous torque generated by the engine. He could feel a lightness to the aircraft, a slight buffeting from the torque, the pilot feeding in more right rudder, stick easing back, the deck dropping away beneath them. The Kate felt sluggish, hovering on a stall, pilot nosing her down slightly, running parallel to the deck for a few seconds so that it looked like they were heading straight into the sea.

Deck behind, Fuchida looked back. He felt a sinking in his gut, the pilot easing the stick back, the control stick between his legs moving, but he kept his hands clear. Today it was not his job to fly. Sitting in the bombardier's seat, now his command perch, his job was to lead. True air speed was now rapidly climbing. A mistake novices sometimes made when taking off from a carrier was to forget they were taking off into headwinds, sometimes as high as sixty knots per hour. A sharp turnout before true speed was up would trigger a fatal stall.

He looked back as they started into a shallow banking turn to port. The next Kate was clearing the deck, another just starting its takeoff roll. Overhead, assembling several thousand feet up with their faster rate of climb, the Zeroes were circling into formation.

Canopy was still back, wind blowing at a thousand feet up, already a bit cooler. Coming out of the turn they flew westward, racing down the port side of the *Akagi,* in the distance, like mayflies rising, planes were lifting from the decks of the other five carriers, circling to form.

He caught sight of the Z flag, and he felt a tightening of his throat. Memories of the academy, where one day of the year the flag would be removed from its sacred shrine aboard Togo's old flagship, *Mikusa,* and brought down to Etajima, the Naval Academy, for the parading ceremony, a lesson to the future of the glories of the past.

He saluted, heart swelling with pride and flashes of memory. Memory of Etajima and those whom he'd met there, some few who in less than two hours would be his enemies.

Mitsuo Fuchida, strike leader for the entire attack, two waves, 363 planes, the largest such carrier-based attack in the history of warfare, circled over *Akagi* twice, waiting for formations to tighten up.

He checked his transmitter, the slip of paper tucked over the transmit switch was still in place, a precaution against accidentally sending a signal; for those planes using telegraphs, pieces of paper were placed between the contact points. Not until the target was in sight would he give the signal.

The groups were now all but formed, circling, waiting, and he knew all eyes were on his distinctively marked plane, sporting a broad yellow stripe around the tail. The six carriers were below, pounding forward through heavy seas, deck crews already bringing up the planes of the second wave and spotting them into position. Farther out, the protective screen of destroyers and cruisers kept watch, far aft, barely visible on the horizon, the resupply ships the admiral had ordered forward to everyone's surprise, the precious oilers ladened with the black gold that in so many ways had become the reason for what was about to begin.

He reached forward, slapped his pilot on the shoulder, and gave him a thumbs-up. A second later the plane rocked back and forth three times and, leveling out, turned on to a heading of south-southeast. Crossing over *Akagi,* now several thousand feet below, he could just see the flutter of the Z flag, ship turning south to move closer to the target while deck crews were already racing to bring up the second strike wave from below.

He looked down at his Swiss chronometer. It was 6:20 a.m. local; in Japan, it was 8 December 1941. The island of Oahu was one hour and twenty minutes away.

■ ■ ■ ■

PART ONE: THUNDER ON THE HORIZON

■ ■ ■ ■

CHAPTER ONE

Etajima — Japanese Naval Academy
10 April 1934

"Mr. Watson, come quick!"

Lieutenant Commander James Watson grinned at the rather foolish joke of his old friend, Cecil Stanford, Lieutenant Commander, Royal Navy, as the two old friends raced toward each other and, in rather uncharacteristic manner, at least for a British officer, embraced heartily, slapping each other on the back, exchanging greetings, "Damn good to see you, old chap," "My God, man, is that gray in your hair?"

James Watson stepped back slightly, hands still on the shoulders of his friend, looking into his eyes, delighted to be reunited with a comrade of old. The last time they had seen each other was right after the Armistice when their office was shutting down and James was returning back to the States. They had worked together in London during the war, a joint British/American code-breaking team, working on German U-boat signals and having precious little luck at their tasks.

And now sixteen years had passed.

Cecil had not changed all that much. Gray around the temples, with blue eyes that still sparkled with delight. Nose a bit swollen and reddened, evidence of his predilection to good single malt scotch (if he could find it here), but still stiff-backed, trim, double-breasted civilian suit looking a bit out of place, made incongruous by the open-faced black robes and hood dangling from his back that denoted an Oxford education.

James was feeling slightly uncomfortable this warm spring day with the high-button collar and dress whites of a lieutenant commander in the United States Navy, but formalities had to be observed, especially on this visit to what was the Japanese Naval Academy at Etajima, in Hiroshima Bay.

His entry onto the academy grounds had been greeted with all the proper formalities, honor guard to greet him. He had to climb the bridge of *Chiyoda* — a dispatch ship from the great Russo-Japanese war, incongruously set on firm soil at the edge of the parade ground — receive formal salutes, then was led to the office of the admiral-president of the academy who, in halting English, welcomed him "aboard" and thanked him for his willingness to address the cadets on American naval doctrine post–Washington Treaty.

The speech was a "cook up," the usual platitudes about bonds of friendship, but he had been cautioned by his superiors to keep it brief, Japan was still deeply rankled about the 5-5-3 provision that limited the number of her capital ships to 60 percent of those of either England or America. The speech, at least, was a task for which he felt ill suited. His ship, *Oklahoma,* was docked in Yokohama on a courtesy call, and at the reception that evening his captain had revealed that James spoke fairly good Japanese, mentioned the academy at Etajima a few minutes later, and the "hint" to their Japanese hosts could not be politely refused. Though it was a bit more than a "setup" for James. His captain had been under orders to pull off the arrangement, that it might be worth the effort to have an American naval officer visit the academy and have a look around, perhaps hook up with an old English friend teaching there.

The speech was for later today. At the moment James was focused on Cecil and like old friends reunited they compared notes, exchanged names of old friends, some greeted with a sad shaking of heads about the mortality of all, and generally delighted in seeing a beloved friend once more after so many years. James did not pull out a photo of his wife. Another bond was both had endured tragedy, Cecil losing his family in an automobile accident right after the war, James, his only son to leukemia but a year back.

"So you're teaching here now?" James asked, and with a touch of humor tapped the traditional mortar board hat of an English don. How incongruous, he thought, even as he spoke. Regalia of an English professor, offset against the background of flowering cherry trees and the white-capped waters of Hiroshima Bay beyond.

"Retired from His Majesty's Service, you know," Cecil said, "but this posting came up just as I was caught in the naval cutbacks, and friends at the Admiralty arranged it. Curious assignment, I can assure you. Lot to learn about these people. A lot to learn, indeed, even as I teach these lads proper King's English and jump down on their predilection for Yankee slang. Blast all, but I wish films had remained silent. Your movies are quite the rage here in Japan, and they are all trying to imitate your gangster talk."

James smiled and didn't ask anymore. Just as his own visit was so "casually" arranged to this place, he could sense that there was more behind Cecil's posting than met the eye.

"Glad though you got here early as I requested, once I learned you were coming," Cecil continued enthusiastically, "give us a chance to talk before your speech, and also for you to have a look around before scooting off."

"My ship departs day after tomorrow. I'll have to catch the train back in the morning."

Cecil looked past James and smiled.

"Ah, here's one of the things I was hoping you'd get to see," and Cecil gestured across the parade ground to an approaching column of cadets of the academy.

A chanting in the distance interrupted their reunion, growing louder, two columns of Japanese naval cadets, dressed in fatigue blues, came marching onto the parade ground at the double, running in that curious short step that seemed unique to the Japanese. White head bands adorned with the red circle of the rising sun were tied around the foreheads of some, while others wore the standard low-peaked cap.

"Glad you got here early as I requested,"

Cecil announced. "Damn all, James, watch this; it's an eye-opener."

"What is going on, Cecil? They sound like a pep squad for a football game."

"Football?"

"You know, our rugby."

"Silly game you play. All that whistle blowing and stopping and regrouping. Have at it, by God, until one side or the other caves."

"So that's what we're going to see?"

"Just watch. I really wanted you to see this. It reveals a lot about these chaps. They call it 'botashi.' "

He thought about the word for a moment, then shook his head.

"They claim I know Japanese, but I'm not that good yet."

"Just watch for a moment."

The two columns approached the parade ground, each several hundred strong, and at mid-field separated. There was a momentary pause, the two sides lining up in block formations, bowing formally to each other. They about-faced, then went to the opposite sides of the field.

At each end of the field a pole was going up, atop each pole a red pennant.

"Now watch carefully," Cecil said, his voice edged with excitement.

The two sides gathered around the opposite poles; there seemed to be little debate, each side had one or two in charge, barking orders that James could not hear clearly.

On each side the teams seemed to divide into two groups, a couple hundred stepping forward a few paces and lining up, a hundred or so staying back, gathering tightly around the pole with the pennant atop.

"Get ready," Cecil whispered, "this is all going to happen dreadfully fast."

A whistle blew. James could not see from where, and it was on.

A thunderous shout went up from both sides and the forward teams charged with mad abandon, wild shouts, those with the headbands in the lead, waving their arms wildly, pointing to the other side. The field was perhaps two hundred yards across. Their speed was building with the charge, and James inwardly winced. These kids were about to run smack into each other.

He could feel the tension with Cecil, whose hand was now resting on his shoulder.

The two lines hit, and went right through each other. There were a couple of tackles, blows exchanged, but nearly all of them ran right past each other as if they didn't even exist.

What the hell kind of offensive rush was this? James wondered, but he was now so focused on the game he didn't have time to analyze.

Passing through each other, the offensive squads, with wild screams, charged at the poles of their opponents. The boys who were now obviously the defenders braced for the onslaught. Some even climbed on the shoulders of others, ringing the pole adorned with the pennant.

At nearly the same instant, the offensive charges of both sides collided with the defenders.

There was no strategy here. No feints, no flanking maneuvers, no organized squads moving to left or right, no diversions, just a head-on assault. The charges on both sides swarmed up onto the defenders.

And James could see there were no rules. Kicks, punches, judo throws, karate blows were the order of the day. Cadets with bloody faces staggered out of the attack even as their comrades, wild with excitement, pressed in. Cadets standing on the shoulders of others leapt into the air, crashing down into the wild melee.

The assault on the east side of the field surged up around the pole, shoving aside the defenders, kicking and punching. The flagpole started to waver back and forth as the attackers bodily tried to tear the pole out of the ground and bring it down.

But then, on the west side of the field, the charge pressed in with wild screams, some of the cadets wearing headbands at the back of the seething mass, shouldering those who showed the slightest reluctance into the fight.

Seconds later the flag atop the pole on the west was snatched down, the cadet who grabbed it waving it wildly while balanced atop the shoulders of a comrade.

Whistles echoed and, amazingly for James, within seconds the fight was over. Cadets first coming to attention, bowing to their opponents, then as one extending helping hands to those who were collapsed on the ground, too injured to move, or who had been trampled under in the battle. There was even some backslapping between the opposing sides, leaders of the two teams shaking hands.

"My God," James whispered, "if that had been how we played Army-Navy games back in my day, every cadet in the stadium would have swarmed down on the field for one helluva donnybrook."

Cecil chuckled loudly. "Definitely not a proper game of cricket."

James looked over at his friend and back to the playing field where, victors and losers, all of them filthy, more than a few limping or having to be carried, began to form up, stretcher bearers loading up four boys who were not moving.

Cricket versus this, he wondered. A glimpse of national character, of how we fight wars?

"I've had boys show up in my English class a couple of hours after one of these, broken arm in a sling, eyes swollen half shut, and not a murmur of complaint, though I could tell the lads were in agony. My first week here, I tried to excuse one of them from class, told him to go to his barracks and rest, and he filled up with tears.

"It wasn't tears of pain. I had humiliated him in front of his comrades, implied he didn't have the guts to take it. A lesson about them I never forgot, and a mistake I never repeated.

"You know about their swim test?"

James shook his head.

"Every summer the entire academy camps out on an island for several weeks," and he motioned across the bay, "wearing nothing but loincloths. The poor beggars get burned as black as an Indian and live just as primitively. On the last day they swim back here, and James, it's a ten-mile swim. Good lord, man, that's half the distance of the Channel in water just as cold.

"They go off in teams of a hundred. It's considered a disgrace to leave a comrade behind. Many of these lads have just come from villages inland, and until they go to the island for the summer camp have never swum a stroke in their life; but they go like all the others.

"Ten miles, I tell you. They have sampans out there with officers on board to pull in someone who is obviously drowning, but if he is pulled in, that's it. Pardon the pun, but he is washed out. Every year a couple of them die. They just quietly go under without a word, not wishing to shame themselves by calling for help, or they just collapse and die shortly after reaching shore from severe exposure. Believe me, when you witness that, the way they finally come staggering out of the ocean, sunburned from the island, damn near blue from the ocean, but still working as a team and not a word of complaint, you wonder just who these lads will turn into."

Cecil looked down at his wristwatch. "Nearly tea time, or would you prefer something a bit stronger?"

James grinned. "Stronger, but I do have

59

that speech after dinner, and it would not be proper for a serving officer to trigger a diplomatic incident, so let's stick with the tea."

The shimmer of moonlight across Hiroshima Bay held a haunting quality, actually reminding James of the old Japanese prints of such scenes as he settled back in his chair, Cecil bringing out the bottle of single malt they had both denied themselves hours earlier.

With a nod of thanks, James let him pour several ounces. They smiled and held their glasses up.

"For the King and President, God bless them," James said, and without anymore fanfare he drained nearly the entire glass in two gulps, Cecil following suit.

"Well, is it fair to say your speech was a bloody disaster," Cecil said, offering a weak smile.

James said nothing, looking off. His audience of cadets, to be certain, had been the model of politeness, attentive, eyes fixed upon him, chuckling good-naturedly a few times when he stumbled a bit on his syntax and pronunciation of Japanese, but he knew the talk had been a lead balloon.

The implication of the Washington Treaty,

now over ten years old, the so-called 5-5-3 agreement, had been bald-faced in its intent. For every five capital ships allowed to the Royal Navy and the United States Navy, Japan was limited to three. The rational argument had been that both America and Britain had multiocean responsibilities, even in this period of alleged peace, while Japan's natural interests were limited to the Pacific.

It was an asinine agreement, James always thought. Though like many he had real reservations about Japan's ever-increasing Imperialistic goals, nevertheless, she had indeed been a loyal ally, especially to England in the Great War. Bound by treaty, Japan had declared war on Germany when the show started in 1914, swept the small German enclaves out of the Pacific, and then dispatched a squadron of ships to help Britain in the Mediterranean. At war's end she had aligned herself with her allies in the expedition to occupy part of Siberia during the Soviet revolution, until all had withdrawn in 1921. Those with a sharp eye toward the geopolitics of East Asia argued that a closer alliance with Japan should be sought as a counterforce to Soviet expansion into China.

There had been several serious bumps in

the situation between America and Japan, dating back to of all things the racism of the city of San Francisco, which had banned Japanese students from their public schools back in 1905, immigration laws that essentially banned Japanese from settling in America, to the current diplomatic flurry about the takeover of Manchuria. But in general, a broad-thinking Occidental could see the potential of actual cooperation, if handled adroitly.

The Japanese were as anxious about expanding communism as were most Americans, and the Soviet Union was right on Japan's back doorstep. With this Stalin now firmly in control and apparently drenching his tortured nation in yet more blood, Japan could be seen as a potential counterforce in the region.

But the 5-5-3 treaty had thrown a monkey wrench in the works for the time being. James felt as if he were navigating through a mined channel as he delivered his talk, having to adhere to policy, not able to mention the Soviets by name, and trying to emphasize points of agreement, all done in a language he had learned from his wife, a Nisei, half-Japanese, whom he had met when stationed in Hawaii right after the war; thus his knowledge was more colloquial than formal, and he knew he was making mistakes.

The whole thing had been a bloody embarrassment, not a single question asked by the cadets afterward, a sure sign they had been ordered to behave thus.

The obligatory reception afterward had been polite but relatively short, the various staff of the academy quickly begging off, claiming papers to correct, reports to write, and given the cool reception to James's speech, Cecil had finally led him out on the excuse that their American guest had endured a most exhausting day and needed to ship out come morning.

"So, how is it here?" James asked. "I mean really?" He paused and looked around a bit cautiously.

Cecil laughed and shook his head. "We can talk freely. No one is listening. They would see that as underhanded and rude to a fellow naval officer to try and eavesdrop or wire my place. Really, on a personal level most of the blokes here have a love of His Majesty's Navy, more than a few of them serving alongside us during the last war. We can talk."

James nodded.

"The lads are a delight to work with, best I've ever seen. Our navies could use a dose of them, and that's no mistake. Most come from the back country, curious, same way you have so many in your navy from the Midwest. Entrance exams are brutally competitive, and as you know more than a few have committed suicide when not accepted.

"They endure eighteen-hour days with no letup. Usual range of subjects, but strong emphasis as well on either English, German, or Russian. Of course that's where I come in.

"English is the most popular, and it does make me wonder is it because their navy is patterned after ours because we helped them build it, even supplied their first ships," he sighed and took a drink, "or is it because they think the next fight will be with us.

"What I would wonder," James paused and instinct actually made him stand up, walk to the edge of the veranda to look over the porch, before settling back down.

"Your houseboy?"

"Gave him the night off."

James nodded.

"All right, old friend," Cecil asked, "out with it."

"Just that some higher-ups remembered you and I worked together in the war. I was asked to come down here and have a chat with you and see what you think. You have your ear to the ground. What do you think?"

"Ah, so you might say I was sent here to spy?"

"Dirty word that," James replied, imitating Cecil's clipped style of speech when stirred, "let's just say, observing."

"But first you," Cecil said, and he reached over, putting his hand on James's knee. "I'm so sorry about your son, James."

James nodded, unable to speak. It had been a year now since his son had died. He knew that if he started to talk about it, he would break down. He coughed shyly, motioning for a refill of his drink, and the two old friends smiled.

Both could be defined as spies, though their specialty was a new field, of radio signal intercepts and cryptology. It had been their job together in the last war, but in peacetime more than a few of the higher-ups were of the old school that "gentlemen did not read gentlemen's mail" or for that matter intercept their signals and try to decode them, especially if the other gentleman was allegedly an ally. It was a specialization that was a guaranteed slow track for promotion.

Cecil looked off, the crescent moon touching the horizon on the far side of the bay. The campus was quiet, lights out having already been sounded.

He sighed. "It'll come," he said softly.

"Go on."

"They think they're us in a way."

"How so?"

"Well, we bloody well ran riot over the world for a couple of hundred years. Plant the flag, build the Empire, assuage any sense of guilt by spreading the gospel and calling it the white man's burden, but it was imperialism plain and simple; and now that's done, we see ourselves as being proper gentlemen having done the right thing in spreading our civilization.

"You could say we did in a way, but still, it was a grab and we made the most of it.

"You Yankees did the same, though to a lesser degree. They were too polite in there tonight to ask the question, but just what the bloody hell was America doing in the Philippines anyhow?"

"We got stuck with it," James replied a bit weakly, "after beating the Spanish."

"And made sure of supplies of rubber, manila, even your busboys for your navy.

"So these chaps see it as the same. Remember, they are the only, the only non-European nation to have successfully resisted European encroachment. Remember, they thrashed the old czar good and proper back in '05, and frankly we all cheered them on when they did it. So now they want, as the kaiser used to say, 'their place in the sun.'"

"Manchuria," James said.

"Oh please, stand corrected, dear friend. Remember, it is Manchukuo now."

"Still it was a grab."

"Who would you rather see have it? Them, that insane Chinese warlord who was terrorizing the place, or the Soviets who were just itching to grab it?"

James nodded slowly in agreement.

"You have to remember that there is a big, deep argument underway in this country. The army sees itself as a continental force and is focused on defeating the Soviet Union and conquering China. The navy sees itself as a Pacific power and has focused on defeating you Americans ever since the end of the World War One."

"They don't let me sit in the courses where they discuss strategy and planning, but it is clear from conversations with both students and faculty that they have been consistently thinking about war with America here at Etajima for over a decade. They think objective reality about resources will force a conflict sooner or later, and they are determined not to be dictated to and dominated by you Americans.

"England had its advantages when this new age started. We had mountainsides of coal, plenty of iron, the building blocks of empire. But by God if ever there was a spot on this earth not to start an Empire from, it's Japan. Smaller than Britain, not counting that frozen northern island of theirs, and yet half again the population, barely 20 percent of the land worth trying to farm, no coal, precious little iron, and yet in sixty years they've tried with success to leap onto the global stage."

"So let them have Manchukuo, if that's what they want to call it," James said.

"Ah, but there's the rub. Did you Yanks stop at the Mississippi? What about all that land you took from Mexico and then Spain back in '98. You called it Manifest Destiny and maybe it was. Well, these folks think they have a Manifest Destiny as well."

"And that is, in your opinion?"

"A unified Asia."

"Under their dominance of course."

Cecil smiled.

"If it was us, would we want it any other way?"

James shook his head.

"And there is the race question. They do ask the logical question, why is Southeast Asia run by the French, the East Indies by the Dutch, you in the Philippines."

"So that will lead to war? Damn all, it would be suicide in the end," James replied.

"There are far bigger worries for all of us. They might have Manchuria, or whatever they call it, but I dare say the Soviets would love payback for 1905. This little corporal in Germany is getting downright bothersome. Why not play on our side?"

He said it with passion because there was a personal reason behind this as well. His wife was a Nisei, half-Japanese, a wonderful racial mix so typical of Hawaii where they had met when he was stationed there in the early twenties. Her father was Portuguese European, her mother Japanese, and Margaret had inherited the best of both in terms of intellect, beauty, charm. He had to say, as well, that he was one of the lucky few, truly blessed with a mother-in-law whom he outright adored. His own mother had died giving birth to him, his father remote, distant, and James sensed deep down resentful of a son who had cost him a wife. So he had grown up with a sense of being alone, until Margaret came into his life and with her a mother who took him in as if he were her own son as well. The thought that Japan was emerging as an enemy, it was hard to swallow in a way. How could the people who had given him such a wonderful family ever truly be an enemy?

Cecil motioned to James's tumbler, and he nodded agreement for a refill.

"Oh, there are many in their government, and in their navy, who would fully agree," Cecil continued, while he poured the scotch. "But it gets strange, to Western eyes. It has to do with race, with the gods, with an image of destiny, with their own individual submersion into a greater whole, a submersion that disdains individual worth for the greater good of the family, of the race, of this mystery of destiny. In some ways each as an individual sees himself as nothing more than a mote of dust tumbling on the wind, and that wind is national destiny. Of himself he is meaningless, but a hundred million such specks of dust, driven by the wind of national destiny, can blast down a castle wall, reshape mountains, change the world."

"You are beginning to sound like some of those mystics from your India."

Cecil smiled.

"That's another problem right there, and believe me, they are quick to point to it and ask if it is alright for England to be in the Raj, then why not they in China, bringing order out of chaos the same way we did a hundred years ago."

"Good points," James said softly, "but damn all, there are rumors about the brutality of their occupation of Manchuria: executions of civilians, beheadings, torture."

Cecil nodded.

"Dare I mention what we did in our not-so-distant past? How we put down the Sepoy Rebellion, or what about your Wounded Knee?"

"I know, I know," James said, sadly, "but this is the twentieth century."

"Exactly their point, and they want a part of that; and our arguments, when pitched on moral grounds, well, they feel they have the counter. Valid or not, it is their own self-justification, and though we might disagree we must understand that is how they see it."

They had been speaking in low tones and therefore the knock on the door was startling, both standing up, falling silent. James felt a moment of paranoia, wondering if Cecil had been incautious.

Cecil went into the house, James following, drink in hand, trying to act casual, though on reflection he realized that their conversation had been completely innocent, just mere speculation, no secrets exchanged or actions agreed upon that might offend their hosts.

The house was a curious anomaly, actually a touch of England in a way. The school had been laid out with advice from the British navy; and as a result several of the buildings, those used by Western instructors and visitors, were European in design, complete to a print over the fireplace of a naval action from the Napoleonic Wars.

With the houseboy off for the evening, Cecil opened the door himself and a smile creased his face.

"Lieutenant Fuchida! A delight to see you!"

Standing behind Cecil, James caught a glimpse of the visitor. It was a naval lieutenant, trim, sporting a narrow, dapper-looking mustache, body lean, and like nearly every naval officer he had met here, obviously in excellent condition. He was a bit tall for a Japanese, and at the sight of James he came stiffly to attention and saluted.

Custom was, James being indoors and with hat off a salute was not necessary, but he returned it anyway.

"Lieutenant Mitsuo Fuchida, may I present Lieutenant Commander James Watson of the United States Navy."

James stepped forward to the doorway, and Fuchida, stiffly formal, bowed slightly, hesitated, then shook James's extended hand. His grasp was warm and firm. Cecil guided their visitor in and held up his glass as a signal.

"If it is your Scottish whiskey, a pleasure," Fuchida said, with a smile.

Again an uncomfortable moment of silence as Cecil filled the glasses again and held his up.

"To the Emperor," Cecil said formally, and Fuchida, smiling, held his glass up and turned to the north, facing toward the Imperial Palace as he sipped his drink, then turned back.

"And the honor of your visit?" Cecil asked. "I didn't even know you were here."

"I came down from the Koyshu Naval Station to talk with the final-year cadets about choosing aviation," Fuchida said. "When I heard Commander Watson was here, I decided to come a bit early to hear his talk. And, of course, to see you as well, my old friend. I was a student here in 1921, and any time I can come back to Etajima I love visiting. The world seemed so young and innocent back then."

"And what did you think of my talk?" Watson asked.

Fuchida smiled and motioned to one of the chairs on the veranda, and the three sat down.

"What I expected," Fuchida said. "Of course you have to follow your orders on such things as I would."

"So, as we Americans would say, it did not scour with you."

"Scour?"

"American slang," James said, "it means that the dirt sticks to the plow rather than dig a good furrow."

"Scour," Fuchida said with a smile, "I'll try and remember that. No it did not scour as you say."

"Why?"

Fuchida chuckled and the manner of his soft laughter made James warm to him.

"The treaty, on all sides, was by and about politicians. I think if they had left it to us naval people, a fair accommodation would have been made. Realize that we Japanese are proud. That treaty says we are not of the same class as you on the world stage."

James said nothing. For the truth was, they were not, though they wished to be. Beyond that, if their aspirations of Imperialism were landward, Manchuria and anyone could guess that sooner or later they would turn to that trouble-wracked insane asylum of China. So why the need for a deep ocean navy equal to that of the West? And yet he could see the issue of national pride.

"So, still flying?" Cecil asked, changing the subject.

Fuchida nodded excitedly. "I was training some of the new pilots for *Akagi*. A beautiful ship, but at the moment I'm landbound, helping to train new pilots on shore," and he shrugged and sighed, "keep your nose down in the turn, go around, let's do it again."

And then he chuckled, the other two joining in at the lieutenant's obvious frustration with breaking in new trainees. No matter what the field, it could be frustrating in the extreme.

"I heard your carrier pilot program is the toughest in the world," James said quietly. "I'd be curious to compare some of your young men with those on our *Saratoga* or *Lexington*."

"An interesting challenge," Fuchida replied eagerly. "I'd like to try my hand at your new Devastator monoplane."

"I can see what I can arrange," James said, knowing it was a lie. The fact that Fuchida even mentioned the new torpedo bomber meant he was current with American naval development. No one would ever clear a Japanese pilot to "try his hand" on it.

"I flew down here," Fuchida replied with a grin. "I can give you a flight back up to Tokyo tomorrow if you wish, save you the train trip."

Absolutely startled, James could not reply for a moment. He hated to admit that he had never flown and frankly the prospect terrified him.

"Capital idea!" Cecil exclaimed. "By God, my friend, how come you never offered a flight to me?"

"Because you never asked!" Fuchida laughed.

Though scared to death at the prospect, how could he keep face and refuse, James now realized.

"You can stay to hear my talk. We can enjoy a lunch together, and I'll have you back to your ship on time."

James could only nod in agreement, and Fuchida smiled with open delight. "A deal then, as you Americans say."

James did not even bother to ask Cecil for a refill of his drink; he poured a few more ounces for himself.

"Your question about our training program," Fuchida continued. "Yes, our program is tough but fair. I wash out three quarters of my students before they have even finished primary training. Better to frustrate them at the start and keep them on the ground then have them wind up killing themselves and destroying one of our precious frontline planes in the process. Three quarters more are grounded or transferred to be bombardiers and navigators, while in advanced training. To fly and land off the pitching deck of a carrier, I believe you have to be born with the instinct, and my job is to find those with that instinct and spare the lives of the rest."

"So you only graduate a hundred or so a year," James replied.

"You have been studying us, haven't you," Fuchida replied, now a bit wary.

"It's just that everyone's carriers seem to be terribly expensive. By the time you are done, the pilots are literally worth their weight in gold. And as of yet, these new ships have yet to prove themselves in battle. My captain on board the *Oklahoma* says he can swat down carrier planes like flies as he closes in, and one salvo of fourteen-inch guns will end it, with the enemy carrier going straight to the bottom."

"Do you believe that?" Fuchida asked, a bit of a defensive note in his voice.

"Just what my captain says," James replied

noncommittally.

"Give us another five to seven years," Fuchida announced proudly, and his voice was now eager, "you and us. The crates we fly now are not much better than what we all used in the last war. But your Devastator is a step forward. When a plane can lift off with a ton of weaponry, fly at two hundred miles an hour, and strike a target three hundred miles away, then your battleship admirals, and mine, will have to sing a different song."

"That American chap, Mitchell," Cecil interjected. "That's what he said after his planes sank that captured German battleship and look what happened to him."

"That was stupidity. A shame how you Americans treated him," Fuchida replied. "He should have been decorated, not dismissed."

James did not reply to that one. The Billy Mitchell incident was still a bit too hot to talk about. It was evident that the destruction his planes had wrought had been something of a setup, sinking a captured and condemned German battleship that was anchored in place and not maneuvering. Mitchell had gone outside the reservation with his outspoken opinions to the newspapers; but then again, maybe this eager pilot was right and progress would overtake the beloved ships of his navy. It was hard to imagine, though, that the old *Oklahoma* could ever be threatened by a crate made of canvas and wood, puttering along at a hundred miles an hour.

"I'm curious as to how you two now see naval aviation and what your admirals are doing with it," Fuchida asked, as he motioned for a refill of his drink, which Cecil quickly complied with.

Cecil and James looked at each other. If this was an attempt to pump information it was done poorly.

Fuchida laughed softly. "I'm not spying on two who more than a few have said are themselves spies. It's just that I knew Commander Watson here witnessed the use of *Saratoga* and *Lexington* in your war games. In a way they are sister ships of *Akagi* and *Kaga,* since all were converted from being battle cruisers after the treaty was signed. Just wanted to catch up with you, Cecil, and hear what Commander Watson has to say."

James could sense a genuineness in this man. He was blunt, direct, and obviously filled with professional curiosity. And it was indeed curious, this relationship between sailors of what might be opposing nations.

Between hostilities they would often openly talk about doctrine, publish articles each other had read in their respective journals, chat at conferences, and do as the three of them were now doing.

"Oh, I guess I could say the usual," James replied. "Though I am not up to speed on such things. That Panama War game was several years back. You undoubtedly have read the journal reports on it. The red team carrier slipped through at a flank-speed run, launched before dawn, and claimed they had blown the locks of the canal by dropping flour bags on them. The judges ruled otherwise. I was onboard *Maryland* at the time and didn't see it. So there is no way I can claim to be an expert."

"But do you think the attack was valid."

James hesitated. But there was something about Fuchida that was so damn disarming, his open, almost boyish enthusiasm about the subject.

"On our side it is the usual debate," Fuchida said. "The battleship admirals claim that their ships were, are, and will always be the deciders of battle. Those who were at Tsushima think the carrier was nothing but a scout ship, to locate the enemy fleet, then to serve as fire-direction control for the battleships once they'd closed to firing range."

Watson chuckled. "Same here. Though remember, I'm signals, not a flyer."

"And are you trying our codes?" Fuchida asked good-naturedly. "You delivered your speech in Japanese, and I must say it was fairly good."

"Just have a knack for language," James said noncommittally. "The Japanese is just sort of a hobby. My wife is half-Japanese, by the way. Her mother was born in Japan, so let's just say it's to get on the good side of my mother-in-law.

"How do you two know each other?" James asked, changing the topic.

"Oh, my friend Mitsuo here and I go back a bit. He comes by on a regular basis to talk to the cadets about aviation and then to practice his English on me."

"And steal some of his scotch," Fuchida replied. "I will say that any talk you might hear about conflict between us and you, our navies I mean, push it aside. We see our descent from the traditions of His Majesty's Navy. Remember, the founder of our Imperial Navy, the Great Togo," and as he said the name he bowed ever so slightly, "long ago trained in England. So there is a brotherhood there."

"And as for us?" James asked quietly.

Fuchida turned to look at him.

"The Pacific is a vast ocean, my friend. There is room enough for both in their proper spheres of influence."

"Which are?"

Fuchida chuckled and looked down at his nearly empty drink, making a motion, and Cecil poured out a few more ounces. The bottle was now well more than two thirds' empty, and James wondered just how many his friend still had in reserve out here.

"The Philippines, I can see what was almost the accidental placing of it in your hands after your defeat of the Spanish. I actually do believe your American idealistic claim that you wish to decolonize as soon as practical, though your big businesses might object.

"But realize, if Japan is to survive in this modern world it needs the same resources your nations already have at your fingertips . . . steel, coal, rubber, various metals, and now, increasingly, oil for both ships and airplanes.

"Let me ask you, Cecil, would your government willingly give up its oil holdings in the Middle East?"

Cecil chuckled. In the old days of Admiral Fisher and the naval reforms prior to the war, seizing and holding secured oil, infinitely more efficient than coal to power a battleship, had been a cornerstone of his policy and, by extension, the British government's.

"We make it fair enough for the locals, and we did bring some semblance of order to the region," Cecil replied.

"Fair enough for you," and he now turned to James, "but it is no question, you Americans are swimming in oil. For Japan, there are a few small wells in the far northern islands, barely a trickle of a few thousand barrels leaking out of them. So there alone we are vulnerable. Nearly every drop of oil that powers our ships we must purchase and at a premium from one or the other of you or the Dutch in the East Indies."

"So you would like to secure these resources?" James asked.

Fuchida smiled. "Trade is better of course," he replied. "And, dear friends, don't quote me, I'm just a naval lieutenant trying to get those above me interested in flying."

"But of course," Cecil replied smoothly.

"I cannot speak for policy," Fuchida continued, "but I think it fair to say that if wiser heads prevail, on both sides, the three of us can find far more in common than what might divide us. There are, of course, the Soviets to contend with; and remember, they are not at your back door, but they are most certainly at ours.

"Though Stalin has backed away from the more radical talk of the International and Trotsky has fallen, still they export their disease into China with this new revolutionary leader there, this Mao. Imagine China as Communist, and you and I might find ourselves side by side trying to block them."

"I would think that the Nationalists have him well in hand," James said.

Fuchida shook his head.

"Give it five years," he replied. "You Westerners do not understand the Chinese as we do. Remember, we have had two thousand years of dealing with them; you have not. Oh, you have your sentimental visions of them from your missionaries; but China can only be ruled by one central authority, and for now, the thought of any democratic rule, the line that the Nationalists parrot to you in order to receive aid, flies in the face of their history."

"So you will go into China?" James asked.

"I did not say that," Fuchida said forcefully. "And besides, even if that did happen, it would not be a naval affair, it would be the army, and they are a different breed."

He fell silent and James registered something in his manner and speech. A hint of disdain in his reference to the army.

"Another?" Cecil asked, holding up what was left of the bottle.

Fuchida hesitated, making as if to stand up to leave.

"Come on, my friend," Cecil said. "I don't have to teach tomorrow, I look forward to hearing your talk, then seeing the two of you off in your plane. Besides, I want to hear about your insanity with this flying. Bad enough getting off the ground, but from the deck of a ship?"

Fuchida smiled and held his glass back up, and there was something in the gesture that made James smile.

Within a minute, loosened up a bit by a few more sips of scotch, the Japanese pilot was talking animatedly about the future of naval aviation, dreams of new designs, of planes that could cruise at four hundred kilometers per hour, how the battleship was obsolete, as proven by the now disgraced Billy Mitchell, and all three were soon sharing the usual complaints about the hide-bound nature of battleship admirals lost in the past.

And as the hours slipped by James found, at first, an admiration for this young man, so dedicated, so intellectual and visionary.

Perhaps it was fueled by the scotch, perhaps by sentiment, but it was not all that long ago that he and Cecil had been like him, though their passion was code breaking.

With the coming of dawn another bottle had been consumed, the three were trading songs, at first traditional ballads of their respective branches, and from there descending into bawdy chanties that seemed to be amazingly universal in their plots and themes, no matter what the language.

Near Tokyo
11 April 1934
2:30 p.m.

"Hung over or not, my friend, I think it's time you saw what we can do!"

James, strapped down in the backseat of the open cockpit American-made Stearman biplane, wanted to beg for mercy.

The flight, well so far, had been relatively uneventful, even though he did vomit within five minutes after they had lifted off from the grass strip, leaving behind Cecil and several dozen cadets who had attended Fuchida's animated lecture about the future of naval aviation.

He tried to conceal what was happening in the backseat of the plane as he clutched the paper bag, losing his breakfast and the very, very light lunch he had all but avoided in anticipation of the flight.

But Fuchida had heard the retching noises, in spite of the howling of the wind around them, and chuckled through the voice tube . . . "still hung over?"

James could only groan, he was indeed hung over, and when finished vomiting, embarrassed, he didn't know what to do until Fuchida had told him to just simply toss the bag over the side.

He had leveled out at seven thousand feet, flying by dead reckoning along the east coast of Japan, and James, after a few more queasy moments, found that with the higher altitude, the cool, actually cold air, and the steadiness of the pilot's hand, his stomach had settled down. After a half hour he was no longer clutching the sides of the cockpit with a death grip, and after forty-five minutes, had even at last taken up Fuchida's offer for him to handle the stick and rudder.

And he was hooked. A scattering of cumulus clouds were forming, the warm air rising up from newly plowed fields below, and Fuchida had guided him through first circling one, then popping through it. At the final second before entering the billowy mass, James had nearly panicked, it looked so solid, and then he had burst out laughing as they blew through the other side a few seconds later. The second time he had actually piloted the plane into the next cloud, before they leveled out and continued on their heading to Tokyo.

Japan from the air was stunningly beautiful. The rich greens of early spring, fields of cherry, plum, and peach orchards startlingly brilliant in their multihued splashes of color. Small farm and fishing villages neatly laid out, the spine of the mountains of the central highlands, the highest peaks still capped with snow. He had hoped to see Fuji, and his friend had pointed out the direction, but it was capped in clouds. Ahead, he could see a distant haze and the outline of the bay. Tokyo was not far off now.

"Hang on!" Fuchida cried, and a second later the plane went into an aileron roll. As it tipped over and went inverted, James could not suppress a gasp of panic as they hung upside down, shoulder straps digging in, then easing as the roll continued and only seconds later leveling out.

He felt a queasiness returning.

"Like it?" Fuchida asked.

"Yeah, sure," James gasped.

"Then another one!"

This time James could feel the stick, which he held lightly, slap over hard, nose down a bit, the rudder petals shifting as Fuchida fed in opposite rudder. And the plane snapped over in a blur, ground and sky inverting, and then rolling back out.

"Now you do it?" Fuchida announced.

"What?"

"You do one. It always feels better when you are in control. Come on, James."

He swallowed hard, the nausea building, again that terrible first warning, cold sweat breaking out.

"Push the stick over to your left and then push the right rudder as you begin to roll, that will keep you from just going into a banking turn. Keep the nose down as you roll, then reverse slightly, pull the stick back a little when inverted, that will keep the nose down, then forward again as you come out of the roll, then level off."

James said nothing, the sweat beginning to soak him.

"Ready?"

"Yeah," was all he could gasp.

"Now!"

He didn't budge the stick for a moment until finally he felt it nudge slightly under his hand, Fuchida up forward urging him on. He had to take the challenge and did as ordered, pushing hard over to his left, working the rudder, feeling Fuchida guiding him there a bit, adding in a little more, and the plane rolled through onto its back. For a second he panicked, feeling as if they were about to just simply fall upside down, but the roll continued and several seconds later they were leveled back out . . . and he felt a pure rush of joy!

"Damn, that was great!" he shouted.

"Another one then?"

"Sure!"

This time he felt more confident and once the roll was completed, he could not resist leaning forward and slapping Fuchida on the shoulder, the pilot laughing.

"I'll take you on as a student and have you flying off carriers in six months!"

"If only," James replied.

Their four rolls had dropped them down a couple of thousand feet so he could now see Tokyo Bay clearly ahead.

"We'll soon be over the bay, so no playing around, but I want to show you something," Fuchida announced.

"Anything."

And James found the nausea was gone and at this moment he wished they could just continue to stay up here, to float through the sky, the roar of the engine now a wonderful harmonious sound.

"Recognize anything?" Fuchida asked.

James looked around and found that he could easily see the vast sprawl of the city just half a dozen miles ahead, smoke from factories, not sure but perhaps a glimpse of the Imperial compound, and then the harbor itself filled with hundreds of ships, half a dozen passenger steamers, dozens of cargo ships, even the dot of sails of sampans and there, in the naval yard, his own ship, the *Oklahoma.*

Fuchida banked slightly and lined up on the battlewagon and throttled up, the pitch of the engine going from a steady reassuring hum to a loud roar, the wind shrieking in the wires and support struts.

Details started to become evident, even the white dots of sailors up on deck.

"You still strapped in?" Fuchida asked.

"Yes, why?"

And with that his stomach felt as if it were up in his throat as Fuchida pushed the nose over into a dive, again a moment of panic, but James rode it out, stunned by the acceleration of speed, the size of his ship growing. They were heading down at a 60-degree dive for the bay below, and though he trusted the pilot, he did wonder for a second if they would just simply plow into the ocean. At what seemed the last possible second he felt as if he were being shoved down into his seat as they pulled several Gs coming out of the dive, leveling out a scant fifty feet above the harbor, racing straight toward the *Oklahoma*.

They were less than a mile out, and within seconds the battleship seemed to fill the world before him, becoming larger and yet larger. He could see some of the sailors on the deck turning, looking, pointing.

"Can't get too close!" Fuchida shouted, "your captain might not approve!"

And he yanked back on the stick, plane soaring back up and then banking over sharply so that James was looking straight down at the deck, five hundred feet below.

"That's what a torpedo attack would be like!" Fuchida shouted.

James could not reply, startled by the moment. He had been caught up by the sheer exhilaration, even contemplating how he would boast to his comrades later that he was aboard the plane that buzzed them, but now he saw it differently.

He could imagine twenty, thirty such planes coming in at the same time and the thought was frightful. And in that instant he knew that the pilot Fuchida was right, and all the admirals were dead on wrong. This

USS Oklahoma *(BB-37) off the Philadelphia Navy Yard, Pennsylvania, on 21 August 1929, following modernization.* **Naval Historical Center**

crate he was in was the future, not the guns down below.

It took years to build a battlewagon and tens of millions of dollars, and millions more just to keep her afloat each year. The plane he was in, how much? Ten thousand at most. The pilot far more expensive than the plane. If twenty such planes could break through, armed with torpedoes, the only thing that could stop them would be other planes, if they reacted fast enough. If not, the battleship was as good as dead.

Their conversation of last night, Fuchida's animated lecture of this morning, he was right. Planes would continue to improve, become faster, more agile, have greater range, be more deadly, while the battleship had reached its climax, nothing could be added to it to make it more efficient other than to just make it bigger, with bigger guns, but what use were those guns against planes? And a bigger ship would simply be a larger target to hit from above.

He said nothing, looking aft as they raced off and then the engine throttled back, speed dropping. They were coming down, and he saw the landing field, a broad open grass plain with a paved strip in the middle.

Nose pitched up, speed dropping, strange for a second, he thought with nose up they should climb but then realized it was actually the throttle that controlled climbing and dropping, by pitching the nose up with the throttle nearly closed, Fuchida was bleeding off speed and the plane was dropping.

The ground came racing up, he braced nervously, and then ever so gently there was a slight lurch, and they were down, rolling straight down the center line of the landing strip, slowing more, then taxiing over to a hangar, and then silence as the engine shut down.

Fuchida, already unstrapped, stood up, then turned to look at James, flight helmet pushed back, goggles off, grinning.

"What do you think?" he asked, and again there was that boyish enthusiasm.

James unsnapped his harness, taking off goggles and helmet, and, a bit shaky, stood up. Fuchida was now out on the wing, extending a hand to help him out, for which James was grateful, his back more than a little stiff. He backed down along the wing and alighted on the ground, knees feeling a bit weak.

Several enlisted men were by the plane, and Fuchida ordered them to refuel and for someone to find a staff car to take their guest back to his ship.

"You didn't answer me?" Fuchida said, putting his hand on James's shoulder.

"The flight, it was beautiful," he said, hesitating a bit.

"Your stomach feels fine now?"

"Yes."

"You seem troubled, my friend."

James nodded, unable to hide what he was thinking, that moment when the joy of flying had changed to something else, the realization of the game they were playing at and all the frightful implications of this machine of canvas, wood, and gasping engine.

"I see your point now," James said quietly.

Fuchida nodded, understanding, and he seemed troubled as well.

"You showed me something I never really understood until I was out there with you."

"And your report to your admirals?" Fuchida asked.

James hesitated.

"Perhaps I shouldn't have taken you on this flight. Maybe I've made you a convert."

James nodded.

"I honestly hope we will not be enemies some day, Commander Watson," and he spoke formally now, using James's official title as if speaking to a superior.

"What could be gained by either side?" James replied.

"But we are professionals and must answer to our orders when given."

"A war between us?" James replied. "Hard to imagine."

"Yes. I hope you convey that in your report as well. Do not underestimate us, that is always a fatal mistake for any country to do. Do not misread us."

"Nor should you underestimate us," James replied forcefully.

Fuchida did not say anything for a moment, then nodded in reply.

"I will remember that as well."

A small car, an American Ford, came onto the field and rolled to a stop by the plane, the driver getting out. One of the ground crew having already fetched James's overnight bag from the small cargo hold while another helped him out of his leather flight jacket, James a bit embarrassed that it was stained with the remnants of his breakfast.

He started to hand over his goggles and helmet.

Fuchida smiled and shook his head.

"Keep them as a souvenir of the flight."

James grinned and nodded his thanks.

He truly liked this man, in fact something had happened in the plane and the night before. Drink with a potential enemy and you might find common ground and that he had done last night. Flying had done the rest. This man loved his work, not just as a warrior, but he could sense the joy Fuchida felt as well, and he had shared that as they had soared over cherry and peach orchards in bloom. They had shared the joy of the moment and in that found yet more common ground. The diving attack on the *Oklahoma* had changed things back.

James looked at him and felt he had to be

honest with this man.

Fuchida formally saluted him and James returned the salute, then they shook hands.

"I'll pray you never have to do for real what we did out in the harbor, my friend," was all he could say and then he got into the car and went back to his ship, there to write a report of all that he had observed, a report he knew would just be simply filed away and forgotten as he slipped into retirement and was forgotten as well.

CHAPTER TWO

Chartwell, England
4 March 1936

"Cecil, glad you could come!"

Cecil Stanford approached Winston Churchill, hand extended, the two shaking warmly, Winston patting him on the shoulder and directing him over to sit by the fire in his study. It was a typical English late-winter day outside, dark, blustery, chilled rain coming down. Shed of his umbrella, hat, and overcoat at the entry, Cecil was glad to settle down into the heavy red leather chair, Winston personally pouring a good two fingers of scotch into an ornate cut glass tumbler for his guest and nearly twice as much for himself. He motioned to the half-open ice bucket, and Cecil shook his head.

"Good man, can't see why anyone would water down a proper single malt."

The room was typical "Winston," overstuffed leather chairs, all four walls lined with bookshelves, in some places the books neatly arranged, the proper leather-bound editions any gentleman might have up for display, in other places books stacked up sideways, slips of notepaper sticking out from between pages, half a dozen volumes piled up on the floor near his chair.

The small table between them held all the "essentials": a heavy cut-class decanter, the leather-clad bucket of ice, a humidor for the cigars, and two ashtrays, both of them overflowing.

Over the fireplace was a typical painting of battle, something from his illustrious ancestor's time, the Duke of Marlborough, lines of cavalry charging forward against the French. The air was rich with the scent of cigar smoke, well-seasoned oak from the fireplace, and that slightly old and musty smell that all such homes of the landed English gentry always seemed to have . . . in short the remembered scent of home. Having just returned the week before, after eight years in Japan, it was a blessing.

Of course he had loved his posting to Etajima, at least up until the final semester. His young charges, almost to a man, had proven to be a delight to work with. Once past their rigid external barriers, so many had opened up. His "tradition" of a Sunday afternoon English tea, his English club he had called it, was often met with an overflow crowd, the boys laughing as they forced themselves to speak only in English, peppering him with questions about everything from cricket, to the king, to Shakespeare. His advanced students would try to tackle *Macbeth,* and it seemed to resonate with them, they exclaiming that it was like many of their own tales.

A bit of a chilling thought for him was whenever he compared their eagerness, dedication, and toughness to his old school chums back home, or the current crop of ensigns being turned out by England and America, it was a frightful comparison.

Among many of his peers, Japanese professors of other subjects, friendships had developed as well. He had been invited, during summer breaks, to all parts of the islands, had climbed Fuji, an experience that he thought would kill him, and even enjoyed a two-week cruise aboard their battleship *Hiei,* amazed with how "English" it felt, except for the cuisine, typically rice balls, and some kind of fish which he often suspected was not cooked, or barely cooked at all. Though as a joke, on the final night aboard, the officer's mess had presented him with a proper serving of fish and chips, complete to it being wrapped up in a copy of the *London Times.*

The friendship was warm, courteous, he would often be invited for evening tea to watch a sunset or moonrise. There had even been polite and very circumspect hints on several occasions regarding his bachelorhood, but mention of Allison, who had died along with the twins in an auto accident right after the end of the war, had stilled those inquiries.

It had been a warm, pleasant assignment, teaching English at Etajima, but of course it had to come to an end, and in the last year, he could sense things changing. His students were, as always, polite to a fault, but the number attending the teas dropped off, and at one uncomfortable session the tradition of not discussing politics had broken down, a firebrand student asking for justifications for European colonialism and why Japan was not viewed as an equal partner in the global community. The others had sat silent, heads slightly bowed, and yet he could sense that what was being revealed was what was being discussed openly when he was not present.

He noticed a certain distancing when in the faculty mess, a few times even an embarrassed silence when he walked in, a sense that conversations were suddenly changed. And thus it was no surprise when, in the middle of the autumn semester, he was informed that his wonderful services were no longer required, regretfully due to budget concerns. No surprise either that a Japanese instructor would take his place.

Though he missed Japan, especially upon returning to London on a raw winter day, not really sure of what his "prospects" for the future held, still it was good to be home again.

They chatted politely for several minutes, catching up on life. Long ago, before going to "Room Forty," a secret naval decoding center, Cecil had first come to Winston's notice as a young adjutant, enlisted then commissioned right after graduation from Cambridge with a degree in Oriental studies, serving in the Admiralty. Upon discovery that he had attended Harrow, the boarding school that had changed Winston's life, a bond formed, since Cecil, though twenty years younger, had studied under many of the same teachers who had guided Winston.

When things started to go wrong in Gallipoli, meaning on the very first day, Winston had dispatched him there as a personal observer of the fiasco that eventually caused his fall from the Admiralty.

Cecil had stayed on in the Med, posted as a liaison to the Japanese naval squadron in the Mediterranean, before transferring to Room Forty for the last year of the war. Winston and he had stayed in touch on and off over the years, and yet Cecil was surprised that Winston somehow knew he was back in England after his long stint at Etajima and had sent an invitation for him to come out to the countryside for an overnight visit and "chat."

Winston had aged tremendously since last he had seen him, nearly a decade ago. It wasn't just the physical aging though, there was a seasoning to him, the youthful enthusiasm had lessened, it was obvious he was burdened down. When Cecil had mentioned to a few friends where he was going to spend the weekend, there had been almost outright horror or disdain shown by them . . . "that madman, he'll get us into another war the way he talks!"

Winston, it seemed, was now something of a social pariah with his outspoken criticism of the government and his calls of alarm over the rising of that "goose-stepping little corporal" as the *Times* had quoted him just a few days past.

They shared their drink and cigars, catching up on family news for Winston, and a respectful avoidance of the subject regarding Cecil's own.

"Guess you know why I asked you here," Winston finally said, cutting to the chase, "delighted to see you, Cecil, but I need to get your insights now."

"You want to talk about the coup attempt by the army in Tokyo last week?"

Winston nodded vigorously.

"Not just that, but things there in general. I'll confess I've been preoccupied with that crew of thugs in Germany of late, but there are far broader issues confronting England in the days to come. I could wander over to the appropriate office along Whitehall for a briefing, but as you know, I'm not all that welcome in some quarters."

Cecil smiled knowingly.

Winston leaned forward, picking up a couple of small logs and tossing them onto the fire, the wood crackling, sparks floating up the chimney.

"I want to understand just what the hell is going on over there. Fifteen years back we counted the Japanese as firm allies. With Stalin in power, I had hoped the Japanese could be a counterforce to any adventures he might consider in China. But there are rumblings, Cecil, rumblings that something over there is going wrong, terribly wrong."

Winston finished his drink and poured a few more ounces, looking over at Cecil, brows furrowed, that look of deep concentration and intensity he was famed for.

"Remember Lawrence?" Winston asked.

"You mean Thomas?" Cecil asked.

Winston nodded.

"Yes, heard about his death while still in Japan. Motorcycle, wasn't it?"

"Sad loss. A good friend," he gazed at the fire. "We all should have listened to him a bit more closely, he had a feel for the Middle East. But too high-strung, eccentric, and, of course, those detestable false rumors that followed him."

Cecil said nothing.

"Don't believe them for a moment, mind you, but still a brilliant man."

He looked over again at Cecil.

"When I read in the *Times* about this coup attempt in Japan, well, I thought of Lawrence for some reason. And that led me to you."

"Me, sir?"

Winston smiled. "You're no swashbuckler in white robes" — Winston laughed softly — "but you have a feel for the place. You're not with the Foreign Office, those bloody fools, and you're no longer in the service so you can speak your mind. And I thought, by God, if there's anyone that can explain it all to me, it's you, Cecil."

"Well, comparing me to Lawrence and all his exploits in Arabia, that is a stretch, sir."

"Find me someone else then who can explain the Japanese and what is going on over there. Find him right now and you're off the hook. Otherwise, for the moment you are now officially my Lawrence of Japan, or should I say Cecil of Japan."

Cecil could not help but smile. When Winston wanted to pour on the charm he could do so in spades. He sat back in his chair, sipping the scotch, trying to collect his thoughts. He suspected, of course, that this was why Winston had summoned him to his private retreat. The army coup plot had made the papers for a day or two, but then was submerged by news from Germany, the crisis in Spain, and the usual foolery about sports, fashion, and film stars.

"Fine then, sir, but let me warn you, I can give it to you two ways: I can tell you who the players are, what happened, and why; but I fear you'll be lost in a sea of names and secret societies, and side-switching that will leave you dizzy. Or another way, what I see as the reasons behind the coup, and what it actually means."

Winston smiled and Cecil relaxed slightly. Though charming, Winston had little time for fools, even those fools whom he considered loyal subordinates or even friends. He could indeed summon a report as a PM but he wanted something different.

"You know what I want."

"Right then, and remember my information is the same as yours in one respect, I had to glean the information from the *Times* and fill in the blanks with what I already knew.

"The hard fact news item is that a small group of army dissidents attempted a coup: several key government officials were killed, and then the coup was speedily suppressed with only a handful of casualties.

"Based on several previous incidents, quite similar to this one, but which did not draw such international attention, the dissidents will go on trial, and a year from now will be quietly released."

"Which means they have support within the government?"

"No, sir, and I think here is where you want some answers."

"The government now, as I understand it," Winston said, "is Western leaning, wants to rein in the army after its romp into Manchuria, and keep good relations with us and America. So if there's hidden support, does that mean the government is about to switch policies?"

"Not quite yet," Cecil interjected. "We define a coup as an actual attempt to overthrow the government, a dissident group trying to seize power and take over. In Japan, that is not necessarily the case. The Emperor, of course, is sacred and immovable; there is absolutely no Western comparison to his position."

Cecil shook his head.

"No sir, it is not about actually overthrowing the whole lot. What happened last week in Japan, their word for it is *gekokujo.*"

Winston mouthed the word silently.

"It means *insubordination,* but not insubordination as we define it. That sir, is always the problem when dealing with Japan. So many subtleties of thought and words fail to translate. We say insubordination and we think of a young corporal gone cheeky to his sergeant, or a government minister telling the PM to go to hell."

Winston chuckled softly.

"And sometimes deservedly so."

"*Gekokujo* is insubordination with a higher purpose. It is actually an act of loyalty, at least to those who perform it, loyalty to a higher ideal, to the Emperor and beyond him to the concept of nation. Even there, the word 'nation' does not translate effectively. It can even be construed, at times, as an act of loyalty to the very man they are attempting to kill, to try and awaken him and have him return to a righteous course."

"Killing him awakens him?" Winston grumbled. "That is one hell of a stretch."

"Not in their culture. Don't get all confused by how some Westerners view Buddhism and reincarnation. The Japanese blend, at least for the warrior class, is strongly mixed with Shintoism, the worship of ancestors and, by extension, the greater concept of national identity. If at the moment of death, the man who is slain faces it with stoic honor and a realization of atonement, then the killers have actually done him a favor. After they kill him, they'll salute the body, even clean up the mess, and apologize to the family for the inconvenience they have created before leaving."

"Bloody insane if you ask me," Winston replied. "Some damn hothead who is pro-Nazi or Communist puts a bullet in me, and I thank him for it? Like hell!"

Cecil chuckled and shook his head.

"I think a story might explain it best. Have you ever heard of the forty-seven ronin?"

Winston shook his head.

"It is, to the Japanese, an epic as powerful to their national psyche as Henry V or the legends of Arthur are to us, or for that madman over in Germany, the Ring cycle of Wagner."

"Too many fat ladies shrieking for my taste." Winston chuckled.

"The story is a favorite kabuki play, told in schools, performed in puppet theaters, held up as a national ideal, and *gekokujo* is at the core of it."

"Go on, you have my attention with this."

"It was several generations after the ending of the civil wars that unified Japan, when the Tokugawa clan controlled the Shogunate. The atmosphere at the court had become highly rarified, filled with intricate rituals, the most subtle gestures conveying great meaning, the slightest stumbling in proper etiquette a source of amusement and disdain. One could perhaps compare it to Versailles on the eve of the revolution. The slightest breach of protocol triggered ridicule.

"A daimyo from an outback region . . ."

"Daimyo?" Winston asked.

"Say our equivalent of a baron from the hinterlands."

"Ireland," Winston said, with a bit of a sardonic grin.

"Exactly. . . . arrives at the court, summoned to do his turn of duty, as were all vassals of the Shogun. It was considered an honor of course, but also a way of keeping an eye on the underlings.

"This daimyo arrives at the court, accompanied by his knights, forty-seven samurai. He makes a shambles of things with his behavior from the first day. He understands nothing of what the Japanese court considers to be the higher arts of a cultured man. It might seem strange to us, but here you have these tough samurai warriors, and I do mean tough. Good lord, man to man, they'd have cut any of our medieval knights to ribbons. Yet they place great stock in being cultured, being able to arrange flowers, to come up with an appropriate poem while watching cherry blossoms fall, to properly serve tea.

"Frankly, we aren't all that different, sir, though, the way we greet each other, the expectations for an officer in combat to show total indifference to danger, the way a cultured man offers another a drink and a cigar, the old rituals of the regimental mess that you once knew. It is a way of marking a man and his social class."

Winston grunted and nodded in agreement, a crease of a smile lighting his features

112

with old memories of long ago in Africa and India.

"So the humiliation gets worse by the day," Cecil continues, "and then enters the Court Chamberlain, the master of ceremonies we would call him."

"And he won't help," Winston interjects.

Cecil nodded. He could see that Winston was getting involved in the story.

"Won't help unless a bribe is paid. The daimyo is from a poor province, but beyond the issue of money, his pride forbids him from lowering himself thus, to pay a bribe to a simpering court official."

"I think I can see where this is going," Winston interjected, pausing then to prepare and light a cigar, thus giving time for Cecil to continue.

"Matters reach a head when the daimyo is humiliated once too often in front of the Emperor, the entire court laughing behind their sleeves when he fumbles a ceremony. Drawing his blade, he turns on the Chamberlain, who flees; the Emperor's guards jump upon the outraged daimyo and disarm him.

"Well now, he has violated a sacred court law. It does not matter the provocation, he has drawn a blade in the presence of the Emperor and there is only one recourse left.

Dishonored, he must commit seppuku."

"You mean hara-kiri? Is it true they actually cut their stomachs open?" Winston asked, and Cecil could sense an almost schoolboy curiosity about the details.

"In the full ceremony, yes," Cecil replied, "but usually there is just a ritual cut, or for the braver, a thrust of the blade into the stomach, and then a second beheads the poor devil. So thus it is done. The offending daimyo dies, and in the West that is where the story would die as well."

"Obviously this leads us back to the matter at hand, this coup attempt," Winston said.

And Cecil realized that though Winston did love a good story, he also wanted the point to be made as quickly as possible, so he nodded.

"It makes a powerful point. The forty-seven samurai who had come with their now dead daimyo are disgraced as well. In their world, they had failed to protect their lord. No other house will take them in, even if they sought that, but they did not. They became ronin. A ronin is a samurai who has no lord to serve. Without a lord he has no colors to wear, he is something of a societal outcast, in fact he is seen as on the borderline of the law, for many ronin turn to robbery and murder.

"The Emperor, upon the punishment death of the rather tragic daimyo, passes a decree that the matter is settled once and forever. Law had been broken in the court, penalty exacted, case is closed.

"The forty-seven samurai, who were the daimyo's retainers, are now completely disgraced by the Emperor's decree. In their culture, it is they who are at fault."

"How so? The bloody fool should have paid the bribe and be done with it, or get someone of influence to put pressure on the Chamberlain. My God, if someone pulled a revolver out in front of the King or in Parliament, there'd be hell to pay."

"Now we are getting into the deeper issues with these Japanese," Cecil said, with a smile. He nodded toward the decanter of scotch, and Winston, smiling, waved for him to refill, which he did. Wreathed in smoke, Winston then nodded for him to continue.

"Disgraced in their world, the forty-seven ronin did not leave the capital. Instead they remained in the city, apparently casting aside their ceremonial robes and selling their swords. They took on the most menial of tasks, gardeners, night soil collectors, wood cutters, drifting to the edge of society, and over time they were all but forgotten."

Cecil smiled.

"They waited for over a year. The Chamberlain was no fool; he knew they were out there, watching, waiting. He kept his guard up, extra samurai to keep watch day and night, so much so that he himself became something of a laughingstock, viewed as a coward afraid of his own shadow. But he had reason to be afraid.

"For finally, he did let his guard down, and then, at last, the leader of the forty-seven ronin, his name was Oishi, summoned his comrades together. In secret, they met in the graveyard where their lord was buried, and from secret hiding places drew out their ceremonial robes of his house and their swords, which they had not sold."

Winston leaned forward, caught up in the tale.

"They stormed the Chamberlain's palace and slaughtered everyone. Cornered, the Chamberlain begged for his life, but they killed him and took his head."

Winston slapped his knee.

"Figured it would be something like that."

Cecil nodded.

"But there's far more, sir. You see they had, in so doing, fulfilled their own sense of honor, and yet had directly violated the will of the Emperor. They were now hunted men."

"The hue and cry went up. There are several versions of what happened next, but finally they are brought before the Emperor himself who orders them to commit suicide."

Cecil nodded and unable to contain his desire any longer he motioned to the box of cigars, which Winston happily offered. He had managed to drop the habit in Japan, good tobacco was all but impossible to find there, but the scent of the smoke, the warmth of the fire, the taste of good scotch, a cigar would make it complete; and Winston sat in silence as Cecil unwrapped the cigar, cut the end, and puffed it to life.

"But, sir, there is far more. A Westerner hearing the story might say it's a rousing good tale but not see the deeper meaning to it, a meaning that relates to what happened in Japan last week."

"And that is?"

"*Gekokujo.* Their actions ultimately were *gekokujo.* Yes, they got the revenge they felt duty-bound to fulfill, but there is also their suicides. It was not just an apology to the Emperor for breaking the law, as some might read it. It was a message direct to the Emperor and the Shogun, an act of rebellion. The message was that they were right, and he had done wrong. The Emperor had failed their daimyo, allowing a corrupt official to stay in the court. He had failed in allowing a good man to be driven to the point of madness by this corrupt official. Killing the Chamberlain therefore was an act the Emperor or Shogun themselves should have done long ago. Their suicide would remain in the national psyche, be a lesson to all, and restore balance and purity."

"Connect the two," Winston said, "this rebellion and the story."

"Easy enough, sir. The coup attempt on February 26 was carried out by a small cadre of disenchanted junior officers in the army and some revolutionary radicals. They are enamored with a mystical sense of a unique and special destiny for Japan. Their concept of nationhood is unlike ours. It is nationalism tied to religion, tied to, for lack of a better term, a racial destiny."

"God save us, not another Hitler and his drivel," Winston growled.

"No sir, very different and one that will make us feel a bit uncomfortable. The Japanese nation is a joined entity. Their religion a dual one, an aesthetic form of Buddhism, Zen Buddhism, which truly fits the warrior code of the samurai. That life is a fleeting illusion, with a reality beyond that illusion. To let go of life is, in a way, to embrace life. Inculcate that into the hearts of warriors, and you have a fearsome opponent.

"Combine that with Shintoism. On the surface it is ancestor worship, a bit like the Romans if you will: the family and its honor is everything. The individual is nothing when compared to the family.

"Believe me, when I taught at their academy I saw it every day. The lads there would endure treatment and schedules that would set off a rebellion in our Sandhurst. And to wash out? Death is better. In fact, when a boy did wash out, a suicide watch had to be kept until he was escorted off the base, and not infrequently we'd hear that the poor boy had killed himself rather than endure the shame of facing his family as a failure."

Cecil fell silent for a moment. The memory of more than one of them was still troubling.

"Potentially a tough adversary," Winston interjected.

"Exactly. But to the point you seek. The coup? A sham. No one in their right mind, at least a Western right mind, would ever see it as having the remotest chance of success."

"What was it they wanted? The reports in the *Times* are not clear at all, just saying some disgruntled soldiers."

Cecil shook his head.

"Oh, there were some tenets spouted, sounded a bit communistic to some. Limits on amount of money a family can have, nationalization of industry, elimination of corruption, and, a key here, a return to a state of national purity."

Winston cocked his head.

"How so? Sounds Fascist to me, this national purity thing."

"Sir, don't confuse the two. They mean it as a true state of purity. Like a minister saying it's time to get right with Jesus. It's about this national sense that Japan is unique, exceptional, the Emperor godlike.

"That one is tough to explain. A bit like the old Egyptians and their Pharaohs, but different. The Emperor is a direct bond back to the creator of all, and since the manifestation of that creator is Japanese, well then, that means Japan is exceptional in the eyes of God.

"Even their dating system is a reflection of their unique ties to the Emperor. They count years from the accession of Japan's first in 660 BC. They consider this to be the year 2596.

"They even name their planes by the year of the Emperor. Their newest bomber was introduced this year as a Type 96 because it is being introduced in 2596. Every time they turn around, they are reminding themselves of the length of their heritage, the sanctity of their Emperor, and the uniqueness of their nation and race. You should not underestimate how deeply this defines them and makes them dedicated and courageous.

"These revolutionaries, these young Turks you might call them, are not about overthrowing the Emperor, rather it is to purify the government, to restore Japan to its proper destiny, and, yes, to send a message to the Emperor that his house needs to be placed back in order, in balance. I daresay that before they shot some of the officials, they most likely apologized first. It was a ritual.

"So, they've been arrested, the trial will be a show trial. The dead will be buried, but mark my words, the national destiny has just changed, even though by our standards the coup was a tragic farce and put down before it even started.

"Even as people publicly shake their heads over the bloodshed, in their hearts, the way they see the world, the men in the coup were purists out to cleanse Japan. We must remember, it is a country that has gone through a stunning cultural shock.

"There are people still alive today who can recall a world where firearms were unknown, no machinery, totally cut off from the outside world. They started their modernization in the 1860s, and in less than forty years trounced a colossal Western power, the Russians. They now race to carry out rapid industrialization, though without the resources inside their borders to do so. Besides looking at any graphs or charts about growth and economics, we must realize the psychic shock to their entire system. They know they have to embrace the future to survive, but within, there is a terrible longing for what was a world of proper order, control, without disturbance from an outside world that did not even exist. That outside has brought impurity and chaos; the rebels wanted order restored, purity restored."

"And the army is the one to do that," Winston grumbled.

Cecil nodded.

"They see themselves as the inheritors of the samurai class system. Through them the uniqueness of Japan will be saved, and add in this doctrine that the ultimate destiny of Japan, now that it has been forced to join the global community, is to free all of Asia of Western influence and unify it, under their leadership of course.

"Expect a sea change, sir. There'll be an awakening of nationalism, a silent admiration for this act of *gekokujo,* even from some of the very people threatened by it. And we, sir, will eventually be the target."

Winston exhaled noisily.

"Go on, it is what I was wondering."

"Remember, they actually admire us. That's something the Japanese are good at, admiring what is admirable in others and then borrowing it. The Romans were the same, remember. Culture, art, religion hijacked wholesale from the Greeks, naval skills from the Carthaginians, trade from the Phoenicians, mysticism from the Egyptians. The Japanese turned to us to help build their navy because we were the best. When it came to their land forces, more than one German was out there as an advisor fifty years ago. And like us, they covet an Empire and see nothing wrong with it.

"Their argument has its points. Imagine if it had been the Chinese coming around the Horn rather than Europeans; and Spain, Italy, and France were now controlled by

Orientals. Might we not nod in agreement if Hitler, instead of preaching his German purity, was instead preaching a white, Western purity, asking why we allowed Orientals to rule us?"

Winston said nothing. And Cecil knew there was nothing he could say. He was a dyed-in-the-wool Imperialist; he had fought as a young man for the Empire; and now, in late middle age, stood firm on the India question.

"They want, as the Kaiser once said, 'their place in the sun' and that is the East. Too bad the world was not bigger, that there was still terra incognito out there that we could point them toward. But it is not so. The sub-text to this coup is about racial destiny, not just in Japan, but across the entire East."

"You mean China."

Cecil nodded.

"It's a quagmire. The Nationalists, the warlords, the Communists all at each other's throats, and the Japanese sitting in their puppet state up in Manchuria watching the show. Nature abhors a vacuum as they say, and to them, China is a political vacuum that they know they can straighten out."

"You mean conquer and exploit."

"I could bring you more than one of their naval officers, good men, many educated right here in England or the States, and they will sip tea with us and ask a blunt question. Would we want them in China or Stalin instead."

Churchill grunted disdainfully at the mere mention of the Soviet leader.

"Bloody butcher," he muttered.

Cecil leaned back in his chair, his cigar having gone out, and he looked over at Winston.

"Sir, you might be focused here, on Europe, on Germany, but believe me. I spent eight years teaching their lads at the academy. I respect and admire them, would go to sea with any of them. But there is a logic building that is vastly different from the way we think. They vividly feel their lack of oil. They know oil is the key to modern power. They are determined to find a way to secure a stable supply. In their minds the alternative is not defeat; it is suicide. They believe they will cease to fulfill their destiny if they cannot find a way out of this box. On the surface, to contemplate a naval war with us, and most likely the United States combined, perhaps even French and Dutch forces thrown in, well that would be suicide. On the surface it would look like that.

"But they have a different sense of their time, their place in history. Suicide perhaps, but they have faced greater odds and won, and I think under the skin of most of them, they are gamblers with fate. Perhaps it's their religion. So what if you lose, but you do so with honor. The wheel of life turns, and you return, and the honor of your family and of your race is made richer by your sacrifice."

"And your conclusions?" Winston asked.

"Sooner or later, we'll have to fight them."

Winston took a deep puff on his cigar, inhaled, and blew out.

"What is your situation now, Stanford?"

"Well, sir, to be honest, at loose ends. The naval pension helps enough. My sister has offered to share her home out near Saulsbury, a pleasant little place. Some friends have encouraged me to try my hand writing a book about my years in Japan, perhaps look at some of the smaller colleges for a professorship."

Winston chuckled.

"Hard way to make a living. Some day I'll tell you about dealing with publishers."

He looked up at the ceiling.

"How would you feel about going back out there?"

"Sir?"

"The Orient."

Stanford didn't reply for a moment.

"Well, sir, I was kind of thinking of some time in England for a while."

"To do what? Get rusty. Eccentric country gentleman, daily walks, wind up talking to yourself. Believe me, this waiting here drives me half mad at times."

"And your proposal, sir?"

"Do what I did."

"And that is?"

"Correspondent, my good man. Gets you into places others could never access. Just say you're a reporter, and good heaven's doors can fly open."

"I never dreamed of doing such a thing," Stanford said quietly.

"You were going to write a book, weren't you? Go back out and write about what is happening now instead. The *Times* might be out, but I think a call to the *Manchester Guardian* might do the trick. Pay won't be so good, but then again, a few friends of mine can always see to things."

Churchill smiled knowingly. "Remember, that little adventure of mine in the Boer War made my career, and a tidy sum from the book sales as well."

"And the real game, sir?" Stanford asked.

Now his features were serious again.

"I'm curious about China, about our own affairs in Singapore, even our business interests still in Japan. You've made me aware of something, and I want to learn more, a lot more. And I trust you, Stanford, rare thing these days, to trust a man."

"In other words, I'd be working for you as a spy. Is that it, sir?"

Winston Churchill looked at Stanford and smiled. "My good man, you will be a correspondent now, you'll have your full credentials and travel vouchers back to the East within the week," and he paused, "but of course your special reports will come directly to me."

CHAPTER THREE

Naval Staff College, Tokyo
9 December 1936

Lieutenant Commander Fuchida looked up with anticipation as Commander Genda Minoru came through the door into the huge conference room. There was a stilling of voices of those gathered around the great table, over twenty feet long and fifteen feet wide, a map of the Pacific spread out upon it.

He stepped up to Fuchida's side, and there was a subtle nod of recognition. The two had become fast friends. Ten years before, Genda had been an instructor at the Yokosuka Air Station, Fuchida one of his students, both students and instructors practicing to perfection medium-level bombing but also beginning experiments with low-level torpedoes and this new doctrine the Americans and others were experimenting with, dive bombing. They

129

had parted ways with different assignments but were now reunited at the War College and were both kicking up quite a stir over air doctrine. The results of the annual fleet exercises were highly dependent on the "referees," since of course only simulated gunfire was used. These referees, all of them adherents to battleships, would judge that an attacking wave of torpedo planes had all been shot down long before coming into range, and the carriers then destroyed by, of all things, naval gunfire since the ships were linked to the carrier battle line, supposedly to launch spotter planes for the climactic conclusion of battleships squaring off.

Genda was relatively tall, nearly the same height as Fuchida, with sharp hawklike eyes and a brilliant intellect. Like Fuchida he had mastered the difficulties of the English language and at times the two would converse in it, especially when discussing the latest American film or their newest plane designs. Genda was the intellectual visionary, thinking in broad strategic and operational terms, while Fuchida was emerging as one of the finest pilots and aerial tacticians in the fleet, the one who attempted to put Genda's theories to the practical test.

They were the perfect team and Fuchida was intently focused on his friend, knowing that he was facing a major challenge within the next few minutes. The room was silent. Those gathered around the table were not just students, such as Fuchida, but more than a few of the senior instructors at the staff college; several of them wore the stars of admirals as well.

Genda first bowed to the portrait of the Emperor, all following suit, and then bows of acknowledgment to their superiors.

"May I have your permission to begin?" Genda asked, and there were nods of agreement. Fuchida could feel the tension in the room, for Genda was about to speak what some would consider to be nothing short of heresy, an attack on "Kantai Kessen," the strategic doctrine that had been the supposed masterpiece of Japanese strategic thinking in relationship to America since the start of the twentieth century.

"Let us open with the following assumption," Genda said, the slightest edge of nervousness in his voice, "that for whatever reasons, be they current situations or those not yet visible, war has been declared between America and us.

"The doctrine we call Kantai Kessen was formulated in the wake of our great victory against the Russians at Tsushima, and the assumption was a fair one to make. Be it the Russians or the Americans, their fleet would have to travel great distances before finally entering our home waters.

"The logistical problems for our foes would therefore be immense. Coal-fired ships with reciprocating engines would need mountains of fuel, and the engines would be worn down after such a lengthy voyage, needing serious maintenance before going into battle. As they approached we would have the advantage, as well, of choosing the time and place of battle, our ships fully prepared, our men rested, the waters known.

"At the appropriate time and place, we could then engage them in their weakened state and destroy them en masse. Once that fleet is sunk, the opponent would seek peace."

There were nods of agreement. It had been a plan honed and refined for over a generation.

"Kantai Kessen postulates the following: that upon the declaration of war, America will react with a forward movement in order to protect its interests in the Philippines and, to a lesser extent, China and the Orient in general. There are two variants but these are actually immaterial in a sense: one postulates that their main fleet is based out of ports on their West Coast, as it now is; the second is that it is based out of Pearl Harbor in Hawaii."

He picked up a long pointer and tapped the eastern edge of the map. "In either case, their fleet will sortie from Pearl, the only difference being a time factor of several weeks if they must first make a forward move from the West Coast and then stop at Pearl Harbor to refuel and refit before moving on.

"Our application of pressure upon the Philippines, in short an invasion, will force the Americans to react, at least that is what we assume."

"And what we do know from their own Orange Plans," one of the admirals interjected. "They believe we will attack, and their action plan is to bring full forces to bear and relieve the garrison in less than three months, in so doing, forcing battle with our fleet and destroying it."

Fuchida was surprised that this revelation about detailed knowledge of Plan Orange was being openly spoken about even within the confines of this room in the Staff College.

"Their own version of Kantai Kessen," Genda said quietly.

Fuchida caught the irony of what Genda

had just said; he was not sure if the others had. "The Americans will be forced to advance through the Central Pacific, securing bases as they advance for the final jump to the Philippines. The root of our plan is to concede the opening moves, to give back, to fall back with the main battle fleet staying within the safety of home waters. Engagements will be fought by light attack forces of destroyers and submarines. Our entire doctrine of submarine warfare is based around this, to go after the enemy's main battle fleet, to ignore his logistical support."

"Commander Genda, if you are going to raise that point again about submarines," came an objection from the back of the room, "please spare us. In the time allotted in this great campaign, our submarines will only be able to fight with the torpedoes they have on board. They are too slow to race back to their bases for a quick resupply of arms. Their role is to get directly in front of the enemy fleet, engage, and communicate the enemy location. If all twenty torpedoes on board a submarine are fired and but one enemy cruiser sunk, or a battleship crippled, that is far more to the advantage of the moment, to the ultimate battle, than harassing tramp steamers far to the rear."

Genda nodded as if apologizing.

"That is not my point today," he said, his voice almost humble.

"The Kantai Kessen plan," came another voice, "is predicated upon our strengths and weaknesses. As the Americans advance through the Marshalls, their only real route of approach, our land-based aircraft will weaken them further, whittling down their strength so that by the time the main line of battle engagement occurs, the numbers will be even, our men and ships rested and ready, the enemy worn and depleted. It will be another Tsushima, and it will end the war in one blow."

Genda sighed and shook his head.

"Please hear my theories. You agreed to attend for that purpose."

There were exchanged looks, one of the admirals nodding in agreement. "Go ahead."

"I maintain that two factors have rendered the Kantai Kessen plan obsolete and thus requires a complete rethinking of our strategy in the Pacific if war should ever occur." He looked around the room.

"When first conceptualized, the battleship was indeed the main strike force of any fleet. Its striking power is still the most deadly at close range, its mere existence, as the American theorist Mahan said, a projection of power in and of itself. But let me not open with what I suspect you think I will say of battleships versus other technologies. Rather, its range has changed. When the Russians steamed from the Baltic under our guns at Tsushima, their old coal-fired reciprocating engines were all but worn out. The ships of but thirty years past required constant and difficult maintenance, nearby bases, and, in truth, had a battle range of only a few thousand miles, with their captains always keeping a careful eye as to the nearest coaling station.

"That was part of our original plan. Our ships would stay close to home waters; the Americans would exhaust and weaken theirs merely by crossing the thousands of miles of water to reach us. That is changed. The new turbine engines, powered by oil with tankers for resupply, render that first weakening point obsolete. Battleships are now capable of steaming at high speed for thousands of miles without need of major overhaul."

He paused, looking around the room, and there were several nods of agreement, even from the known battleship admirals.

"Now to changing technologies. As the plane evolved in the 1920s, our plans incorporated it. Land-based aircraft would keep track of the approach of the enemy fleet and bomb it, thereby further weakening the approaching enemy. Some took heart from the American Mitchell's experiment. When a squadron of land-based bombers sank the hulk of a German battleship, skeptics called it a stunt and even claimed that Mitchell had explosions rigged on board the ship."

"A sham," one of the admirals exclaimed.

"I fully agree," Genda replied with a smile, and his comment caught many by surprise because they figured he was leading into the already known argument that aircraft would be the deciders of the next battle.

He nodded to Fuchida.

"Perhaps my friend, Lieutenant Commander Fuchida, can expand on this point."

Fuchida cleared his throat nervously.

"For several years I have been involved in experiments in a wide variety of aircraft, from seaplanes to land-based twin-engine bombers. It is our firm conclusion that land-based bombers, attacking horizontally at the standard accepted altitude of two thousand meters or more, which is required for the dropped bomb to accelerate to penetration speed, will be all but useless against ships capable of maneuver. An adroit ship's captain can easily outmaneuver individual planes and even small groups from the time the bomb is released until its impact. Even if, by remote chance, a target is struck, structural damage will be minimal and the cost in aircraft lost prohibitive."

"So aircraft are indeed ineffective against battleships," one of the admirals exclaimed with a smile, slapping the table.

"Respectfully, sir, I did not quite say that. I described land-based army aircraft attacking horizontally, which is currently how they are trained.

"However, we have seen tremendous strides in the last several years with the practice of dropping torpedoes from low level. As you know, a torpedo strike below the waterline is infinitely more deadly than a blow from above, even from that of a sixteen-inch shell, for the explosion is contained by the water and bursts inward. In turn, the attack would be supported by a new type of bomber, a dive bomber, which we know the Germans are learning to use with great effect in Spain.

"Commander Genda and his team have war-gamed the following scenario: a combined strike of one hundred aircraft striking a main battle fleet simultaneously from several directions. The result would be devastating, with the potential of sinking capital ships." Fuchida looked over at Genda and nodded, relinquishing his role.

"Lieutenant Fuchida is, without doubt, one of the finest pilots of our fleet, experienced in all types of aircraft and has personally developed some of the tactics we are now studying. Projecting forward several years, with heavier aircraft, faster aircraft, capable of carrying more deadly weapons, the results could be profound."

No one spoke for a moment.

"Then consider submitting a report to that effect, Commander Genda, and we shall study it," one of the admirals replied. "We are always open to the applications of new technologies."

"If we really accepted the power of airplanes, we would not be building more battleships," came a voice from the back of the room.

All turned in the speaker's direction, some with looks of respect, others not so respectful as the navy's new vice minister, Admiral Yamamoto, stepped forward.

All well knew the game within the game here this day. Genda and Fuchida were protégés of Yamamoto, and, in fact, were speaking for him, an ancient game of a younger samurai voicing the opinion of an elder and thus deflecting direct counterattack.

"They are a huge waste of resources," Yamamoto said forcefully, his open statement catching many by surprise. "If we really trusted in this analysis, we would immediately convert the seventy-thousand-ton battleships we are currently planning into giant aircraft carriers, capable of carrying two hundred or more planes each. Then we would have a real chance of winning naval dominance in the Pacific."

Several of the more traditional admirals exploded in anger at Yamamoto's heretical views. They had been engaged in this fight for several years; and even though they were getting the money to build the battleships they cherished, they simply could not stifle the voice of the former head of the technical division of the Aeronautics Department. Yamamoto was rising because of his sheer ability, despite the hostility of much of the more conservative wing of the navy.

No one spoke back directly to the vice minister, but the looks of hostility were barely concealed. He stood ready to accept a challenge, and then finally smiled and simply nodded.

"My apologies for interfering in the presentation. Mr. Genda, please continue." Yamamoto nodded toward the younger man.

Genda nodded politely, took a deep breath, and then pushed into the opening his "master" had already created.

"Sirs, I think I must express the deeper concern here. Even more than our ship-building program, our strategies and planning needs rethinking. The Kessen Plan projects a certain wearing down of the Americans as they move through the Marshalls and on to the Marianas. The potential of an overwhelming air strike might inflict such losses that they would halt, even withdraw, concede the Philippines, but then apply their massive industrial strength to build up, even if it took six months or a year."

There were looks of confusion.

"You present a contradiction, Genda," came a reply. "On the one side, Fuchida states that bombers are ineffective, but in the next breath declares them deadly."

Genda nodded.

"Carrier-based aircraft would be deadly: naval aircraft trained to fight against other ships, to strike them and sink them even as they maneuver. The army does not concern itself with such training. They might make some polite gestures, but their concerns are elsewhere. I maintain that carriers, properly employed, will profoundly change the entire focus of any future campaign at sea."

No one spoke in defense of the army, as he fully expected, but at the mention of carriers several shook their heads.

"Carriers though?" came a reply from one of the admirals. "Our numerous war games have always shown that the carrier, unarmored, loaded with highly flammable aviation gas, if struck by but one bomb can be placed out of operation for hours, days, perhaps even lost."

Genda nodded.

"And therefore, to commit them, unsupported or lightly supported, into a campaign against the Americans advancing through the Marshalls is too risky a venture, especially if scattered and ill protected as the main strike force is held back."

"No, I propose something far different," Genda replied, now speaking fast for he sensed he was about to lose his audience.

"Again, I must maintain that a delaying campaign through the Marshalls, having the Americans come to us, ultimately will play to the American strength of recovery and industrialization.

"No, instead the opening move should be that we strike first, strike hard, and strike with total surprise."

He looked around the room.

"How?" someone asked.

He picked up the pointer and again swept it to the eastern end of the table.

"If war against the Americans, which personally I would find to be regrettable, becomes inevitable, our move should not be to wait but rather to strike first. And not with battleships, but with carriers and not one or two carriers but six or eight carriers, capable of putting three hundred or more planes in the air. And in that first strike, destroy the American Fleet, in its entirety, in the opening blow."

His pointer came to rest in the waters around Hawaii.

"This should be our new plan, and Kessen should be laid to rest."

"Absurd," came a heated reply. "They will advance toward us; we know they will do that. Why venture far out, thousands of miles forward, in such a risk-laden venture, without nearby bases for support and repair. Let them come to us and walk into our trap."

"If one sets a trap for a fox, no matter how elaborate, and the fox declines to enter, the trap is a waste, even if built of solid gold," Genda replied forcefully. "What then? We all agree that if hostilities break out, time will be on the Americans' side. Suppose they decide to sit back and first build up."

"They must defend the Philippines; to lose them without a fight is a loss of face the U.S. Navy will never accept."

"Perhaps, ultimately, their navy will be focused more on victory than what we define as saving face. I therefore still maintain that it is we who should strike first."

He fell silent, looking about the room hoping that now debate would open up; that perhaps someone would ask for greater elaboration, but there was only silence and, after a moment, muttered comments about other meetings, a clearing of throats, nods of thanks, and the gathering broke apart, heading toward the door.

The room quickly emptied out.

Genda looked over at Fuchida and forced a smile.

"It's a start," he said, and Fuchida could only shake his head.

Finally only one other officer remained, and he stood across from them, looking down at the map table, and sighed.

"A good start and most courageous," Yamamoto said.

"Thank you, sir, I'm sorry it was not more successful."

"Personally I hope it never comes to it," Yamamoto continued. "I served in Washington, D.C., as an attaché, traveled extensively around the country, count many in their navy as my friends. For me, war with them would be unthinkable; there are far greater concerns, the Soviets for one.

"Genda, you are on the right track. You know I opposed the building of these new superbattleships. They are a waste of money. The key to the future is airpower, and the key to naval airpower is the carrier. I really came to understand that when I commanded the *Akagi* back in 1928. Here was Lindbergh crossing the Atlantic nonstop, and our hidebound admirals refusing to believe airplanes would matter.

"Something else for you to ponder. I have always been a gambler. I actually developed a system for roulette that made me a lot of money in Monaco when I was touring Europe. I like the gamble inherent in your plan. It fits life as I understand it. If possible, we should never fight. But if we have to fight, let's do it boldly and with courage and audacity.

"I'd like to see your written report on this," the admiral added, "and believe me I will not file it as many will do. Good day."

There was a polite exchange of bows, and the admiral left.

Fuchida watched Yamamoto depart with

open admiration and turned to Genda. "Now there is a leader I would follow into battle against anyone."

"Perhaps someday we will," Genda said quietly.

The Yangtze River above Shanghai
12 December 1937
3:45 p.m. Local Time

He didn't need binoculars to see them, and he felt a tightening in his gut. They were coming straight for him.

Though technically superior in rank to the captain of the river patrol boat *Panay,* it was not his place to give orders. The navy had placed him in Shanghai to head up the Small Signals Division there that was monitoring Japanese naval transmissions and, with his knowledge of the language, to act, if need be, as interpreter for the American Consulate Office to which he was officially attached. He had briefly stayed on with the Consulate Office when it was in Nanjing, but the navy had ordered him to report back to Shanghai . . . he was supposed to be going home, back to Pearl, back to retire, his last physical finally catching up with the arthritis he had tried to conceal. With the utter chaos of the Japanese invasion of

146

USS Panay *on standardization trial of 17.73 knots, on 30 August 1928, off Wosung, China.*
Naval Historical Center

coastal China now in full swing he felt it best to get aboard a ship of the United States for the trip back, and the gunboat *Panay* had now been his home for several days as it shepherded several small oil tankers and stayed just outside of Nanking to pick up the last Americans who wanted to get out.

It had been a good posting, but when the war between Japan and China started up in Peking in July and rapidly swept this way, he felt it best to send Margaret back to their home in Hawaii. Anti-Japanese sentiment was high, and though she was but half-Japanese, he didn't want to take any chances either with the Chinese, or, for that matter, the Japanese themselves.

He regretted not perhaps staying on in the city longer. His old friend Cecil was there, now working as a correspondent, and they had managed to share a couple of meals and drinks together, both not believing, as of yet, the horror stories that moved along the front lines as the Japanese overran the Nationalist army.

Though he was loath to admit it publicly, he was so fed up with the corruption of Chiang and the Nationalists and their inability to effectively cope with the Communist threat, that secretly there was part of him that kind of hoped the Japanese would just pull it off and be done with it. If they fought it the way they had the war with Russia in 1904, honorably and with boldness and then brought stability and peace to the region, in the long run it might be for the best after all.

Word, however, of their brutalities had run before them, and it was shattering to hear, in fact he did not want to believe it, for in so many ways he felt they were his people too. His lost son, part-Japanese, the woman he loved, part-Japanese, the language now as familiar to him as his own native tongue.

He did not want to believe it, but as he studied the approaching planes, several fighters, his gut instinct was a grave warning.

The "captain" of the gunboat, actually a fairly young lieutenant, had his binoculars raised, saying nothing, and when finally James cleared his throat, the lieutenant lowered the glasses to look at him.

"I don't mean to interfere, sir, but it might be trouble," James said softly.

He was breaking naval protocol. An officer in transit, even if he was an admiral, still deferred to the commander of the ship he was aboard, though once off that ship, he could tear him up one side and down the other. It was a delicate situation.

"They wouldn't dare," the lieutenant responded loudly and brashly, then raised his glasses back up.

But they did dare. . . .

The first of the fighters rolled over into a shallow Split S, while still a mile out over the river, then pulled out, dropping in low over the water. No sound yet: It looked to James like one of their new Type 96 fighters, sleek, a match for anything in the air, a glint of sunlight off the propeller; it was coming in fast, nearly four miles a minute, and then he saw it . . . like Christmas tree lights winking on either wing.

A split second later, water foamed on the river surface, geysers from the 7.7-millimeter rounds fountaining a dozen feet into the air.

"Jesus Christ, they're shooting at us!" someone screamed.

James caught a glimpse of some of the civilian refugees on the deck, who had been casually strolling about watching the approach of the fighter plane with interest, begin to scatter.

The fountains of water "walked" right into the *Panay* and suddenly there was the sound, the machine-gun firing, the roar of the plane's engine, the sound of bullets smacking into steel, ricocheting off, huge flecks of paint flying up, pockmarking the hull, and then the main deck cabin, windowpanes shattering.

The plane bore in, then roared overhead, the red rising sun painted beneath each wing.

The lieutenant stood, gap mouthed, unable to respond for a moment. "They're shooting at us . . . ," he gasped finally, unbelievingly.

James felt, for a brief instant, a strange,

almost surreal detachment from it all. Part of his mind refused to believe that this was happening at all, that the Japanese would dare actually attack an American ship. He spared a glance aft. The American flag was standing out in the noonday breeze . . . there was another flag painted atop the main deck cabin to clearly identify the ship from the air. No, it couldn't be . . . and yet even as his mind rebelled, he saw the second plane leveling off just above the water, boring in, again the fountainlike geysers kicking up, this time coming straight at him.

And the strangest of thoughts then struck him. I've been in the Navy for over twenty-three years and this is the first time, the first time I'm actually being shot at. They are trying to kill *me!*

There was no melodramatic instant of life flashing before his eyes, thoughts of Margaret, or even of his lost son, just that each geyser erupting was stepping closer, marking the converging fire of 7.7-millimeter machine guns coming right at him.

Someone knocked him hard, sending him sprawling, knocking the wind out of him. It was the lieutenant, finally reacting. The bullets stitched up the hull, tearing up deck planking on the diminutive bridge, shattering more glass, sparks flying. The plane roared over, followed by another right behind it, strafing the bow. He caught a glimpse of a sailor doubling over, collapsing. Screaming now, civilians scattering in panic around the deck, sailors, some moving to their general quarters' position, though it had not yet been sounded, others just standing like statues, as unbelieving as James had been.

The three planes soared upward, gaining altitude, and for a moment he thought that somehow, just somehow it was a mistake, that they would climb out, realize their error, and leave. But no, the lead plane did a wingover, now coming down steeply from several thousand feet, guns again firing.

"General quarters!" He heard the order picked up, shouted, men running.

How many drills had he been through aboard ships such as the *Maryland,* the *Lexington,* the *Oklahoma,* where it was all done so smoothly in such orderly almost stately fashion . . . but they had never been under fire, so caught by surprise . . . by terror.

The lieutenant was back up on his feet, someone tossing him a helmet, as if it would actually do any good.

"Sir, could you get those civilians under control . . . get them below decks!"

James came to his feet, not sure where to

start; it was not as if he could pass a simple order and they would all just follow along.

The lead plane was firing again, shot plunging down, several more dropping, including one of the civilians, which set off hysterical screaming, the plane roaring out low over the water and then immediately beginning to climb back up.

"Below, damn it, below!" James shouted. Grabbing the nearest civilian, he vaguely recognized him as a secretary from the embassy; he shoved the man toward the open doorway of the main deck cabin.

There was a moment's hesitation, but then the second plane came in for its strafing run, and as one man went below the others raced to the doorway, shoving to get under what James knew was nothing more than the false protection of the overhead deck. The *Panay* was no battleship; it was a river gunboat.

"Below decks! Below decks!" He stood by the doorway as the last of them piled in, a couple of sailors carrying a man wearing a clerical collar, a missionary knocked unconscious, bleeding profusely from a head wound.

He heard a crack of a rifle, a lone sailor standing on the deck, armed with a Springfield '03, swearing, firing as the first plane continued to climb away.

"Bombs!"

He looked up and saw yet another plane, not one of the fighters, now coming down on them, pulling out of its dive, two dots detaching.

He needed no urging. This time he flung himself flat on the deck, only to be met by the hard steel as it was flung upward by the two bombs bracketing the gunboat.

The three fighters wheeled, coming back in for yet another strafing run. Stunned by the blast, soaked by the cascades of water coming down, he suddenly no longer cared, standing back up, filled with rage.

Atop the main cabin he heard someone swearing and, looking up, saw a sailor actually holding an American flag up, waving it, as if the bastards would somehow now see it at last. He started to shout for the man to get the hell down, but his cry was drowned out by the roar of the planes, the staccato snap of bullets, the sailor diving down for cover, flag falling from his hands.

"Abandon ship!"

Startled, he looked back to the young commander of the *Panay,* hands cupped, shouting the order; but already men were going over the sides. Actually there was no need to do so, the bracketing of the bombs had stoved in the fragile hull, the *Panay* already settling to the bottom of the muddy river, water beginning to cascade over the railing. All he had to do was just simply step over and into the Yangtze. The water was cold, damn cold, startling him. A sailor tossing a life jacket to him, which he simply grabbed hold of, to keep afloat, kicking the few yards to the weed-choked riverbank.

Another of the fighters wheeled in like a vulture over a dying beast and rolled in for a strafing dive. James pushed the civilian by his side down into the weeds, diving to get under the muddy water. An instant later it felt like he had been kicked by a horse, shoving him down into the mud, no pain, just numbness. He convulsively gasped, the filthy water of the Yangtze flooding into his lungs.

In four feet of muddy water, he began to drown. He felt hands around him, pulling him up, rolling him over. Panicked, he kicked, struggled, the pain suddenly hitting, agonizing. He vomited, aspirating more water and filth as he did so, choking. He heard voices, someone shouting, still struggling he felt land under him, mud stinking of human waste.

Somebody rolled him on his side, slapping him on the back, gasping, he was finally able to draw a breath.

"Down!"

More gunfire, a plane racing over low, a split second of shadow passing like an angel or demon of death, the roar of the engine, someone swearing.

"That's it, sir, take a breath, that's it!"

The voice was almost gentle. He had lost his glasses, the world looked fuzzy, but he saw the stripes of a chief petty officer who was kneeling over him.

"Let me get your tie off, sir," and the officer snaked it loose, popping a few buttons off his uniform, taking the tie.

"This might hurt now, sir, hang on." And damn it did hurt. As the sailor raised James's left arm, it felt like someone had driven an ice pick up it. Blood was pouring out of his hand. He tried to move it, winced, the last two digits dangling loosely. The sailor wrapped the tie around the hand, tight it felt, too damn tight; he gasped slightly, but said nothing.

"That'll do for the moment, sir."

It was still hard to breathe. "Thanks," was all he could gasp out.

"I'm going back in now, sir, there're still people out there. Stay low."

James could only nod, suddenly feeling small, helpless. Like anyone with astigmatism, the loss of glasses made him feel naked, vulnerable. *My other glasses, in my luggage.* He looked up, absurd. *Panay* was settled to the gunwales, smoke pouring out of her.

"I can't believe it," the petty officer gasped, "the bastards. I can't believe it."

One of the fighters banked over low, circling, and he could catch a glimpse of the pilot in the open cockpit looking down.

The petty officer stood up, raised his arm in the classic gesture of insult, finger extended, shouting obscenities.

James said nothing, looking up, at the circling plane, the face of the enemy above him.

We're at war now, he thought. *America would never accept this, could never accept this. They had fired on the flag, on a ship of the United States Navy. It could only mean one response now — war.*

The White House
Washington, D.C.
14 December 1937

"Sir, I know you are furious about this Japanese attack on the *Panay,* but there is just nothing practical we can do about it," Secretary of State Hull wearily asserted to an angry President Roosevelt.

"Cordell, this is *my* navy, and they have sunk one of *my* gunboats. We have to do something."

"Mr. President, Gallup reports 70 percent of the American people want us to withdraw from China, not just the military, but everyone, every civilian, every missionary, the logic being if none of us are there, no one can get shot at and thus we avoid a war."

Disgusted with this bit of intelligence and the logic it implied, the president could only wearily shake his head.

"Congress is even more isolationist than the American people. There would be no congressional support for a real confrontation with Japan. The American people oppose the Japanese aggression and sympathize with the Chinese, but they simply do not want to get involved."

"You may be right for now, but I have a feeling time is going to teach all of us some very painful lessons about aggressive dictatorships in both Tokyo and Berlin. For the moment, you are right. You and Joe Grew work up some strong statement, and raise as much Cain with the Japanese as you can without getting us into a shooting match."

As Hull turned to leave, FDR couldn't

resist one last parting shot. "Just remember that I am going to watch them constantly and take advantage of every mistake they make to teach the American people that we have to stop the dictatorships before they threaten us directly."

CHAPTER FOUR

Nanking, China
15 December 1937
Staggering with exhaustion, Cecil Stanford, correspondent for the *Manchester Daily*, pushed through the terrified, jostling mob. Attached to a bamboo pole, held aloft in his right hand, was a makeshift British flag, painted onto a torn bedsheet. In his other arm, nestled in tight against his breast, two small Chinese girls, ages most likely about two, both of them soiled, covered in feces and vomit, both screaming hysterically even as they clung to him. Clutched around him were several score of people, terrified, pressing in tight, all but climbing on top of him, petrified to be at the edge of the group staggering through hell.

The children had been pressed into his arms a couple of blocks back, a woman, horrific looking, blood pouring in rivulets down both her legs, had staggered up to him. The cause of the bleeding was obvious, far too obvious because she was naked. She had pressed the two screaming children into his arms, staggered back away, and collapsed in the gutter.

They turned the corner, his goal only a few blocks away, and there they were — half a dozen Japanese soldiers.

They were obviously drunk, be it drunk on liquor, drugs, or some primal insanity was immaterial now. He braced himself, unashamed to inwardly admit that he was terrified. If only Winston could see him now, what would he think of his choice of "spies." For that matter, if Winston could see, at this moment, the goddamn nightmare of this city, what would he say, what would the entire world say.

He had come to Nanking shortly after the incident at the Marco Polo Bridge up in Peking, since it was the purported capital of the Nationalist forces.

The bridge incident had exploded into what was officially being called the "Second Sino-Japanese War," a polite reference to the fact that the two sides had a brief skirmish back in 1894–95. But that war had been fought with at least some dignity; this, this was beyond any imagining, beyond anything he had believed in and loved about

161

the Japanese.

Within weeks after the takeover of Peking, Japanese armored columns had poured into the central China plains, the forces of Chiang Kai-shek, ineffective at best, cowardly at worst. Four weeks ago he had been in Shanghai, covering events there, but felt it best to try and make it back to the temporary capital, perhaps to even seek out an interview with Chiang Kai-Shek. To no avail.

The siege of the city had caught him and nearly all the defenders of the ancient walled city off guard, the Japanese army rushing forward with lightning speed. In less than three days the defenses had crumbled, and the Japanese army had poured in. For a few brief hours, very brief hours, there had been an uneasy tension, Japanese commanders purportedly declaring that they came as liberators, that personal property and rights would be respected, but that fleeing soldiers disguised as civilians must be turned in. And then, it seemed in a matter of hours or minutes, the army had given itself over to a medieval pillage, the likes of which transcended Cecil's worst nightmares.

A small committee of Westerners, a few missionaries with the guts to stay on, a couple of consulate officials who had stayed on either by choice or by being simply trapped, and a half-dozen correspondents like himself had formed what they called the "International Committee." It was all a bluff. A few dozen Westerners roping off an area, putting up their flags, standing guard at each intersection, and declaring that to cross the line would trigger a war with their respective countries.

It was a bluff, born of madness, and it had united together Brits, Italians, Americans, Portuguese, and all of those led by a German business executive from the Siemens Corporation, John Rabe, a member of the Nazi Party. It seemed that the display of the swastika, hand-painted onto strips of cloth and tied to rope blocking off the streets, was more of a deterrent than anything else.

Rabe had been everywhere since the madness started, sending demands to the Japanese commanders, organizing the cordon around a section of the city where Westerners lived, cajoling and rallying the few exhausted Europeans and Americans to redouble their efforts as tens of thousands died, literally right in front of them.

What had driven Cecil outside the barrier line was the sight of half a dozen Chinese schoolgirls and a nun, Chinese as well, be-

163

ing dragged off just a block outside the cordon. Grabbing his makeshift flag he had run out into the street in pursuit.

In a far saner world he would have stood riveted, waiting for someone else to act. But within that small cordon of several dozen blocks, hundreds of thousands of terrified civilians had now sought refuge from the rampaging Japanese troops. In that terrible instant, he knew there was no one but himself.

He had stepped forward, running down the street, turning the corner, pushing past a terrified family running in the opposite direction, running blindly. Several buildings were burning, agonized screams coming from within; two drunken Japanese soldiers staggered out of the inferno, one of them pointing at Cecil and shouting an insult about English dogs.

The small procession of horror turned a corner and he raced after them, following, closing in. And horrified, he slowed at the sight he now beheld. The nun had tried to fight back even as two of the soldiers started to push the girls through a shattered storefront window, a small furniture store, the beds and sofas within obvious for what was to be done. The nun had clawed at the face of their leader, a lieutenant, and Cecil, horrified, saw the sword come out and, in one blow, the nun decapitated.

The girls, her charges, were screaming, shrieking wildly. The lieutenant looked at the corpse lying on the sidewalk, head having rolled into the gutter, the lieutenant swaying slightly on his feet.

Cecil slowed, trying to still the pounding of his heart.

He thought of all the fine young men he had taught at Etajima. Boys who would ask for help translating a Shakespeare sonnet to send to a hoped-for beloved back home, or a letter to a mother or father in English to demonstrate their skills, knowing that the proud parents would parade from neighbor to neighbor, showing off the skills of their honored son.

Were these one and the same? Could the boys he had taught ever do this, ever condone this? Where was the honor of Japan this day?

He slowed, drawing in his breath.

"Lieutenant!"

He drew himself up, trying to remember the housemaster at Harrow who, at not much more than five feet, could strike terror into the heart of any boy. He stepped closer, letting the bamboo pole with the crudely drawn British flag atop it come to a rest position.

"Lieutenant! Face me and come to attention before a superior."

The lieutenant was obviously drunk, not much more than a boy, twenty-two or -three at most. The sharp command, given in Japanese, had caused him to instinctively turn and come to attention. The half-dozen soldiers, the rapists with him, paused, the schoolgirls still shrieking hysterically; and he wished that for the moment they would shut up.

"I am a duly appointed representative of the government of Great Britain," he lied. "Those girls are students from a school sponsored by my government, and they are now in my charge."

He did not ask; he knew enough of what he faced not to do that. He ordered. Orders for the Japanese, whether legitimate or from someone who appeared legitimate, were to be obeyed without hesitation.

The lieutenant gazed at him, suddenly unsure. One of the soldiers started to pull a girl in closer and muttered, "This one is mine, round eyes."

Cecil turned and faced the soldier.

"Let go of her now or face a firing squad come morning. Obey me now!"

His command so sharp and in such perfect

Japanese caused the soldier to release the girl.

As if the man no longer existed Cecil turned back to the lieutenant. "Your name?"

"Hashima Mitsushi," there was a pause, "sir."

"Return your men to order immediately," Cecil roared. "I shall personally report you, come tomorrow morning, to your superiors."

He gestured at the dead nun, suddenly struggling to suppress a gag as blood slowly continued to pour out of her body.

Without looking over at the enlisted men, he snapped his fingers. "Release the girls."

"White devil, who is he . . . ," one of the enlisted men growled, but the lieutenant turned and barked out a command. "Release them!" Cecil commanded.

He kept his gaze fixed on Hashima, then ever so slowly turned to the six terrified girls.

"Walk toward me," he said, speaking slowly, still not sure of his Chinese after almost a year in this country. "Stop crying and come to my side."

They did as ordered.

He wondered if the Japanese could see that he was actually trembling, his entire body shaking, his knees near to jelly.

It was one thing to play the white knight on the mad impulse of the moment, to cross over the protection of the barrier line and go racing off. Now it was all literally balanced on the edge of a razor blade. If Hashima should come to his senses, realize there were no witnesses, a flick of his wrist and Cecil knew he would be dead, the girls alive a bit longer, but then, hopefully, mercifully, dead as well.

He felt the girls crowd in around him, and kept his gaze locked on Hashima.

And then he knew he had him. Hashima dropped his gaze, looking sidelong at the body of the nun, and then lowered his head farther. He felt almost a touch of pity for the young man. Would what was happening here eventually inure him to suffering, to agony; or might, perhaps just maybe, he might realize the madness that he had given himself over to and spend a lifetime of regret.

"Stay close to me," Cecil whispered to the girls, but he did not need to tell them. They clung to him in desperation. He turned away and without a backward glance tried to retrace his way back to the safety zone set up by the German.

Right up to the street corner he more than expected that the lieutenant might rouse himself or his men rebel.

"There are plenty of other bitches," he heard one of them say as he turned the corner. He dared to look back and saw Hashima still standing in the street, blade drawn, gaze lowered, fixed on the body of the nun.

For a moment he feared he was lost. The street was choked with smoke, fires spreading, a panic-stricken crowd of several dozen running past him, pursued by several laughing Japanese soldiers armed only with bayonets, rifles slung, waving the blood-soaked blades high. But with each step people fell in by his side, racing out of hiding places; the tragic woman with the two small children emerging from an alleyway and then staggering back to collapse.

He turned the corner ahead and never in his life did he ever dream that he would be glad to see a swastika; but there it was, tied off to a telephone pole, a silken rope blocking the street beyond it, a sea of humanity packed together, huddled back.

Safety was but fifty yards away, and then from a smoke-filled alleyway, six Japanese soldiers emerged, laughing, one of them carrying, of all things, a large clock, another a pile of silk robes slung over his shoulder, no officer present.

At the sight of Cecil and his pathetic knot of refugees they slowed, pointing, laughing. And then one of them boldly stepped forward with a swagger. "You there, stop!"

Cecil did not slow, pushing his group on.

The soldier unslung his rifle and pointed it straight at Cecil and looked up at the roughly made flag. "English dog, stop!"

"Stand aside, soldier," Cecil snapped back in Japanese. "These people are under the protection of the British government."

His command of Japanese caused the soldier to pause, and Cecil moved to shoulder him aside. Just thirty yards more and they would be through the barrier.

"A toll then!" someone shouted, and an instant later a loud scream caused Cecil to turn. The Japanese soldier had stepped around the edge of the group and even now was dragging off one of the schoolgirls Cecil had just rescued. His comrades closed in, laughing.

"Merciful God," Cecil whispered, as he started to turn to try and intervene.

"Mr. Stanford!"

He looked to the barrier rope. It was the German, John Rabe, Nazi armband prominently displayed on his right arm.

"For God's sake, man!" Rabe shouted in

English, "run for it now! Or you'll lose them all!"

Torn, horrified, Cecil looked back at the schoolgirl being dragged away. One of the other girls was starting to break from the group, to try and help, others grabbing her, holding her back.

"Save my sister!" the girl being dragged away screamed, even as the Japanese soldiers circled around her and pulled her back into the alleyway like spiders engulfing their prey.

From farther up the street Cecil could see more soldiers approaching, pointing in his direction.

It was a moment of horror he had never dreamed he would ever face, a slowing of time, the look of resignation and despair on the one girl's face, the screams of her younger sister, the screams of the two toddlers in his arms, the weight of an old woman, near collapse, clinging to his belt.

He had to make his choice.

"Run!" he screamed.

The small pitiful circle about him staggered forward, several of the Japanese soldiers from farther up the street laughing, moving to block them off; but Cecil and his group were ahead, John Rabe holding up the rope, the group collapsing underneath it. John stopped at the edge of the rope, looking up at the tattered Union Jack.

"Get in!" Rabe shouted, and reaching over he pulled Cecil over the rope to safety.

The Japanese in pursuit slowed, one of them making a show of saluting the German flag but then spitting on the ground in front of Cecil, who stood just a few feet away.

Cecil fixed him with an icy gaze.

"By God, someday all of you will pay for this, you bastard," Cecil snapped.

The Japanese soldier, having just endured the worst of insults, an attack on his lineage, the honor of his mother and his father, leveled his rifle and worked the bolt.

Rabe stepped between them and pushed Cecil back into the swarming crowd. And at that moment, all Cecil's self-control began to crack and break apart.

He had loved these people, he had taught their sons for eight years and seen in so many of them the son that God had taken away from him in one tragic instant. Boys who he would always call "his boys," who were now in the navy of this country. He did not want to believe that "his boys," of what he almost considered to be his adopted navy, would ever have allowed this, tolerated this.

Rabe grabbed him by the shoulders and

pushed him farther back into the crowd.

"Why did you step over the barrier line?" he shouted, trying to be heard above the bedlam, the terrified screaming and sobbing of those around him, the rattle of gunfire, the crackling roar of the fire spreading across the city.

Cecil couldn't speak, the two toddlers still clinging to his arms.

Rabe looked around, shouted something in German, and a woman, Chinese, came up in a soiled, blood-soaked nurse's uniform and pried the screaming children out of his arms. She looked at Cecil.

"Namen?"

He looked at her and could only shake his head.

She nodded, her features implacable, the tragedy of two orphans, now nameless, but another fragment of anguish blowing in a maelstrom of agony.

He watched as they disappeared, and his control began to break. The memory of the nun, the girl being dragged off . . . he bent his head, shaking. "Goddamn all this!" he cried, "Goddamn all of them." He began to sob, unbelieving that soldiers of Japan could actually have sunk to this level of brutality, of sheer raw bestiality.

He felt strong hands on his shoulders and

he looked up. It was Rabe, who then reached into his breast pocket and pulled out a flask, uncorking it.

"American whiskey," he said, trying to smile.

Cecil nodded. Hands trembling, he took the flask and drained nearly half of it in two strong gulps, the drink hitting him hard; within seconds he felt as if he were about to collapse.

"You are a madman for stepping out there," Rabe said in English. "I thought you were dead. You English!" And he smiled.

Cecil nodded, handing the flask back, and Rabe drained the rest, the two gazing at each other, holding an island of refugees in the middle of Nanking, where three hundred thousand were being slaughtered; hundreds of thousands more terrorized, tortured, raped by an army that had gone out of control in a frenzy of drunken killing, pillage, and hatred; an army that claimed to have come as liberators, the bringers of justice, of a new order.

Cecil looked into Rabe's eyes and could see the man's anguish. They had known each other casually, crossing paths several times since his own arrival here in China back in the spring.

He suddenly felt weak-kneed, about to

collapse, and Rabe braced him up.

"Go back to my quarters, take my bed," Rabe said. "You've done enough saving for one day; try and get some sleep and something to eat."

Cecil grabbed hold of Rabe by his forearms and again noticed the swastika armband, which Cecil knew his friend now wore in order to intimidate the Japanese and to save the lives of what would ultimately be a quarter of a million Chinese. He sighed. "I wish the world was different, my friend," Cecil whispered.

Shanghai
17 December 1937

Through the haze of fever he knew they were working on his hand, something about how they could not give him a general anesthetic and just knock him out. The water he had taken in had helped trigger a dose of pneumonia, compounded by the raging infection from his wound.

He felt something, the local they had shot him up with, helped somewhat, but still he could feel it and winced.

"A few more minutes, sir, just a few more." He looked up, a naval corpsman was leaning over his side, hands resting gently on his shoulders, ready if need be to restrain him. More pain, worse now, the sound, he didn't like it, like a wire clipper snapping something, he felt another wave of pain, dulled but still there.

Muttered conversation, the doctor, a naval surgeon from the cruiser now anchored in Shanghai harbor. The bright light of the surgical light overhead forced James to close his eyes.

Fevered thoughts, memories, lying in the feces and mud of the riverbank, the artillery shelling that raked the area, a ship, British, pulling in close to retrieve the survivors, returning fire. At first he had tried to fool himself. The wound hurt like hell, but surely they'd fix it up, some stitches. The thoughts of that turning into a haze when, by the following morning, he started to run a fever, lungs beginning to fill up, too painful even to breathe. The British corpsman on board redressing the wound, whispered conversation with someone helping him about the filth of the water, infection.

Another snipping sound.

"What the hell are you doing?" James gasped, voice slurred from the morphine they had given him.

"Almost done, sir," the corpsman said, a huge, bluff-looking fellow, but gentle with a soft Southern drawl.

A sound of instruments rattling, steel being dropped on steel, a sigh.

"Stitch it up. I've got to get to the next case," he heard someone say, and then another face, removing a surgical mask, the doctor he thought.

"Can you hear me, Commander?"

James nodded.

"We have this fever under control; you'll pull through okay."

He caught an exchange of glances between the doctor and the corpsman. Even in the haze, he knew that look. How many times over Davy's bedside had he seen those glances, Davy learning to read it as well, the reassurances, even as the leukemia destroyed him.

"Straight," James whispered.

"What?"

"Straight answer, no bull, straight answer," was all he could say.

The doctor nodded. "You're one hell of a sick man, Commander. You swallowed half that damn river and have pneumonia, but I think you'll pull through."

"Know that. My hand?"

The doctor hesitated for a second. "Gangrene was setting in with all that filth. It was take the hand, sir, or you'd die. It was pretty well shattered anyhow. I'm sorry, sir."

James nodded, not saying anything, drifting.

"You're going home, Commander. I'm giving it to you straight like you want. Retirement, sir, but a Purple Heart; they'll promote you. Where you from?"

"Hawaii."

The doctor patted him lightly on the shoulder. "You've got your life ahead of you, sir."

"Next one's prepped."

The doctor looked up, nodded. "Coming."

"Goddamn slants, those Japs," the doctor said.

James looked up at him, not saying anything. My wife is half-Japanese he wanted to reply, but then remembered the red "meat balls," as the men had taken to calling the rising sun painted on the wings of their planes.

"Bastards," was all he could whisper as the morphine caused him to drift off. The doctor turned to his next patient, a chief petty officer, an eye gone, the infected wound — nearly all of them infected due to the river water — still under a rough bandage, the man sitting up, waiting stoically for what was to come.

"Please admit him," Ambassador Joseph Grew said to the staffer at the door to his office.

Grew debated for a moment whether he should remain behind his desk but elected to stand. He knew the intent of the message that was about to be delivered; a slight gesture of standing rather than remaining seated was in order.

If ever there was a man who looked to be the stereotype of a senior American diplomat, it was Joseph Grew. Born of a patrician Boston family, tall, gray-haired, sharp-angled distinguished features, he had been a schoolmate of the president at both Groton and Harvard, though his rise to his current posting as Ambassador to Japan had nothing to do with his lifelong friendship with the president.

After graduating from Harvard he had traveled the Far East, a grand tour for a member of the elite pre–World War I social set before settling and then authoring the obligatory book, *Sport and Travel in the Far East,* which had been moderately successful and was a favorite of yet another traveler and hunter, "Teddie" Roosevelt, who had sent him a fan letter. Joining the diplomatic service, he had served in Denmark, Switzerland, and Turkey until finally achieving a long-sought-after posting, as Ambassador to the Court of the Emperor of Japan, assigned by another presidential friend, Herbert Hoover. It was an assignment he felt was the capstone of his career. He and his wife loved the country, admired the people, their industrious nature, which in some ways was so American, and the beauty of the country. Having first traveled there nearly thirty years earlier, he was awed by the Westernizing transformation that had taken place in little more than a generation . . . railroads, factories, shipyards, even an increasing number of privately owned automobiles of Japanese make. Close friendships had been formed on that first trip and more now across his last five years of service. He was well liked by those both Oriental and Occidental, who interacted with him. Invitations to his parties and receptions, official and unofficial, were highly sought after. One night his parties might feature the performance of a famed "No" play, the next one, a showing of the latest Hollywood musical in the embassy's highly prized and envied theater room, which even had a modern 35-millimer projector.

Above all else, he had a deep empathy for the Japanese, a genuine attachment that was obvious, and a profound desire to smooth over troubled times and eventually cement a lasting friendship.

In spite of the aggression of the Japanese army, acting on its own authority to seize Manchuria in 1931, he at first tried to rationalize it as a rogue group of the military exceeding authority, and what had happened was now an accomplished fact that was futile to attempt to change.

Though he would never voice it publicly, he felt analogies could be drawn to Andrew Jackson as a rogue military leader, all but stealing Florida, and later, in a base, cruel act, taking the land of the Indians in the Old South. Beyond that there were so many other such actions during the Mexican War. Beyond those issues, he did see a Japanese presence in Manchuria to be preferable to that of Stalin and his henchmen. The Japan he had returned to in 1932 was bursting at the seams, but at a hard price, for the island was a net importer of nearly every essential item required for industrialization, and for just simple survival as well. Like England it could no longer feed itself without massive imports. Manchuria, it was claimed as justification, was a depopulated land cruelly ruled by a tin-pot Chinese warlord. Japanese officials, many of whom had traveled in America, tried to draw the analogy to the American West of sixty years past. Manchuria would be a place for settlers to pour into, for resources to be exploited, the land to be civilized and made prosperous.

Grew hoped this would be the limits of the desires of the Japanese military, and for five years those he worked with claimed that Manchuria was indeed the end of their "need for growth."

That was now unraveling. First the absurd but dangerous attempted army coup of the previous year, which did have the effect of shaking up the government, bringing in officials who were increasingly "hard line" about the "destined role" of Japan, including the current foreign minister, Koki Hirota, who for a brief period after the army coup had been prime minister with the army's approval.

In the year after the coup, the army had begun shifting an increasing number of troops to Manchuria, Manchukuo as they now called it, claiming a need for security both against Chinese banditry and Soviet threats.

The tension had finally exploded early in July in Peking at the ancient, famed Marco

Polo Bridge, so named because the Italian traveler had described its splendors in his writings. A Japanese garrison was camped at one end of the bridge, Chinese Nationalist troops at the other. The garrison was not unlike the small outposts of the U.S. Marines, British troops and Royal Marines, other European forces stationed in key locations around China, supposedly there to react, if needed to protect the property and lives of their own nationals while the civil war between the Communists and Nationalists raged.

In all cases it was, of course, a cover, a showing of the flag and its always potential trigger points.

Apparently the trigger was all a mistake. A Japanese soldier turned up missing at roll call one morning and then during the night a shot was fired across the river. No one was sure who fired it, many felt it was some fool tossing fireworks. Regardless, it escalated. The commanders of the two sides met the following day, the "lost" Japanese soldier was found drunk on the wrong side of the river, salutes were exchanged between the two commanders; but then, within hours, rumors exploded of provocations, insults shouted, discipline broke, and a full-scale battle exploded.

Such actions, real, planned, or conspired in by some officers in the field, trigger wars. No one would ever know who fired the first shot at Lexington Green; most likely it was a mistake, but nevertheless it had rendered an Empire and created a new nation.

And regardless of original intent at the Marco Polo Bridge, the Japanese army reacted with such stunning speed that it was possible to believe the provocation had been deliberate, though Grew had reliable reports that the first incident was indeed an accident that higher-ups decided to exploit the following day. Accident or not, it now threatened to destabilize the entire Pacific region.

The war triggered by the stupid misunderstanding at the Marco Polo Bridge had, within days, escalated into a campaign that was stunning in speed and scope. Peking fell within the month, and from that vantage point, Japanese armored columns poured down into the central plains. Seaborne assaults seized Shanghai and were now pushing inland, Nanking having just fallen. Reports of the brutalities committed were now leaking out of both cities, one of those reports sat on his desk; it had left him sickened.

His own position in all this had been made

more difficult by his president, though of course he would never admit this in public.

In a speech on October 5, in Chicago, the president had bitterly denounced the rise of aggressive acts around the world and had all but directly linked Japan to Germany and the other Fascist states and then spoke of a "quarantine" of such nations. It was tantamount to a threat of an economic blockade.

All of this was made even more complex by the Japanese-German Anti-Comintern Pact signed the month before. On the surface it was supposedly an agreement to contain Soviet aggression, but nevertheless, to the world it appeared a linkage between Japan in the East and the ever more aggressive Hitler in the West.

But that was not the reason for the visitor who was now being announced at the doorway to Ambassador Grew's office, bad enough as the initial crisis was, what happened on December 12 on the Yangtze River had been infinitely worse as far as America was concerned. The two nations were tottering on the brink of war.

"Mr. Ambassador," he looked up, his thoughts interrupted, and he braced his shoulders back, checking to make sure his suit coat was buttoned. His aide standing in the open doorway stepped politely aside, "Foreign Minister Koki Hirota."

The Japanese foreign minister came through the doorway, dressed in the formal morning coat that the Japanese felt was the proper uniform for an official meeting between government representatives. There was nothing truly distinctive about Hirota, of medium height for his race, on the surface he could be mistaken for some middle-level businessman or official, but his gaze was icy, hard, and he was noted for sharp anti-Western commentary when aroused.

He was followed by a young interpreter, and at the sight of him Grew gave a subtle nod to his aide to remain and act as interpreter as well. Though his command of Japanese was fairly good and though he knew Hirota spoke English, at such a delicate moment, it was best to have experts on hand to ensure that not even the slightest inference or subtlety of language be mistaken or misinterpreted.

There was no handshake between the two, though Hirota did bow formally, and Grew nodded a reply and then gestured to the heavy leather sofa that was against the far wall of the office. Hirota and his interpreter sat down stiffly; Grew and his aide sat down on a second sofa that faced the first one, an ornate Oriental carpet and delicate teak-wood table separating them, tea having already been set, but there was no offer of pouring or small talk first.

There was an awkward moment of silence, Grew deciding not to allow the slightest opening. The incident to be discussed had been unprovoked, triggered by Japan, and historically such an incident usually started a war.

Though he pretty well knew the content of the message that Hirota was about to deliver, nevertheless, there could always be a surprise, a very brutal surprise. Hirota shifted uncomfortably and nodded to his interpreter, who opened an attaché case and drew out an envelope of heavy silken paper, affixed with a red seal, and handed it to Hirota, who stood up, walked the few feet to Grew, and bowing low, presented the envelope.

Grew stood to accept it.

"To your President Roosevelt," Hirota said, through his interpreter, "but please open and read it now."

Hirota retreated back to his sofa and sat down, Grew doing the same; and without waiting for his aide to fetch a letter opener, he broke the seal and opened the envelope.

Inside were two letters, neatly folded, one in Japanese, the other in English. He drew out the letter in English, scanned it quickly, and could not conceal a sigh of relief and then slowly, carefully, read it again, the only sound in the room the ticking of an ornate porcelain clock on the fireplace mantel and the crackling of the pine logs that were crumbling into glowing ashes.

It went far beyond what he had expected, far beyond it. Finished with reading the letter he carefully folded it along its original creases and placed it back in the envelope.

"I am certain a written reply shall be speedily arranged after I consult with my government," Grew said, noncommittally.

The two diplomats were silent for a moment, looking at each other. Only weeks before Hirota had made a bitter speech in response to Roosevelt's accusations, declaring that what happened between China and Japan was not the affair of America and, if anything, the president's words would only create more bloodshed by encouraging the Chinese to continue to fight a war they could not win.

Total victory in China against the Nationalists and, after them, the Communists was all but a foregone conclusion. Japan would not retreat, and ultimately Japan's presence in China would restore order and end the generation-long chaos that had cost the lives of millions.

Sarcastic comments were in the press as well, obviously engineered from Hirota's office, that America showed no interest regarding the Italians in Ethiopia, the current war in Spain; therefore why this browbeating over a China racked by bloody civil war? If anything, Japan brought with its actions the promise of peace and stability to the region.

Grew did find it ironic that the death and suffering of millions in China, had, in these last few days, taken a backseat to the death of four American sailors on the Yangtze River, which was now the topic of this confrontation.

"I must speak frankly," Hirota finally said, breaking the uncomfortable silence.

Grew nodded, saying nothing.

"I must express my personal shame and deepest regret over this entire incident. I can assure you, Mr. Ambassador, that if any of us in the government had even been remotely aware of this action being planned, we would have used all means possible to stop it. All of Japan is shamed by what has happened."

He paused, Grew looking sidelong at his

aide to ensure that the translation by Hirota's interpreter had been accurate. There was a nod of agreement.

Grew cleared his throat. "Sir, nevertheless I must express my government's grievous shock and anger at this wanton action of aggression."

Hirota lowered his head, and Grew pressed on. "Our naval gunboat *Panay,* an official representative of the United States of America, was on the Yangtze River in order to protect American property and, if need be, evacuate American nationals caught in the middle of the war that your nation now wages in China. Our presence there was with the full knowledge and permission of the Nationalist government.

"Our ship was clearly marked with American flags. We were openly on that river for humanitarian reasons and in no way whatsoever attempted to hide our presence. Its presence was known by all, including your forces in the days prior to this wanton and unprovoked attack by your naval air force."

Hirota said nothing, merely nodding with lowered head.

"Four dead, over forty wounded in the attack. One of our men was wounded while holding the American flag aloft, trying to wave your planes off and yet still they attacked."

That incident had at least been reported in the popular press, and the imagery of it was riveting. American newspapers were running drawings of the sailor, holding the flag up, staggering from his wounds, and whether the report was true or not, it had aroused bitter public opinion against Japan. And yet, there was, stunningly, no depth to that bitterness.

Grew was amazed by the poll. If the Japanese ever learned of it, in spite of their abject apologies now, they would read it as nothing short of craven cowardice and it would embolden them to further acts of aggression.

Hirota raised his head to speak, but Grew pressed on, knowing he had to at least put up a strong front, regardless of what some damn poll said.

"The excuse offered by your military that it was all a mistake is ludicrous and shameful. If for no other reason than the fact that Japan prides itself with the repeated claim that it has the best pilots in the world. How can one of the best pilots in the world not see what he is shooting at? How can he not see it was Americans he was shooting at? And furthermore, it was not just your pilots who attacked us. Your army's artillery shelled the wreckage, with survivors still in the water, wounding yet more of our citizens. If it had not been for the timely arrival of a British gunboat, which had also suffered attack, I think it is clear that every American aboard the *Panay* would have been slaughtered. The actions of your army and navy are shameful beyond belief."

Grew knew he was letting emotion get the better of him. He fell silent, fearful that he might say more.

"I am having a very difficult time," Hirota said slowly in English. "Things happen unexpectedly."

Grew said nothing now. The letter he had just been handed by Hirota actually surprised him by its almost abject tone. The government took full responsibility, stated that those involved in the incident would be punished, and surprisingly were offering an indemnity of well over a million dollars to be paid to the families who had suffered losses.

More amazingly, the marines stationed outside the embassy all day long had been coming back inside, carrying bundles of letters from Japanese citizens and even school groups, expressing their shame over the incident and asking for forgiveness. It was a strange, and yet touching outpouring.

To an American, the offering of money as some sort of compensation for men so cold-bloodedly murdered was an insult; but to this culture it was a humble way of offering atonement, not unlike the "blood gold" of old Norse tradition, where a family prevented a feud by admitting the wrongdoing of a killing and providing a lifelong income to the bereaved as settlement.

"So now what do we do?" Grew asked.

Hirota, a bit surprised, looked at him. "Sir?"

"Just that, sir," Grew pressed. "I cannot speak officially at this moment, but unofficially I believe my government will ultimately accept this letter with the spirit intended, that what occurred was a terrible mistake. But frankly, sir, we both know it was not a mistake, as far as some in your military are concerned. Already we are receiving reports from American missionaries that the display of our flag over churches, hospital compounds, schools, and refugee centers, rather than deterring attacks, are triggering them."

Hirota reddened. "Sir, in the confusion of war, tragedies happen."

"And that is precisely what I am addressing. You know me, sir. You know my desire from the day I first stepped foot on your shores was to work with all my powers to ensure peace between our nations. How do we move from here to ensure peace?"

Hirota shifted uncomfortably, and Grew studied him carefully, very carefully.

Grew stood up and returned to his desk, picked up a file folder and, returning, handed it to Hirota.

"Sir, please examine the contents. Those were transmitted from Singapore, having just been delivered there from a British citizen returning from Nanking. They are wire service photographs that at this moment are going around the world."

Hirota opened the folder and visibly paled as he turned the sheets of paper.

Though grainy as typical of wire service photographic transfers, the contents were clear enough. A pile of corpses being thrown into the river by Chinese civilians while Japanese guards stood about; another of two Japanese officers grinning, holding their samurai swords, the caption accompanying the photo explaining that the two were in a competition to see who could decapitate the most victims in Nanking, the winner so far was claiming 105. At their feet were half a dozen heads. Most horrific, a sequence of half a dozen photographs of a Chinese male, naked, not tied but instead tethered to a pole, and then being used for bayonet practice by several laughing soldiers, the last photograph the corpse of the man curled up in a fetal position, his "victors" standing around him holding bloody bayonet-tipped rifles high in the air.

Sighing, Hirota closed the folder.

"Oh, do take it with you," Grew said coldly. "Believe me, everyone in the world will see those. I have additional copies already. Magazines in America in a few weeks will publish them, *Life, Time, Look*. Think of how that will impact American public opinion, compounded by this *Panay* incident."

He was bluffing again. If the *Panay* incident resulted in the majority of Americans saying it was best to simply cut and run, get every American out of China so there can be no more "mistakes," he knew the sight of Chinese civilians being decapitated, being used for bayonet practice and reports of children as young as six being raped, might cause moral outrage, but within a day it would be pushed off center stage to be replaced by some frivolous news about the latest going-ons in Hollywood or society affairs in New York.

He wondered if there was anything, after

this, that would finally cause the country to awaken and realize their collective reaction would only serve to embolden the radicals in Japan to take the next step, and then the next, misinterpreting just how angered America really would become if pushed too far, and believe instead that we would always cut and run. The result, in the end, would be tragic, for both sides, and come at a far bloodier cost.

He felt he had to push the bluff as far as he could, to try and give some kind of warning with the hope that it would strike to the core. "I can assure you, though some view my people as uncaring of the situation beyond their borders, this will generate, at some level, a reaction that will imprint and stay with my people for a generation to come. And thus my question, How do we stop this? How do we stop this from devolving into a war between America and Japan?"

Grew looked over at his interpreter, realizing he had been speaking so rapidly that something might have been lost, but the young man spoke quickly, and the interpreter sitting by Hirota nodded, indicating that the translation had been accurate.

Hirota raised his gaze from the closed folder. "I am shamed."

Grew knew enough not to press the issue,

but Hirota said no more.

"How do we step back from this, sir? We are at the brink. You know my love of your nation. You know I wish to view that," and he cast a disparaging wave of disgust at the folder filled with images of atrocities, "as an aberration. You know that since my arrival here five years ago I have sought better understanding. And you know the deep love I have developed for your country, its people, its culture, its remarkable history."

In spite of himself there was a husky tone to his voice as he spoke the last words.

"If we cannot reach accord," Grew said, "I fear for the future. You and I must rebuild that accord, sir, otherwise there shall be a cataclysm."

"I fear the same," Hirota replied.

Grew sat back and exhaled noisily. It was a remarkable reply on Hirota's part. "I think the core of the issue is this. Your military, with its increasing political power, believes that it has the right to act as it pleases in China. That your government, in turn, does not respond to rein this in, out of concern for another coup attempt like last year or because it actually wishes this imperialistic act to continue."

Hirota stiffened. "Sir. I do not recall any American objections when the English were carving out their Empire in India, nor English objections when you so aggressively seized your control of an entire continent, rich in all the resources you coveted."

Grew nodded. "Yes, that is true. But, sir, that was the nineteenth century. This is the twentieth. Imperialism in this modern age is not as it was. The reaction of the global community is not as it was."

"Is it not?" Hirota replied. "It is easy for you to say now. But there are no photographs of England's Opium War against China, where it was nothing less than, how do you say, a drug dealer. Nor are there photos of your treatment of your native population, nor of your brutal occupation of the Philippines back in 1900. Are they not the same?"

"No sir, they are not," Grew replied sharply. "All nations have done wrong. I want to think my nation has the courage to admit that. Your government has shown courage in admitting that it did not plan the attack on the *Panay* but is willing to make amends. I commend you for that. But sir, the past is dead; the mistakes of the past are dead. I fear for our mutual futures. We are heading on a path, sir, that could annihilate hundreds of thousands of our young men, perhaps millions, if we do not tread carefully."

"I came here to seek your nation's forgiveness for the terrible tragedy regarding your ship *Panay,* which I must say was in Chinese waters in the middle of a war zone," Hirota replied.

Grew was silent, hoping for more, far more than this response. He felt if only he could get through to this man, bring him into personal alliance, the growing control of the army over their government could still be reined in.

"Sir, may I speak frankly before you leave?"

"By all means, Mr. Ambassador."

"We have our differences. I have read every word of your public utterances since you took office and in them your support of your army's occupation of China. And yet, I suspect it is your military far more than your civilian government that has so ordered things."

Hirota did not reply.

"You and I must continue to talk. We both know how some military men, once set on a course, will follow it without regard to the consequences that can echo for generations. You and I must be frank with each other. There is far more that can bind us, than separate us. We can form an understanding that will ensure peace in the Pacific and prosperity for both nations."

"If that is based upon our withdrawal from China, which your president has demanded," Hirota said stiffly, "those talks will be difficult indeed."

So saying, Hirota stood up as if to leave, and Grew came to his feet as well.

"Sir. Those photographs," and he pointed to the folder containing the images from Nanking that Hirota had left on the sofa, "will strike hard, both with the citizens of my nation and with my president. I beg you, rein your army in. You must convey to the world that what happened at Nanking was an aberration to the code of honor of the Japanese army, which in previous conflicts, such as the war with Russia, gained a reputation for fair play and honorable treatment both of civilians and captured military personnel. Though it is beyond my authority to even suggest to you how you manage your internal affairs, I beg you, a public display of discipline for all officers involved with Nanking would serve you well. That and a public apology as you have now done regarding the *Panay*. Do that and you will serve your country and, yes, mine as well, making it easier to assure peace. If not," and his voice took on a harder edge, "such horrors will turn the world against you."

Hirota looked at him coldly.

"We shall clean our own house," he finally replied, "but we do not need the advice of others, no matter how well meaning, to bring us to that action."

Grew nodded, unable to reply.

Hirota bowed formally, signaling that the meeting was at an end.

Grew, grasping at straws, retrieved the letter from his aide and held it up.

"This, at least," he said, "I think will be greeted with the spirit of understanding conveyed."

"Thank you," Hirota replied, and with his interpreter in tow, he left the room.

Grew exhaled noisily and looked over at his own interpreter.

"Did I miss anything?" he asked.

"Sir, that is difficult to answer."

"How so?"

"He was shamed. That is certain. I think the *Panay* situation was a shock to him and to his government and the Emperor. Yet again, some hotheads fired up with the anti-Western nationalism and racism that some of their press and leaders keep spouting. In a way it was tacit permission for them to strafe our ship, and now they are scrambling to cover themselves."

Grew listened carefully and nodded in agreement. "I could sense that in his careful choice of language," Grew replied, "but the overall intent?"

The interpreter fell silent.

"Go on."

"Frankly, sir, I think the message is, we can go to hell. They will conquer China whether we like it or not. Their army is now running the show. The nuance of words chosen. He never once said that the Emperor himself was outraged, that there would be swift punishment. It was, instead, just an apology, a standard procedure here as you know."

"Yes, I do know," Grew replied.

Damn all, he thought to himself. Both of us are beginning to box each other in. There will be less and less room to maneuver diplomatically. The situation was getting out of control.

CHAPTER FIVE

Nanking, China
30 March 1938

As chief flight officer to the Thirteenth Naval Air Corps, currently stationed at a captured Nationalist airstrip just outside the city of Nanking, Lieutenant Commander Fuchida's participation in this raid was not really necessary.

But he was up anyhow this morning, dawn just breaking the eastern sky, the air smooth, no turbulence, like sliding on an icy pond, his Type-96 Mitsubishi responding to the lightest touch of stick and rudder as he went into a sharp, banking turn a thousand meters above the burning target below.

His job was to help plan operations, train his pilots, and see to the overall operations of his squadron; in private he had been sent over from the staff college to make sure that another "*Panay* Incident" did not happen.

Several days after that attack, Rear Admiral Zenshiro Hoshina, chief administrator of the Naval Air Corps, had summoned him personally. "We cannot afford another such," Hoshina started, hesitating, "incident with Westerners. It was utter rashness for it to happen. One would expect it of the army, but not of our own pilots whose discipline is higher."

Fuchida said nothing, for after all, every navy pilot held their counterparts in the army in disdain. Let them try and land on a pitching carrier deck in a force-five blow, or for that matter carry out a disciplined attack and actually hit their targets with precision.

"So I am sending you over to ride herd on those men for a while," Hoshina had continued, and Fuchida's heart sank. It meant he was being taken out of his class at the War College, a definite step backward in his career.

Hoshina had sensed his dismay and smiled. "Don't worry. You'll still be on the rolls as part of the training here. Clear up any problems with discipline in China, and you'll be back here in six months and finish your studies by the end of the year."

He had sighed with relief and actually bowed in thanks.

"I've watched you, Fuchida. You have

judgment, discipline. I want someone out there to watch things directly, to make sure there are no more such," and again he hesitated, " 'mistakes' and besides, the combat experience will do you good."

So now he circled over the blazing village in his Type-96 Mitsubishi, fuming with anger.

The bombing had been poor, no excuse, he had already marked the crews of three of the bombers for a solid chewing out, having obviously dropped early, their loads simply cratering paddies and an orchard.

As to the target, whoever had designated it was a fool, or, as he suspected, the enemy had been forewarned. It was obvious there was nothing down there but yet another burning village, now most likely littered with a couple of hundred dead, and not a single uniform in sight, not a single secondary explosion. If Nationalist forces had been hiding ammunition and supplies there, as Army Intelligence had informed them yesterday, requesting the strike, someone had either second sight or found out about the raid and moved the supplies out.

Security around the base, on the outskirts of Nanking, was still far too lax. Chinese laborers working to keep the runway operational with the onset of the spring mud, coolies delivering food, even those working in the kitchen. He had tried to push them all out, to have everything done by Japanese troops, but the base commander said it was impossible. So he was willing to bet that word had leaked out, yet again.

The last of the bombers turned back to the south-southeast, ten minutes to cross the Yangtze, and ten minutes beyond to their base. As the bombers started for home, he decided to drop down for a closer look, his wingman, Lieutenant Masatake Okumiya, closing in on his starboard wing. As a squadron leader he had a radio, but Masatake did not, so it was still communication by wing wags and hand signals. Yet another thing that he felt had to be modernized at once.

Fuchida nodded, pointed to his eyes and then up, Masatake saluted in reply, pulling back up to keep high cover and a lookout in case an enemy fighter actually did appear.

There had been several tangles over the last few months with Nationalist fighters, old Curtis Hawks flown by Chinese pilots, and reportedly there were even some Soviet "volunteers" flying I-16s for the Communist forces. He had yet to tangle with either, and this morning's raid was as uneventful as the dozen others he had flown on so far. The few Chinese fighters that were encountered now either fled or were shot down, the 96s far superior in all respects. The enemy pilots usually kept their distance, especially when it was Japanese naval planes doing the job.

He rolled from a sharp banking turn into a split S, inverting, going over on his back, pulling the stick back sharply, easing back on the throttle slightly.

The plane was a joy, fast with a maximum speed of nearly four hundred kilometers per hour, able to go through a 360-degree roll in just seconds. As he pulled the stick back into his stomach, the horizon disappeared, several Gs pressed him into his seat, he was coming straight down on the burning village. He could see people scattering. He continued to hold the stick back then eased off slightly. If a student pilot had pulled this stunt with him at this altitude there would have been hell to pay, but he knew what he was doing, knew his plane, and didn't pull out from the inverted dive until he was less than fifty meters from the ground, racing at near the V_NE for the plane, "velocity do not exceed." The moment felt good, plane stable, no tremor, the stick solid in his hand. He was now just above the road leading out of the village, heading up toward the front lines. He caught glimpses of peasants scattering in fear. He tried not to think about that. All too often the army pilots, when coming back from a mission, would empty their remaining ammunition on the terrified peasants. He had forbidden that practice and was amazed when several had questioned him one night at evening mess about the order and he found that he had to justify it, not morally, but rather as a "waste of expensive ordnance."

There were tracks on the muddy road, the early morning light sparkling off the water that filled the ruts. And in an instant he knew. Damn, next time, from now on, someone would fly in first on these damn raids against a target that wasn't fixed in place and check before a single bomb was dropped.

A couple of kilometers ahead was a bamboo grove, to either side the ground open, all of it farmed. He raced toward the grove and then caught a reflected glint of light. He banked 45 degrees as he thundered over the grove, and there he saw them — four trucks, crews already jumping out of the vehicles that had obviously come from the village, cut bamboo piled atop them in a vain effort at concealment, but the ruts a beacon straight to the target.

He banked up sharply, circling, gaining a hundred meters so when he went into his strafing run and nosed over, he'd still have plenty of ground room on the run in. Too many pilots had been killed on strafing missions when, so intent on their target, they forgot that to keep the target in their sights it meant they had to be in a shallow dive and would pull out too late.

He lined up on the east side of the road half a kilometer away and raced in, cover on the trigger flipped up, finger poised, ready to brush against the hard metal, just the slightest touch and the machine guns would ignite, the cold morning wind whipping past to either side of the open cockpit.

Another few seconds . . . a Nationalist soldier out in the middle of the road, running in blind panic . . . bad luck for you, fellow . . . he brushed the trigger, ready to walk the tracers into the truck park, ready to flip sharply and bank if secondary explosions should light off.

A glimpse of the terrified Nationalist, staggering backward, rifle raised . . .

And then the blow . . . forward windscreen shattering, shards of glass blowing back, wind howling at over three hundred kilometers per hour blasting his face. Thank heaven my goggles are down was the flash thought; a split second later black oil was flinging into his face, blinding him.

He yanked back on the stick, one hand up to try and wipe his goggles clear, not even sure if he was hit. Disoriented now, he looked to one side, saw he was in a high banking turn. Impossible to see his instruments, sensing the controls going sluggish, losing lift in the high banking turn, starting to head into an accelerated stall, at this altitude no time to break the stall, especially if it snapped into a spin.

His heart was pounding, he pushed the stick forward and to the left, feeding in left rudder as well, wondering for a second if the controls would even respond. They did. Rudder was working, ailerons, elevator, no damage there. The plane leveled out. Oil was still streaming back, smashing into his face, filling his mouth and nose, almost impossible to breathe. He fumbled for his oxygen mask. Somehow it was knocked off, not clipped to the side of his helmet, maybe shot away. Again he looked to his port side to try and orient himself. Horizon was nearly level now, sense of control returning, but smoke was now making it hard to see. The big radial engine forward was rougher by the second, a cylinder or two beginning to misfire. It was impossible to see his instruments, to check oil pressure, engine temperature, temperature. Smoke was pouring into the cockpit, smelling of burning oil.

Damn, damn all! A bullet, one damn bullet fired blindly, most likely had pierced the cowling, severed an oil line, then smashed into his windscreen. One damn bullet and he had a flash memory of his English instructor at Etajima, the Kipling poem about the Sandhurst graduate, the thousands of pounds spent on his education, to be snuffed out by an Afghan taking a potshot with a bullet costing one rupee.

A shadow. He looked again to starboard, it was his wingman! Up so close the planes were almost touching. He could barely make him out through the oil-covered goggles, but he could see that Masatake was wagging his wings — follow me.

Fuchida let go of his iron grip he had been keeping on his stick with both hands, waved, pointed to his goggles, shook his head to try and signal he was blinded.

Masatake ever so slowly went into a banking turn with a gentle climb.

He finally leveled out but continued to climb.

Good old Masatake was leading him home and going for altitude. Every meter gained was six meters of glide if and when the engine cut out.

The engine was getting rough. When would a piston finally seize up? He slowly worked the throttle back, dropping rpms, leaning the fuel mixture out, working cowling flaps wide to force as much cooling air as possible into the engine, a trade-off since if there was fire the extra rush of air would fan it. If a fire was igniting, all hell would break loose, and his sense of smell was alert. It still smelled like hot boiling oil, hopefully from the ruptured line spraying onto the engine and manifold, but if it caught into an open blaze, it was time to get the hell out; and, unlike some, he had no qualms about using his parachute that others disdained as cowardice. Fools, a pilot was worth his weight in gold, in fact, actually most likely far more than his weight in gold when the cost of training him across the years was actually calculated.

But he had no idea where in hell he was, if over Nationalist lines, the prospect of being a prisoner was unacceptable. There were rumors circulating that the Nationalists were torturing then executing prisoners. It's what we do, he thought, a grim irony, trying to argue with them that he was a naval pilot and thus different than the army. A poor excuse, he knew. No, the engine had to be nursed along.

Rougher engine and still rougher. Shut it down now and avoid fire. No, wait . . . the minutes dragged out, engine sputtering, sounding like it was going to seize, then kicking back in. Mitsubishi made an engine that could take punishment, oil starved it'd still keep running. He was still flying.

Again good old Masatake by his side, wing tip tucked up close, and then a wave, barely visible, pointing down, and then he slowly began to drop. Fuchida nodded. They must be close. More smoke. He cut the throttle completely, working the hydraulic pump to feather the prop, then turned off the magneto switches. The engine stuttered, there was a shudder and it stopped, but the smoke continued to cascade into the cockpit, it was all but impossible to breathe now. He fumbled around, trying to find the oxygen mask again, and at last grasped it, pressing it to his face . . . damn, it had indeed been shot away, a hole through the hose, and that gave him a cold chill, it meant the bullet had missed him by no more than a fraction as the mask hung to his side.

He couldn't judge altitude, had no idea where he was, he just stayed focused on Masatake who was bleeding off speed. A wave from Masatake, a gesture as if pointing down, and he thought he could see the flaps on Masatake's plane cranking down, and he followed his lead. The plane had fixed landing gear, so no worry there. Air speed dropping off, slowing, stick heavier, the edge of a stall approaching, nose pitching up, imitating Masatake.

Then an instant of panic as Masatake suddenly accelerated and started to pull up.

And at nearly that same instant there was a hard slap, the ground! His plane bounced, hung for a second. Smoke was dying off. He stuck his head over to the side, caught a recognizable glimpse of the control tower; another slap, all three wheels down, no need to work rudder against torque from the engine; he rolled past the tower, looked up, saw Masatake now flying above him thirty feet or so higher, acting as a guide for directional control, but he no longer needed that, he pulled his goggles back, able to see, eyes stinging from the smoke, but he could see as he rolled out to a stop.

Silence. Absolute silence.

He was shaking, fear now really digging into him and a few seconds later, still strapped in, he tried to lean forward as he vomited and then gasped for air.

Hands around his shoulders, shouts, sound of a truck pulling up, men leaping out, someone, his crew chief, pulling him out of the cockpit and down the wing. Gasping for air he vomited again and felt complete and utter shame at doing so, worried that those gathered around would think it was fear. It was the damn oil.

"Water," was all he could croak out. And a canteen was pressed to his lips. He rinsed, spat it out, someone was wiping his face even as they led him away from the side of the plane and over to the truck.

"Sir, let me rinse your eyes," someone said. He nodded, cool water splashing on his face, a towel gently wiping the oil away, more water, more wiping.

"Try and open them now, sir."

He opened his eyes. They stung like hell, but he could see. Breathing was still difficult, someone pushed an oxygen mask to his face and he took the air in, breathing deeply, coughing, half vomiting again, black oil clearing from his throat.

An engine. He looked up, it was Masatake, taxiing in, swinging to one side of the runway. A fire crew was hosing down Fuchida's plane, engine hissing under the cascade of water.

Masatake climbed up out of his cockpit, jumped down from the wing, and came running over. Fuchida suddenly realized that dozens, maybe a hundred or more, were watching. He had to play the role again, hoping that the trembling would just be seen as illness from breathing and swallowing oil.

Masatake slowed and Fuchida did not salute, instead he bowed formally.

"I owe you my life, my friend."

He felt Masatake's hands on his shoulders pulling him back up, and he looked into the grinning face of his comrade who let all formality break and hugged him, then stepped back.

"Hey, you got oil all over my new flight suit," Masatake joked, and there was a thickness to his voice as the two gazed at each other.

Fuchida could not speak for a moment, embarrassed by the emotional display, and then turned away, walking over to his plane where a crowd was gathered around. The crew chief, up on wing, soaking wet, leaned up over the forward cowling and exclaimed: "You can see it, one damn lucky shot, cut open an oil line, up through here," and he pointed to the hole in the cowling, "and through here." He pointed to the oil-caked remnants of the wind screen and then looked back with amazement at Fuchida.

It was unspoken but both knew what the

other was thinking. A few more centimeters to one side, and that bullet would have shattered his skull, and he would be tangled into a burning wreck eighty kilometers to the north on the other side of the Yangtze. Funny, he could not even remember crossing the river now.

"Sir, I think we should get you back to the infirmary," one of the medical staff announced, still holding the oxygen bottle.

Fuchida shook his head. "I'll be all right," he replied, his voice raspy. Actually something to drink would be better medicine.

Within seconds half a dozen eager hands were offering small flasks of sake. He took one, the owner grinning and bowing slightly. He forced himself to gulp it down, even though it burned. Again, part of the show of command, something the men would talk about later.

The drink hit his head, and he swayed slightly, everyone now laughing good-naturedly.

Air crewmen gathered around as he forced himself to walk to the control tower and his barracks just beyond. A shower, change of clothes, then quietly over to the infirmary afterward.

Eyes still burning, he looked around at his comrades and then stopped short, surprised beyond ability to speak. It was a Westerner, tall, and immediately recognizable — his old friend Stanford.

What the hell was he doing here? Fuchida wondered in confusion, and then remembered. The base commander had informed him that a Western reporter would be allowed onto the base to interview him. Another gesture after the *Panay* situation to try and smooth the waters.

He had no idea that it would be Stanford.

His old friend approached a bit hesitantly, the pilots and ground crew gathered around Fuchida falling into silence, some nervous, more than a few features going cold as if this man were an intruder.

Fuchida broke the tension, stepping forward, hand extended. "Sir, my old friend," Fuchida said.

Stanford smiled and extended his hand, and Fuchida started to pull his back, realizing he was covered with oil; but Stanford took it anyhow, shaking it warmly, so un-Britishlike, and then actually patted him on the shoulder.

"So does this happen often?" Stanford said in Japanese.

Fuchida chuckled. "Fortunately, no."

"I'm glad you are safe, my old friend," Stanford replied, and the tension of the group eased slightly.

Fuchida nodded, suddenly unable to reply.

"Perhaps we should arrange our interview for another time," Stanford said, but Fuchida shook his head. "Unthinkable," he replied in English. "Let me shower, have a drink, and give the doctor a moment to poke around. My friend here, Lieutenant Masatake, will take you over to my quarters."

Masatake came stiffly to attention and saluted, Stanford nodding.

Fuchida suddenly realized his diplomatic mistake and prayed that Masatake would not reveal it. Masatake was one of the pilots who had machine-gunned and bombed the *Panay*.

Cecil Stanford sat uncomfortably in the straight-back chair in Fuchida's office. Flight Lieutenant Masatake, sitting across from him, saying little other than to answer with short yes and no answers so that after ten minutes or so there was silence. An enlisted man came in, bowing low to Cecil, offering tea and some hardtack like linseed cakes with jam on them. They were actually quite good and standing he took his teacup and slowly walked around the room, look-ing casually at the photographs lining one wall. Fuchida from earlier days in a biplane, his infectious grin lighting the picture, of course a picture of the Emperor directly in the center of the room, the far wall lined with charts. He could sense Masatake's gaze boring into him, and he steered clear of the charts, walking over to the window to look out at the airfield.

A small truck was towing Fuchida's plane over to one of the hangers, the sides of the plane streaked black with oil.

"I saw the way you guided him in," Cecil said, looking back to his temporary "host." "Absolutely masterful flying, just superb."

"Thank you, sir," was the laconic reply.

"You took a risk there it seemed, coming down like that off the edge of the landing strip while guiding him in."

"I knew what I was doing."

"Of course. Lieutenant Masatake, isn't it?"

"Yes, sir."

Cecil looked away, acting casual, sipping his tea.

Masatake said nothing.

And both knew the game. Naval pilots had participated in the *Panay* attack, and he had heard the rumor that Fuchida had been sent over to tighten discipline. Was this man one of the attackers?

He looked back but Masatake sat, impassive, that studied pose that Cecil was all so familiar with from his days teaching at Etajima. Calmness in the face of threat, absolute and utter control of all features and gestures.

The door into the office flung open and Masatake leapt to his feet, obviously relieved. Fuchida came over to the lieutenant and slapped him affectionately on the shoulder.

"Thank you, my friend, and thank you for taking care of our guest."

Masatake nodded, turned, offered a slight bow to Cecil, and left the room.

Fuchida was dressed in loose-fitting flight overalls, hair still wet, streaks of oil still under his neck and caked under his closely trimmed fingernails. It was obvious he had rushed to clean up.

"Been to the infirmary yet?" Stanford asked.

Fuchida chuckled and shook his head and for this moment the bond was there, that wonderful infectious grin, the open smile, the searching eyes.

"I'm dying for a cigarette," Fuchida said, motioning for Cecil to sit down. Fuchida pulled his chair out from behind his desk to create a more comfortable setting and to be closer to his friend.

Cecil shook his head. 'That medic was right. You breathed in a lot of gunk. You should be in the hospital now on oxygen for the next day or so."

"Just one," Fuchida said, forcing a smile. "Since this war started, Dunhills are impossible to get here."

Cecil hesitated, reached into his breast pocket and pulled out his silver cigarette case, and opened it, helping Fuchida to light the smoke.

He inhaled slightly and then was hit with a terrible coughing jag, Cecil pulling out a handkerchief which Fuchida grasped at and then, embarrassed, balled up in his hand; it was stained black.

"Told you," Cecil said quietly, as Fuchida stubbed out the cigarette and sighed. "If it had killed you, your comrades would claim I was an enemy provocateur and most likely shoot me."

The humor fell flat but then again, Cecil knew it was not all humor now. The barely concealed hostility between the Japanese armed forces and the few Europeans left was palpable and rumors were coming in of disappearances, of mission churches and hospitals flying American or British flags being shot up.

Fuchida fell silent, poured a cup of tea for

himself, and then offered to refill Cecil's cup, which he gladly accepted.

"I'm slightly confused," Fuchida said. "I thought you were still in the navy. I was told a reporter from a British newspaper was being allowed onto the base to meet with me and my pilots and now you are here."

"You're correct on the latter point," Cecil replied. "Retired from the navy, was going to write a book about my days at Etajima and other things about Japan, but the pension for a retired lieutenant commander are short rations at best. A newspaper offered me a correspondent's job, so here I am."

Fuchida nodded, still smiling. He had been told that the correspondent was, as well, most likely a spy and to be cautious.

There was an awkward pause and Cecil finally broke it. "Tell me about what happened out there?" and he pointed to the plane now being backed into a hangar.

Fuchida chuckled and gave a short account. "Just a damn lucky shot, or unlucky one could say, depending upon which side you are on," as he finished up.

"Your target was Nationalist supplies."

"I'm sorry, my friend, you know I can't discuss that."

"There have been numerous reports of the

bombing of unarmed villages, strafing of innocent civilians working in the fields, terror tactics."

Fuchida stiffened slightly. "Whose reports?"

"Other Westerners here, missionaries; when I was still inside Nationalist lines I witnessed some of the air attacks."

"Can you differentiate between Japanese army and naval aircraft?"

"Yes, of course. And yes, from what I've seen it was Japanese army aircraft doing the attacking."

Fuchida nodded. "There are strict orders with naval units to engage only against legitimate targets as defined by the rules of war."

"The attack on the *Panay* was by naval aircraft; they were clearly identified."

Fuchida did not reply.

"Do you remember Lieutenant Commander Watson?" Cecil asked, voice calm.

"Of course I do." Fushida grinned. "We corresponded for a while. Said when he retired he wanted to take up flying as a hobby, and I was his inspiration."

"That might be a bit hard to do now with one hand."

"What?"

"He was on the *Panay,*" Cecil replied bitterly, and Fuchida visibly paled and lowered his head.

"Damn near died. Had to amputate his left hand, had pneumonia from nearly drowning. He's been beached, retired out of the service as disabled."

"I'm sorry, so terribly sorry. Perhaps I should write to him."

"I doubt if he'd even open the letter now," Cecil replied. "How would you feel if it had been you as a target?"

"I wish I had been out here before it happened," Fuchida said softly.

"Word is that the plot was hatched out here among the pilots themselves, another act of *gekokujo;* higher-ups knew and said nothing, which is the same as saying yes, and your government seemed damn quick with its ready-made apology. There was no disciplining afterward, hell. If that had been a pilot of the Royal Air Force, he'd be stripped of rank and sitting in prison right now, not out flying."

Fuchida sighed and drew a bit closer.

"Are we talking as friends, Professor Stanford, or as a reporter, Mr. Stanford."

Cecil said nothing.

"We've known each other how long now, nearly ten years?" Fuchida asked. "Can we make it as friends for a few minutes, off the record, nothing that will go into the newspaper."

Fuchida finally nodded. Cecil suddenly felt like a heel liar. He had said nothing about what he might report to Winston.

"You saw what happened with the coup two years ago," Fuchida said softly. "It was a minority, but the message was clear and it took effect, the army wanted a free hand in China to do what the civilian government did not have the courage to do . . . to end the civil war in China, restore order, and build out of it a modern state."

Cecil shook his head.

"You believe that? Oh, not about the coup; I agree with you on that. But your presence here in China; you make it sound like you come as friends."

"Did you come as friends to India or South Africa?" Fuchida snapped back.

"You believe in this campaign, don't you," Cecil asked.

Fuchida nodded.

"I believe it is Japan's destiny to rule in the Western Pacific. My friend, we are you, England, of a hundred years past as it built its Empire. There is still much that can bind us, an English dominance in the West, Japan in the East."

"You seem to have forgotten the French,

the Dutch, the Americans in this."

"If England should see fit to join hands with us, the others will follow."

Cecil shook his head. "You know the alliance between America and us is firm, unbreakable."

"Let us see how strong that alliance is when finally you must face German expansionism. They will run and hide. America has lost its moral courage."

"You think the *Panay* proved that, don't you? Is that why your pilots did it, a test to see if America would run, a statement for them to get out."

"I'll not comment," Fuchida said, after a long hesitation. "Rather than speculate on your allies, let's continue to talk about here, what is happening in China and why."

"Go on then."

"China is a vast pool of hundreds of millions still in the medieval world, as we were but eighty years ago. We can lead the way. You did that to India and South Africa. South Africa is now independent, and I dare say in another generation so will India be; but you will be bonded together.

"And besides, China is in a vacuum. Does anyone in England want to see the Communists win? You've tacitly thrown your lot in with the Nationalists. The corruption of

Chiang Kai-shek is already the stuff of legend. If you want to see disciplined cadres, look to Mao and his Communists, and believe me, in the end they will win if someone, meaning us, does not intervene."

"I cannot deny that the Communist troops are better led, better disciplined."

"There, you have it," Fuchida said, slapping the table. "Let Japan take control here. Yes, there will be tragic fighting, but in short order that will end and stability will return. We'll bring order, law, industrialization, the same as your people have done, and the English can look to us as being like England but on the other side of the Continent."

"An interesting proposition," Cecil replied coolly, "but again, I doubt if the French wish to be dislodged, the Dutch and the Americans express their own interest in China . . . and this *Panay* incident struck dangerously close to triggering a war."

Fuchida said nothing for a moment then sighed. "We are talking now as a reporter, are we not?"

"Yes, Lieutenant Commander Fuchida."

"And might I therefore reply that in the opening days of the war, Nationalist planes attacked a British ship, but fortunately, due to their terrible bomb aiming, no damage was done."

"A mistake in the heat of action is one thing," Cecil pressed, "but the attacks on British ships on the Yangtze at nearly the same time as the *Panay* seems rather a coincidence, wouldn't you agree?"

Fuchida shifted uncomfortably.

"And the same apologies and restitution have been made. I see no further use for an inquiry in this direction."

Fuchida remained silent for a moment, not adding that he felt it was Western arrogance to sail ships right into the middle of a war zone and then, in all that confusion, cry foul if one was hit.

"Another question," Cecil asked, breaking the silence.

"Go on."

"Nanking, have you been down into the city of Nanking?"

Fuchida shook his head. "I have been on the base here since my arrival."

"I want you to come with me."

"Why?"

"Because I want you to see what the hell your army is doing," Cecil snapped angrily. "I was there in December; I witnessed it. I saw children being raped, nuns decapitated, old men used for bayonet practice. I saw it!" Cecil sat back, angry with himself, his last words nearly shouted.

Fuchida stood up and stepped away from Cecil.

Cecil continued, "Do you know that at least two hundred thousand, maybe three hundred thousand or more have been murdered there? No, I shouldn't say murdered, rather tortured and executed by your Imperial Japanese Army. Do you know that?"

"The navy is here to provide air support only and patrol on the rivers," Fuchida said defensively.

"It is still your country, your army, your war. It is barbarity not seen in hundreds of years. But this time, this time the entire world is watching. I have filed my reports with my newspaper along with photographs of the dead. Newsreel footage is being shown in theaters around the world. But a few years back many looked upon your nation with favor, even saw it as a block against Stalin and his henchmen moving east, but now?"

He hesitated. "Now they see you as conquering, Imperialistic barbarians."

"And do you see me that way?" Fuchida cried, voice rising.

"Come with me to Nanking today, walk the streets with me and see."

Fuchida shook his head.

"I have my duties here to plan for and

then to the infirmary."

"I was there," Cecil said, shaking his head, voice thick. "I will continue to report what I see. I was hoping that at least with you, an old friend, I might hear something different. The voice of a Japan I respected and loved."

Fuchida stood looking at him, uncomfortable, recalling so many evenings over a good scotch, talking history, the theories of war, but those were always abstractions. "Is there anything else?" Fuchida asked.

Cecil slowly shook his head. "Why bother. If you take me around the airfield, I'll see the usual planes, the usual fresh-faced kids, hear the usual platitudes. But the reality of it all? No, I don't think so, my friend. What did you bomb today? What did you bomb yesterday? I've walked through some of those villages, the stench of bloating bodies making me vomit. And I was at Nanking, and that I can never purge from my mind.

"No, if you will not walk the streets of Nanking with me, then the interview is over."

He jotted something on a piece of paper, tore the sheet out, and leaning over placed it on Fuchida's desk.

"Your old friend Commander Watson's address. Perhaps a letter of apology is due.

Let the man who saved your life this morning send him a note as well, if he has the courage to do so."

Fuchida looked at him coldly as Cecil folded his notebook and stood up, ready to leave.

"You do not see our side of it," Fuchida replied sharply. "China will rot in anarchy for a hundred years to come or fall to the Communists if we do not intervene. We will restore order and bring peace."

"Your army murders hundreds of thousands as a bringer of peace?" Cecil Stanford shook his head. "We are all tottering on the edge. This will go out of control. You do not have the manpower, the equipment, the army to conquer all of China. It is simply too much for Japan to swallow and then hold. I'll bet some damn fools with your general staff said it will be over in six months. Make it six years, more like sixty years, and you'll still be fighting and sooner, rather than later, it will just expand, like a cancer. With the drain created by this, your eyes will finally be forced to turn elsewhere, to gain the materials needed to wage this war, and that will mean more war.

"I'm sorry if you believe what you just told me and will not face what your military is doing, I am sad to say we are no longer friends." He waited as if expecting a reply, an appeal in response.

"You press too far, Commander," Fuchida hesitated, "I mean Mr. Stanford." His voice was cold now, distant. "You asked me to imagine how I would feel if I was Commander Watson. How dare you ask me to refute my nation? If it was I who demanded that of you, what would be your answer?"

Cecil remained silent, not replying.

There was nothing more to be said, Fuchida looking straight at him, expressionless.

"I congratulate you on surviving today. I hope you survive all that is to come. Farewell." Cecil turned and walked out of the office.

Fuchida watched him go, saying nothing, for indeed, there was nothing more to be said.

An escort accompanied Cecil to his car, a navy vehicle that would take him back to the international quarter in Shanghai.

Fuchida turned away, walking over to the far wall, gazing at the maps, local tactical maps, and then, pinned to one side, the map of all of China. He felt cold, distant. He knew that in a few more months his tour of duty here would be finished, the promise already made that he could return to the

War College in the fall to complete his studies there. Then most likely back to either a carrier offshore, perhaps his old beloved *Akagi,* or to yet again train new pilots, for the navy now needed them by the hundreds.

And he knew that his former friend was right. In spite of all the promises of the chiefs of staff, the generals, the admirals, he would most likely come here to China yet again in a year or two, the war still raging, like an open sore that would not heal, that the decade would turn, and still there would be fighting . . . and it would spread, like a cancer.

He felt bad for James, though they had met only twice, the bond they had shared in the flight had continued, the love of flying that can always bring pilots together, even if one had flown but for the first time.

But Cecil was American and, incredulous as it seemed, America had not reacted to the war that his friends had tried to provoke that day with the *Panay.* It had revealed much about the character of America. They could be pushed, and if need be pushed hard without reacting. They had built their Empire and expected the world to accept it, and then tried to hide behind their moral platitudes. But it was now Japan's turn and in that he had utter faith, feeling a flicker of anger toward Cecil for even daring to ask him to make a choice. Two thousand five hundred years of history were behind Japan and her unbroken line of emperors.

If it took sixty more years to fulfill that destiny here in China, then so be it . . . and he knew with utter certainty that neither England nor America would have the courage to dare to stop them. Other storm clouds were on their horizons and, hopefully, soon the Westerners would turn on themselves in their own frenzy and thus leave Japan to pick up the pieces that were left. He was Japanese, and no one from the West could ultimately understand the true meaning of that, even those whom he had considered to be his friends.

He returned back to his desk, sat down, and begin to write up the report on the raid, noticed the address of James sitting on the corner, looked at it, hesitated, then balled it up and dropped it into the trash.

The White House
Washington, D.C.
16 May 1940

"General Marshall, I know you do not agree with my proposal for building fifty thousand aircraft a year. As commander in chief I have to follow my deepest instincts, my own judgment. It is clear from what we have seen in Spain during the Civil War, in China during the Japanese invasion, and now in Western Europe and North Africa that airpower is the dominant force. Germany and Japan have it and they are dominating. China, Republican Spain, Poland, France, all failed to have effective airpower, and now they are suffering. We must have dominance in the air if we are going to defend America." Roosevelt looked up at Marshall from his wheelchair with an intense gaze.

"Mr. President, we will implement your order if you insist. However, I feel obligated to point out that our war plan calls for a two-hundred-division army. If you insist that we build fifty thousand airplanes a year, we will have to divert so many men to the Army Air Corps and even more importantly to an industrial base big enough to build that many planes, that we will have a dramatically smaller ground force." Marshall looked determined and spoke with sober precision.

"General Marshall, I am afraid you will have to reshape your plans and reduce the number of divisions. I am going to issue an executive order today calling for fifty thousand aircraft a year," FDR replied.

Marshall could offer no reply, and the president offered his best winning smile.

"I'm betting on the future here, General, and my instincts tell me that the future is with airpower."

CHAPTER SIX

London Bridge
7 September 1940
1730 hours

The noise was deafening, all encompassing, as if the world was indeed ending . . . and he could not help but be thrilled by the power and intensity of it.

"You there, you ya bloody idiot, just what in hell are you doing?"

Minoru Genda, stationed in London for the last two years as naval attaché to the Japanese Embassy, turned to face the air raid warden, crouching low, running toward him. The cacophony of noise continued to swell, the continual trembling wail of the air raid sirens, the pulsing thunder of thousands of engines overhead, and the ever-expanding concussion of explosions washing up the Thames River from the East End, which was taking the brunt of the raid.

"Off this bridge now, you bloody fool!"

and the warden reached out to grab him by the shoulder. Genda raised his hand, black leather of the oversized wallet containing his identification card and credentials flipped open, and stuck it in front of the warden, only inches from his face so that he had to step back.

It identified him as a member of the diplomatic staff of His Imperial Majesty's Government of Japan, one document in English, the other in Japanese, all of it very official looking and proper and guaranteed to intimidate a lowly air raid warden and for that matter many a member of the British government as well when used correctly.

The warden stared at it for a few seconds and then the attention of both turned toward the river. A German twin-engine Heinkel 111 bomber, twisting and turning as it followed the banks of the river, was screaming straight toward them, skimming the river so low that as it turned it seemed as if its wing would dig into the water. A trail of black smoke was streaming out of its port-side engine. Behind it, a Hawker Hurricane was fifty yards off its tail, following every twisting turn of the desperate German pilot, cutting inside the turns to squeeze off short bursts, some rounds hit, sparks flying off the wing, others missing, stitching into the river, each round sending up a geyser of water ten feet high, coming straight toward them.

Genda and the air raid warden ducked down behind the stone siding of the bridge as the Heinkel 111, at more than 200 mph, screamed over the bridge, just feet above them, the thunder of its passing shaking Genda, the exhaust of its engines, the pungent smoke from the oil-starved pistons darkening the sky. It was so close that for a second he could actually see the face of the tail gunner, swinging his weapon around firing off a burst. The German pilot was now pulling up, struggling for altitude. Genda knew why; the drama was nearing its end.

The sound of it all sent a corkscrew thrill down Genda's back. The roar of the engines, the smell of the exhaust, he was back on the deck of his beloved *Akagi* or *Kaga* again. Planes revving up, preparing to take off. Soon he would be back there, in another week he was leaving London to return home, and he had witnessed what was now being called the Battle of Britain from its opening stage to now, this moment, to what some would think was its dramatic climax, most of the staff in the embassy exuberantly betting that the Germans would come marching past Whitehall within the week.

A split second later the Hurricane screamed over the bridge, banking in tight onto the tail of the 111, tracers slashing into its victim. A few rounds from the tail gunner of the 111 splattered the stone bridge the two were standing on, fragments of stone kicking up.

The 111, now maybe five hundred feet up, began to roll into a sharp, banking turn, fragments tumbling from the port wing and fuselage, the turn taking it toward the south bank of the Thames. It wasn't a controlled turn, Genda could sense that. Either the pilot was dead, or the aileron cables had snapped, that and the port wing was beginning to sheer off, flame erupting from the ruptured fuel tanks. A body fell out of the bomb bay, then a second, the chute of the second jumper instantly opening, the other struggling for a few tragic seconds too long, even as the chute started to blossom he slammed into the mud of the embankment on the south side of the river. The open chute of the lucky one drifted behind the trees lining the river.

The Heinkel 111 fireballed along its port-side wing, which now sheered off completely and the plane went into a tumbling spin. Seconds later there was a rumbling explosion and sheets of flame erupted near Waterloo Station.

The Hurricane turned in a sharp bank to the north, the pilot, obviously unable to contain his exuberance, doing a victory roll as he climbed heavenward over Parliament, soaring upward to rejoin the fray.

"That's the stuff!" the warden screamed, jumping up, clenched fist raised in the air in salute. And Genda could not help but feel an exuberance as well as envy for that pilot at this moment, having made his kill like a samurai, clean, efficient, and with all of London watching below; and in spite of the overwhelming noise of battle, he could hear cheers: "That's our boy! Get another Jerry, lad!"

The warden half turned back to Genda.

"That's why you should be off this bridge. Get yourself killed out here like this."

Genda again held up his diplomatic pass, saying nothing, and the warden shook his head.

"Bloody stupid slant eyes. If you want to get killed out here, that's your business."

"I speak perfectly good English," Genda said slowly. "And I am an officer in my country's navy."

The warden, embarrassed, actually raised his right hand and offered something of a salute, mumbled an apology, and moved on, disappearing into the smoke from the burning Heinkel that still cloaked the bridge.

Genda turned back to watch the unfolding battle. The main action was down along the East End, from Tower Bridge three miles away clear down to Greenwich. With the well-made excellent Zeiss binoculars that he was using to observe the fight, he estimated at least two hundred or more German bombers were at work, dropping their loads from what appeared to be several thousand meters up, above the range of the lightweight 20- and 40-antiaircraft guns, which were basically all that the British could muster for the defense of the city except for a few batteries of heavier weaponry clustered around the center of the city and government buildings.

The concussions from the heavier bombs, 500 kilos or more, slapped against him, even from this distance. Smoke was columning up, darkening the skies. A huge secondary lit off. He saw the fireball soaring heavenward, counting the seconds until the blast washed over him. It was staggering even from miles away. Most likely the Woolrich arsenal he thought. Still operational from the reports he had received but a few days before most likely a thousand tons or more of explosives had lit off with that one.

A high, almost bell-like tinkling interrupted him for a moment, and he saw a scattering of shell casings hitting the pavement in the middle of the bridge, bouncing, coming to rest, cast-offs from .30-caliber and 7.7- and 20-millimeter guns, hundreds more were pocking the water of the Thames. High overhead the sky was a latticework of contrails, the battle up there between Spitfires and ME-109s raging at twenty thousand feet or more, remote from what was transpiring down here, and yet still a deadly struggle for control of the air over London. Nearly invisible dots twisted and turned, as if their intent was to weave an elaborate pattern of contrails in the skies. It was beautiful to watch, and Genda, head tilted back, focused on it for a moment.

Any semblance of formations seemed to have broken down, the heavenly battle a hundred duels, a puff of smoke, a flash of flame, the dot disappearing, contrail following it turning away, German or British he could not tell. Three contrails were streaking down from the west, up there, far away up there, coming out of the sun, pouncing, another flash of flame, the three continuing on into a sharp spiraling turn, looking for more prey. And how he wished with all his heart to be up there now. It almost didn't matter which side, just to be up in the thick of it, pitting his skills against any who would dare to challenge him, again the thought of the samurai duels of old.

There must be a thousand planes in the sky overhead, Genda thought, filled with a sense of wonder, the greatest air battle in the history of warfare was taking place this day, and here he was, stuck on the ground. Overhead, just from the German side alone, more aircraft than his entire navy could ever hope to launch.

An explosion directly above and he looked up to see what appeared to be a Hurricane, disintegrating, both wings sheering off, plummeting down in a nearly vertical dive, a 109 pulling out behind it, engine scream-ing loudly as the pilot leveled off and began to climb, heading southeast, apparently rac-ing for home, fuel most likely short.

With a sense of horror Genda watched as the wreckage of the Hurricane tumbled down to fall somewhere along the north side of the river; and there, just above the burn-ing fuselage, trailing smoke, was the doomed pilot, parachute tangled into a burning streamer like a candlewick about to snuff out, arms and legs flaying. The wreckage of the burning plane, and the man who had flown it but seconds before, crashed down on the north side, somewhere up near Trafalgar Square. He felt a wave of pity for the man, more likely a boy since it was known that the RAF was indeed scraping the bottom of the barrel, putting up barely trained youths of nineteen with less than twenty hours of training in their planes. In the Japanese navy, it was expected that a pilot would have at least three hundred hours or more in a combat aircraft before he was deemed ready for battle. Planes and pilots, for Japan, were too valuable to be wasted lightly. But for England, they were on the desperate edge.

He wondered if the doomed youth had been the same pilot who but a few minutes before had, with such high zest, pulled a victory roll over Parliament, climbing back up to meet his fate in the tumult raging above.

More explosions from the East End drew his attention, while overhead the pulsing roar of hundreds of engines grew in intensity, the vast German air armada banking, turning about to head back southeastward to reload and, most likely, return come night, the fires of the East End now their beacon.

He shook his head.

The clattering of a bell sounded behind him. He saw a white ambulance racing across the bridge, behind it three fire trucks and several lorries loaded with infantry. Downstream, a fire boat was at work, streams of water arching high in the air, trying to douse a fire consuming a burning freighter, a bomb detonating near it, rocking the boat, yet it kept to its duty. Down on the river embankment behind him, half a dozen men, up to their thighs in muck, were dragging out the body of the dead German from the Heinkel. He turned away from the chaos to walk back toward his embassy, the report already forming in his mind.

To have such power . . . to have such power and not to squander it as it was being squandered this day by the Germans, that would be the key to a Japanese victory.

Oahu
11 September 1940
7:00 a.m. Local Time

James Watson, former naval commander, now associate professor of mathematics at the University of Hawaii, eased in a little more rudder to counter the engine torque, eased back on the stick, not too much, just a touch, and the Aeronca Chief with all its fifty horsepower floated off the dirt strip and into the air. Nose down slightly, build up climb-out speed to sixty, then stick back again, best rate of climb a stately four hundred feet per minute. Not like the first ride he had been on, but still such a joy, a slight buffet from the gentle trade winds coming in from the northeast. High enough now to circle out over the ocean, if the engine cut off more than enough altitude to glide back to the private landing strip at Kaneohe, just south of the naval air station there.

A lone PBY Catalina twin-engine recon plane was taking off from the small bay, white foam spraying out, and James felt a touch of real envy. If only he had discovered flying back when at the Naval Academy twenty-five years ago, how different his career might have been. It took a Japanese pilot to show him the joy of it, and as he did nearly every time he took off, he wondered how Fuchida was.

Cecil had written him a note about Fuchida, describing their last meeting, and James knew why Fuchida had stopped their correspondence. After getting his private license and buying the Aeronca, he had actually sent a photo of himself with the plane to his old friend. The motivation why, he wasn't sure. Part of him could never forgive nor forget what happened that day, but on the other side, Fuchida had not been personally involved and according to Cecil had most likely been sent out to rein in the hotheads who had launched the attack. Part of it, as well was, he knew, to send a message.

Navy rehab had done some fine work with him. The rubberized hand looked fairly lifelike, fit over the stump comfortably. When he flew he used the mechanical claw hand, it was easier to grasp with and fortunately with flying he only needed his left to work the throttle and trim tab, master switch, and there was always someone around to throw the prop for him. Nearly everything else was done with his right, once he demonstrated he could do so to his instructor, an old retired army pilot from the last war, he was cleared to solo and then got a license. His instructor, Don Barber, had an artificial foot, the real one he said was lost in a cloud somewhere over northern France back in 1918 and was still floating around up there, looking for its owner. It took one of Don's friends to coax out the real story. How he had been pounced, shot up, his right foot damn near blown off, and he had started for a cloud, looking for cover, only to realize his wingman was in trouble, then turned about to go back for him, dropping both Germans they had tangled with. He escorted his wounded wingman back and then passed out from loss of blood after landing his shot-up Spad. Somehow James felt his own injury paled in insignificance next to this man, at least Don had been able to fight back. All he had managed to do was be in the wrong place at the wrong time and had a hand blown off. He had not been able to do a damn thing in reply. Sure, the navy had made a big to-do over his Purple Heart, a Bronze Star for supposedly helping to pull a drowning civilian out, he was ashamed for ever allowing that medal to be forced on him, and then promoted and retired out as disabled.

Learning to fly had been his real therapy, rebuilding confidence, giving him a goal, and his instructor had been the therapist, coaching him along, understanding the need, the two talking about the strange phenomena of "limb memory," how Don said he still woke up in the middle of the night, foot itching like hell, and would actually reach down to scratch it, the same for James who still at times forgot he was missing a hand and actually reached out to pick something up, or got a damn annoying tingle that could never again be scratched.

He knew that was the other reason he had sent the photo to Fuchida. He made a point of wearing the mechanical claw rather than the cosmetic rubber hand, the claw holding the leather flight helmet and goggles Fuchida had given him. He wanted him to see what his comrades had accomplished when they hit the *Panay*. He never heard back from him.

He leveled off at three thousand, cruising

USS Lexington *(CV-2) off Honolulu, Oahu, Hawaii, with Diamond Head in the background, 2 February 1933.* **Naval Historical Center**

comfortably down the east coast of the island, his favorite flight, following the coast toward Diamond Head. Still early enough that he didn't have to worry about the turbulence that would build up to gut-wrenching levels by midday. It was a great day for flying, peaceful, like sliding on glass, the way he loved it. He wished he had dragged Margaret along. She had begrudgingly accepted his new hobby, the seventeen-hundred-dollar cost of the plane, and even gone up a few times, but the slightest bump and back to the airport they went. Today, it was just so damn beautiful, the white surf, startlingly blue ocean, even up here the air rich with that smell of the sea, side windows pulled back to let the breeze in, the lush tropical green clinging to the mountainsides. It was still three hours before he had to be on campus to teach, plenty of time to just cruise around and enjoy the early morning light illuminating the mountains. He gained another five hundred feet, easily clearing up over the east rim of Diamond Head, the breathtaking view of Waikiki Beach beyond. Off in the distance he saw something that made his heart swell; it was distant but clearly visible . . . a carrier putting out to sea from Pearl.

He saw a plane coming in from the east, a

beautiful sight, one of the famed Pan American clippers, which now flew a regular route from San Francisco, coming in a bit early he figured, now down to a thousand feet, passing to the south of Diamond Head, ready to turn into the main loch at Pearl Harbor for final approach and landing.

Now that was flying, he thought. Hard to imagine almost, though *Life* had done a big spread on the luxury to be found aboard, the full-time chef, sleeping berths, even a lounge and bar aboard. Pan American was boasting how they would ring the entire world with their huge four-engine "Clippers" named, of course, after the legendary tall ships of a hundred years past, and soon no spot on the earth would be more than a three- or four-day journey away.

A touch of envy, but his little Chief was enough for now.

It all looked so peaceful, the war news distant, remote, on the other side of the world, he circled Diamond Head once and then turned back for his little dirt strip and another quiet day of teaching.

Two hundred miles west of Lisbon
19 September 1940

Lieutenant Commander Genda still could

not quite believe the experience he was having. The waiter, proper and correct looking in his dark blue Pan American uniform, bent over slightly with tray extended, offering him the famed drink of the plane, the Clipper Special, a mix of vodka, gin, and grenadine.

Nodding his thanks he took the drink, leaning back in his luxurious well-padded seat, the décor a rich turquoise blue carpeting, seats, and even padding of the walls and ceiling, an effective sound barrier that drowned out the pulsing roar of the four Wright Cyclone 14-cylinder engines, each of which delivered 1,600 horsepower to lift this giant of a plane, the famed Boeing 314 Clipper, on its voyage across the Atlantic.

He never dreamed he would ever be aboard such a plane, the greatest transoceanic aircraft ever built, and most likely ever to be built. Capable of carrying seventy day-flight passengers, or forty overnight passengers, each of whom would have their own individual sleeping berths, the plane was richly appointed in every detail.

He had assumed that at the end of his tour of duty in England he would return as he had arrived, by very slow boat, a journey of a month or more. But someone back in Tokyo, most likely Admiral Yamamoto, had seen otherwise, and now he was to be rushed home, first the Clipper to New York, a train to the embassy in Washington to report there, another train to San Francisco, clippers to Hong Kong, and then a waiting Japanese plane for the final flight home.

It was all so breathtaking and actually exciting that some felt that his thoughts, his reports, were worth the expenditure of such money to whisk him home in little more than a week.

It told him as well that something was afoot, something was changing in Tokyo and he would have a role to play in it, and if the Emperor commanded, so he would obey.

As his gaze drifted around the richly appointed plane, the turquoise carpeting, alternating with rust color in the next compartment aft, the heavy leather lounge chairs, the brass-railed spiral staircase that led to the flight deck above, the thick-cut and beveled glass in the lavatory . . . this is something only Americans would build, even while the world plunged into war. The thought of Japan having such aircraft filled him with envy. The range alone was staggering, two hops to refuel, first the Azores then Bermuda, then on to New York, each leg less than twelve hours. Stripped of all its luxury and weight, the bomb load it could carry, or a full company of Imperial marines . . . the thought was staggering what such wealth implied, what five hundred planes such as this could do in time of war.

The interior was divided into six passenger compartments, color scheme arranged in alternating turquoise or deep rust color. Just aft of the spiral staircase was the dining lounge, exceeding anything he had ever experienced aboard ship or train, a full-time chef onboard to tend to the passengers, and he had immediately demonstrated his skills when he produced a light lunch just before takeoff from the mouth of the Tagus River in Lisbon. The menu had offered a selection of fresh fruit, Spanish and Portuguese cheeses, the chef personally apologizing that because of the war, you know, French cheeses were no longer available, a fine selection of wines, thin slices of veal and asparagus, and for dessert, iced sherbets and, of course, the usual brandy and cigars.

It had been a feast straight out of fantasy. Regardless of the diplomatic status of the embassy in London, the cook there was finding it increasingly difficult to obtain meat, eggs, fresh fish, even rice. One day there had been fish, aplenty, only to find out that a stick of German bombs had landed in the Thames, hundreds of dead bottom dwellers rising to the surface. He had passed on that meal, going out instead to find a corner dealer in fish and chips, not bothering to ask where her fish came from, most likely from the same source he realized later when struck by the after results of the meal.

After takeoff he had even been invited to go upstairs to the flight deck, a spacious affair with pilot, copilot, relief pilot, flight engineer, and navigator greeting him. Typical Americans in their friendliness and when they found out he was not just a diplomat on his way home, but a naval pilot as well, the conversation had opened up, with discussion of range, the reliability of the huge Wright-Cyclone engines, the unique tri-boom tail, "could not get the damn thing to turn otherwise," the copilot had quipped, and even discussion of hopes, once things "settled down," for flights routing directly to Japan. The copilot knew the Pacific, having helped to lay out some of the routes, and spoke about the potentials of a base at Okinawa or even at Tinian . . . Genda was surprised the man even knew of those places.

Later into the flight, the head pilot promised him that when the rest of the passengers were settled down and asleep, he'd let Genda take the controls for a bit, on the sly of course since it was against company rules; but it was obvious that Genda, who actually produced his battered logbook tucked into his carry-on briefcase, with over five hundred takeoffs and landings from carriers, knew his stuff. He nearly had the entire plane to himself. There were only eighteen other passengers aboard, all of them gathered aft, in the deluxe luxury suite and sixth compartment.

They were all Americans, two of them generals, the third a colonel that he had vaguely heard of, "Tooey" Spaatz, a pilot from the last war and advocate of the Douhet theory of strategic bombardment.

Conversation over lunch before takeoff had been polite and almost in the tradition of a regimental mess, business was off the table, instead it was about the luxury of the plane, Spaatz comparing it to the Sopwiths he'd flown in the last war and a wish to have a chance to try a little hunting up in the hills of Portugal before leaving, another officer talking about a desire to visit the sites of Wellington's battles against the armies of Napoleon.

"Another tin-pot invader who thought he could take on England," Spaatz growled, the closest they ever got to the real reason why they were all aboard this plane, flying back to the States.

Once in the air the Americans had gone aft to the luxury suite and left the rest of the plane to him. It was almost amusing in a way, all this vast plane to himself, the stewards and chef waiting for any request he might have.

And so the request was yet another Clipper Special, and he settled down in the luxury of the forward compartment in one of the huge oversized chairs, on the starboard side, facing aft to avoid the late afternoon sunlight streaming in through the window.

Setting down his drink, he pulled the attaché case out from an overhead rack, first checking to make sure that the small yellow grease pen dots on the latches had not been smeared. No one had touched it.

Producing the key attached to his watch chain he unlocked the case and opened it, pulling out a sheaf of papers, the start of his written report, which when completed would be nearly the length of a book.

His initial impressions of England's response at the start of the war were that it was woefully foolish and shortsighted, an aggressive response in the first weeks might very well have overrun Germany clear to the Rhine, or at least taken out the Ruhr industrial basin, that in itself ending the fight.

Its remarkable failure of intelligence, preparation, and coordination of command with her allies when the Germans finally turned their gaze westward on May 10 and the obvious consternation within the government in the weeks that followed when France collapsed, something any astute observer should have easily foreseen.

And yet, on the other side of the coin, he admired their masterful handling of defeat, the evacuation of an entire army literally under the shadow of the Luftwaffe, something that was still a mystery to him as to why the Germans had not closed the trap. But much of that was old news, other observers, the entire world had been watching for months. His interest, of course, was supposed to be naval, but his actual travel was severely restricted due to England's wartime security. Still, he had a perspective now that only a few score of his countrymen could lay claim to, he had witnessed the summer of German air assaults to destroy the RAF and thus open the way for a seaborne invasion.

Here was a case study to note in detail, and he started to shift through his papers, carefully stored in individually sealed folders related to various subjects ranging from effectiveness of German weaponry; to the delayed-action bombs, which were interesting, at times creating far more disruption than the explosion itself would have achieved, but of course not viable in any way whatsoever against a naval target; on down to his personal observations regarding the Spitfire versus the German 109s and 110s.

He caught movement from the corner of his eye and looked up. An American, Spaatz, was in the main lounge, which would soon be converted over to where dinner would be served, a steward handing the American a drink, two drinks actually.

The American looked his way and then started forward. As he cleared the spiral staircase to the upper deck the American slowed, motioned with the second drink in his hand.

This could be interesting Genda thought, and he nodded agreement, pushing back the nearly empty glass on the sidearm of his chair. He quickly closed up the folder he was about to work on, put it back in the attaché case and snapped it shut.

Spaatz had sharp, rugged features, a bit of an oversized nose, whether from drink or a good fistfight, it was hard to tell. But it was obvious he was "hard," though most likely around fifty, he moved with the ease and tone of someone in top shape, even as the Clipper bounced and sideslipped slightly as it momentarily went into a bank of clouds.

He kept the two drinks balanced and smiled.

"Speak English?" he asked.

Genda smiled and nodded. "But of course."

"Don't worry about the turbulence, always get a bit of a bump when you fly through a cloud."

"I know," Genda replied, "I'm a pilot as well."

The American smiled and Genda could see the appraising look. He was dressed today in what the Brits called "mufti," dark double-breasted suit with vest and tie, while Spaatz was in uniform.

Genda stood up and bowed slightly. "Lieutenant Commander Genda Minoru, until this week naval attaché to the Japanese Embassy in London."

"Carl Spaatz, Colonel United States Army Air Corps."

There was a momentary pause, and then Spaatz extended the drink, and to Genda's relief it was not the slightly fruity-tasting

Clipper Special. It was honest to goodness scotch, neat.

"Excellent choice in drinks, Colonel," Genda said, motioning for this colonel to sit down across from him.

"So, you said you fly," Spaatz asked, first raising his own scotch in a friendly salute that Genda replied to. "What?"

Genda laughed. "Everything the Japanese Navy has put in the air since the early twenties."

"I've heard about this new plane you have coming out, the Zero, you get your hands on one?"

"I've been hearing about your new P-38. Is it a match for the German twin-engine 110s?"

The two paused for a second, then both laughed.

"Touché," Spaatz said softly.

"Actually the Zero is superb, I think a match for the Spitfire in a dogfight, at high altitude, though, it might be more even."

Spaatz nodded. "If a German ever comes up against a 38 in those 110 crates, it's their funeral. That plane of theirs is a mule."

"A mule?"

"Neither horse nor donkey, a mule. Designed as a long-range fighter escort for their bombers, it can't get into a tight fight;

in fact it needs its own escorts if it is to survive. Use it as a bomber it has no load-carrying capacity. The worst of both. They should trash them all or simply use them for low-level ground support or perhaps as night fighters."

"I agree. The same for their Stukas. I heard they were torn apart and withdrawn from the main battle by early August," Genda replied.

"Looking for information on that?" Spaatz responded.

"But of course."

The American chuckled. "It'll be public knowledge soon enough. The Brits claimed that unescorted the Stukas were like fish in a barrel, dropped dozens of them. The Germans certainly screwed that, sending them in without heavy escort."

"What were they hitting?" Genda asked.

Spaatz smiled.

"I'll have to leave that for you to find out."

"Touché," Genda replied with a smile and Spaatz smiled.

"When did you start flying?' Genda asked, figuring it was best to shift targets and put his companion back at ease. Besides, he already knew, the Stukas were slaughtered trying to take out the new British radio-guided directional towers, what the Americans were calling radar. The entire British coast was ringed with the towers, which looked like radio towers, but strung with a tangle of wires. He wondered how far along his own government was in developing them, such a tool, to be able to detect enemy planes from a hundred miles out, would yet again change the entire nature of carrier-based warfare, all but eliminating the element of surprise, something to be sought by the attacker and dreaded by the defender. Suddenly the balance might shift toward the defender if this new radar worked. Something more to think about on the way home.

Spaatz grinned and sipped his drink.

"Actually flew support for Pershing back in our little romp through Mexico in 1916. Saw some action on the western front, 1918. Things sure have changed since then."

He paused. "I mean, look at this plane. It's just thirteen years since Lindy crossed the Atlantic, and the whole world was mesmerized by the feat. Now we cross in luxury, complete to flushing toilets, and a chef on board. Who'd have thought it.

"Give it another three or four years and planes will be flying the Atlantic nonstop, maybe even the distance from San Francisco or at least Hawaii straight on to Tokyo."

Even as he finished speaking there was a slight stiffening between the two, and Genda wondered if the implications both thought of were the same. This size plane, perhaps bigger, perhaps six engines, stripped down as a bomber, carrying five, maybe ten tons of bombs across an entire ocean, five hundred of them could level San Francisco or yes, Tokyo, in a single night. He knew that Yamamoto had been worrying about the implications of Japanese paper and wood houses if such a bomber could hit their cities with incendiary weapons. It would be a disaster. But it was the type of weapon he knew his own country, for now, could never afford, only the profligate Americans had such surplus of wealth, of aluminum, and above all else aviation gas. A fleet of five hundred such bombers, flying such an attack, would consume more fuel in a single night that every plane in the Japanese navy would use in half a year.

"Did you see much of the air battles?" Genda asked.

Spaatz looked out the window, gently swirling the drink in his hand.

"A bit," he said noncommittally.

Genda did not need to ask. Reports had come into the Japanese Embassy throughout the summer of teams of Americans coming

266

over to evaluate the fighting and set up conduits for supplies. Already replacement aircraft, parts, ammunition, tanks, and artillery were flooding across the Atlantic, making good the losses of the spring in Belgium, Holland, and France.

"And your thoughts?" Spaatz asked.

Genda hesitated. After all, he had downed three drinks in the last couple of hours and the nonpressurized cabin, flying at eight thousand feet, lowered oxygen just enough to affect inhibitions as well. He wondered just how strong his drink was relative to that of this sharp-eyed colonel. He wondered, as well, what he'd be like to face out there among the clouds.

But what the hell, as the Americans say. It was no state secret and perhaps a bit of truthfulness might reveal something in return.

"The Germans have lost, at least for the moment they have lost."

"I agree," Spaatz replied sharply, "but I'm curious as to your observations, you being in the navy."

"Two weeks ago I would have said the Germans had won. After much negotiation I was allowed out of London, under escort, to go to the Kentish coast to observe. The British were rightly engaging the Germans over their own territory, not venturing out into the Channel to seek engagement."

"Why do you see that as good. It could be called a lack of forward defense. Their airfields near the coast have all been nearly pounded out of existence.

"Every British pilot shot down still had a chance of bringing a crippled plane in, or to bail out to fight another day."

"I understand you Japanese do not like to bail out," Spaatz said softly, looking at his drink."

"To fall into the hands of the Chinese? Some of our pilots have been found crucified."

"And the Nationalist pilots that fall into your hands?"

"The navy has captured very few, and they have been treated with respect while in our control," Genda replied defensively, "I cannot speak for the army."

"I guess you've heard of Chennault."

"Of course," Genda said coldly. He was the loudmouthed, arrogant American advisor to the Nationalists. Of course he was strictly "a volunteer," no official connection to their military or president, and yet through private venture firms, a lot of American supplies were now flowing over a road through Burma and rumors were, more and yet more American "volunteer" pilots were showing up to fight, having supposedly resigned their commissions with their own service to do so.

"Chennault supposedly tells his people to save the last bullet in their side arm for themselves if they get shot down."

"Exactly what our pilots are told," Genda replied, his voice pitched even.

Spaatz nodded.

"Perhaps we should turn back to here and now," and leaning over from his chair he caught the eye of the steward in the main lounge and held his glass up and then two fingers.

Genda wanted to refuse, but the scotch did taste good and he would nurse the next one. The neatly attired steward promptly arrived with two more drinks and took away the empties.

"So the British apparently are conceding the Channel just for the moment," Spaatz said.

"And on the invasion day, if it should come, I would pity the German glider troops and paratroopers, an essential first wave for securing the coastal airfields and perhaps even the harbor at Dover. The Germans had never developed the airlift capacity for a large-scale invasion, whereas a hundred planes such as this giant we are now in, properly covered by fighters, could place an entire division across the channel in thirty minutes."

"An interesting concept," Spaatz replied, and neither spoke of the giant gliders that both knew about, the huge Me-321s under construction in Germany and capable of bringing in upward of 150 men — but also a death trap if a single fighter got on to it or the twin-tow planes needed to haul the giant.

"The Germans have not actually seized control of the air. Achieve that on the first day of battle, and the conclusion is ultimately foregone.

"You and I are both airmen," Genda continued. "Perhaps the new doctrine is to totally seize control of the air on the first day, and victory is inevitable. The Germans pretty well did achieve that over France and definitely over Poland; they have failed in England."

"But you saw the raid on September 7," Spaatz said, and there was an edge of excitement to his voice. "My God, I have never seen so many planes in the air at the same time in my entire life."

"And they were bombing the wrong targets," Genda said quietly.

Spaatz looked at him.

Genda shook his head, perhaps he was indeed saying too much.

"What target would you have chosen instead?" Spaatz pressed.

Genda smiled and held up his drink in a salute.

"Perhaps it is only fair that I ask that question of you."

Spaatz chuckled. "I think we are on the same wavelength. I'd have put that power out there the first day. The Germans have proven the genius of the tactical application of airpower directly onto the battlefield. There is no denying that. But this is more a strategic objective. And they have missed the point. It is not about the factories that make planes or engines, or even process the fuel. It is about the young men inside those planes."

Genda nodded. He thought of his own comrades, those who had first sailed aboard *Akagi* and *Kaga,* testing out the new theories of air war at sea. There wasn't a man of them still alive who did not have eight hundred, even a thousand hours of flying time. Reports indicated the British were indeed at the bottom of the barrel, having shaved off dozens of hours of training time to rush air crews into action, some going up with as little as fifteen hours' experience in their planes.

Cecil added, "I'd have kept pounding the airfields, their command centers, naval targets along the coast. Their bombers have been taking such heavy losses though that it seems the German fighters are increasingly tied to protecting the slow, lumbering aircraft bombers, not even designed for the mission of a heavy bombardment of a city. No, I'd have had pure fighter sweeps going in, looking for fights, and if the Brits didn't come up, catch them on the ground. Once superiority there is won, then let the bombers be used judiciously to prepare the way for the attack. They've done it ass backward."

Genda smiled at the "Americanism" of ass backward and chuckled.

His analysis exactly, and this little conversation would go into his report as well. The Americans were perhaps thinking along the same lines. They must see now the deciding factor of airpower. The German air force was not designed for strategic operations, that was something that most likely only the Americans could ever afford to purchase, fleets of heavy four- or even six-engine bombers.

Japan could never afford it, and he felt a

wave of envy. And yet that envy had to be transcended. If a potential opponent had a distinct advantage, which the Americans so obviously did — just by the sheer massive size of their country — then one had to think around that advantage, to a path that would defeat them nevertheless. No, Japan's planes would have to be light, at least for the start if war was to come, and light meant fast, swift, and slashing in hard.

The Germans had missed their chance. Granted they had to play against the tricky weather of the region, the need to build or occupy French fields, move up logistical supports before launching their attacks, but those attacks should have come on day one, with overwhelming force and aimed at but one target, the Royal Air Force and the young men inside the planes. Kill them and the battle is won.

In a carrier strike it should be the same. Take out your opponent's airpower first, then whatever is on the surface of the sea can be destroyed by the bombers and torpedo planes that follow.

That would be his report back to the staff college and his admiral. Airpower would be the key, but it must not be squandered. They could never hope to have the massive air fleets he had witnessed over London, witnessed being so miserably used. No, it would have to be a lightning strike on the first day, designed to first and foremost cripple the enemy airpower, that would mean catching their army air forces on the ground, or just barely getting up; and as for their navy . . . the carriers, break through the fighter screen, then sink their carriers on the first day and their entire fleet would be naked from above, to be picked off at leisure.

He looked over at Spaatz and nodded. He found he actually liked this man, another pilot and pilots, no matter what divided them, could always find one common love to talk about, a favorite plane, a near escape to be chuckled about, and both shared that inner realization, the joy of floating in the heavens at dawn, or in evening twilight, or to dance between mountains of billowing white on sunlight afternoons.

And so they talked awhile longer as the Boeing 314 Clipper raced westward, chasing the retreating sun, leaving the war zone behind, and the tension between the two dropped when they talked of these things rather than calculated all that might yet come or maneuvered to wrangle just a little more information from the other. Yet another drink eased the mood more. He could sense that Spaatz had been ordered up here to "pump him," as the Americans would say, but that part of the conversation was past, unless one or the other, with a bit too much drink, made a mistake, and now they just relaxed and talked flying.

"I've traveled a bit in America," Genda finally asked. "Where are you from?"

"Beautiful little village outside of Philadelphia, Boyertown. A great place for a kid to grow up. Been stationed a lot of places, but still kind of call that home. You should come visit the area some time, glad to take you up, say, in a nice open cockpit. I got a friend there who'd loan us his Stearman. I'm stopping over there for several days to visit family and friends before reporting back to Washington for my next assignment."

"And where might that be?" Genda asked good-naturedly.

Spaatz smiled but did not reply, merely holding his heavy glass up in silent salute.

"I wish I could take you up on the visit," Genda replied, "but my duties require me to press on to Washington to the embassy and then to home."

"And where is home, I mean in Japan?" Spaatz asked.

"I was born in Hiroshima," Genda said, a touch of nostalgia in his voice. "It is a coastal city, peaceful, on a bay, not far from our naval academy. You should visit Hiroshima some day, sir."

"Perhaps I will some day," Spaatz said quietly.

CHAPTER SEVEN

Kailua, Oahu
6 January 1941

Incredulous, James Watson looked at the telegram that Margaret handed to him. She had been waiting for his return from work, standing at the doorstep of their beautiful home set on the east shore of Oahu, in the town of Kailua, just north of Fort Bellows.

It was a home typical of the community, up against the mountainside, garden a cascade of flowers, fantastic view of the ocean, a fairly contemporary design with open lanai where they spent most of their evenings, listening to the radio and reading, the interior an open design, cooled day and night by the trade winds coming in off the ocean. Margaret, at forty, still looked in his eyes to be twenty, having inherited that beautiful mix of a marriage between an Anglo-European and Japanese, dark nearly black hair, the slight Oriental cast to her eyes, nearly five eight and still slender.

She knew his schedule almost to the minute on his daily commute back from the campus on the other side of the mountains in Honolulu, weaving his way down the side of Pali Highway, and he often joked that she must have a telescope hidden away to watch for his approach and to make sure he wasn't dropping off any girlfriends. Damn how he loved this place. Late afternoons, almost like clockwork, clouds would build up along the crest behind the house, a warm tropical rain washing down, usually breaking apart by sunset, shafts of golden light illuminating the jagged peaks.

It was such a moment now, at least as far as the rain as he stepped into the lanai and looked at the letter before opening it. He scanned the contents.

He looked at Margaret and forced a smile. "Guess I'm back in."

Office of the Fourteenth Naval District, Combat Intelligence
Pearl Harbor
7 January 1941

The telegram had been sufficient to get James through the outer gate of the base and nearly within hailing distance of the squat concrete building he had been directed to, where a well-armed marine, .45 at his hip and a Springfield '03 over his shoulder, had stopped him and asked for his identification.

The marine had handed off the telegram to an assistant, a seaman second class, who went into the building. James was told to wait outside and the marine just stepped back, obviously not interested in any small talk.

He had not been on the base since his retirement and thus this afforded the first closeup look in over three years.

Nearly any vantage point from the central part of the island gave a magnificent view of the harbor. Since the fleet had been moved out here, the previous year, forward positioned from San Diego, the harbor was packed with ships, especially on weekends, and Honolulu had been overrun with eager young sailors. The vast majority of them were fairly clean-cut types. The army boys from up at Schofield Barracks had always been a bit more hardscrabble, most of them on long-term enlistments, and had always carried a tougher edge than these fresh-faced sailors, many of them kids barely out of high school. Though the Depression was all but over, thanks to the war in Europe, jobs had still been scarce up until a year ago and many a boy had been lured into the navy with the promise of seeing the world. And for someone from Des Moines or Jersey City, Honolulu was indeed seeing the world, a true paradise.

The once sleepy town of Honolulu of but a couple of years back, which might perk up a little bit when a couple of ships came in from the States loaded with vacation seekers, had taken to "their sailors," with generally a positive attitude, though many was the father of a teenage girl who made sure his daughter stayed close to home on a Saturday night.

The boys had money in their pockets to burn and fresh in from the West Coast the obligatory photos with hula girls, sentimental silk pillows for moms and girlfriends, and ridiculous-printed shirts had sold like crazy.

There was a bit of a seedier side now to certain quarters, booze joints that didn't look too closely at IDs; so-called private clubs that were fronts for gambling, liquor, and girls; and no weekend complete without a couple of fights between the tougher sailors and brawlers of the army's Lightning Division, usually the only disruptions to this paradise. In general most of the boys on weekend leaves, which were distributed liberally, went for the beach, looked for girls, and tried to master the unique Hawaiian sport of riding a wooden board on the surf off Waikiki, or just lounged in the sun before returning shipboard for Sunday evening roll call.

For the officers there were several golf clubs to choose from; private parties at beach-front homes; a regular social whirl of dances, receptions, and parties; for the bachelors a paradise as well, especially with the local girls attending the university. And on Monday the ships would weigh anchor and head out for training maneuvers, usually to return by Friday afternoon for another weekend of pleasure.

Given his job of long ago during the last war, in a sense he was appalled by it all. Anyone, sitting on a nearby slope, could on a daily basis count which ships were in, and which were out, at times battleship row as it was called was packed with all the heavy battlewagons of the main Pacific Fleet. Walk into any bar in a few hours, have your eyes and ears open, and you knew exactly which ships were in, where they had been, what they had been doing, and where they were heading come Monday.

Enterprise, deck loaded with planes, was

out in midharbor, guided by tugs, heading back out to sea. A few sailors nearby were watching the show, chuckling.

"Old Bull got a hair up his butt again," one of them said, "those poor bastards, another weekend out there steaming in circles just to make his point. Launch and recover, launch and recover, you'd think there was a war on." The other laughed and they walked on.

Across the bay, at Ford Island, a PBY was coming in, low and slow, descending from the north, dropping down, flaring, water spraying up, recovery crew waiting by the ramp to guide it up onto land, another minute and a second came into the pattern, this one from the west, morning patrols returning, work done for the day, pilots and crews eager to fill out their reports and get into town.

"Mr. Watson?"

He looked up. The marine who had gone inside was approaching.

"Sir, sorry to keep you waiting out here, but the admiral will see you now."

James followed, the doors into the main administrative building opened by the marine, and to his surprise the corridor was cool, the luxury of air-conditioning.

There was another security check at the

doorway, this one a formality, the marine escorting him leading the way, straight to the end of the corridor, an end office, name stenciled on the door CIC 14 NAVAL DIS-TRICT, ADM. BLOCH.

James took a deep breath, nodding his thanks as the marine opened the door and stepped back. A petty officer at the outer desk stood up and motioned to the inner office where Bloch waited, on his feet, smiling. He motioned for James to close the door.

"Sir, good to see you," James said, wholeheartedly. He had served under Bloch before and had the utmost admiration for the man. He looked every bit the admiral, in his mid- to late-fifties, features still trim, eyes deep set, shoulders square, and James wondered just how he looked in return. The last couple of years as a professor was not necessarily conducive to good fitness. A month's warning about this interview, and he'd have gone to work on trying to drop those extra few pounds, so the double-breasted suit he wore this morning was deliberately chosen with broad shoulders and a bit of cover for a slight paunch that had been developing.

"How's Margaret?" Bloch asked, coming around from behind his desk to shake

James's hand.

"Lovely as ever. I'm blessed."

He could see Bloch pause for a second, wanting to ask but deciding not to, no there were no other children now. There had been no others, and the void was still a daily ache. Bloch most likely knew, word like that traveled through the old network, but sensed it was better not to ask and James tried to smile.

"Margaret and I are okay," he finally said.

Bloch offered him a seat and James sat down, resting his left arm with the rubber artificial hand on his lap.

Bloch nodded.

"I heard about your getting wounded on the *Panay*. Damn bastards! I'm sorry it cut your career short."

"Thank you, sir. But after our boy died, I should have retired anyhow. It was tough on Margaret. Maybe it was for the best."

"That's the spirit, James. Now I'll cut straight to the point," Bloch said. "You know we are mobilizing backup. Orders for new ships pouring in, manpower just exploding, and I need every fit young officer I can find out there, training the new men, getting ships ready for sea duty, and all the time trying to keep what is out there afloat and battle ready.

"CinCPac, Admiral Kimmel is up my backside nearly every day on manpower, expansion of facilities here, you name it, it somehow falls on my desk."

"So you want me back, sir?" James asked.

He wasn't sure just how to react. Yesterday morning he had left campus having finished his syllabi for the next semester. Wrestling as well with whether he should take the dean's offer of a promotion to department chair, an extra four hundred a year, which they could use, but a job with endless headaches and petty squabbles, especially since he only held a masters in higher mathematics and probability theory and the younger PhDs in the department would surely kick up a squawk about his "qualifications."

"Definitely want you back," Bloch said enthusiastically, and he made it a point of picking up a file folder and opening it.

"Annapolis, 1914, eighth in your class, MIT, 1921, your advanced degree in probability theory and statistics," he put the folder down for a moment, "definitely not a career builder but interesting I dare say."

"Just one of those things," James said with a smile, "and the navy was willing to spring for it. They saw some uses for it."

"Several sea tours, the *Oklahoma, Lexing-*

ton as their signals officer . . ." he paused, "and that interesting assignment in London in 1918. Something called Room Forty."

He looked over the folder at James.

"Interesting experience?"

James smiled and said nothing. Though the story of Room Forty was no longer classified, still he was always reticent to talk about it.

He put the folder back down.

"How are you physically."

"Fit as a fiddle."

"Well, James, I'll be blunt. I didn't call you in here to reactivate you for sea duty."

Again, a mix of feelings. He let it register for several seconds. No, sea duty was out, besides, even as he drove over here, he dreaded the thought of telling Margaret he was going back to sea. He knew though that the prospects of that were absurd. It had been a long time ago since one-handed sailors had put to sea.

"I didn't expect that, sir."

"Fine then. I wanted to make that clear at the start. You'll be behind a desk, and from what little I understand of the job, a lot of hours behind a desk most likely bored silly or driving yourself half mad."

Bloch smiled.

"Still interested?"

"Well, sir, you aren't giving me much of a lead."

Bloch leaned back in his chair.

"Funny position I'm in, Watson. You see, your name's come up several times for this, shall we say, thing. The problems are two-fold. First of all, there isn't a medical board out there that would pass you based on current standards, but I can pull that string easy enough. Second, until you say yes, I can't say a word; and then when you do say yes, you'll have to go through some clearances and even then they might wind up saying no, and that can take weeks."

Watson leaned back in his chair now and stared out the window, which gave a panoramic view of the fleet. More Liberty Boats were plying the narrow channel to the mainland, sunlight reflecting off the water, a sparkling glorious "winter" day for Hawaii. And the war, the threat of war seemed a million miles and a million years away.

"It's going to come to us," James finally said, breaking the silence. "Anyone with their eyes open can see that; before the year is out we'll be in it up to our necks."

Bloch nodded in agreement.

"I'm not offering glory, James. It's a job, a very important job, but from what I'll call the team you'll be working with, and believe me they've looked at hundreds of files, you fit the job."

"What about my professorship, the semester starts next week. Mobilizing up or not, it'll put the university in a tight spot finding a replacement."

"I can give the dean a call, he's an old golf buddy."

"Good enough."

James did a quick mental calculation. Tenured, offer of department chair, it was going to be a tough hit financially.

"I can make the patriotic appeal," Bloch said, "don't worry, I already know what you are making now and it isn't all that much for a man with your knowledge. Back in the forty-eight you'd be making double, triple in some industries right now, but I know that's not where your heart is."

James looked back out at the fleet and took a deep swallow. "Let's get started," he said softly, taking his glasses off and pulling out a handkerchief to wipe them clean, doing so adroitly with his one good hand.

It was turning into a very long day and he was exhausted. The life of a prof had indeed softened him, perhaps too much for what was going to be expected. Once he said yes, the interview with Bloch was over, his chief petty officer came in, led James out, marched him over to the infirmary, and without fanfare, twenty minutes later, he was standing stark naked, being poked and prodded, the admiral's chief standing to one side, staring at the ceiling during some of the more humiliating moments of this "interview."

"The admiral really wants him passed?" the doctor asked.

The chief simply nodded.

Sighing, the physician scratched a signature on a form and handed it back to the chief.

"Get dressed, drop this with the nurse at the front desk on the way out. You are passed for limited duty and, frankly, God save this country."

From there it was over to administration to get started on the mountains of paperwork, though the petty officer, with thirty years of hash marks on his sleeve, finally just scooped them up and said someone in the Admiral's Office would take care of them later.

Back to the Admiral's Office, and it was now one in the afternoon and he was starving. Standing in the Admiral's outer office, the petty officer wished him luck, dropped the mountain of paperwork on a desk, and walked out, and James stood there for a moment, thoroughly confused. Hell, one doesn't just go up to an admiral's closed door and knock on it uninvited and ask what he should do next. Was the day over? Was he to go home and wait?

"Mr. Watson, I presume?"

He turned sharply, half expecting the absolutely wearisome jokes about Sherlock Holmes to now start. The sight that greeted him was a bit startling. The officer, a captain, extending a greeting hand was several inches shorter than James, eyes enlarged by thick glasses, dark mustache with flecks of gray not at all neatly trimmed. His uniform was rumpled, as if he had been sleeping in it for days, a very visible coffee stain on his pants, he was every bit the antithesis of what a naval officer should look like.

"I'm Captain Collingwood, Tom Collingwood. Figured you might be hungry," and he held up a battered lunch box and two opened bottles of Coke.

A bit taken aback, James simply nodded and followed Collingwood out of the building, his guide walking past security as if they didn't exist and, in turn, they didn't even take notice of him.

"Nice little spot down by the waterfront," Collingwood said, pointing the way. They weaved their way across the base, Collingwood barely acknowledging the salutes of enlisted personnel, a couple of lieutenants passing, faces deeply tanned, snapping off salutes and then one loudly saying after they passed so that he and Collingwood could definitely hear the comment, "I'd love to see his ass at sea; do that slob some good."

Collingwood ignored them. They reached the waterfront, a small parklike area shaded by a few trees and a couple of benches to sit on. The two settled down.

"A couple of ham sandwiches, hope that's ok, wife always packs the same."

James nodded his thanks, opened the wax paper and looked a bit suspiciously at the offering, it looked to be a day or two old and suddenly he had a real longing for the faculty dining room on campus, always a good selection of Western and Asian food to chose from, darn good conversations to be found, and here he now sat with a disheveled captain who, with the added realization, due to the direction of the wind, was in serious need of a good shower.

He ate half the sandwich and politely put it down. It definitely was a day or two old, maybe longer. Collingwood ate his without comment, looking out across the narrow loch to the battleships anchored along the east shore of Ford Island.

Finishing his sandwich, he finally stirred. "Tell me about your work in London during the last war," Tom asked, smiling in a friendly manner.

"I'm not really sure if I can discuss that . . ."

Tom waved his hand dismissively.

"Let's spare ourselves the walk back to the Admiral's Office to review what I should know. I'm more than cleared for anything you might have inside you." He smiled openly. "And no, this is not some sort of trick test to see if you are a blabbermouth or not. Scout's honor."

Disarmed by the boyish gesture of Collingwood raising his hand in the Boy Scout pledge, he nodded.

"I was part of a joint team in London. Sort of an experiment actually. We and the Brits never really did work well on those sorts of things in the last war but a few wiser heads made a stab at it. Seems that our undersecretary of the navy," he paused, "now our president, suggested it to someone in the Admiralty."

"Churchill?"

"No. From what I understood those two didn't see eye to eye at the same time then. Churchill was gone from the Admiralty before we came into the war. But anyhow, rather than being out to sea, I was stuck in a basement for the duration."

"You missed being at sea?"

James was silent for a moment. To give the truth would almost be like a priest saying he did not believe in the Trinity.

"Honestly, most of my time at sea I was sick as hell. The thought of patrolling the North Atlantic in winter?"

Watson chuckled softly.

"Same here, and remember, the great Alfred Thayer Mahan, praised forever be his name," and he made a half-joking gesture of praying at the mention of the famed naval strategist, "would damn near die sitting in a rowboat on a mill pond. He threatened to retire rather than accept sea duty."

"And your job in that basement?"

James hesitated but then relented. Hell, the information was over twenty years old and when retired from the navy, there had been no cautioning even then about talking. It was just he felt naturally reticent about it.

"Trying to crack the German U-boat codes in 1918."

"Any luck?"

"I suspect you know as well as I do."

"Go on."

"I was assigned as an American liaison to what was called 'Room Forty.' The Brits

293

had gotten lucky right from the start. The German navy relied on code books. They got a copy from a spy out of Brussels early on in the war. Later, divers actually made it to a sunken U-boat and recovered the code book. Finally, of all things, the Brits captured a another code book in Persia, and just what the hell a naval code book was doing with a German consulate officer in Persia is beyond me.

"But then, in 1918, the sources dried up. They actually built an encrypting machine, primitive, but effective for those days. So that's how I got into it all."

"And how is that?" Collingwood asked, eyes fixed on him owl-like.

"Statistical analysis was my field, running calculations, trying to find statistical linkages between messages that might lead to the coding source. If you know the language, know the syntax, structure, even the metaphors and have a good analysis of probabilities of word usage you at least have a start.

"Some thought they might have gone back to old-style code, very simple actually. Take a copy of *Wuthering Heights,* for example, same editions in the boat and back at headquarters. Numbered to a page, then numbered to a line and word. You can even jumble it any number of times. Number one actually means number 99 on Tuesday and number 65 on Wednesday, and so on. Simple, but clumsy to use, slow to transfer, prone to mistake, and it's breakable."

"How so?" Collingwood asked quietly.

"Statistical analysis of course, guess that's where I came in. Have a knowledge of the language, percentage of word usages, get a handle on some of the code words, for example whale means battleship, dolphin means cruiser, et cetera. A previous message says whale, we've figured that out and we figure out the latitude and longitude, those usually stand out, and sure enough one of our battleships is there. So whale equals battleship and we have a word broken. Cipher that out from one message and you got a few holes filled in on another. Ideally, you can go on and crack the book they are using. Absurd example but say someone on our team has pretty well memorized *Moby Dick,* or Goethe's *Faust* and someone on the other side's code room gets lazy and uses four words in a row. One of our whizzes remembers the quote, cracks that, and we have the book. But that's the stuff of bad spy novels. No one is stupid enough these days to use book codes anymore or for that matter even specially designed code books, too prone to espionage. Fair to assume everyone is using some sort of encoding machine now, though for lower priorities code books still might be done temporarily.

"Oh, Room Forty was an amusing place, Oxford literature dons mixed in with biblical experts, and statistician types like me. It was all very interesting, but it wasn't book codes. We finally figured out that it actually was an encrypting machine. Got our hands on it after the Armistice. Primitive but believe me, we were impressed. It drove us near to distraction in the final months of the war."

"You have a thing for languages don't you, James." He smiled and nodded.

"I was hated at Annapolis you know. I don't know why, but hear a language once and it sticks. Give me a few months and I can read it. Maybe not speak it like a native but can read it. Whizzed through German and French and could nearly sleep in the class. Was first in my class in both languages and boy did the other guys resent that, especially because I never had to study. I just read it and it stuck. Maybe it hurt me in the long run, had a reputation for being something of a grind as they used to call my types."

"Eighth in your class."

"Men five years behind me are now captains and angling for commodore and rear admirals now with this expansion."

Collingwood nodded sympathetically. "We serve as we are able to serve."

James said nothing, stomach growling with hunger. He looked at the half-eaten sandwich but decided against it. "I understand your Japanese is rather good. You even speak it with some of your students at the university."

"How do you know that?" James asked, a bit defensively.

Collingwood smiled. "Don't ask."

"Well, it's in the family, my wife and mother-in-law speak it all the time, and even when we were dating I was curious if they were talking about me or not," and he waited a moment. "My wife is half-Japanese, is that a problem?"

"No, James, no problem at all. That's been checked."

Though Hawaii was a place where races did so freely mix, the prejudice was still there. In some ways it could be said it was not helped by the local population who had immigrated directly from Japan in recent years. The local language newspaper actually referred to the campaigns in China as "another victory," and to the Japanese army as "our army." Some families had actually sent their sons back to the homeland to serve. Rumors were rampant about alleged tourists down by the harbor every day, taking photographs, with families conveniently posed to one side of course, if questioned.

"Margaret's mother came over back in 'ninety-six as a girl. She has absolutely no contact with any relatives back there, for that matter she doesn't even know if she has relatives there."

"It's okay James, relax," Collingwood said. "Just the question was raised and had to be answered."

"What question? Why? Frankly, I think it's time I got to ask a few questions."

"Shoot."

"What the hell are we talking about? Am I being recruited for cryptanalysis?"

"I can't say yet."

"Well, I'd like to know."

"Hypothetically, let's say you were. Would you take it?"

"I don't know. It was migraine work. Bust your ass for weeks staring at hundreds of pages of numbers, trying to trace patterns, you start to crack it, and then the bastards on the other side change the game around and everything is for naught. Sleepless nights 'cause you can't get it out of your head. It makes you crazy."

Collingwood smiled and looked down at the coffee stains on his lap in a bit of a self-deprecating manner.

Jame added, "And, my God, to do it in Japanese? A pictograph language converted to Western alphabet just within the last hundred years? Unique letterings that we don't have, idioms and complex syntaxes unknown to any Western language, definitions of words absolutely blurred, at times nearly impossible to translate effectively. It makes cracking German look like a breeze, which it is in comparison. Plus, I'm willing to bet they've created hundreds of obscure metaphors for everything related to naval affairs. The Japanese love poetic metaphors that we would never dream of using. You're talking a code-breaker's nightmare."

Collingwood just looked at him, hands clasped between his legs, head half lowered, looking at James over the rim of his glasses.

His gaze lifted from James to the battleships, more Liberty Boats coming in, excited young sailors whooping and hollering.

"Some think that's our first line of defense out here," Collingwood said softly, nodding to the tethered ships, anchored to their moorings.

He looked back at James.

"But it's not."

"That's what this job is, isn't it," James asked.

Collingwood simply smiled.

■ ■ ■ ■

PART TWO: THE COUNTDOWN

■ ■ ■ ■

CHAPTER EIGHT

Battleship Nagato, *Flagship of Admiral Yama-moto*
Kure Harbor, Japan
3 February 1941
Saluting stiffly, Commander Genda stood in the open doorway to Admiral Yamamoto's private quarters. The room was plain in its appointments, a standard table covered with green cloth dominated the center of the room, surrounded by eight chairs, charts laid out upon the table. The portrait of the Emperor hung upon the inner bulkhead wall, a bookshelf beneath it filled with works both in Japanese and English. Yamamoto looked up from the far end of the table, acknowledged the salute, and motioned for Genda to enter and close the door. The admiral was sitting comfortably, wearing a heavy quilted kimono rather than standard uniform, the steam heat turned down so that the room was cool. It was frigid outside,

the wind blowing a mixture of sleet and snow straight down from Siberia, and Genda felt he would freeze to death during the open launch boat ride across the harbor to where *Nagato* was anchored. He had neglected to wear an outer coat and gloves, and was now somewhat embarrassed as he removed his cap and slushy water ran off it, splattering the floor.

"Be at ease," Yamamoto said, with a warm voice, and motioned for Genda to come and sit by his side, and without even inquiring poured a steaming cup of tea, sliding it over to where Genda took his seat.

"Thank you, sir," Genda replied, gladly taking the ornate fragile cup in both hands, letting the warmth seep in for a moment before taking a sip.

A rattling of sleet echoed against the porthole windows, bolted down tight, and the admiral stood up and went over to one, wiping the moisture off from the inside with the sleeve of his kimono and gazing out for a moment.

"Straight in from Russia," he said quietly, almost meditatively, Genda nodding, saying nothing, keeping eyes focused on the admiral as he himself sipped down his tea.

The admiral turned and smiled.

"Terrible place to fight a war. Manchukuo

is bad enough, but Russia? Our troops who occupied the trans-Siberian railroad during the revolution there suffered the agonies of hell: more died from lung disease than Communist bullets. It is not a good climate for us."

Genda still said nothing, sensing that the admiral was speaking metaphorically about the current crisis, the debate between "north or south." The army, in spite of its disastrous setback in Mongolia the previous summer, a campaign that had cost them over fifty thousand casualities against the combined Soviet and Mongol forces, still clamored for a northern expansion to take on the might of the Soviet Union for control of eastern Siberia and Mongolia.

The logic of it completely eluded Genda. What was there in Siberia worth the risk to Japan? Lumber, some ores to be certain, and a vast trackless waste of thousands of miles that could devour entire armies to no effect. And even the army was finally forced to admit that Soviet armor and artillery was vastly superior. There were nearly a million men already in China and Manchukuo; a Soviet campaign would eventually require a million more. And for what gain other than the army's self-aggrandizing dreams?

Maybe if the pact between Germany and

Admiral Isoroku Yamamoto, Imperial Japanese Navy portrait photograph, taken during the early 1940s, when he was Commander in Chief, Combined Fleet. Original photograph was in the files of Rear Admiral Samuel Eliot Morison, USNR. **Naval Historical Center**

Russia collapsed, then it might be a temptation to attack, but only if the Soviets lost, but even then the army would be bogged down occupying a frozen nightmare of little immediate value. It was oil, rubber, tungsten, food surplus, rare metals, high-grade coal, and yet again oil, these were the things the nation needed and it was not in Siberia but elsewhere that such could be found. And besides, what role for a navy there, other than perhaps in an opening stage against Vladivostok?

Yamamoto shook his head and returned to his seat, graciously offering to refill Genda's cup, an offer which he gladly accepted.

"I've studied some of your reports, Commander," Yamamoto said, and he motioned to bound copies marked top secret and even though inverted he could see their titles, his report on the idea of concentrating all of Japan's carriers into a single strike force, rather than dispersing them across several groups, which was still the current thinking, his analysis of what was now called the Battle of Britain, and even his observations about his trip across America on his way back from England.

"I am honored and humbled, sir, that you would spend your time thus."

"You know, of course, I spent years in America, studying at Harvard," Yamamoto said, switching to English as he spoke, and Genda's own knowledge of the language was sufficient enough that he could actually pick up the broad vowels of a Boston accent.

He could not help but smile.

"A fascinating country. Vast, wealthy, a force we should never underestimate," Genda replied in English as well.

"What fascinated you?" Yamamoto asked, now falling back into Japanese, having obviously tested Genda's ability with the language.

"The size of course. The train journey took nearly a week from Washington to San Francisco. We can traverse Japan in but a matter of hours. Their openness, I could photograph anything I chose to do so. Their lack of any sense of danger. I suspected several times that one of their agents from their Federal Bureau was following me but half felt it was more to just simply keep an eye on me rather than to actually spy. I could not resist the joke of buying him a drink aboard the train from Chicago to San Francisco, and chatted amiably for several hours, though he never dropped his guise that he was simply a college professor specializing in the Far East. His Japanese was actually fairly good, he claimed he was the son of missionary parents in Korea. But we both knew the truth and maintained the game."

"Maybe he really was just a professor after all," Yamamoto chuckled. "The Americans have such a sense of invulnerability that their naiveté in issues of security, which we take for granted, is amazing at times."

Genda nodded, wondering if that was indeed true. A couple of times aboard the train he had endured racial comments that were insulting, spoken behind his back by passengers who did not know he knew English, and he noticed that the "professor" just shrugged when hearing them and shook his head, as if signaling him not to even bother. In Japan, such an insult to a traveling dignitary would have been jumped on by the police to avoid any incident or embarrassments. If allowed to pass, it was a signal of official policy, and he knew the Americans would not do that. This insight from the admiral was fascinating. Were the Americans really so unskilled and foolish? Surely they would have placed agents on him, hope to get him drunk, perhaps entrap him with a woman, to blackmail him and thus gain secrets. Did they really feel so comfortable and arrogant to let a known agent bearing secret documents traverse their entire country without the slightest concern? The thought was fascinating.

"I want to put two things together here," Yamamoto said, "and then lead you to a third. You and I are talking informally now, how shall I say . . . 'off the record.' "

He spoke the last three words in English.

"You'll have a formal meeting tomorrow through the proper chain of command, but I wanted to sit and talk with you first before having those orders delivered."

Genda waited, suddenly filled with anticipation. Something was developing, and the admiral was coming straight to the point.

"Your report on what you observed during your two years in Britain is priceless information. You are, perhaps, the only trained observer from our country to directly witness the event. As for the diplomats," he chuckled derisively and from the pile of documents on his desk pushed one aside, most likely a report from the embassy in London.

"I've read your report, but I want you to state clearly the most important lessons you felt you learned from observing the fighting."

Genda smiled and bowed slightly at the compliment and for the opportunity. He had feared that what he wrote would simply be filed away and forgotten, like so many hundreds of other reports from trained observers, who because of their lower rank, politics, or interservice rivalries were just simply filed and forgotten.

He paused for a moment, organizing his thoughts. He did not want to ramble into a long discourse. He knew enough of Yamamoto that this man insisted on brevity and coming straight to the point without all the foolishness of protocol. He disdained most of the rituals of rank. A trait that was endemic in the service was a near terror of delivering bad news, or news that might be feared as being not what the listener wanted, instead couching the information in oblique terms or vague metaphors. Yamamoto hated that, he wanted the truth given sharply and directly . . . a very American way of thinking.

Genda cleared his throat.

"Perhaps I should go from the tactical to the strategic," Genda opened, and Yamamoto nodded.

"The Spitfire is a superior plane at nearly all altitudes and aptly designed for its mission, short-range defense and the gaining of aerial supremacy against similar and numerically superior enemy fighters. Against a formation of bombers its light-caliber weapons do not rapidly inflict killing damage, while in turn it is hit by the bomber's defensive fire. Other than that weakness, it is a formidable opponent. The disadvantage the British had was their lack of a number of trained pilots, in desperation they were throwing boys up with but twenty hours in their planes. A wasteful school of training in terms of loss of both planes and pilots; but within days, the survivors were as hard-edged as the Germans. But it is a profligate approach. Better to have spent the time and money beforehand to train; I'd say half their combat losses were due to this factor alone.

"In contrast the German 109 is a superb fighter as well and does carry heavier armaments, if a pilot could turn inside his target and get off a good deflection shot, it usually was a kill, especially against the slightly slower Hurricanes."

"Your conclusion."

"Speed and heavier weaponry are crucial for our fighters."

"And defense?" Yamamoto asked. "Some complain that our new Zeroes are superb as long as it is we who are doing the hitting, but collapse or burn if but a few hits are taken." Genda nodded in agreement. The Zero had come on-line during his tour in England. He had finally gotten his hands on one only a month back. It was stunning when compared to the old Model 96, over 50 percent faster, but that speed came at the sacrifice of any type of defensive armor. Ironically in simulated combat, the slower

96 could actually evade the Zero then turn inside it and more than a few of the naval pilots, though proud of this ultimate achievement of Japanese aviation design, expressed concern about the Zeroes' ability to stand up to a head-on attack or being jumped in a hit-and-dive attack. Training now was emphasizing luring the enemy into a turning fight, the old traditional "dogfight" as the Westerners called it, where it was believed it could outfly anything the West had, even the Spitfire.

"We could sacrifice speed for more crucial armament, but that I fear would be a false path," Genda continued. "Speed is everything, both for choosing when to attack and, if need be, when to run. I think a neglected lesson of the fight between the English and the Germans is the engines. Their Rolls-Merlin engine is beautiful in design, elegant, inline rather than radial so there is a significantly smaller profile when approached both head-on and from astern and less torque as well. From what I was able to learn, it is a tremendous power plant. If we could match the design or exceed it, that would give us the additional power to improve defensive armor without sacrificing speed. On the other side, both the Spitfire and the German 109s lack range. Our Zeroes have them truly beat in that. Their designs are for short-range tactical support, ours is for longer-range strike, and that is crucial. If we ever met a British carrier with Spitfires we could easily stay well out of their range and strike at our leisure."

"So you maintain that speed and range, for now, are the crucial factors, along with superior pilots in numbers."

Genda nodded.

"The bombers?"

"I did not get any opportunity to observe the British bombers, but all reports are they are abysmal, wedded to their doctrine of strategic bombing rather than tactical support.

"However, the German bombers, especially their Heinkel 111s, which is good tactically, appeared to me to be very vulnerable to air attack and lack the ability to absorb punishment."

He remembered the lone Hurricane downing the Heinkel above the Thames. More defensive firepower astern, twin 12.7s, or even a 20-millimeter gun and armored engine protection on the Heinkel might have saved it.

"I saw some limited use of their new JU-88s, and that plane is a superb model. It can function as a medium-altitude bomber, as a dive bomber, or a low-level strike bomber. It is fast, maneuverable, and though not heavily armed, survives better due to speed and a less bulky profile. If I was to pick one plane from the German air force for our army or navy it would be their 88 . . . it'd be a superb torpedo-attack plane and, without any conversion, on its very next mission dive-bomb carrying an armor-piercing weapon. It is a plane too large though for carriers, but would be superb as a ground-based weapon."

Yamamoto nodded and jotted down a few notes on a pad of paper.

"Your report was damning of the German strategy, explain why?"

"Their faults were twofold, sir," Genda said, now warming to the heart of what he had hoped would be asked.

"And they were?"

"The first attack. I understand the logistical problems the Germans had, of first occupying France, repairing damage to airfields, then establishing lines of supply from Germany for fuel, weaponry, ammunition, spare parts. But still it did give the British a crucial breathing time of well over a month and a half from the end of the fighting in northern France until the first blows were delivered."

"And you would have done what instead?"

"Placed the highest priority on massing every single plane available along the coast, from Dunkirk down to Rouen, even if it meant removing air cover from what was left of their campaign against the French in the south, for that fight was already a foregone conclusion. Mass all of it, as quickly as possible. And then strike with everything, every single plane on the first day. Not just one strike, but as quickly as planes returned, if still flyable, to reload, and put them back up so that it was continual waves unrelenting from dawn 'til dusk."

"A tall order regarding logistics?"

"An advantage our carriers have and land-based planes do not," Genda said, with a smile.

"Elaborate."

"Our ships sail fully loaded for numerous strikes; our deck crews trained for rapid recovery, turn around, and relaunch; all weapons and fuel stored but a few decks away. The Germans should have planned better for this air offensive and had the stockpiles already in waiting, prepared to rush forward the moment resistance in northern France and Belgium collapsed, ready within four weeks of the beginning of their offensive to bring the coastal airfields in France back into operation and then start pounding the British airfields on their home island. Such a strike, with such speed might very well have shattered morale even before Churchill could have, with his defiant words, rallied England to the fight.

"I know it is disrespectful, but their Goering is a strutting poppinjay," and Genda used the English word for there was no real equivalent in Japanese.

"Once he allowed the English to escape Dunkirk, he should have devoted the next month to the buildup of a truly massive strike, the single killing blow. Instead he wasted away the best weather of the summer in trying to lure the British air force into fighting out over the Channel.

"No," Genda said forcefully. "I would have put fifteen hundred planes over the coast of England on the first day, and delivered five thousand sorties by the end of that first day."

"The target?"

"Sir, why their airfields, of course. The Spitfires and, for that matter, the Hurricanes have limited time in the air. If Goering had come on in waves, after but an hour or two the British pilots would have been forced to land, while under attack and then surely be destroyed on the ground, or forced to flee farther inland to refuel and rearm while what was left of their forward airfields was totally destroyed.

"The following day repeat the process, pushing farther inland if need be until finally a zone a hundred miles deep from the coast was swept clean of any ability by the British to launch aircraft. At that moment, the invasion could go forward, the few surviving British pilots and aircraft now forced to fly a hundred miles into the fight where swarms of German fighters would meet them. Once the first lodgments were made on the coast, even the most tenuous of holds by paratroopers, glider troops, and sea-borne attack, forces could start landing German planes on English soil and continue the push farther inland. He could have done that in a campaign of less than two weeks. Instead he wasted away the best weather of summer with probes, and feints, and coastal attacks on shipping, rather than concentrating on one target and one target only . . . the Royal Air Force."

Yamamoto nodded.

"Also, as the British gained proficiency, due to the slow start of the German campaign, the British learned to send their Hurricanes in against the bombers while the

Spitfires fended off the fighters. I could see where the Germans were putting more and more of their fighters into a defensive role, covering only the bombers that were taking heavy losses.

"And you would have done what instead?"

"It never would have happened that way if the Germans had used the strategy I just outlined. Let us say on day one the German bombers took heavy losses pounding the British airfields and this wonderful defensive device of theirs, the ability to use radio waves to track incoming planes. I would have held the bombers back in the morning and early afternoon, simply sending in wave after wave of fighters to exhaust the British fighter command in all-out fighter-to-fighter battles without the need for the bulk of planes designed for offensive strike delegated instead to defend the bombers. Then the final punch of the day with all bombers massed and protected, the British fighter pilots, those left, going into the battle exhausted after having flown three or four sorties earlier in the day."

"I agree fully. I do not understand how a man of Goering's experience did not see that," Yamamoto replied, warming yet again to this young, intelligent, aggressive pilot before him. He had admired his courage when presenting his unorthodox views at the conference at the War College more than three years back and had marked him in his mind for greater things yet to come.

"And your second point? The strategic view?" Yamamoto asked.

"Sir, there is where I am still amazed. In spite of the German failure in their application of force throughout July and August, they did pound into submission most of the airfields in southeastern England, forcing their abandonment. Granted, the British dispersed planes to smaller, concealed airstrips useful for just a squadron or two, but nevertheless superiority was in the German hands and then, just when victory was at hand, their utter foolishness of turning their force on London."

"We all know that now," Yamamoto said. "I would think that the day the Germans started their terror bombing of London, Churchill breathed a sigh of relief."

"Exactly, sir. But the deeper point is that here was the moment where the Germans still might have delivered the knockout blow. They had finally learned not to send their attacks in as smaller uncoordinated waves of but two or three hundred planes. I witnessed their biggest attack, somewhere around fifteen hundred planes in the air at once."

He stopped for a moment, the memory of standing on the bridge, the massive air armada passing overhead, and its targets a waste. Never had he dreamed of such power in the hands of Japan. Over a thousand planes in the air at the same time. By all the gods, if given such power for a month, swarming forth from a dozen carriers, he could conquer the entire Pacific, giving to his beloved Emperor the most stunning victories in the history of warfare.

"If, on that day, they had sent that tremendous stream of bombers against the surviving major airfields, Biggin Hill, Duxford, two, three hundred bombers hitting each, followed a half hour later by low-level raiders strafing and disrupting the salvage effort, and perhaps catching surviving fighters back on the ground," he sighed, "they would have shattered British fighter command that day, and the invasion could have followed the day after. Instead they bombed wharfs and warehouses, invasion or not, a waste of effort and sir, as we both know, there was never the invasion that should have ended that war, which might now very well drag on for years."

He sighed, as if the wasted opportunity

were his own personal loss.

"Victory or defeat in that battle over England, it was entirely about airpower, the first such battle in history, but most definitely not the last. If the Germans had built a dozen battleships, what good would they have been, other than to serve as targets to be hit. If they had five hundred more fighters instead, and the understanding of how to use them, the swastika would be flying over London this day.

"Sir, I think you know of my statement, which has caused me some embarrassment."

Yamamoto smiled.

"I think so, but go on."

"The three most useless follies of humanity: the building of the pyramids; the Great Wall of China; and now, our building of the *Yamato* and *Musashi*."

Yamamoto kept a straight face. More than one of his battleship admirals had howled for Genda's blood when he dared to say that in public. And yet he agreed. If *Yamato* and *Musashi* had been laid down as carriers, construction time and cost would have been cut in half, and at 72,000 tons each, the greatest carriers the world had ever seen, capable of launching two hundred or more planes each, would already be ready for sea.

"The Germans failed in delivering the one single strike that can bring victory and that, sir, is the key to airpower: that first killing strike with massive, overwhelming force."

Yamomoto refilled his cup and Genda's.

"Your report on massed carriers used to deliver an opening strike is of great interest," the admiral said, "a profound change of doctrine."

"Sir, if all six fleet carriers, the ones we currently have and the two new ones about to be commissioned were in a single mission we could put four hundred or more offensive planes in the air, have a reserve, and maintain as well an impenetrable cover over that fleet."

Yamamoto sipped his tea and stood up, leaning over to look at the map of the entire Pacific region, spread out on the table.

"We must strike hard, we must strike first, we must strike in such a way that will so provoke them that they will not wait, they will sortie with whatever survives our first attack and we then annihilate that. Only when the American navy in the Pacific has been sunk will we be able to force the Americans to agree to a negotiated peace. That must be our goal. Japan cannot possibly win a long war of attrition with the Americans. Their production capabilities will simply drown us. We must hit them so hard in the first round that they decide negotiation is the only realistic response. Anything less than that will lead to our ultimate defeat," Yamamoto concluded with quiet but deep conviction.

Genda smiled and nodded. "Pearl Harbor," he whispered.

Yamamoto, who was famed for his "poker face," said nothing as he stepped back from the table.

"You will soon receive official orders to help draw up plans for such an attack. It is just that I wanted to hear your thinking first, and I see now that it matches mine."

"Sir, I do not have access to whatever intelligence has been gathered regarding what the Americans station there."

"You will now be included."

"I've studied what is open information. The army airfields and naval airfield will have to be suppressed. It will mean at least three hundred or more strike aircraft to do so and I would estimate our losses to be heavy."

"That is anticipated and will be provided for."

Genda could not suppress a grin. As a professional challenge this was the pinnacle, years of study, of lecturing, of observing, and now at last, the chance to test his theories. "I do not take this lightly," Yamamoto said. "Both of us know America, both of us know the weaknesses she has shown, but we also know the hidden strengths. If drawn into a protracted war with her, eventually we will lose. It is impossible to match her numbers, her strength, unless somehow we can rally all of the Orient and define it as a war of liberation from Western Imperialism."

Genda sat back saying nothing.

"But the army, its brutish behavior in China, has only served to enlist more enemies rather than friends, and I fear that wherever we go, it will be the same, so this will be a fight we must fight alone to victory or ignoble defeat. The army has only served itself and to instill in all who meet it terror and hatred. Nanking is a blot on the national soul that can never be erased. Never was it such in the days of the traditional samurai. It is a sickness that I fear will haunt us for a century to come. Let us at least hope that the navy shall fight with honor and chivalry as it was in the days of old. We must strike America in such a way that will cripple her ability to wage a war at sea and then annihilate what they have left, the same as we did with the Russians, first at Port Arthur and then when their Baltic and Black Sea Fleet arrived off Tsushima, but in so doing, not create a rage that few understand. The Americans can indeed be roused if they feel themselves morally offended. If we can achieve a complete early victory, then we can negotiate with honorable concessions offered to achieve the security we desire."

Yamamoto looked back to the sleet slashing against the porthole window.

"Achieve that, and then let us assume, just assume that in the years to come Stalin actually does fight against Hitler and defeat him. Perhaps at some future date, after establishing parity with the Americans, we might actually find ourselves side-by-side to face the Communist threat. Stranger things have indeed happened. If it should turn the other way, there would be time enough later to pick up the pieces in Siberia after Stalin's collapse.

"That is our task, to wound, to defeat, but not to so enrage America that regardless of loss, regardless of the folly of attempting to totally destroy us while the Russians smile and wait to fill in the vacuum . . ." and his voice trailed off.

He looked over at Genda.

"I want a comprehensive campaign plan within ten days."

His words carried with them a note of dismissal.

Genda stood up, formally saluted, and taking his hat he stepped out of the room into the blast of sleet and icy rain. The entire ride back in the open launch, he did not feel the cold.

Pearl Harbor
24 June 1941

Lieutenant Commander James Watson wearily sat back in his chair, looking at his wristwatch, 4:00 a.m. He should have gone off duty ten hours ago. Any other woman except Margaret would have been motivation enough for him not to go home now. He had promised a Friday evening in Honolulu, a movie, she liked musicals especially with Astaire, he preferred Westerns and historical pictures. Standing her up thus, he knew it would be musicals for the next month or so as payback. But otherwise she understood, amazingly understood, even to the fact that he could only tell her he was working at CinCPac and nothing beyond that.

The cautionary tales had already been circulated to him on day one how more than one man had been washed out of the intelligence business because his wife finally coaxed the information out of him, often because the poor guy could not explain why he would often disappear for two or three days at a stretch without a mistress hidden away somewhere, and then when told what he was really doing she went and shot her mouth off to neighbors or friends.

The Japanese had changed their naval code yet again.

Everything was in an uproar since the evening of June 21. Half a world away it was the morning of 22 June 1941 and Hitler's legions had crossed into the Soviet Union. Former allies, one of which was a potential foe of the Japanese, were now at war, and three days later early reports were that the Soviets were reeling from the hammer blows of the blitzkrieg.

And the following morning the Japanese navy had changed its code yet again. It was maddening. The hundreds of laborious hours to even partially crack a single message, cross-comparing that to other messages to see if the decoded words matched up and might then yield another few words. The complex cataloging of each message received, often with typos since the listeners on the radio rarely had a good grasp of Japanese and would often make mistakes as they tried to keep up with the streams of telegraph and occasional voice transmissions.

It was like running a marathon race, you see the finish line just ahead, and then the bastards run out and double the distance to be run yet again.

The big question was, would Japan now jump and turn against the Soviets? The code change within hours of the start of war between Germany and the Soviet Union could either be a standard precaution, perhaps prearranged weeks ago, or a stepped-up security move on the eve of launching a strike.

If the Japanese attacked the Soviets, then what, he wondered? Would the president respond with a tougher embargo? The thought of Japan and Germany dividing up the corpse of that colossus was frightening, but what exactly would Japan gain?

In the face of increased German activity, President Roosevelt kept shifting ships out of the Pacific and into the Atlantic. It was clear that Washington thought the threat from Germany was a lot bigger and more urgent than any problems with Tokyo.

Somehow the view from this basement was a lot different from the view from the White House.

Still, it was his job to focus on his immediate world and not worry about the larger challenges President Roosevelt seemed to be worried by. And there was more than enough to focus on.

Everyone in the basement office this morning seemed disgusted, exhausted. He heard mutters of frustration. One possible source, the Japanese Consulate Office right in Honolulu, was off-limits. They actually sent messages via Western Union and repeated, secret appeals had been made to the State Department to ask Western Union for just a "peek" at the messages before they were sent. Both the State Department and Western Union were absolutely appalled by the suggestion, pointing out that it was against the law for any agency to read texts sent under diplomatic seal. For after all, who would trust Western Union with their business if word ever got out of such distasteful going-ons and besides, as repeatedly said, it was against the law.

Half crazed with frustration, Collingwood had even sent an enlisted man to secretly loiter behind the Western Union office, if caught to make sure he smelled of cheap booze, and go through the trash every night for a week, hoping to pull out at least one message sent by the consulate, but those papers were either incinerated or shredded beyond recall. Western Union did not want anyone reading their trash. A congressional investigation had already been threatened against the navy for its secret attempts to intercept private communications via Western Union and the various companies that owned the crucial cable lines, even though such intercepts might very well be essential for national survival. It was beyond absurd. So the Japanese continued to freely use American communications systems to send their secrets, without fear of intercept. It was the same across the board. Intercepts of transmitted messages in the clear were okay, but cable lines could not be tapped. The FBI might have some people keeping a watch on local Japanese living on the island or visiting, but the information was never shared, even though he had actually seen one man posing a woman by the waterside in a park at Pearl City while having a picnic lunch there with Margaret, the photographer going through great pains to position his beautiful model, but then shifting his camera with a large lens straight at the ships anchored but a half mile away and running off several rolls of film, of course that rather pretty Japanese girl smiling all the time as if her photo were being taken.

He went over to the coffeepot, tilted it to get the thick near-syrupy liquid at the bottom, someone had brought in a cake, a few crumbled pieces were left, he absently bolted down the stale "meal" and went back to his desk.

The Soviets or someone else? Which would it be?

Off the coast of Kyushu, Japan
29 June 1941

They were four thousand meters out from the target.

"Now, dive now!"

The six Kates with Fuchida in the lead plane nosed over sharply, rapidly dropping down from a height of five hundred meters.

It was difficult in one sense for him to watch. He was in the aft seat, actually the tail gunner's position, converted over to his special use as an observer, sitting in direct line ahead was the pilot. He had no control over the aircraft but knew he could trust the pilot, his old friend Hideo, even though his fingers tingled with the desire to have them on the control stick; Hideo was not diving steep enough.

"Throttle back! Throttle back!" he snapped. The trade-off of altitude was of course increased air speed.

"One hundred and eighty kilometers per hour, fifteen meters altitude. You know how to do it!"

He turned in his seat to look back at the other five Kates flying in echelon to the right behind him. They were his best, they were keeping formation well, but still they were coming in too fast.

"Three thousand meters to target," Hideo shouted.

Fuchida looked forward again, half rising out of his seat. The target was straight ahead, but he could tell they were still flying too high and too fast. .

"Lower, and slower!" Fuchida snapped into his mike. "Still lower, not more than fifteen meters above the water!"

Even for skilled pilots this was becoming dangerous. Judging height over water, especially the flat calm of the bay but minutes after sunrise, was tricky work. Sunlight was reflecting off the ocean, nothing to gain perspective from, far too low to trust any altimeter. The slightest mistake and the pilot would ram into the sea.

They ignored the risk; they had to. He had worked out the calculations; and if this was to work, it had to be no more than 180 kilometers per hour at fifteen meters

Japanese Navy Type-97 carrier attack plane (B5N1 "Kate") takes off from the carrier Akagi *during the filming of the motion picture* From Pearl Harbor to Malaya, *circa March-April 1942. This scene is frequently used to represent the launch of torpedo planes to attack Pearl Harbor on 7 December 1941. However the plane is the older B5N1 model, not the B5N2 used for the Hawaii Operation. Its torpedo is an exercise unit (note its dented nose and lack of "air box" aerodynamic fins at the tail).* **Naval Historical Center**

above the ocean.

He could sense the plane slowing, Hideo cutting the throttle back to idle, a bit of a stomach knot as he nosed over slightly, then leveled out, throttled back up slightly.

"No deflection," Fuchida announced, "no deflection!"

The target was not moving, that made the calculation far easier, no need to estimate target speed and then lay in the proper deflection for a hit as the enemy attempted to maneuver out of harm's way.

Straight ahead was the target, and his heart swelled at the sight of it, a carrier, anchored in the shallows just below Etajima.

Releasing his shoulder harness Fuchida half stood, canopy was open, wind blast buffeting him as he turned and looked at the formation and then back forward.

"Fifteen hundred meters," Hideo announced, "fourteen hundred . . ." every two seconds another hundred meters closer.

"Eleven hundred meters . . . !"

"Release!"

The Kate surged up as the half-ton torpedo slung below their belly dropped away.

Excitedly Fuchida turned to look back at the other five planes, spaced out correctly, at one-second intervals each released in turn, torpedoes dropping, splashing into the sea. He held his breath . . . make it work . . . make it work!

A few seconds later he saw a trail of

bubbles, the oxygen driver of a torpedo, then a second one . . . and no more.

"Damn!" he snarled.

His plane surged up, and he dropped back into his seat.

The bulk of the target, the carrier *Akagi,* was just a few hundred meters ahead. They were heading straight at it, still below the level of the deck. It was doctrine to fly so low that the anti-aircraft gunners could not depress low enough to hit them. Now they were surging up, Hideo pulling back on the stick, full throttle, a heart-racing instant where he thought Hideo had miscalculated and would ram into the side of the ship.

Then a glimpse of men on the deck waving their white forage caps, some ducking low as Hideo cleared the starboard side of the deck by not much more than half a dozen meters.

"Bank to port!" Fuchida snapped.

If simply a practice attack, Hideo would have skimmed across the enemy deck, so low that no one could effectively shoot at them, clear the port side, then dive down to skim the waves, then race off pulling evasive turns until out of gunnery range. But he wanted to see the results.

Hideo went into a sharp banking turn, the force of it pressing Fuchida down low in his seat, as they pivoted above the deck of his beloved carrier, men on the deck now running to the starboard railing to watch the results of the attack.

There were only two tracks of bubbles approaching the *Akagi*. The torpedoes were approaching at just thirty kilometers per hour, barely half speed, throttled back so if they hit the torpedo net deployed out ten meters from the carrier, they would simply snag without damage.

It took nearly two minutes for them to reach the target, one slicing fifty yards behind the stern, to his shame, it looked to be the one launched by Hideo, the second striking amidships a few seconds later, head crumbling in the torpedo net. Of course there was no hundred-meter-high pillar of water from the explosion, just a dull thump, and seconds later the inflatable bladder, set in the torpedo so it could be recovered, brought the bent weapon to the surface.

"The rest of you, head back to base," Fuchida announced sharply to the squadron while he ordered Hideo to circle back over the drop point and skimmed in low. A small tender was already approaching the area. One torpedo was on the surface, bladder inflated, why it failed completely would have to be carefully studied. Bubbles were surfacing from the drop point of two others. The sixth torpedo, no sign of at all, most likely broken apart on the bottom, shattering as it hit.

Damn, damn all, he sighed. The torpedoes were obviously stuck in the mud at the bottom of the bay.

It was another failure.

The drop point for the attack and positioning of *Akagi* had been carefully selected. The bottom at low tide, exactly thirteen-meters deep, the depth of Pearl Harbor's main channel and anchorage.

Four torpedoes damaged by the drop or hitting the bottom, only two successfully launched, only one striking the target, a huge carrier, stationary and only a thousand meters away.

What do I say to Genda, he wondered. He had hoped that the lower, slower approach into the target, the diving planes on the torpedoes calibrated so that it would not sink more than ten meters after drop, rather than the usual twenty to thirty before surfacing back up for the run into the target would work. It had not worked. They could go no slower without stalling, and for that matter making themselves absolutely nothing more than suicidal targets before even launching, and they could go no lower.

Damn all, some other way to launch the torpedoes had to be found, otherwise all of Genda's elaborate plans would be for naught.

"Take us back in, Hideo," he said dryly, dreading the report he would have to file upon return to base.

Tokyo
2 July 1941

The years of debate within the army, between its young aggressive officers and older conservatives, between army and navy as to potential directions to take, between military and government and within government between conservatives such as himself and hotbloods like Foreign Minister Matsuoka, so enamored with Hitler . . . had now at last come to this moment.

Prime Minister Prince Fumimaro Konoye felt trapped, as he most certainly was, trapped into the ritual now about to take place and at such a moment, as they stood waiting, he knew there was no room for maneuver this day.

The side door to the audience chamber opened and all bowed low, from the waist as first the President of the Privy Council

Yoshimichi Hara entered the small room, followed then by the Emperor himself.

Related by blood to the Royal line, Prince Konoye had, since childhood, always felt himself in somewhat of a unique relationship with the Emperor. They were nearly of the same age, knew each other as boys, and in the privacy of some inner chambers of the palace the relationship was as close as possible to what a living God could call a friendship. The prince would tell jokes, gossip, play Go, and felt a close kinship, though even then, there was the sense that here must be the living presence of all that was Japan, the manifestation on Earth of Japan's unique position in all the world, the one nation blessed and entrusted with the "eternal presence," a presence which all Japanese shared, from prince to the lowest peasant, and which therefore placed upon them a mandate unique in history.

And this new age might very well make manifest that destiny intended by the gods. Isolated, remote, while the rest of the world grew, expanded, fought wars, empires rose and fell, Japan had always been remote, and in that remoteness had honed its own steel against itself, the tradition of the samurai, the ultimate example of the warrior ideal, cultured, refined, faithful and yet when called upon, deadly, with the quickest of strokes barely seen. In the two hundred plus years of the Tokugawa regime, Japan had safely insulated itself from the rest of the world while the Westerners ran greedily rampant through the world. In this, the time of Meiji, Japan had stirred out of its self-imposed isolation, for to not do so would mean ultimate submission to the vastly superior technologies of the West.

And now, was the moment at last arriving when the nation with the living presence of a God begin to achieve its destiny?

Konoye knew that all around him felt he was a cipher. He could be urbane, witty, even Western in style, dress, manner, and humor. He had traveled the world and knew the world and enjoyed the latest in gadgetry and luxury the West had to offer. Yet he could also appear to be so traditional, frequently preferring the kimono to the three-piece suit, a quiet evening at home with wife and family rather than the accepted practices of spending those evenings in the geisha houses. Some thought him weak, for whoever came before him to press a case, he always seemed to agree. And yet none, not even the Emperor himself, truly knew his heart; and at this moment, his heart was filled with infinite sadness, even as he fully prepared to perform the ritual forced upon him.

Foreign Minister Matsuoka had been the one, at last, to force the crisis and decision to take place this day. Several months back he had crossed Russia to visit Berlin there to meet with Hitler and Ribbentrop, and there he had been mesmerized by the power and glory of the Reich, triumphant on every field of battle. On his return, ironically he had been hosted by Stalin as well, even publicly embraced by the wily dictator when departing and boarding his train in Moscow. Stalin had personally come to see him off and swept him up in a bear hug, while dozens of photographers recorded the moment of the diminutive Japanese foreign minister enfolded in the dictator's friendly embrace. Matsuoka was the opposite of everything Konoye felt himself to be admired, brash, crude, a show-off, given to extremes, and above all else a manipulator without any finesse and thought for the higher ideals of Japan. Boasting for weeks of his friendship with "Stalin-san and Hitler-san," he pushed his proposal that now was the time for Japan to finish with the Western presence in the Pacific and the army radicals had gladly embraced him, talking of a vast axis of power, stretching from Europe to the Atlantic to the Pacific, the three great new powers humbling forever the effete and decadent democracies of the West.

Thrown momentarily off guard by the stunning turn of events of June 22, when one of the proposed great allies had turned on the other, with Hitler turning on Stalin (something Matsuoka's own professional diplomats had warned of months earlier), he had barely missed a beat, again joining hands with the army, this time with the slogan "Don't miss the bus," a slogan ironically based on Chamberlain's famous remark about Hitler.

Absurd, Konoye thought as he remained bent low, waiting for the Imperial Presence to come to the center of the room and sit down, the signal for all of them to resume an upright position and then sit as well.

Join the bus, join the bus and it did not matter in which damn direction it was going. At this junction some in the army had shouted that now was the time to jump out of Manchukuo and expand into Siberia, perhaps in their wilder dreams meeting the Germans along the slopes of the Urals.

Madness! To do what? Conquer a frozen wilderness into which a million additional troops might disappear forever, breaking the budget, and bringing back not one yen of true profit, as was still the case in China after nearly four bitter years of fighting.

But in a way, it was Hitler against Stalin that Konoye knew had finally forced his own hand as well. He had never been totally dismissive of the use of war, for after all, he was Japanese and the code of the samurai, of courtly patience but if need be of swift direct action in service to the Emperor and to the ideal of what it was to be of Japan, was in his blood.

If there was to be war though, to what purpose? The fire-and-blood youths of the army, caught up in some strange almost cinemalike illusion of being warrior samurai of 350 years past, eager to fight, and frankly to hell caring not with whom it was they fought, just simply to fight, now held a strange perverse sway, so powerful that even the upper ranks, the older heads, some of them who actually had seen total real war back in 1904–05 were now swept up in the fever as well.

China was a deadlock, the analogy of the serpent and the pig so apt. Japan had swallowed the pig halfway, but it was so big it could never fully be swallowed, nor could it be disgorged. Any realist knew that for a generation to come, if they should decide to try and stay on, it would be a long, twilight struggle. If not against the Nationalists then the far more deadly Communists, so adept at dissimulation, the dagger in the night, thousands of good soldiers dying to no possible gain other than more reprisals and blood . . . and still no profit.

Why the Americans were so damn insistent to pick a fight over that godforsaken country of China was beyond him in spite of all his years of professional experience and his current tenure as the prime minister.

He was trapped. In the week after the German invasion, the army had actually argued to reconsider the "northern approach," to take on the Soviets, though of course, ultimately there was no logic to it beyond the grabbing of territory, since it would take billions of yen in capital investments across a score of years before even the remote hope of a profit to the Empire could ever be shown.

And in this now insane topsy-turvy debate it was the navy that presented the counter argument . . . if there was war let it be to the south.

He was boxed. The army wanted war, at least the middle-level rankers did, and there was still the haunting fear of another February 26 coup if they did not get their way. The upper echelon paid lip service to the "revolutionaries out of fear" as well, but also saw the potential political power within their grasp if war should indeed be declared and it did not matter if it was the Soviets, the British, the French or the Americans. The navy saw no future in a war with Russia, but most definitely power, and with it a logical goal of seizing Indochina for all its resources and bases. Once bases were established there, Malaya and Singapore, the Gibraltar of the East, and ultimately the oil-rich Dutch East Indies would be ripe for the taking.

At this moment the entire oil usage of all Japanese coming from their possessions and reserves was but eighty thousand barrels a day. Barely enough to keep the fleet afloat, let alone a modern army of nearly a million in the field in China, and that would run completely dry in less than a year if the Americans, sitting atop their vast reserves of billions of barrels, should turn the flow off.

Every barrel was rationed, every barrel balanced between turning it into aviation gas for a plane to fly for an hour or a battleship to cruise but for a minute or two at flank speed. The Americans most assuredly knew this.

That was his frustration now. It was foregone that the army's next move would be into Indochina. There was no stopping that now, their appetite for a quick acquisition from a weakened and nearly craven Western opponent too much to resist. And yet his conversations with Ambassador Grew made it clear that such a move would trigger President Roosevelt to a rage, and the taking of the next step could be a full oil embargo, and at that moment war would be inevitable. Otherwise within less than two years every ounce of fuel reserve would be gone and Japan, in an instant, thrown back to a powerless medieval kingdom, ripe for the picking.

It was an impossible impasse, and he was trapped in the middle now with no real recourse. Resist the army and there would be another February 26 and he would be dead. Not that he feared that death, but he did fear the thought of Matsuoka somehow then seizing his post.

And there was the other thought as well, one with a faint glimmer of optimism. Was this indeed the moment that Japan must risk all, that in spite of the known risks, to seize the destiny that had awaited it for two thousand years, to bring to the rest of the world the realization that their nationhood ultimately represented the living manifestation of God on Earth? That there could be a new Golden Age, a unification of all the Orient under a single banner, the expulsion of the exploiting West, the establishment of Japan's proper "place in the sun," and from that, after but a brief struggle, the realization by America and Britain that a new equal had emerged upon the global field and out of that, a lasting peace with each cooperating with the other in their destined spheres of influence?

There was a sharp hand clap, the signal by the privy seal that the Emperor was seated.

Prime Minister Prince Konoye raised his head, upright gaze turned toward the Emperor. It was a breach of protocol, to look directly at him was uncouth, but after all, as boys they had once been friends.

He sat there, so curious looking. Pale porcelainlike skin, dressed in the field uniform of the cavalry, thick glasses distorting his eyes, almost fragile. Dare he think it, if met on the street in other circumstances the Emperor might be mistaken for a bank clerk, a professor, or the owner of a dusty book store. And he wondered if inwardly this man, the grandson of the great Meiji, might not have secretly wished for a fate different than this one.

Bowing formally to the throne, Konoye

bent over stiffly and picked up a report, its cover bound in ornate red silk. Turning back the cover he began to speak formally, in the ritual language of the court, ignoring the eyes of the others upon him, that of the President of the Privy Council, of Matsuoka, the assembled heads of the army and navy.

It was July 2, 1941, and Konoye began to read: "Outline of National Policies in View of Present Developments . . ."

French Indochina was to be occupied within the month, under the pretense of establishing more bases to wage the campaign against China, and also to interdict the road across Burma, built with so called "volunteer help" from America, that was feeding supplies to the Nationalists. But the move was a cover as well to establish bases for the eventual attack on Malaya, Singapore, and from there on into the oil-rich Dutch East Indies.

Such a move would surely provoke America to war, and it was now stated that such a war must open with a blow that would cripple the Americans in the opening minutes of battle, and thus in one strike finish their will to fight . . . then to seek a generous, negotiated peace, perhaps even to make concessions about partial withdrawal from the quagmire of China, a concession that could never be made now with the Americans insisting upon such without any concessions from them in return.

He read the report, forcing his voice to remain calm. It was, he realized, without doubt the boldest move Japan might very well have made in over six hundred years, since its rejection of the demands of the Mongol emperor Kubalai to swear submission or face an invasion of annihilation. They had resisted, the gods had intervened with the sending of the Divine wind, the typhoon of legend, the Kamikaze, and Japan had survived. May the gods intervene again, he prayed even as he read his report.

He knew what would transpire once he was done speaking. The privy seal, always the cautious one and in such a meeting the voice of the Emperor, who by tradition would remain silent, would argue against, suggesting instead to wait to see if Hitler's legions did succeed in collapsing Stalin, thus leaving the back door open to take Siberia, or at least to continue negotiating with the Vichy government, and each argument would be shot down in turn by the army and or the navy, now set on their course.

The Emperor would say nothing, it was

all but unheard of for him to do so. The meeting would wind down, for after all, it was already mere ritual. The decision had been reached days ago. Once the report by Konoye was accepted, it would be taken to the secretariat who would transcribe it into traditional form on the finest of silk paper. It would then be signed by Konoye, the representatives of the army and navy, presented before the Emperor to gaze upon without comment, then taken before the keeper of the Privy Seal who would stamp it with the Royal seal of the emperors. And at that moment, on July 2, 1941, it would become official policy. Japan would seize French Indochina by force before the month was out, and then prepare for war with America, Britain, France, and the Dutch before the year was out. The move to the south was now official policy and was as certain as the juggernaut rolling forward toward its destiny.

Hanoi
Vichy French Indochina
23 July 1941

This was beyond ironic, Cecil thought as he stepped off the plane and into the boiling heat of Hanoi on a late summer afternoon.

Six months ago he would have been arrested and thrown in jail the moment the plane landed, because Vichy France and Great Britain were at war. But now, technically though still governed by Vichy France, this was as much Japanese territory as Nanking, Formosa, or Manchukuo.

Japanese planes, mostly twin-engine transports but also some bombers and their new Zeroes, lined the far side of the tarmac.

The half dozen other passengers getting off the flight from Hong Kong, flown by a Portuguese airline based out of Macao, were all Westerners and several Japanese businessmen.

Walking the short distance to the terminal he was already drenched in sweat and once inside endured fifteen chilled minutes of questioning at the customs gate by a typical French official.

The French were still seething with anger over what they deemed as the British betrayal of sinking their main fleet shortly after France's collapse last year. For Churchill to have left that fleet intact, most likely ready to go over to the Germans, would have been madness, but it had triggered the declaration of war against England by the Vichy government.

But in the outer colonies there was still a

strange flow of traffic, smuggling, looking the other way if the proper bribes were offered. And besides, his visa was stamped by the Japanese Consulate Office in Hong Kong, listing him as a British correspondent, with documentation that he was there as a guest of the Japanese consulate in Hanoi. In other words, this French official had to dance to the tune of his new masters and did not like it.

Cecil's French was barely adequate at best, and, of course, the customs officer refused to speak anything other than French at top speed, so the interview was going nowhere fast.

As the officer played out his usual officious role, shaking his head, slowly reading each word of the attached documents, while two of his lackeys, both subservient Vietnamese, took his single piece of luggage and shoulder bag apart, the small line of disembarking passengers sweltered in the heat, swearing under their breath, the Frenchmen in the crowd becoming increasingly irate, until final a Japanese official came over, made a quick scan of Cecil's passport and documents, said something in French, which made the customs officer give Cecil a withering glance, and Cecil was ushered out of the terminal to a waiting car.

As the Japanese official opened the car door he smiled, and in perfect English introduced himself. "I am Shogo Mikawa," he announced in perfect English. "I'm with the Consulate Office here in Hanoi, I was sent to bring you to our office and will serve as your guide for the next day."

Cecil nodded his thanks, tipped the Vietnamese porter who brought out his bag, a shirt sleeve sticking out of the bag, all the clothing inside now rumbled, and placed it in the boot of the rather nicely appointed Citroën. Cecil and Mikawa slid into the backseat, Mikawa ordering the driver to leave, the driver doing so with gusto, as if eager to get out of the airport as quickly as possible before someone changed their mind and came out to collar the Englishman and drag him back in for more questioning.

A small cabinet set into the armrest between Cecil and Mikawa was opened, and inside was a bottle of Vichy water and of all things one of bourbon and, mercifully, an insulated bucket of ice. Cecil gladly made himself a drink.

So far, so good, he thought, looking over at his host who, so typical of such officials, had a permanent smile frozen on his face.

"Rather unusual for a British reporter to

request a visit here in these times," Mikawa opened, dropping all the protocols of inquiring about health, family, the prospect of mutual friends, and, so typical of Japanese who spoke flawless English, a discussion as to which school he had attended in Britain or the States.

"My newspaper wanted an article on the operations here, the obvious cooperation of the Vichy government with yours. I promised to write a balanced report."

"Such as the ones you filed from Nanking?" Mikawa interjected, his smile not breaking.

Cecil looked at him steadily, not breaking eye contact. "I was there and wrote what I saw. Did you see what happened in Nanking?" Cecil shot back.

Mikawa hesitated and then lowered his gaze. "No, and many of us were shamed by the revelations. It shall never happen again."

"But the officers in command are still in command, with only a mild public reprimand that carried no meaning."

Mikawa nodded and looked away as they drove through the airport gate and merged into the traffic made up primarily of bicycles, carts drawn by oxen or humans, and the occasional car, usually a Renault, but also half a dozen open trucks loaded with

Japanese soldiers. The Citroën was such a curious contrast that the gendarme directing traffic at the intersection outside the airport gate, obviously French, gazed intently at it, making it stop for a moment before finally waving it through the intersection, turning his back as it passed.

A Japanese flag was mounted to the front fender, marking it as a diplomatic vehicle, and Cecil found it amusing how Mikawa's frozen smile shifted for a second to anger at this deliberate display of disrespect. As they circled along the edge of the airport before turning in toward the center of the city he saw a flight of half a dozen bombers coming in, one of them trailing smoke from a feathered engine, two Zeroes were weaving back and forth above the damaged plane, which was touched down with obvious skill on the part of the pilot. On the far side of the tarmac were a row of newly constructed hangars, dozens of Japanese planes drawn up in front, twin-engine bombers primarily and some of the new Zeroes.

Cecil knew better than to even think about reaching into his shoulder bag for his notebook, but still he did a quick mental count.

"I can provide you later with any information you might have as to how many aircraft are based here," Mikawa offered in a friendly tone.

"Thank you, I'd like that."

There was a moment of awkward silence.

"Your real reason for being here?" Mikawa suddenly asked, and Cecil was startled by the directness. There was a change in tone and a bit of a chill. Was this man an agent of their secret police?

Mikawa nodded as if reading his mind.

"Yes, I am with our security police, but do not worry, my assignment is to ensure your safety, not to interrogate you and you will safely board your plane tomorrow back to Hong Kong."

"My visa allows me to stay a week," Cecil replied sharply.

Mikawa finished his drink, refilled his glass with ice and then poured some more bourbon, offering to do the same for Cecil, who refused.

"I'll explain that in a minute, but let us not waste time on game-playing and fencing," Mikawa said. "Our purpose for allowing you to visit here, on what is technically the territory of an enemy of Great Britain, is for you to return with a message."

"For whom, my readers?"

Mikawa smiled. "No, for the prime minister."

Cecil kept his best bridge player gaze locked on Mikawa as if the words had not even registered.

"Go on, then," Cecil said noncommittally.

"The mere fact that you are here is an interesting paradox that Great Britain should take note of."

"How so."

"Until our movement here into northern Indochina, this was territory that you were technically at war with, a government that had gone over to Hitler."

"With whom you have an alliance as well," Cecil replied.

Mikawa nodded and then waved his hand dismissively.

"If we were truly allied with that madman you are fighting, we would have attacked the Soviet Union last month. Stalin is now putting up more of a fight than many thought those first few weeks when some analysts were claiming that the Nazi columns would be in Moscow by now. But we did not enter that war, though I can assure you, there were some who wished to do so."

"I agree," Cecil replied, "but there could be some who might say that Japan stayed its hand against a crumbling Soviet Union because it is casting its gaze elsewhere."

Mikawa again nodded.

"Yes, that is obvious here and will be even more obvious in a few more hours."

Cecil stiffened at that, "a few more hours." What did he mean?

Mikawa smiled.

"Ah, now I really have your interest. Perhaps you really are a newspaperman and think you have, as the Americans call it, 'a scoop.' "

"What is it?" Cecil asked, not able to contain himself.

"Ah, give me my moment for fun," Mikawa said, "but first, a genuine question for you."

Cecil tried not to let his frustration show.

"Of course, go on."

"You filed a report from Thailand back in January, that you had witnessed the brief war fought between that country and France. Were those your true impressions?"

Cecil nodded, surprised at how good a dossier this agent had on him.

The short undeclared war between Vichy France and Thailand had all but been lost in the background at a time when war raged across Europe and China. A border dispute had developed in a remote corner of Southeast Asia and flared into a brief but bitter conflict of several weeks' duration. The Siamese thoroughly trounced the French. It was stunning, an Oriental nation that most Westerners dismissed as quaint with a certain storybook quality to it, taking on the French and shoving them back in a humiliating rout. "The Siamese proved to be tough. After all, it is their land, their environment. I did not directly witness any of the fighting but could see where the French were completely out of their league against the guerilla tactics of their opponents."

"And as a Westerner, who were you cheering for?" Mikawa asked.

Cecil smiled. "I prefer underdogs."

"The way England now is against Hitler?"

Cecil did not reply and looked out the window.

They were now pushing into the center of Hanoi, encountering a confusing myriad of traffic, the cooling breeze of earlier in their drive, and conversation, replaced now with boiling heat. Mikawa refilled his cut-glass tumbler with ice, a splash of bourbon, and the rest Vichy water, Cecil doing the same. He wished he could scoop out more of the ice and rub his neck and forehead with it, an absurd thought, but he did wonder how anyone could stand this place for long in midsummer; it felt worse than India. He looked ahead, to the confusion of traffic, the ox carts, the shops closed now during the midday heat, and yes, the beautiful young women on bicycles slowly weaving their way past the car which had been reduced to a crawl.

"This big event you mentioned," Cecil asked, breaking the silence.

"Oh yes, you did answer my question, so now it is my turn," Mikawa replied.

Cecil looked back at him.

"Starting at midnight tonight Japan will occupy all of French Indochina." Stunned, Cecil could not reply for a moment, his mind racing. Their move of earlier this year forcing the French to allow air bases in the north of Indochina to prosecute their war in China proper had triggered a firestorm of protest from Roosevelt. America had notched up its stance, now openly sending supplies to the Nationalists through Burma, and contrary to accepted international law, was allowing its military officers to take "leaves of absence" without loss of seniority or benefits, to volunteer as pilots and advisors to the Nationalists.

It had angered him as well for it showed how craven the Vichy government truly was, to cave in to Japanese demands without a fight. For all practical purposes it meant that here, in the Pacific, France was now openly allied with Japan.

But the blowback from such a move, he did not understand.

"Our transport ships are already approaching the harbors at Hue, Haiphong, and Saigon. There will be no conflict. By this time tomorrow naval units will be in the harbor, troops occupying key positions and aircraft moving down from China and launched from carriers to establish bases. The French administration will stay in place but will now be assisted by us in an advisory role."

Cecil could hear the touch of mocking disdain in Mikawa's voice when he said "advisory role," it meant that Europeans were now puppets answering to their new master in the East.

"Why?" Cecil finally asked. "You and I both know that Roosevelt has already made it clear that such a move would provoke the harshest of economic embargoes on your country. Is the trade-off really worth it?"

Mikawa stiffened slightly.

"Always it is Roosevelt. What right does America have to meddle in our affairs and relations with France here in the Orient? A colony is always more advantageous when it comes to such things," Matawa replied, "would you want your India as a colony or an independent nation making far more difficult trade agreements? We are at war and we need Indochina, it is that simple. Why this should upset America is beyond us."

"Because America sees it as yet another step in your Imperialism and will wonder what next. It is the same question we had to ask ourselves three years ago when Hitler kept making one demand, and then another, and another and each time Chamberlain backed down, until finally there were no more corners to back in to."

Their car, which felt like the inside of an oven, finally crawled up to the jammed intersection at the center of the city, a mad swirling kaleidoscope of carts, cycles, autos, the occasional rickshaw and a lone French gendarme signaling and waving his baton like an orchestra conductor. He saw their car, the flag on the fender, and like the previous policeman, turned away and made them wait.

"Damn French," Mikawa muttered and though he did not say it, Cecil felt the same, even more so now with the news just given. Their caving in of the previous year had left England alone, to survive by the narrowest of margins, their actions here now in the Pacific might very well be the domino falling that would truly trigger total war in the

Pacific. The gendarme finally turned back to them and with a dismissive wave, gestured for them to cross the crowded intersection. A few blocks ahead Cecil could see the flag of the Japanese Consulate Office.

"What about my hotel?" he asked.

"Oh, given the sentiment in the streets these days by the French, we thought it safer if you would be our guest for the evening before your return flight tomorrow."

He paused for a moment, smile still the same. "And besides, it would be tiresome for all concerned. You'll be tempted to somehow try and make a phone call or get a message out regarding the secret I just shared with you, and I'd have to place a dozen agents to watch you, when I prefer to see them used elsewhere today."

"You mean I flew all the way down here to be your guest, and tomorrow will be sent packing?"

"Please don't see it that way, sir," Mikawa replied softly. "You will have your byline of reporting from Hanoi on the day we occupy this country, which shall make your newspaper happy with your scoop, and as first alluded to, we would like your message to your friend to move as swiftly as possible."

"With your occupation of Indochina," Cecil said sharply, "my government can but see one thing clearly. The bases you now have will be seen as a direct threat within striking range of our interests in Malaya and Singapore. I think you will hear a very sharp reaction from Parliament the moment this becomes public."

"And that is precisely why our government was more than happy to allow you this visit here at this time. We want a message conveyed back personally from a Western observer to his trusted friend." Cecil did not respond for a moment. Of course they knew, they most likely knew ever since Nanking, that he was in the employ of Churchill. First privately when Churchill was out of office, and since May of 1940, officially part of British intelligence in the Far East, still maintaining the guise of a correspondent while having the unique portfolio of reporting only to, and directly to the prime minister.

"Go on," he finally said.

"Our move into Indochina should in no way be construed as a buildup to a threat against your holdings in the south. The last thing we desire is a conflict with England. Our primary concern is to finish this war in China. The economic burden it has created for us is crippling, and unless soon brought to a successful conclusion will bankrupt us.

"That is revealing much to you and showing even our weakness. We ask that if the prime minister can use his influence to stay Roosevelt and his threats the situation can be resolved to the benefit of all."

"And if not?" Cecil asked, "assuming somehow that I actually can convey this message of yours."

"We prefer the message be a positive one, speculations about 'if not' as you put it, are fruitless."

Mikawa acted as if he were hesitating but then continued.

"Sir, the performance of your air force in defending your home island was superb, the entire world watched with awe. But as to your army and navy on distant fronts? Dare I mention the complete debacle of but little more than two months ago in Greece, Crete, the current rout in North Africa? Does England really wish to engage in yet another war, a war against a modern navy and not just a motley collection of ships that the Germans have, and to do so on a front ten thousand miles away. I daresay your government must realize that peril and I daresay as well that your public would wish to avoid such a conflict at all cost, given that you are still fighting for your life with an enemy but twenty-five miles off your coast.

"Please think on that and please convey our desire for your government's understanding regarding the action to take place tomorrow, and the consequences if they do not, and please convey our strongest wish that your government move to bridle in Roosevelt."

Cecil bristled at what was now an open threat but said nothing. There was nothing he could or should say now. The message was what should concern him. But the term "bridle," he wondered if that was deliberate with the insult fully intended.

"After all, for both you and America, the real enemy is Germany, not us. Let us fulfill what we must and then perhaps a warmer understanding between us can be achieved."

Cecil looked at the agent sitting beside him and could sense the cynicism behind the offer. There was but one reason for Japan to occupy all of Indochina and to ignore the threat, which Roosevelt would fully carry out, regardless of what Churchill might say . . . to impose an oil embargo, which most certainly would trigger a war.

The bastards no longer care, he realized, and they actually think they can beat us. And there was a moment of fear in Cecil's heart. If their full fury was turned against Singapore, the East Indies, and any sortie offered by the Americans, at this moment, they most likely would beat us here. It means war is inevitable, Cecil thought to himself as the car finally lurched to a halt and he was shown in, with great ceremony, to the Consulate Office, his prison for the night, before being sent back the following day as messenger boy, bearing a useless message which he knew with utter certainty was a lie.

Aboard the USS Augusta
Argentina Bay, Newfoundland
12 August 1941

"Franklin, I will miss you when we part today." Churchill smiled warmly at his friend and ally. "Our new Atlantic Charter sets the moral stage for what we must do. Now our staffs will have to think through all the practical steps to make our victory certain and our future desirable."

"You have to return to the war in London, and I have to return to a different war in Washington. We just got word that the draft was extended by one vote in the House of Representatives. Can you imagine it! One vote! Here we are in the middle of a world at war, and my friends in Congress cannot see their duty with any clarity," the president asserted with vehemence.

"What's even more amazing, Mr. President, is that the American people are now ahead of their elected representatives," Harry Hopkins leaned into the conversation with familiar ease. "Fortune has a poll in which three out of every four Americans believe Hitler is trying to conquer the world, and a solid majority believe we will have to defeat him militarily."

"Mr. President, I feel that despite all our problems in Russia, North Africa, and the Atlantic, I also have to remind you that we could face a very nasty situation in the Pacific," Churchill replied, his eyes focused on FDR.

"I have a source I trust who has been touring French Indochina and other places and he is convinced the Japanese are going to move south soon to grab the oil of the Netherlands' East Indies. We shall have to support our Dutch allies, and we have very little to send to stop the Japanese. I am scraping the bottom of the barrel. I think I can find a few ships to establish a presence, but I cannot build a Pacific battle fleet capable of defending the East Indies region. I can hold Singapore, which we have spent twenty years building up, but I am afraid your forces will have to do any heavy lifting in the Pacific."

FDR nodded yes and pointed toward General Marshall and Admiral Stark.

"We have already decided to quadruple the number of B-17s in the Philippines to thirty-six. Those strategic bombers will serve as strategic deterrent to the Japanese because we will be able to bomb their supply lines if they try to move south. I would send some battleships, but as Stark told Admiral Pound we have a big problem with the mechanical systems on our newest battleships, and they have to be refitted. We simply have nothing to send.

"Maybe you could send a few key ships such as that beautiful new battleship you came over on." FDR motioned toward the *Prince of Wales* lying at anchor a few hundred yards away.

"Together, my friend, we will draw together the will and the forces to stop the Japanese. I just hope we can convince them to accept peaceful negotiations. Britain does not need a second major war at this time, and we do not need your strength diverted to the Pacific," Churchill responded.

"You have my word, America will continue

to focus on defeating Germany no matter what happens," FDR responded.

The day was boiling hot, more like Washington in August than Japan, which usually gets some cooling breaks. Dressed in formal diplomatic attire, Ambassador Joseph Grew felt as if he were already swimming in a sea of sweat beneath his suit, vest, button-down collar, and tie.

His limousine, parked in front of the office of the foreign minister, had the traditional American flags mounted on the front. A cordon of security guards kept a watchful eye as a servant of the foreign minister opened the car door for him, bowing low. Passers-by paused at the sight of him and his cane. An elderly couple, making eye contact, stopped in their tracks and bowed low, and he returned the gesture with a polite nod. Several army officers were walking by, there was a whispered exchange at the sight of the flag and they slowed, but a security agent quickly rushed up to them, snapping an order for them to move on. Reluctantly they agreed but the eye contact with Grew was cold, icy. He ignored them.

At the open doorway, in a most unusual gesture, stood the new foreign minister, Teijiro Toyoda, a former admiral of the navy, a replacement for the hotheaded Matsuoka who had so aggressively dragged their two countries closer to the abyss.

Teijiro even made the unusual gesture of coming down the steps to greet him, old training first causing him to begin to raise his hand in a military salute, but then it fell to his side as he bowed formerly, then offered his hand to shake.

"The heat, it is killing," Teijiro offered, and Grew nodded in agreement as they walked into the ministry and quickly down the hall to the Foreign Minister's Office, the hallway cleared of all traffic as the two passed.

If anything, once inside the office with doors closed, the heat was even more stifling. The new luxury of air-conditioning was all but unknown yet in Japan, where such days of intense heat were relatively rare. Already waiting and standing politely to one side was Teijiro's interpreter and, as usual, Grew had his own young assistant following in his wake.

The formalities disappeared within seconds.

"Mr. Ambassador, may I make a friendly suggestion," Teijiro offered, "let us get out of these ridiculous coats, and ties. I'll have ice and towels fetched for us."

Grew smiled and found an instant liking for this man. He was not a bureaucratic climber such as the detestable Matsuoka; but instead a military man, one who had come up through the standard ranks to command of a battleship in his Imperial Navy. He had that weathered look of a man who had seen many years at sea on the bridge of a ship, keeping watch, someone who instantly struck Grew as no-nonsense, with the reputation of a straight talker rather than a smooth one.

All four shed their formal clothing with sighs, Teijiro going so far as to unbutton the two top buttons of his shirt. Iced tea was brought in on an ornate silver tray along with a large silver bucket, beading with moisture, small hand towels on another tray. Teijiro, without ceremony, scooped out a handful of ice, wrapped a towel around it and rubbed it against the back of his neck and face, sighing audibly. "Sir, I thought I was about to faint while waiting for your arrival."

"And I, sir, thought I'd faint when caught in traffic getting over here," Grew said, with a smile, warming to this man.

Their two assistants had sat motionless, at least shedding their jackets, and Teijiro, shaking his head, told them to pick up some iced towels as well and drink their iced tea, speaking with a slightly booming voice, like that of a commander at sea, the two a bit nervous but gratefully complying.

Teijiro had already redecorated his office in the short time since the Emperor had requested of Prime Minister Konoye that the old cabinet be dissolved and a new one called to order. Gone were Matsuoka's collection of antique prints and numerous photos of himself with various dignitaries, including Hitler and Stalin. Instead there was simply a map of Japan, another one of China, and various nautical prints, some in the traditional Japanese style, others Western looking, along with several photographs of ships he had once commanded.

After draining a glass of iced tea, and taking a minute to let the rapidly melting ice in his towel soak through, cooling his neck so that a rivulet of cool water trickled down his back, Grew felt it was time to bring the meeting to order. Given that it was he who was asked to "attend to the Foreign Minister," protocol was for his host to open the main point of discussion.

"I believe I can speak plainly and to the point," Teijiro opened, and Grew nodded encouragingly.

"Though now, in this office, my training of a lifetime was in the navy. We do not mince words; there is no time to do so when a typhoon is about to strike and you must prepare your ship or all will perish."

"I concur," Grew said softly, nodding for him to continue even as his own interpreter translated what Teijiro was saying.

"The embargo of all goods, but especially oil, laid down by your president will force a terrible crisis. Japan must import a minimum of eighty thousand barrels of oil a day just to barely sustain itself, anything less and reserves, precious reserves saved up over years, must be tapped.

"Such an amount of oil for you Americans is trivial, your citizens most likely burning ten times that amount each weekend merely to go to the beach or mountains. For us it is now a lifeblood, which is a stranglehold upon us. Blockade us from your oil, for which we are willing to pay fair market value, and in short order our economy will collapse entirely."

"Withdraw from Indochina and I am

certain my government will reconsider the actions it felt were necessary to protest your takeover of a neutral country."

"Neutral?" Teijiro asked and shook his head. "The British are at war with the Vichy government, already engaged in combat against them in Palestine, Lebanon, Syria. One could see this as the removal of a potential enemy for your side."

"I doubt seriously if that was your government's true motivation for yet another act of imperialism," Grew replied, but casting his voice carefully so as not to sound accusatory. If it was to argue about Indochina, the foreign minister would never have called him here, that issue for both sides was now set in place and obviously neither would back down unless some major gesture was made.

Teijiro sighed and shook his head.

"We had to take Indochina in order to provide secured air and naval bases for continued operations to suppress the rebels in China. It had nothing to do with German pressure as some now argue, which is most strange given that Germany and the Vichy are tacit allies. It is about China."

"And my government must question this, sir," Grew replied, as he put his soaking wet towel on the tray and picked up another one, wrapped it with ice and continued to cool his forehead and neck.

"Of what good are bases in Haiphong, in Saigon, when it comes to China, hundreds of miles of away. For that matter you have already seized the island of Hainan, and thus secured bases enough for both your navy and army in that area to operate from. If I represented the British, I would of course wonder if you were not, even now, casting eyes farther south."

Teijiro sighed, following suit with the ritual of using another towel to cool his brow.

"Do you honestly believe we seek another war, while still caught up as we are in the one in China?"

Grew nodded slowly in reply.

"One could argue that point. China has become your tar baby."

"What?" Teijiro asked, looking in confusion at his interpreter.

"I'm sorry," Grew replied. "An American Negro folk legend. How a wily fox tried to trap a rabbit by making a dummy out of tar. The rabbit grew angry with the dummy, struck him, and became so entangled within the tar he could not escape."

Teijiro smiled.

"And so the fox ate him?"

"No, the rabbit was able to talk his way out of the trap and escape. Perhaps China is the same. You are entrapped now in a war without end. It could be 1960, 1980 and you will still be fighting there without a final ending in sight. My president is more than willing to help broker a deal for you to disenthrall yourself from China, but my government cannot stand idly by while innocents by the millions are slaughtered, while America and British missionaries who are there out of the most altruistic reasons are attacked as well. Do you know that when the war started missionaries painted their nation's flags and red crosses on the roofs of hospitals, schools, and churches they had built to signal to your pilots the neutrality of such places? They have erased them, for it seems such flags only drew more attacks, an insult to the most common ideals of humanity, let alone the rules of war."

Teijiro lowered his head, saying nothing.

Grew nodded his head.

"I know there are profound divisions between your navy, which you honorably served in, and your army which seems hellbent on refusing to admit the stalemate in China, and as a result now turn covetous eyes elsewhere."

"I speak for my government and the

Emperor," Teijiro replied stiffly, "not for any branch of service."

"Withdraw from Indochina and perhaps that can be an opening to the lifting of the economic embargo," Grew said forcefully. "Otherwise my government has no recourse but to interpret that invasion as an act preparatory to a great expansion of the war against British and Dutch holdings to the south. There is no other reason for the occupation of such territory than that." Teijiro sighed and slowly nodded his head.

"I feared you would say that, but that is not the main reason I asked for you to meet with me today."

"Go on then, please."

"Are you aware of the secret negotiations opened by the prime minister, Prince Konoye, and your Secretary Hull?"

"What?" Grew could not contain his surprise.

Teijiro smiled. He knew Grew to be an honorable man, representing his own government, but also a man who had a deep and abiding ideal that there was still a way for Japan and America to reach an accord. The stain of Nanking, the continued slaughter in China, the Panay incident had wounded his position, and the ever-increasing influence of the military in the affairs of the diplomacy and government of Japan had troubled him. Teijiro watched him carefully. Though Grew suspected that war plans were already being laid out, he had little idea that since early July the navy and army were moving full forward with the strategic and operational plans for a massive strike to topple American, British, and Dutch holdings in the western Pacific. As a military man, the offering of a chance to combat did hold appeal, but now, in his role of foreign minister he could see the other side.

Tojo and others in their war-plannings envisioned a quick victory. Britain had stripped its forces in the Pacific to the bare minimum, its Commonwealth troops and even their navies committed to the campaign in North Africa and the Middle East. America, though having moved its forward base to Pearl Harbor, still wished to be isolationist, the embassy in Washington reporting that on a daily basis peace protestors ringed the White House, calling for an end to Lend Lease, the withdrawal of American garrisons in the Pacific to avoid "provocations," and a general wish just to be left alone. Konoye had been maneuvered into a corner to agree with the meeting of July 2, that set in motion a chain of events that would lead to war by the end of the year. But in secret he had also sent a direct communication to Secretary Hull, asking for a personal meeting with the president. Anchorage Alaska had been suggested, as had Hawaii.

Hull, the embassy in Washington reported, had rejected it as another "Munich," a meeting where Japan would wrangle concessions that would only build its strength.

The foreign minster saw it in opposite terms. If a peaceful settlement was not reached, and reached soon, either America would stir itself and truly begin to rearm, an effort that within months could outstrip anything Japan could achieve, or explode into war.

"Exactly that," Teijiro continued. "Several weeks back he sent a private note to your secretary of state, suggesting that he and your president meet, in secret, to discuss a way of defusing the growing crisis between us."

Grew sat back, incredulous, putting the wet towel he had been rubbing his neck with on the table.

"This is incredible," Grew said softly. "Why was I not informed of this?" He felt silly asking the question. He was never one for the strict and often suffocating protocols and rules of diplomacy. A more proper procedure should have been a consultation between himself and the Japanese prime minister and foreign minister and the note going through his office. Instead, it was obvious that Prince Konoye felt the issue to be so urgent that he had gone straight to Hull.

"It caught me by surprise too," Teijiro offered, almost by way of apology.

"And this would be an official meeting? May I ask, is it endorsed by your Emperor?"

Teijiro at the mere mention of the Emperor's name instinctively lowered his head slightly.

"Yes, the Emperor knows of this and sends his wishes that the meeting should be arranged with all possible speed."

This was stunning news, enough to make Grew feel giddy. It meant the Emperor, in spite of rumors, was willing to defy the army.

Grew gathered his thoughts. The implications were profound, but he could see the pitfalls as well. The president did not fly about from meeting to meeting lightly. As a close personal friend he knew the full extent of the president's disabilities. Yes, his polio was public knowledge, but the public was led to believe as well that he was semimobile, able to walk, and supremely fit. He knew otherwise, with every public appearance carefully staged and limited. He would never let the leader of another country, particularly a nation that they could very well be at war with in short order, see him stagger into a room, leaning on his son for support, not able to walk a single foot without the help of others, his legs encased in twenty pounds of steel braces that must be locked into place so that he could stand upright at his rare public appearances.

The public had only been informed just a few days ago about the secret meetings between the president and Churchill aboard the *Prince of Wales,* anchored off the coast of Canada. That in itself was certain to escalate the growing tensions with Germany. For all practical purposes the navy was already fighting an undeclared war in the Atlantic, unofficially escorting convoys to England. Grew was surprised when he learned of the meeting and the portents it held. And he wondered, as well, how Franklin had been physically maneuvered about, though aboard a ship of an ally, anchored at sea, so that it could be choreographed. It was doubtful that Konoye would agree to a similar arrangement.

The mere logistics of such a meeting

would be monumental. Konoye would most certainly not agree to a meeting in Washington; to his own people, and especially the army that would smack too much of their leader going hat in hand to the White House to beg that the oil be turned back on, any concession then seen as cowardice. Chances were, he'd be assassinated before even leaving the country.

Hawaii would most likely be the place to meet, an arduous journey for Franklin and then what? After Munich no Western leader would ever make such a concession again and expect to survive the political price. It would have to be Japan that makes the concessions.

He could not resist.

"How far is Japan willing to go?" Grew asked.

"Sir?"

"Both sides must make concessions if we are to calm the troubled seas that we now steaming into," Grew said, happy to use a nautical analogy with this former admiral.

"I do not think I am really at liberty to discuss possible terms in a serious way," Teijiro replied.

"Then off the record, as they say," Grew pressed. "You have my oath I will not reveal this conversation other than to communicate to my government the prayerful wish that this proposal of a meeting between our two leaders be embraced and moved upon as quickly as possible."

Teijiro smiled and nodded.

So here was the real reason for this meeting, Grew realized. It was to get his endorsement, for him to appeal to his old childhood friend in the White House to agree.

"I can in no way speak officially to you now on this," Teijiro replied, "but it is obvious that your complete embargo, which is nothing short of a blockade, will strangle my nation within the year. We are as dependent on trade as any island nation would be."

He sat back in his chair, still rubbing the back of his neck with a cool towel, his shirt nearly soaked, and Grew was conscious of just how boiling hot the room was. The temperature had to be hovering at well over ninety.

"Disengagement in China," Teijiro finally said.

Grew waited for more and there was a long silence.

"And that is it?"

Teijiro sighed.

"What more can we offer?" he said carefully. Grew could now see the other reason for this meeting, to fish for terms, the parameters of what America would expect and then offer in return.

"Disengage?" he finally replied. "Sir, your nation went into an unjustified war in China over four years ago. Your army said it would be finished in six months. How many hundred thousand dead on your side and still no end in sight? Can you not see the quagmire you are in. Disengage now and though I cannot speak for the president, I suspect he would be most heartily ready to extend a hand of understanding in return."

Teijiro said nothing for a moment. He knew the true reality, the dream of Konoye to forestall, at the last minute, a war that he himself had been cornered into proposing by the military and Nationalist radicals. He knew as well the reality from the other side, the side he had served for so many years.

"Disengagement will take time."

"How long?"

"I cannot say."

Grew sighed.

"Then I cannot say what will be the answer to your prime minister's proposal."

The two took turns fishing out pieces of ice, now floating in the silver bucket, wrapped the small chunks into their towels and sat back trying to stay cool.

"I will contact my government as soon as I return to my office," Grew finally said, breaking the silence. "I will give my warmest endorsement to your prime minister's proposal. I think you know me well enough to know that I have a deep love and respect for your country. War between us would be the most horrible of tragedies. The reasoning of good men must prevail, and I will try my best to see that this meeting takes place. But I must also know clearly from you. Is your nation, even now, planning hostile action against us?"

Teijiro fixed Grew with a stare.

"I know of no such plans," he said.

There was a long moment, both looking at each other, neither breaking eye contact, both looking for the subtle clues, the slight shift of eyes, like two poker players both wondering just how far they could bluff.

"Then let us hope that the good intentions of honest men prevail, otherwise I fear for the lives of millions of young men, both yours and mine," Grew said.

And in his heart he knew. Teijiro was indeed bluffing. His intention was honest, to see that the meeting of leaders might just take place, but even now they were preparing, planning, getting ready, a madness stretching back years, of a few who sought war, and so many good men afraid to defy and stop them, or if need be to stand up to them in force, and now the price could indeed be a terrible one to pay.

CHAPTER NINE

Tokyo
5 September 1941

It was his second time before the Imperial Presence in as many hours and weary with exhaustion and nervousness Prince Konoye waited outside the doorway of the audience chamber. Beside him were the chiefs of staff of the army and navy, General Sugiyama and Admiral Nagano.

Nothing was said between them.

The liaison conference of two days before had turned into an utter fiasco as far as Konoye was concerned. It had all come down to a fundamental point. The army was not willing to openly concede to the American requirements to cease expansion, to withdraw from Indochina, and then China . . . and even if then the oil would flow again. The argument Sugiyama had shouted back was that now the clock was ticking, with every day of delay, another fifty thousand barrels of their precious reserves were consumed. All the Americans needed do was sit back and drag out negotiations for six months, a year, until the reserves were dry, and the Japanese army was reduced to a medieval force on foot, the navy reduced to sails.

It was now time to present before the Emperor the alternatives: and though Konoye had always felt a closeness, even an informality when before the Emperor, today he did not.

As the door opened the Emperor was already waiting, and at their entry all three bowed low, he barely acknowledging their entry with a mere nod of the head. There was no need for Konoye to reiterate what he had explained to the Emperor but two hours earlier, an explanation that had resulted in a near angry dismissal for him to fetch back the chiefs of staff. Negotiations had borne no fruit. His effort to meet with President Roosevelt had so far failed, that therefore left but one alternative.

Konoye could feel the Emperor's eyes on him, even as he bowed yet again then slowly came back up, their gazes locking for a second before Konoye looked down at the polished marble floor.

"You came to me to speak of diplomacy,"

the Emperor began, a most unusual move for him to open a meeting thus; normally if there were questions the Privy Council would offer them.

"And yet you spoke of war as if you had already agreed to it," he continued.

Face reddening, Konoye looked back up at his Emperor. He could see the frustration and confusion in the young man's eyes.

"Has it truly come to this?"

"I fear so, sire," was all Konoye could say in reply, and then he looked over at Sugiyama who stood unmoving, erect, eyes straight ahead.

The Emperor was silent for a moment, then nodded toward Sugiyama.

"I want to hear this from my chiefs of staff," the Emperor said coolly, coldly. "For months I have been told that diplomacy was the path all of you sought, the army, the navy, my foreign service. And now this? That war is the only alternative?"

"With your permission, my lord?" Sugiyama asked.

There was merely a nod of reply.

"The response of the Americans is an insult we can no longer bear. It is a maneuver on their part to reduce us to a third-rate power, impotent in a world that even as we speak is being reshaped by war. If Japan does not act now, we shall be left behind forever. We would appear impotent, humiliated in the eyes of Germany, which even now is moving toward its ultimate victory and domination of the Western landmasses of Asia, while America tricks us into abandoning what we have so valiantly tried to gain for our own security in the East."

"And yet is there no harm in waiting but a bit longer?" Hirohito asked. "I have been told repeatedly that you, your staffs, have set a date of October 10, others say 15, as the day of decision to war or peace. That is still a month away."

"Sire," Nagano interjected, when Sugiyama did not immediately reply. "Yes, we said that would be the day of decision, but we must prepare now for that decision."

"This would then be the day of decision," Hirohito said quietly, "not October."

"Sire, it is evident that the Americans wish to play a fools' game upon us, to drag out negotiations, to pile demand upon demand, and thus wear us down. The moment is upon us, the moment when we can achieve the destiny of Japan and take our proper place in the world."

"And you believe we can win?"

"We have studied the problem for months," Sugiyama replied, "the southern operation has been thoroughly evaluated, repeatedly tested in war games. It is ready."

He fell silent for a moment as if offering the Emperor the polite opportunity to reply, but Hirohito merely nodded.

"The operation will open with forces landing along the Malay Peninsula, moving south rapidly to envelope Singapore by land, a move the British are not prepared for. At the same time air strikes will cripple the American air fleet based around Manila, and any ships based there, followed immediately by landings along the north coast of Luzon, to move south and take the Americans, again, by land. With those two key positions under siege, our fleet can then move unhindered into the South Seas to take the vast riches of the Dutch, especially their oil."

"How long?" Hirohito asked, "before the oil flows back to Japan, freeing us from our fears?"

"Five months, sire. Singapore and Manila will fall within six weeks. We must assume some sabotage on the part of the Dutch oil supply when they realize their oil fields are to be taken but we are prepared to rapidly repair that damage and begin shipments back to the home islands and to our forces in China."

"Are you sure only five months?"

"Yes, sire."

Hirohito sighed and sat back in his chair, slumping over slightly, breaking the rigid, erect stature he usually maintained. Konoye studied him closely, with shoulders hunched his awkward frame looked more like that of a boy filled with self-doubts than the living embodiment of the god he was supposed to be.

"The South Seas are vast," he said quietly.

"And we shall own them," Nagano replied forcefully.

"As vast as China," Hirohito replied, "and I recall, after the incident on the Marco Polo Bridge, the same assurances from my army, that though China was vast, it would all be ours in five months, before the end of the year."

He straightened his frame and looked at the three.

"That promise was given to me over four years ago. A million of our young men now fight in China, a hundred thousand have died, and still half of that vast land resists us."

Nagano looked over at Sugiyama, saying nothing. China was the army's battle, not the navy's.

"Sire. The unforeseen happened as it

always does in war."

"And the unforeseen can happen yet again, can it not?"

"Sire. No one could have foreseen that the Communists and the Nationalists would form a truce. No one could foresee the rash interventionist attitude of the Americans, British, and even Russians smuggling supplies in to sustain that fight. If the Nationalists had shown even the remotest of logic, they would have finally rallied to our side in a fight to destroy the Communists, and thereby gained in us a friend."

"And why do they not see us as their friend?" Hirohito asked sharply.

"They are irrational."

"I would think, given the rumors I have heard, that they have reason to be irrational regarding our good intentions," the Emperor replied sharply.

There was an intaking of breath by Sugiyama and no one spoke. The Emperor knew of what happened in Nanking and other cities across China, the entire world knew and though there was the tacit understanding it would never be spoken of directly in front of the Imperial presence, it was now clearly on his mind.

"I would expect better of our men, the tradition of the samurai is one of chivalry.

What shall happen if that is not displayed when we move to free the peoples of the Philippines and the East Indies of their Western occupiers? What then?"

"Sire, the army has always fought by the code of the samurai and will do so in the future," Sugiyama replied, and there was the slight edge of defiance in his voice.

"I expect nothing less," Hirohito retorted. "But you have not answered my question of the moment. You promise five months, but war is never a matter of promises fulfilled, it is an arena of the unexpected."

"Sire, your grandfather faced the same question against the Russians thirty-seven years past. There was no absolute promise of victory. In fact, the odds were higher against us then as compared to now."

Konoye looked sidelong at Sugiyama. Was there a veiled insult there, a statement that the Emperor lacked the fortitude of his illustrious grandfather?

Hirohito did not respond.

"I can promise you, sire, that in five months all that we seek in the South Seas will be ours and then our position impregnable."

"Your Majesty," Nagano interjected. "We are like the patient that has been found to have a cancer. The situation is grave the doctors will tell us, but if we operate now, immediately the odds are good that the cancer will be removed and our life saved. That cancer is the ever daily growing of the strength of other powers in the world at our expense. The economy of America booms because of the war. Even Great Britain holds out, and marshals new strength. We, however, with each passing day will grow more vulnerable. Operate now and we survive, delay but a little while longer and the chance will be gone forever."

"The Americans, and what of them?" the Emperor asked. "You have focused on the South Seas. What they have in the Philippines is of little real consequence to them. A mere extension of a finger with no worth. Their strength is coiled and waiting elsewhere."

Nagano nodded.

"Sire, the opening blow will destroy that. Once destroyed it will take a half year or more for them to marshal a response, and by then, as General Sugiyama has pointed out, all that we need for a prolonged struggle, if need be, will already be flowing to our factories here in Japan and Manchuria."

"A prolonged fight then, is that what you promise?"

The two military men looked at Konoye, who remained silent for a moment, then finally raised his head to speak.

"According to the plans to which the army and navy have committed themselves to, the total destruction of all major American forces in the Pacific will be achieved in the first days. If they venture a retaliation strike it will take half a year or more. In that interval two new carriers will join the fleet. A thousand more planes and their pilots will be ready for battle, with all the fuel needed. A second battle will go as the first, the same as with the Russians at Tsushima. Defeated thus a second time, the Americans will see the inevitable. The negotiations that are now stalled will always be waiting and known to them through contacts in neutral countries. We shall then offer honorable terms to them, that if they simply accept our position in the western Pacific there will be peace. It is that simple."

"The difference between the position of my grandfather and I myself is this," the Emperor replied, his gaze fixed upon Sugiyama, obviously the veiled insult not forgotten.

"The plan of my grandfather was adroit. The illustrious Admiral Togo promised him victory at sea, our ships were known to be superior to those of the Russians in armaments, training, speed, and gunnery. But on land, if sufficiently aroused, the Russians could drag the war on for years. The adroitness was his knowledge of the Americans and the vanity of their president Roosevelt. So even before the war had started, this first of the Roosevelts was cultivated and once war started already approached to act as a negotiator to the unpleasant crisis that had suddenly appeared. And he played his role and negotiated a peace after we had defeated the Russians at sea, but before they could overwhelm us with their endless supply of men.

"I will concur with the opinion of some that we conceded far too much to this Roosevelt to gain that peace, but nevertheless most of our goals and position was thus established and with it respect for Japan as a nation among equals."

"But our goal was achieved. Your plan is predicated upon an eventual negotiated settlement with the Americans. I see no reference to that here now. Who will negotiate? Who will be the facilitator between us and the Americans and British? Surely not Russia, nor Germany?"

"Sire, that is why I argue that we still pursue the diplomatic up until the actual moment of battle," Konoye replied forcefully. "If war then does come, we can present to the world the argument that negotiations have broken down for the moment, and we are willing at any time to return to the table and seek a just and honorable peace." Hirohito nodded in agreement.

"You have traveled extensively there," the Emperor said, "I have not. Will they accept such an offer after we attack?"

Konoye hesitated. And knew that here was the central core of the issue of war and peace with America.

They, the Americans, were different; they saw the world in a different light. They wished to believe, they actually did believe, that they could represent some higher order of things in this world. War to them was not a norm, a continuum of an eternal struggle for survival in this world; it was an aberration to be avoided. They had stayed out of the last war until nearly the bitter end, and thus paid but a fraction of the price in blood and treasure as result, in fact had emerged in a way as the ultimate victor.

Even now though their president was all but engaged in an undeclared war in the Atlantic against the Germans, still the vast majority of Americans were vocal about their desire to stay out of any war, no matter where, unless it came directly to their shores. Would they perceive an attack upon their fleet as such a violation, to be answered with vengeance, or would they still remain detached, fight halfheartedly for a while, then be swayed back to the negotiating table with words of peace.

There would be no persuasive third power to be the negotiator as the first Roosevelt had been between us and the Russians, Konoye realized.

Would they be willing to talk at all or would they finally bestir themselves and, if so, that was truly to be feared. Nagano could speak proudly of the two new carriers about to be launched and the two mighty battleships all but completed, their eighteen-inch guns the greatest ever put to sea. And yet there were ironies. To conceal the building site of the battleships a vast screen had been erected around the harbor, made out of bamboo, canvas, and rope. Merely to build that had stripped all of Japan of rope and canvas for months. America? America could build a dozen such ships and it would be but a drop in the bucket for them as far as national effort went, and there would be no absurdity of a rope shortage as a result. Even now, their naval liaison in Washington was reporting that the Americans planned to construct another dozen carriers, launching one a month starting late next year, ships far more modern and capable then *Akagi,* and *Kaga,* the current backbone of the Imperial Fleet.

If whatever they start on moved yet faster on that path, he realized, what then could he say to the Emperor seated before him.

"Sire, I suggest we continue negotiations right up to the day of attack, if indeed such attack should prove necessary. It can still bear fruit as I have said, if not, it can still leave the door open afterward for a settlement honorable to both sides." He regretted it even as he said it. He had not said clearly enough the third consideration . . . that perhaps the Americans might not want to negotiate once hostilities had started.

Hirohito slowly nodded and then reached into his breast pocket and drew out a crumpled sheet of paper, taking a moment to flatten it out on his knee before holding it up close to his eyes so he could read.

"All the seas, everywhere,
Are brothers, one to another
Why then do the winds and waves of strife
Rage so violently through the world?"

Konoye immediately recognized the poem. It was by the Emperor's grandfather, the Emperor Meiji.

No one spoke, awed by the strange gesture.

"From time to time I remember that poem," the Emperor said, "reminding myself of my grandfather's desire for peace even as war approached."

The three stood silent.

"I still prefer the path of peace," Sugiyama announced, "even as I prepare for war."

"As do I," Nagano chimed in.

Konoye looked back and forth at the two, unable to conceal his amazement. They had agreed, even as they disagreed and at that moment Konoye could see all so clearly what was about to happen . . . and it did.

"Can you assure me of victory if diplomacy fails?" the Emperor asked yet again.

The two military men gave sharp nods of assertion.

"Then, if such is the case, diplomacy shall continue. If by October 15 the Americans have not accepted more direct and meaningful offers of settlement, you are released to fulfill you duties as men of war."

The Emperor now looked directly at Konoye and nothing more needed to be said.

There would be meetings and more meetings, but the decision had just been reached. It was not done with the sharp drawing of a sword to then be held high. It was couched in terms that spoke of peace and regret of strife and yet led to the same conclusion. There was a nod of dismissal, and the three left the audience room; as the privy seal closed the door behind them, the general and admiral both exhaled noisily, looked at each other, and nodded.

"It is done," Sugiyama whispered.

"There is still time though," Konoye replied, "you heard that clearly as well."

Nagano smiled and shook his head. "Do you honestly think talk will change anything now? The Americans have refused to meet you, their ignominious demands to humiliate us we have refused. Your continuing to talk is meaningless, sir."

"Are you saying my position is meaningless?" Konoye snapped back angrily.

Sugiyama stepped between the two, but it was obvious he was now standing beside Nagano and not trying to intervene.

"If your talk succeeded today with the Americans, what then? Do you honestly think I could go back to my comrades fighting in China and tell them that four years of blood and sacrifice were for naught? That we should retire with heads bowed low in abject apology and abandon China to the brigands and Communists? Never!"

He snapped the last word out loudly, so loudly that Konoye looked back nervously to the door of the audience chamber.

"And if you asked that of us, do you honestly think you would survive or I would survive for long?"

"Do not forget February," Nagano whispered.

"Is that a threat?" Konoye replied.

"No, just a statement of reality," Sugiyama retorted. "The army, as an act of honor, would rebel if so asked, rebel to save the honor of Japan and the Emperor himself."

Konoye looked one to the other and saw the openness of it now. A coup by a deranged group of young radicals had indeed created what they had desired. Though denounced by the leaders of the army and navy, it had given them ever-increasing power, the threat always in the background. From that day forward, with their platitudes about national destiny and honor, it was they who had come to dictate power. Creating the paradox of a war in China they claimed they did not seek, and now by extension, a war with Britain and America. To withdraw backward was impossible.

He could see now that his days were numbered. It would be Tojo and the army who would now openly lead the nation. If negotiations suddenly did break open and the Americans came to the table, willing to make concessions, he would be assassinated before he could ever get to that table. If he stayed, he would be the prime minister that would lead Japan into a war not of his design. Assassinated or forced to resign, that would be the next step and he could see so clearly, waiting in the wings, it would be either Sugiyama or the minister of war in his own cabinet, Lieutenant General Hideki Tojo.

CHAPTER TEN

Combined Fleet Headquarters
3 October 1941

Standing to greet the two, Admiral Yamamoto waited for them to begin, half suspecting the reason behind their "urgent need to talk."

After the usual greetings it was Captain Kusaka, chief of staff for Nagumo, who came straight to the point.

"Sir, we feel so deeply opposed to the Hawaiian attack that we have brought a letter stating our joint opposition. We simply think it is wrong and very likely to fail in a manner disastrous to Japan," Kusaka held out an official document.

Yamamoto took the letter and read it slowly and carefully. Once or twice he stopped and looked at one section or another. Once he went back and reread a section.

"I appreciate your courage and your

professionalism in handling this in such a thoughtful manner," Yamamoto indicated the letter, which he had placed on the table between them. "I take very seriously your concerns, and I agree with you that this is a real risk. However, let me ask you a few questions.

"If we follow the advice of those who want us to focus the fleet on the south what happens to Tokyo if the unharmed American Fleet decides to come here? We have a plan to sail from Japan to Hawaii. What if they have a plan to sail from Hawaii to Japan?

"Much of Tokyo is paper and wood. Ask Commander Genda what he saw in Britain of the German bombing campaign. Their homes tended to be brick and stone and still they were destroyed. Can you imagine what would happen to Tokyo or any of our great cities if our wooden and paper structures were bombed?

"Are you prepared to tell the Emperor that we will go chasing the Dutch and the British in the south, but the Americans might soon have carrier aircraft flying over the Imperial Palace? But he should not worry?"

Neither could reply as he invoked the name of the Emperor.

"Gentlemen, I am deeply opposed to fighting America. I have great respect for the power and the determination of the Americans. If they have the capacity to hit us, they will take great risks to do so. If we are forced to fight them, I want to limit their capacity so decisively that it affects their will. Otherwise we will inevitably be defeated by their industrial capacity. You are both right. This is a daring and dangerous plan. Other plans would have fewer tactical risks.

"However, this is the only plan. I repeat, the only plan that gives Japan a chance to win the war.

"If you decide you cannot implement this plan with full enthusiasm I suggest you ask for a transfer, and I will ensure it is granted today."

Neither spoke in reply and with a curt wave, he indicated their dismissal.

He settled back behind his desk. Such a strange evening. If victory is achieved, the letter would be forgotten of course and all would be eager for reward. If failure resulted, then they had their cover, their proof . . . damn them.

Hiroshima Bay
15 October 1941

Heart pounding, commander Fuchida pulled back on the stick of his Zero, feeding in right rudder and then stick over, turning into a sharp banking circle directly above the Kate torpedo bombers.

Formation was excellent, perfect after the relentless drilling of the last two months.

He did not need to give the command, it was instinct now, the first torpedo dropped away, two seconds later the next, then the third, fourth, and fifth.

He held his breath, waiting.

Yes!

He could not contain a shout of triumph, radio switched on, all hearing it, both crews on the planes and on the deck of the *Akagi*!

It had worked. One after another the five torpedoes surfaced in the shallow thirty-five feet of water, high-pressure oxygen-powered turbine engines running true, foaming wake visible . . . and at each point of impact a spreading wake with four simple slabs of wood bobbing on the gentle waves of the harbor.

It had been so simple, the British having invented it a year ago for their raid against the Italian fleet at Taranto. Strap breakaway

Akagi *(Japanese aircraft carrier, 1925–1942) at sea during the summer of 1941, with three Mitsubishi A6M "Zero" fighters parked forward. Donation of Kazutoshi Hando, 1970.* **Naval Historical Center**

wooden paddles fore and aft on each torpedo. Upon impact, the light wooden strips of bent lamented wood holding the paddles to the sides of the torpedoes would sheer off, having served their purpose, absorbing a fair part of the energy of the drop, acting as brake, thus slowing the descent of the torpedo as it then dived under the water, but now they would be going down only twenty-five to thirty feet before leveling out and then rising back up to the predetermined depth for their run into the target.

It meant they could launch torpedoes in the confines of a shallow bay . . . such as

411

Pearl Harbor. The target ship, an old destroyer, was steaming at ten knots, its starboard side draped with heavy matted padding. The ship steamed on, the crew aboard standing on deck, watching, the captain most likely more than a bit nervous, not sure of the promise of Genda and others as to what would happen next.

Four of the five torpedoes were running true, racing forward at nearly forty knots, the fifth one, apparently with rudder jammed, was sheering off into a left-turning circle. Troublesome, but still 80 percent were on target.

They closed in, the planes having dropped their loads, following proper evasion tactics, racing straight at the target destroyer, pulling up to barely clear the deck, roaring over the ship, dropping back down to near surface level then kicking into evasive turns to throw off antiaircraft fire. The Zeroes, assigned as escorts to keep off enemy fighters, flew higher and astern; mission done, they too broke away, swinging wide to avoid the destroyer but then ready to drop in behind the Kates they were assigned to protect.

The four wakes closed in on the target ship. The first one passed just astern, continuing on. The second . . . a hit! Followed two seconds later by the third torpedo

. . . another hit!

There was no explosion of course, just the bubbling wake converging on the destroyer slamming into the side.

For the men aboard the ship, it would be something of a shock. Half a ton of metal, racing at forty knots, even without an explosive warhead could punch through the thin skin of a destroyer but the heavy padding slung over the side took most of the blow, the torpedo shattering on impact.

Expensive, damn expensive, they could not be retrieved like standard training torpedoes but the test had to be done under real conditions and not just at a static target. The fourth torpedo passed fifty meters in front of the bow. Actually not a wasted shot for in a real situation the target would have been maneuvering violently, in the thirty-second interval between drop at six hundred meters and impact, enough time for a ship to start to turn, to speed up, bracketing fore and aft ensured it would not escape unscathed.

The old ship would most likely have to go back to dry dock after this, have plates below the waterline repaired, but it was worth it.

They had done it!

He could not resist the joy of throwing in

a touch of reverse rudder and then stick hard over into a victory roll, excited voices on the radio breaking silence, exclaiming over the triumph until Fuchida ordered them to silence.

Granted the radios were short-range plane-to-plane, but still, stranger things had happened with atmospheric skips, or perhaps an observer on land, listening in.

Akagi loomed straight ahead, several miles farther out to sea, steaming leisurely at fifteen knots, the Kates turning wide to go into landing formation, Fuchida announcing he was taking the lead, feeding in throttle, swinging out wide to the port side of the carrier steaming south, tip of his wing just barely obscuring the view of the ship as he raced down her length, three hundred meters above the ocean, clearing the aft end of the ship, counting to five, then banking over sharply. It was a little too sharply, but he could not resist showing off a bit.

Coming out of his 180-degree turn, the deck was lined up straight ahead.

He ran through the final checklist, switching to main fuel tank, checking oil pressure, temperature, air speed, throttling back, nose high to bleed off speed, leaning to one side of the cockpit for a better view past the engine cowling. Air speed dropping, plane sinking, no challenge bringing a fighter in to land on a carrier in the calm seas of Hiroshima Bay.

He cleared the threshold, ready to slam the throttle up if something went wrong at the last second, felt the arresting gear snag a cable, a point of pride that it was almost always the first one, and then lurching to a stop. The deck crew chief was standing to one side, arms raised and crossed as others pulled the cable free of the tail hook, signaling now to throttle up, taxi forward, and to the starboard side, clearing the path for the first of the Kates coming in. The safety barrier net was dropped to let him pass, raised up again, and then the signal to throttle down, cut magnetos, shut down.

The propeller whirled down to a stop, noise and vibration stopping, that strange instant of silence until one of the deck crew was up on the wing, helping to slide the canopy back.

The boy looked down at him, excited, helping him to unsnap his shoulder harness, offering a hand to stand up.

"Congratulations, sir!" the boy gasped, and Fuchida smiled, slapping him on the shoulder, and then stepping out of the cockpit, springing down to the deck, all around him gazing with admiration, stifling saluting, then closing in with shouts of laughter. Because of the highest level of security, only half a dozen men on the entire ship knew the truth of the mission they were training for, though speculation was rife and more than one, he had heard, had correctly guessed the target. To try and stop the rumors was impossible, to come down hard on those who had guessed right would draw attention, but the order was strict in one sense, not a word of anything they did or saw to be spoken while ashore. Secret military police would indeed trail some of them, and if they spilled anything, anywhere, it would be transfer to a discipline battalion in Manchukuo, or worse. Several had already suffered that fate, including one pilot who got drunk at a geisha house and boasted how he would sink an American carrier at Pearl Harbor. That man was going to spend the war, or at least until after the attack, in an isolation cell.

He stepped back around his Zero to watch the first of the Kates come in, less than a minute behind him. If this were a full combat rehearsal, it would be one plane every thirty seconds, but then again *Akagi* would be cruising at flank speed to ensure slow landing speeds for the planes. The cost in fuel even for half an hour was a major concern and thus this more leisurely approach.

The landing was perfect, as he expected.

"Congratulations!"

He looked over to the entry to the conning bridge. It was Genda!

He had no idea that his friend was aboard *Akagi,* and the two raced toward each other, both stopped for a second to go through the ritual of saluting, before embracing and slapping each other on the back.

"You did it!" Genda cried excitedly. "Two hits it's reported. The captain of that poor old tub already complaining he has to go back into port for repairs."

Fuchida grinned.

"Imagine what they would have done if loaded with explosives rather than sand."

Genda smiled and made a motion with his hands like a ship sinking.

"Even a battleship," Fuchida said quietly.

Genda's features stiffened for a moment then relaxed.

"Come below where we can talk more freely. I have some things to show you."

They entered the doorway onto the bridge, and Fuchida followed Genda down a flight of stairs, which emptied out into the vast cavernous hangar deck. Dozens of aircraft were lined up, Vals, Kates, Zeroes, still a few of the older M96s, more than one with mechanics and crews laboring over them, cowlings pulled off, inspection plates removed from wing and fuselage surfaces, every plane constantly being inspected and reinspected.

Everyone knew something was building, and the mere sight of the legendary Fuchida walking with Genda over to a side room guarded by marine sentries would of course set the whole deck to buzzing with speculation.

Genda pulled the door shut behind him and locked it. It was one of the briefing rooms, but the large table used for maps had been broken down and removed. An object a dozen feet square covered by canvas filled the middle of the room, another object, rounded, a couple of meters in length and as thick around as a barrel was to one side, the heavy dolly it was resting on barely concealed beneath. "I wanted you to see it first. Once our pilots start to study it, they will be confined to this ship until the operation ends. Just one look at it, and their liberty ashore is finished until the mission is completed."

"Including me?" Fuchida asked, with a grin, "I can already guess, at least, what is under one of those tarps."

Genda nodded and with no slight fanfare, gently started to roll the canvas cover back off the tablelike object filling the middle of the room. He motioned for Fuchida to help on the other side. One turn of the canvas back and he could see it was an exquisitely made scale model, hills painted green and water blue, a true work of craftsmanship.

The canvas was rolled back to reveal a model of Pearl Harbor, exact, Fuchida could see, in every detail.

Ever since he had been let in on the secret back in the spring by Genda, he had studied the photos and maps made available to him, but this was the first time he saw it thus so perfectly displayed.

There was Ford Island, the narrow sounds, miniature scale models of PBYs lining the tarmac of the naval air station on the island, and there, to the west of Ford Island, in what they were calling battleship row, the berths of the great battleships of the American Pacific Fleet, with three models representing the carriers *Enterprise, Lexington,* and *Saratoga* anchored to the north of the island.

"It is exact to the scale of how you will see it at three thousand meters above the base when the model is resting on the floor. Shortly, squadron leaders will be introduced to it, and then we begin to plot out attack routes. I think, already, that the only way for the torpedoes you tested to be launched correctly will require some remarkable flying. You will have to approach here, and he pointed out a narrow sound to the east of battleship row. Your torpedo bombers dropping down to fifty feet above the water and throttling back, perhaps bracketed by anti-aircraft fire from gun positions flanking that sound and the ships within them.

"Clear into the main sound, align, and drop. They will have less than ten seconds to acquire target and release; it will be no open approach by sea."

"No chance then for their battleship gunners to fire back."

Genda nodded.

"Let's hope so."

"My men are like racehorses," Fuchida announced. "They are training for a race, but they know not when or where. Delay too long, and they will be overtrained, anxious, and could make mistakes."

"We follow orders, remember?"

Fuchida nodded reluctantly, then seeing the "package" sitting in the corner of the room he gestured to it.

Genda grinned. "Thought you might want to see this, but before we do so, a question."

"Anything, sir."

"Your training of horizontal bombers. It is still not where I want it to be."

Fuchida nodded. "If I had limitless fuel and practice bombs, it would be where we both want it. Still, we are scoring 30 percent hits at 3,000 meters on targets 40 meters wide."

"I want 50 percent."

Fuchida nodded, taking it in, hesitated for a moment. "Can you release more fuel? If I could raise training flights from two to four a day, I think we could reach your goal in another month."

Genda nodded.

"Done."

That was forty thousand gallons of aviation gas a day, he thought. Absolutely profligate for the Japanese navy. If Genda could pull that off, then indeed he was a miracle worker.

"Deliver that, and I promise you the goal of 50 percent in thirty days."

"Fine, then," and Genda walked over to the long, bulky object and pulled the tarp back. Fuchida could not help but whistle with amazement and then squatted down to look more closely. "As you know," Genda said, "our current bombs are but 250 kilograms, a few 500 kilograms armor piercing. The decks of the battleships are all but proof against that. We could blow superstructure away, but to render a fatal blow . . ."

His voice trailed off.

"You are looking at the fatal blow."

Fuchida ran his hand along the long, tapered object, taller than a man, machine-milled to perfection, stabilizing fins aft, obviously welded on after the fact, the welding then polished down to mirror smoothness.

"You are looking at a sixteen-inch artillery shell. Weight, one thousand kilograms. Armor piercing."

"Dropped from an altitude of 2,500 meters, it will achieve a velocity of over 700 kilometers per hour in its fall to the target, enough for it to penetrate the armor of any American battleship afloat. Armed with a delayed fuse it will detonate after penetrating halfway through the ship. The destruction wrought will be nearly total."

"The weight, though," Fuchida interjected. "It exceeds by 250 kilograms the carrying capacity of the Kate."

"Every extra kilogram will be stripped out of the plane, armor, ammunition for the rear gunner will be minimal, we've already run some tests with dummy loads, and if our carriers are moving at flank speed into a 15-knot wind or higher, the plane should be able to get airborne. After thirty minutes of cruising with normal fuel consumption, the weight should balance out. It will require exceptional skill from our pilots, and they are to be trained for overweight takeoffs."

Fuchida nodded. It was a tough order, but could be done.

"We will have sixty of them ready by the time the operation commences. Nearly all will be carried by the first strike wave. I want you to train and organize the horizontal bomber force from your best pilots and bombardiers. These are the only such weapons we will have. They must be used to maximum effect. If you can give me 50 percent hits, that means thirty will strike the six to eight battleships in port, two to three for each target. That combined with the torpedoes will complete the task."

"A carrier though," Fuchida replied. "It will pierce right through the unarmored deck."

"And most likely go clean through, but then detonate underneath the ship on the harbor floor, the explosion breaking the back of the carrier."

"But not at sea."

"No, not at sea, so let us pray that their

three carriers are in port, for if so, one of these bombs will shatter it."

"When?" Fuchida asked, running his hand along the flank of the one-ton artillery shell.

Genda smiled.

"When we are ordered to, but I think that it will be soon, very soon."

Fuchida again ran his hand along the artillery shell that was now a bomb, then looked back at the model of Pearl Harbor. He knew it was not his place to say anything, but the issue had been boiling inside him for weeks, ever since he had learned of the glory of Genda's plan, the combining together of the smaller carrier units of two to each "fleet" into one combined fleet of six carriers for this mission. It was one crucial issue that had kept him up at nights thinking but to dare to speak it?

They had worked together for so long that Genda picked up on the cues, the look of hesitation, the way Fuchida's eyebrows would furrow, head lowered slightly. They had been friends for well over a decade and a half; and bonded as they were, in the air, where one could easily spot the other by the way he handled his plane, to staff meetings on the ground, the signals were clear.

"Out with it," Genda said.

"What?"

Genda put a reassuring hand on his shoulder.

Fuchida hesitated. "It is inappropriate for me to raise it."

Genda gestured to the model of Pearl Harbor. "If it in any way might influence the chances of our success there, it is your duty to tell me."

Fuchida sighed and lowered his head.

"Come on, my old friend."

He knew it was melodramatic, but he felt he had to. Leaving his friend's side he went to the door and pushed on the handle, the door was still latched.

Genda chuckled. "This must be serious."

"It is. And I have your promise that it is between us only. What I am to say could remove me from this mission if it is repeated."

Genda hesitated, his features now serious as well. "Out with it," and it was more an order now than a friendly request.

Fuchida walked back over to the table, hands resting on the edge of the model. "I have no confidence in our commander."

"What?" and there was a true note of shock in his voice.

Fuchida hesitated, then looked straight back at him.

"Out with it," and this time it was snapped

out as an order.

Fuchida nodded and sighed. "When you first approached me for this mission to test out the tactics, to do the minute planning, never have I been so honored by you, my friend, and with it, a realization of the honor given to me by my nation, to trust me with such a task. It is not my place to question at all the reasons of our superiors and, forgive me, my Emperor, to reach this conclusion. But their reasoning must be sound, and I know that the survival of Japan rests upon our shoulders."

Genda nodded. "But?"

"I was overjoyed when I learned, at last, that our carriers were not to be broken into smaller groups, merely to support the battleships, but instead to become a great independent strike force, a dream you and I have shared for years. But," and he hesitated, drawing in his breath. This was worse than anything he had ever ventured before. The incident in China, the fear of that moment, in a way trivial in comparison. If his friend followed what should be proper procedure after he spoke, he would be removed from this mission. "It is Admiral Nagumo."

Genda said nothing for a long moment. "Go on."

As he had once heard his English friend Stanford say, it was now "in for a penny, in for a pound."

"I do not think he is the right man to lead this strike."

"Why so?" Genda asked with a strange look on his face.

"We have both served with him in one capacity or another," Fuchida said, now at last finding strength in his voice. "At the War College we both found ourselves in opposition to him at times. He had never embraced carriers and air strike as the means of achieving ultimate victory, instead he has always viewed us merely as the auxiliary, the secondary attack, the harassment or raid until his beloved surface ships closed for the killing blow. His specialty is torpedo attacks, cruisers, and to a lesser extent submarines. I was therefore stunned when I learned he would be the operational commander of the strike force destined for this target."

As he spoke he pointed to the model of Pearl Harbor. "I fear, sir, that ultimately, in his heart, Admiral Nagumo will view our attack not as the killing blow on the first day of the war, but instead will see it as a spoiling raid, to set our opponent off balance for four to six months, and then the battle he dreams of, the great encounter with surface ships that will finally decide this war with America.

"No sir," and he felt emboldened. "Pearl Harbor must end the war, not start it. Admiral Nagumo will hesitate if things should turn against us, or if when we arrive the fleet is not there, but out to sea. He will turn back rather than press in, or do but a half measure."

He felt as if he had said far too much, and fell silent.

"If you wish to relieve me, sir, I will accept that fate without complaint, but I realize now, my duty to my country and my Emperor compelled me to voice my concerns."

Fuchida fell silent, looking straight at his friend, his superior, awaiting his fate now that he had spoken.

There was a long moment of silence. "You are dismissed," Genda said quietly, his voice barely a whisper.

Fuchida, feeling sick inside, knowing that he had crossed a line that he never should have attempted, came to attention and saluted, something he had not done with his friend in private for years.

Genda returned the salute, went over, unlocked the door, and motioned for him to leave.

And then, alone, Commander Genda returned to the table, lighting an American cigarette, and stared at the model, lost in thought.

Tokyo
Embassy of the United States
17 October 1941

The knock on the door stirred Ambassador Grew from his thoughts, and he called for Eugene Doorman, his young assistant and interpreter, to enter. Grew looked up from the newspaper that had been absorbing his attention, the English language *Japan Times & Advertiser.*

Lyrics of a song that had swept the airways in the last week had been translated and printed:

We will win, we must win
What of air-raid?
We know no defeat
Come to this land to be shot down.

Madness, the evidence clear enough of all that it portended. He looked up from the paper, knowing as well what Doorman was there for.

Gene stood in the open doorway, clutching an ornate silk-embroidered envelope, the kind that Prince Konoye was so fond of using in his correspondence. The letter was secured with a red wax seal, and as Gene placed it on the table he could see the elegant "To Ambassador Grew," written across the front, in English, in Konoye's spidery and well-practiced calligraphy. Fascinating, Grew thought, how the Japanese took such pride in their penmanship, be it their traditional calligraphy or in Western Latin lettering. The typewriter was changing that now for so many Americans, an art form of a more refined time being lost.

Not wishing to damage the envelope he took a pen knife out of his desk and worked the seal open, drawing out the letter.

"It was just delivered by one of Prince Konoye's staff," Doorman said.

The letter, in English, was brief, having both the formal style of diplomacy but also something of a personal aspect to it, for he and Grew had known each other for years, the one man Grew felt who could have successfully stayed the course of the military . . . and it was a letter regretting his acquisition to acceptance of the Emperor's call to form a new cabinet.

He read and reread the letter. Konoye's hope was that negotiations would still move forward as they had both so vigorously had worked to achieve. But it was evident what the portent was.

"I'll need to send a secured cable to Washington," Grew said wearily, putting the letter down. "It is only a matter of time now."

Akagi
18 October 1941

He was drunk, and the knowledge of that disgusted him. He usually could handle his liquor, something few of his countrymen could do when a bottle of Western liquor, in this case scotch, was placed before them. Over half the bottle was empty. Sitting on his bunk, he uncorked the deadly stuff and filled his teacup back up.

A bit sloppily he raised the cup in a toast to the two portraits on the wall of his tiny private cabin, the portraits of the Emperor and his commander in chief of the navy, Admiral Yamamoto.

"What do I do?" he said, not really aware that he was speaking out loud.

Fuchida had not said a word to anyone about his concerns since their conversation of the day before. And it had haunted him, for the deep-seated fear he carried was the same one, though he never would have dared to express it to a subordinate, even one as close to him as Fuchida. He knew his friend was right. For the strike force destined for Malaya or to the Philippines, if that was the case, then Admiral Nagumo would be well suited to the task.

He feared, in fact he knew, that at heart, Nagumo did not have the stomach for this mission. He still thought of carriers as fragile auxiliaries, nor was he a battleship man who, bullheaded, would forge straight in. His specialty was cruisers, destroyers, what some still considered to be the surface scouts of the fleet, a task that anyone with sense knew the airplane had long overtaken. To raid, thrust in sharp, but then to run away.

"Like a small dog," Genda muttered, "bite then run away."

But how do I tell the boss, my admiral, he wondered, looking at Yamamoto's portrait again.

"How do I tell you?"

To go before the Commander in Chief of the Navy, to tell him to his face that his choice of Nagumo was the wrong one. There would be only one recourse left open for the admiral, to remove him from the operation for insubordination. No one would dare, in this navy, to go not just over the head of their superior, but to go all the way to the top and say such a thing.

No one. It would mean the end of a career, beached just as the greatest naval war in history was about to unfold, one that he had personally helped to plan.

"No, I can't," he sighed, draining the teacup, then refilling it yet again, this time so that it overflowed and spilled on the deck. He didn't care, he was so drunk now that all he needed to remember was that a trash bucket was beside his bunk as he drained the cup and then fell back to try and get some sleep.

Tokyo
18 October 1941

The newly selected prime minister of Japan, General Hideki Tojo, with head lowered approached the steps of the Ise Shrine. The crowds that waited for him outside the gate had broken into thunderous applause at his arrival, the guard detail struggling to keep them back, to provide for him the quiet needed for the ceremony of this moment, where alone, he would enter the temple to kneel and pray, as custom demanded, to the Sun Goddess, guardian of Japan.

And yet even as he knelt he could not conceal his inner sense of pride, of fulfillment, how by the most remarkable of ironies he had risen through the ranks to that of war minister and then in the most ironic twist of all, had been called for by the Emperor, not as a prime minister of a nation now fully bent on war, but instead, as a military man who still just might be able to broker peace.

Even Konoye had reluctantly gone along with the choice. The logic of it was convoluted, as were nearly all decisions of this government. As a known war leader, who had advocated an aggressive stance, he could as prime minister still seek a negotiated peace, and if achieved, if negotiations actually yielded fruit that was not a humiliation to national pride, he could accept it without any real fear from the military extremists.

The Emperor had exacted from him a promise that he would continue to seek to try diplomacy even as they prepared for war. A paradoxical decision, for surely as they prepared for war and the evidence of that became clear, the Americans and British would surely see the signs and prepare as well, further accelerating his own officers' demands to end the farce and move to the killing blow.

How strange it all was, as he bowed low, alone in the ornate temple, even the monks and priests having withdrawn to give him privacy. He had sworn eternal obedience to the Emperor, the Emperor still desired peace, asking for a rescinding of the decision of the previous month that the middle of October would end any attempt of real negotiation.

And yet, he knew that as of this day, war was inevitable, that the time to fulfill the destiny of Japan had come.

Flagship of the Imperial Fleet
Battleship Nagato
19 October 1941

Standing stiffly at attention Commander Genda stood in the doorway, heart racing. Admiral Yamamoto returned his salute and motioned for him to come in. But Genda could not bring himself to sit. In their long months of planning for the campaign, especially after the man seated before him said it was no longer just a theory now, or a possibility, but that the Emperor had approved, they had worked together closely

435

and in some ways there was almost a father-to-son relationship between the two. He would, without even a flicker of hesitation, die defending this man.

The fact that he did not sit down was signal enough that something important was to be discussed.

The admiral, who had been studying a report on deployment of auxiliary and fleet oilers for the fleet through the first sixty days of the campaign, looked up. The report was bad enough, the consumption in relationship to reserves would be prodigious, draining off well over a quarter of all their reserves.

"What is it?" the admiral asked, looking up, and feeling under his gaze, Genda felt his stomach tighten, a bit of nausea hitting him. He wondered in that instant if he was still, in fact, a bit drunk from his binge of the night before.

"Sir . . . ," his voice trailed off, unable to speak.

Yamamoto glared at him for a moment and then his features softened ever so slightly. "You look like hell. Have you been drinking?"

"Yes sir." There was of course, no sense in lying. He knew the man before him was a hard drinker himself at times and could easily detect it in others. In his infamous poker games, when the stakes were high and he was the host, he was more than liberal with the saki for his guests, and all knew the ploy.

"I can smell it from here," Yamamoto announced, leaning forward as if to sniff the air, then sitting back, now a trace of a smile.

The smile cut into Genda and gave him courage.

But still the words could not form. "Well, have you come over here, just to report yourself half drunk? If so, I have more important things to attend to," and he gestured back to the report.

"No sir."

"Well then, out with it."

Genda took a deep breath, and then felt it best not to exhale swiftly.

He had indeed gotten sick during the night, and was fighting a terrible hangover now. But it was those facts which, in the raw light of dawn, had actually given him courage. The fact that he had tried to bury his fears with liquor, rather than face them head-on, had forced the realization of where his duty did indeed rest. For what he had done was the act of a coward trying to hide, not that of a man who had sworn an oath to the Emperor. He had given his all to the planning of the attack; to do anything less was a dereliction of duty. If I am willing to die for the Emperor, then I must now be willing to destroy my career as well. If by some remote chance, it changed the odds, if it saved but one more pilot, or perhaps even meant the death of more pilots, but in so doing ensured a final victory.

I watched the Germans make their mistake and shook my head, he realized. I cannot shake my head now, I must act, for I do now believe that the fate of our nation might rest on this.

"Sir, may I speak freely," he finally said, nervously clearing his throat first.

"Of course, damn it," the admiral replied, and Genda could see that his hesitation was now starting to annoy him.

"Sir," he took in another deep breath, "I do not want to be impertinent or to be out of place, but I feel I have to insist that you personally lead the attack on Pearl Harbor."

Yamamoto was actually starting to look back down at the report, as if Genda would make some minor statement, he'd nod agreement, and then go back to work. Startled, he looked back up. "Did I just hear you correctly?"

Genda nodded. "Sir, I believe you should personally lead the attack on Pearl Harbor," Genda said, repeating his words.

There was a moment of stunned silence. Yamamoto then put down the pen he was using to make notations on the report and now it was his poker gaze, unflinching, almost serpentlike in its coldness.

"Do you realize what you are saying? Are you questioning my judgment?"

"Yes sir. I do. No sir, but —"

"I would advise you to leave here now, report yourself to the infirmary as drunk, and that will be the extent of the action I would be forced to take against you." He ever so slightly shook his head.

"I am sorry, sir. Please do not construe my refusal as being impolite. I am perfectly sober."

"In essence, you have just told me that you do not have confidence in your commander, Admiral Nagumo, nor confidence in my choice of him to command the mission."

"No sir, I did not say that," Genda replied, glad now that he had spent some time dwelling on this moment, and the responses he had to give in order not to be ejected and relieved of command, to stay in the fight as long as possible.

"Sir. I have said nothing regarding Admiral Nagumo; he is your choice for the strike force, and it is not my place nor position to question his ability."

A lie to be certain. He questioned every-thing about Nagumo the more he thought on the subject.

The admiral stood up, chair sliding back noisily, and he came around from behind his desk. His approach seemed overwhelm-ing, his presence powerful. "Explain then, and no foolery with words. Your intent is clear enough."

"Sir," and at that moment he knew that this was as much a battle as any he had ever trained to engage in, but ultimately far more important. With that thought he actually felt a calmness take hold, and he was able to hold Yamamoto's gaze unflinchingly.

"I will cite but two historical examples to you. At Trafalgar, Lord Nelson was at the front of the fray and paid for it with his life; but his presence at that moment, the cour-age of his decision when the wind all but failed, and he ordered his line to go straight in, ensured a victory for England that day, and with that victory more than a hundred years of domination of the seas."

Yamamoto nodded slightly, but did not reply.

"Our own greatest hero was at Tsushima. And dare I ask, sir, was the presence of Admiral Togo not an inspiration to you? You fought in that battle and bear the honorable wounds of that fight. What did he mean to you?"

"He was an inspiration to all of us," Yamamoto snapped, but Genda could sense in that reply an agreement.

"I therefore rest my case, sir. You are our Togo, sir. Of the main missions to be carried out on the first day of the war, I believe that Pearl Harbor will clearly be the most crucial. I therefore implore you to lead us from the front, sir. It will be an inspiration to every man of the fleet to know that you are on the front line of battle with them and will in turn inspire all of Japan."

He fell silent, there was a moment's hesitation, the poker gaze seemed to flicker ever so slightly. "You are, by implication, saying that Admiral Nagumo is not competent to command."

"Sir, I must forcefully reply, I have not said that. It is just, sir, that given modern communications, your flagship need not remain here in Japan. Once the campaign is launched on all fronts, your direct intervention is finished, you leave to your commanders at sea the decisions we have planned upon for months on other fronts. That therefore frees you to directly lead the attack on Pearl Harbor.

"You have been the key visionary regarding the use of aircraft carriers for our fleet, sir. It is you who was the first admiral to agree to reconsider our war plans not to be on the defensive against the Americans and instead taking the aggressive route of neutralizing their fleet, especially their carriers, in the opening strike.

"Sir, in the battle soon to take place at Pearl Harbor, a new age of warfare will be introduced, the same as it was at Tsushima, where wireless telegraphy and modern fire control were used for the first time by Admiral Togo and granted us a victory as great as Nelson's. Your presence at Pearl Harbor will ensure that all is done as you have planned for, and if contingencies change, you will be on the spot to address them directly."

"Ah, see, you are saying Nagumo is not capable of making those decisions."

He had not expected that sharp a reply but he was ready. "Sir, Admiral Togo laid down the plan to meet the Russians; when he had the Z flag hoisted each ship's captain knew his duty. It was then merely his presence that instilled greater discipline, the spirit of bushido, complete and total confidence in victory. Every pilot, of all my groups, looks to you as their direct leader.

Your mere presence on the bridge of *Akagi* will fill them with even greater desire to strike for victory.

"Sir, this will be your battle. I implore you. You are the one to lead it; no other man alive can lead it as you can. This will be the one and only chance we shall have to deal such a crippling blow that the Americans will be forced to sue for peace. If we do not completely destroy them on the first day of the campaign, then, sir, we shall be in for a long and bloody war. Your presence can change that."

He fell silent, and then as a gesture of submission, lowered his head. "If I have spoken out of turn, sir; if I have insulted you, or the honor of Admiral Nagumo, I shall accept without complaint your punishment, whatever it might be."

There was a long moment of silence. "Look at me."

He lifted his gaze. Again, it was impossible to read the man before him. "You have a touch of the ronin in you," Yamamoto said, and there was an ever so slight easing of the tension. "You actually came in here, expecting me to dismiss you from command for what you just said."

"Yes sir, if need be, but I felt the fate of our nation might rest on what I have just said to you. I can stand here and implore you yet more, but I have spoken what I came to say. You may call it *gekokujo,* but I did it for you, and for the Emperor, sir, and for Japan."

Again the long silence and then the slightest of nods.

"You are dismissed. Return to your duties. For the moment I will say nothing of this nor will you. Now leave."

Genda came to attention and saluted, but the admiral had turned his back and walked back to his desk. Yet still he remained until Yamamoto looked up, half raised his hand in salute, and then sat down, picking up the report he had been studying.

Genda turned, left the room, sought the nearest head, slammed the door shut behind himself, thankful that no one else was within, and vomited.

Alone in his cabin, Admiral Yamamoto picked up the report, but no longer was reading it. His thoughts back at Tsushima, the opening moment of the battle as he absently rubbed the stumps of his two missing fingers of his left hand.

That had indeed been the moment, knowing that it was Togo himself in the middle of the fight, personally ordering the deployment of the fleet, so confident were his men in his genius that none doubted the victory that was to come; and in war, such confidence, when played correctly, can indeed be the deciding factor.

Though he hated to admit it to himself, young Genda had touched upon his vanity. The greatest mass carrier battle in history, in fact, the first true carrier battle, and his name would be forever attached to it. Yes, his name would still be attached if he was here, back in the Inland Sea. But out there? Of all his various subcommanders he had no concerns about Nagumo's courage or competence . . . but did he truly understand? His elaborate plan for the use of midget submarines struck him as incautious, only a bid by another branch of service to claim its role. They were vulnerable, could be discovered beforehand, perhaps provide warning. But Nagumo insisted upon it, saying they would block the harbor of any ships attempting to escape.

Exactly what would be his role now on the first day? He remembered the story of the American Civil War. He had visited some of their fields of battle. In the last year Grant had achieved overall command, though he had stayed with the main army, that of the one before Washington and

Richmond, even as he directed actions by commanders a thousand miles away.

What is my role, he wondered, once the day comes and battle is joined? To sit in this room and just listen as the reports come in? Or do I lead from the front, as the true warlords of old always did.

He opened his desk drawer. The letter from Nagumo's chief of staff, and therefore by clear implication from Nagumo himself, was still there, voicing grave concerns about the risks of the attack, but no grasp of the potentials to be gained. Defensive rather than offensive thinking. Back at Etajima, Nagumo as a cadet most likely guarded the pole rather than led the headlong attack.

He read, and reread the letter, folded it up, and placed it back in his desk, took out a sheet of paper and with his famed style of calligraphy, began to write out a formal note.

CHAPTER ELEVEN

London
30 October 1941

The distant thump, that one he could feel in the soles of his feet, caused him to look up. Winston did not even notice. Settled back in his thick leather lounge chair, a scotch in one hand, cigar in the other.

The chair was the one luxury of the room, which was painted a dull institutional green. Studies had shown that was the best color for those doomed to live perhaps for days, even weeks underground. It was a tiny alcove, room for the chair, a cot to sleep on, a small side cabinet filled with the required scotch and cigars, a desk, and the straight-back chair that he now sat on.

Another thump, this one closer, and Winston chuckled at Cecil's obvious discomfort.

"A mile or more off, just a nuisance raid, keeps us on our toes; you should have been here this time last year."

Winston chuckled and pointed up to the ceiling, a crisscross of pipes and wires lacing back and forth.

"My engineers didn't tell me until later that a good drop down some ventilation shafts would have blown us all to hell. This bunker is nowhere near as safe as most believe. I wonder if Hitler has the same design problems. Would love to know that," and he grinned.

He looked at his drink and swirled it in its glass before taking another sip.

"Now Stalin, rumor is he has one a hundred feet deep under the Kremlin. Heaven knows he might need it or just simply get out if the weather turns back to Hitler's favor and the ground freezes."

Winston looked off.

"He could still collapse, you know. Oh, he talks a great game of reserves, and of course his demands for supplies and yet more supplies from us and the Americans, but all that is saving him now is mud. Freeze tomorrow, and I dare say they'll be in Moscow in a fortnight."

Another thump rattled the room.

"Six months after that, and the Luftwaffe will be back with a thousand planes a night."

Cecil was still in shock from his ride down from Biggin Hill. It had been his first time back to England since leaving at Winston's behest nearly five years ago. Entire blocks of once familiar landscapes had been turned to rubble. Though exhausted after a week of flying across the Pacific, the United States, and then on back to here, he had sat erect throughout the last hour of drive to this concealed command bunker. A day and a half ago he had been in New York City, its port crammed with shipping, streets bustling with renewed traffic after the long Depression, but here, it truly was back into a war zone. Not as bad as Nanking, but shocking none the less, a different kind of destruction because this was once home . . . and his own flat had been one of the victims just off from Paddington Station, a direct hit he had been told, the tenant an old friend from school days, engaged in some hush-hush job like himself, never found in the blown-out wreckage.

Well, if one had to go, better that then all the horrors he had seen in China and had just finished telling Winston about.

"If Stalin should indeed fall," Winston mused, "it could still change the complexion of what we must assume Japan is preparing for."

"Going north, even in winter?"

"The temptation for their army would be

too much, even now. Most certainly the Soviets gave them a good and proper drubbing two years back and showed Japan its weakness in armor and aircraft. They have rectified the latter. I could see them delivering the stab in the back, the way Italy did to France last year, come in to scoop up what spoils they can once the real fighting is finished. That still might be possible."

Cecil did not reply. If Germany did topple Stalin and the Japanese then moved in from the east, what would that bode for England, for the world, a year hence? The full fury of the Nazis would be turned again upon this island and then all Japan need do is sit back awhile longer. England, in the end, would have to strip itself bare out of the Pacific, perhaps even India would then be in jeopardy.

Churchill smiled as he looked down into his drink.

"I've read your report though, my friend, and I dare say it is already too late. The die has been cast, and now we must wait to see what it produces." He had traveled nearly fifteen thousand miles to deliver but several dozen typewritten pages, feeling the information too sensitive to transmit, or even to hand off to the Americans to deliver. No, this was something he felt Winston had to see directly. It was his assessment that the Japanese would strike toward Singapore and the Dutch East Indies within the month, two months at the latest.

"Devilish bastards," Winston grumbled. "They think we are on the ropes. Now is when they will move."

"And Stalin and the Soviets?"

"Take Moscow now, the edge of winter," Churchill laughed softly, "you were the one who excelled even above me in history back at Harrow."

"Napoleon," Cecil replied. "Stalin will order the entire city burned if need be then retire back to Gorky or Kuibyshev to continue the fight. The Nazis will occupy a burned-out shell at the end of a thousand-mile supply line."

Churchill nodded in reply and offered to refill Cecil's drink. He refused, fearful he would fall asleep if he had but a few more ounces. Winston poured himself several fingers' worth in his glass and smiled.

"If it should come to that, in the spring Stalin and his cutthroats will drive out the starving bastards who are left. No, that old devil will never give up, unless there is finally a coup and a bastard as dark as him, Beria for example, murders him then takes his place, and then they will disintegrate into civil war. The army would love nothing more than to take down the NKVD. The same with the Wehrmacht I daresay when it comes to their SS and Gestapo. A complicated mess, but I doubt if it will come to that."

Cecil looked back down at his own drink, regretting he had not asked for more. After the long strain of the trip by American clipper plane, then a twenty-four-hour flight across the States, and then another day and a half to here, he could stand to get drunk, properly drunk.

The world was a madhouse and only America, in a perverse sort of way, seemed removed from it all. They were profiting, out of the doldrums of the Depression, thanks to the emptying of the British Treasury for arms. They were even mobilizing, halfheartedly, but still at every airport where the DC-3 he was traveling aboard stopped to refuel, he saw bustling activity, trainer aircraft by the scores, new barracks going up by the edge of airfields, at their stop in St. Louis, a score of their B-17s warming up for a training flight. But as for the rest of the country, it was still locked in an opium-like dream of peace. Just arm and sit back, waiting it out. Snatches of overheard conversations dwelt on new cars, the latest Western pic, the trivial going-ons of Hollywood celebrities, the casual talk of peace. Only on the flight from New York to Newfoundland, to Iceland and then London were the passengers somber, most of them obviously military men, dressed in civilian garb, tight-lipped other than the most casual of conversations, but then again he was tightlipped too, simply a reporter returning back home with little to say about all that he had seen. During the night someone reported a flickering glow to the south and all had gathered at the windows, gazing out across the black Atlantic and there was indeed, a pulsing fire in the distance that suddenly winked out.

"Tanker most likely," someone whispered, "sunk, poor bastards."

As they flew peacefully along through the night, he had been suddenly aware that directly below, at this very moment, U-boats were on the surface, charging their engines, prowling, hunting for their prey, perhaps a lookout hearing the drone of their distant engines, calling a warning as the darkened plane droned overhead and then passed on.

And now here, another shudder rumbling, this one closer, he could almost sense the overpressure of the bomb striking nearby. Winston did not even notice. "If they strike us before the new year," Winston finally said, "there is precious little we can do about it. The crisis is still on in North Africa, even though Rommel has been forced back. If Hitler does push to Moscow and does not overreach, it could free a dozen of his divisions to turn south, to overwhelm us and take the Suez come spring. We have nothing to spare for the Pacific; I fear we can barely hold in India. It will be an American fight."

"But suppose they don't directly strike the Americans," Cecil ventured. "They just hit us and the Dutch. Do you think President Roosevelt could rally the support necessary to enter the war?"

Churchill grumbled and shook his head.

"I doubt it. The isolationists will point at the map, how far distant it all is, how meaningless to American interests. Far better for us that a U-boat sinks one of their destroyers off the coast of New York City, but even then, there would be some screaming that Roosevelt and his Jewish friends had warmongered it."

Cecil looked at him, slightly shocked. "Oh yes, that propaganda line of the Nazis is heard by more than one in America. Filthy tripe all of it, but some hear it and repeat it. No, it will take a blow, a very hard blow to bestir them. Tell me, do you think the Japanese will hit the Americans as well?"

Cecil sat back in his chair, nursing the last few drops of his drink, and without prompting Winston uncorked the scotch and refilled his glass, and he now gladly accepted it.

"They will."

"Why so?"

"They cannot bypass the Philippines in their drive south. Second, the embargo of oil has become an issue of national pride. Finally, though some in the navy are indeed for peace, far more moderate than the army, there are others who believe one killing blow can shatter the Americans. It is a testing that some have itched for for nearly forty years."

"Two boys on the block and sooner or later they'll test each other's mettle, is that it?"

Cecil nodded.

"It is the weakness of the samurai way. I saw it when I taught at their academy. Their strange game of all offensive and precious little defense. Their thinking is to strike first, the single killing blow. You see it in their sword fighting versus ours. Our dueling is fencing, strike, counterstrike, maneuver, thrust, counterthrust to finally the kill. To the samurai, for one blade to even touch the other is considered a lessening of victory. The true victory is the serpentlike strike, lightning speed in the very first strike, so fast the opponent's blade falls to the ground, dead, before it has even touched the other blade or armor of his opponent. That is considered the true glorious victory. They believe it is their destiny; they will fight for that destiny in the manner in which they think. No, they will not attack us and leave the American threat to their flank and rear. I dare say the first blow will fall there because that is potentially the strongest opponent. We, I am ashamed to say, are seen as secondary."

"And where will they strike?"

"The Philippines obviously. I am not privy to the American war plans, but everyone can surmise them. Strike the Philippines, then wait for the American Fleet to sortie from Pearl Harbor. As it transitions, the Marshall Islands their ground-based planes, destroyers, and submarines will harry and weaken. Then once into the open seas beyond, the main battle fleet will come forth to finish the job. Then the Americans, defeated, sue for peace."

Churchill snorted derisively. "They don't know the Americans, if ever aroused. Lured into a fight or not, they sink a fleet and the

Americans will build another, just as the Romans did against Carthage."

"We know that, many on their side know it, but they will do it nevertheless."

Churchill nodded, taking the information in. "I'll talk to Roosevelt about it again tomorrow," he finally said. "Get some rest, go to number ten, they'll have a room for you there."

Cecil hesitated and Winston chuckled. "It's only been hit once and besides, those pesky flies overhead are just a nuisance raid. Keep us up, keep us on edge. You'll sleep like a baby. We'll talk more tomorrow, and then I want you to go back."

"Back, sir?" Cecil asked, unable to hide his dismay.

"But of course."

"Sir, may I speak frankly."

"By all means."

"I'm sick of it all. I've seen far too much. Whatever love and respect I once held for the Japanese died at Nanking and was buried deep in the four years since. I'm sick of the Orient, the brutality, the war, the blindness of more than one on our side out in Singapore who chortle and say all will be well, that the little yellow buggers wouldn't dare strike England."

He sighed.

"Couldn't I have a posting here for a while."

Winston smiled and laughed.

"But you're my expert out there now; my eyes and ears. Your report is damn good and damn smart of you as well to bring it direct. If you had mailed it, I fear other eyes might have read it first. I wanted your impressions directly, to hear your voice and all it implies as you speak. Take a few days to rest, then I want you back out there in Singapore. If the show is to start, I want someone outside the loop to report to me and you I trust."

Cecil sighed and wearily shook his head.

Winston looked at him coolly, as if examining him for some test.

Cecil wanted to tell his old Harrrovian schoolmate to bugger off, but he could not. He was not just Winston, he was the prime minister and even the closest of friends did not speak thus to the PM.

"Go on now, off to bed with you. We'll talk more tomorrow. Do this favor now, my friend, and then, well perhaps after the show starts that you predict, I might have other ideas for you. You're too old now to go running around in the middle of a war zone," he smiled, "but then again, this is a war zone."

Even as he said it, there was another

thump, this one fairly close. "On your way back there's an American I'd like you to talk freely with. Interesting chap named Donovan."

Cecil sat up at the mention of the name.

"Has a friend, Hollywood director. Remember that terrible movie about the Welsh that they lavished awards on this year? Such sentimental rubbish."

"You mean John Ford?"

"That's him. Like you to meet him as well on your way back, talk things over a bit. Maybe something there a bit farther down the road."

Now he was curious. A Wall Street lawyer, hero of the last war, now supposedly heading up some hush-hush operation, and a hard-drinking Irishman with little love of the English, who nevertheless made damn good films. What was Winston thinking of?

"Off with you now and get some rest. We'll talk more tomorrow before you catch your flight out."

Finishing up his drink, Cecil stood up, and a Royal Marine guard outside the door beckoned the way up the long flight of stairs to the outside. An antiaircraft gun lit off over in the small park in front of Parliament, a stream of tracers going up, the flashes illuminating the grounds. He paused to watch.

"Not much of a show tonight, sir," the sergeant announced cheerfully.

There was a flash across the river, a thundering explosion rolling over them several seconds later.

"Nothing at all, a miss is as good as a mile, sir."

The guard walked him up, through the blacked-out streets to Number 10 and handed him off to another guard who guided him into the residence of the PM. He knew he should be honored by this, few were granted the privilege of staying in Winston's private quarters. The windows, of course were all cross-hatched with tape, inside, blackout curtains darkened the room. An all-so-proper butler was waiting, asking if he needed refreshment before retiring, perhaps a cup of tea with something in it, sir? Cecil politely refused and minutes later was up on the third floor, door closed, the room decorated in late Victorian, heavy on knickknacks and pastoral paintings.

The bed was already turned back, and he barely took the time to take off his shoes and jacket, collapsing atop the bedspread.

But sleep was impossible. Back to Singapore, damn it. His subterfuge, and Winston most likely had seen clear through it, was that by personally delivering his memo, Winston would ask him to stay on here, rather than go back to what he suspected would be a hellhole under siege come spring. It was not that he was afraid of a fight, far from it. A posting now to Spain, Turkey, for that matter even back into the secret activity he knew must be going on up at Benchley Park was more his ideal line now. And this talk of Donovan and John Ford was interesting stuff. But Winston wanted him back in Singapore for now and he could not say no. And sleep was impossible as well, for at regular intervals, every ten minutes or so, another bomb whistled down, sometimes far, sometimes near enough that the blackout curtains rustled and though disgusted to admit it after all he had been through . . . he was afraid.

Pearl Harbor
9 November 1941
9:30 a.m. Local Time

"Sir, there's someone waiting outside to meet you."

James Watson looked up from his desk, bleary-eyed, as usual. He had been working since . . . well, he wasn't quite sure when, on several naval transmissions triangulated out of Manila as coming from Formosa, indicating an increase of traffic. There had been talk of trying to sneak a reconnaissance flight up to just off the island for a look around. MacArthur had vetoed the idea as too provocative.

Provocative, hell, the Japanese were wandering "by accident" into Philippine airspace nearly every day, popping in along the entire west coast of Luzon. Commercial flights between Hong Kong and Manila were disgorging what was now the usual array of alleged businessmen who seemed a little too fit and trim, several cameras in their luggage, who would stay for a day then fly back out.

And yet he was still hampered by the absurdest of controls. In fact, an investigation team led by a senator and federal judge had been sent out on the behest of the Senate to see whether the navy and army out here were breaking any laws regarding trying to look at outgoing mail and telegraph messages from Japanese who seemed more than a little suspicious. It was promised that if the slightest impropriety was uncovered, heads would roll, perhaps all the way up to CinCPac himself. Fortunately they had not heard about James and Collingwood's little venture of sending an enlisted man down to prowl through Western Union's trash, that lad had been quickly transferred off to an outgoing destroyer, bound for Manila, so he would not be forced to perjure himself.

He pushed back from the desk, rubbing the stubble of his chin, again, a couple of days worth of growth and he knew, without even raising his arm for a quick whiff, that he most likely stank. The air conditioner, a great luxury that everyone else on the base was envious of, wondered about, and grumbled about regarding those "weird birds in the basement," had gone on the blink again and the temperature in the room was somewhere in the low eighties.

He went into the washroom, splashed some water on his face, toweled off and wove his way back down the narrow corridor, past dozens of others, some bent on the same task as he, others laboriously working on translations of what little they had, looking for any finer nuances, well-worn Japanese-English dictionaries open by their side, in the signals room, to his left, behind a closed and locked door, a dozen operators were monitoring a dozen frequencies around the clock, some of it in the clear transmissions, weather reports from commercial Japanese ships, messages back to the mainland that might have, concealed within them, some hidden text or clue, others the laborious process of taking down each Morse dot and dash, not really understanding the words at all, just jotting them down as fast as they were received to be passed on to someone like himself. Still others listened to the commercial and state-run radio stations, enduring the at times god-awful screeching noise that the Japanese claimed passed for music, and on rare occasions even a Western piece, though decadent American jazz and big band had been banned. Of late the song about the air raid shelter and ignoring the bombs had found new rivals extolling the prowess of the army as it fought to free innocent China from the brigands and Communists, another something of a recruiting song about the joys to be found aboard a ship on the high seas, defending Japan. All of it had to be monitored; but not all of it was. Navy simply didn't have the money, the equipment, nor manpower to monitor all possible sources of information twenty-four hours a day, seven days a week. So every few days "the chief" as they called him would hold a quick meeting, educated guesses would be presented as to which frequencies and stations might bear fruit, and personnel assigned, and the rest of the traffic went unlistened to, perhaps bearing a message that would fit into another message and together would help crack the newest code, which the Japs were changing ever more rapidly of late.

It was like watching a dozen leaks in your ceiling, but you only had one bucket to run around with, trying to catch the drops; and it drove them all mad, made worst by the four-and-a-half-hour time difference, which meant they lived on Tokyo time rather than Hawaiian.

Opening the door, he stopped before the marine guard, the two of them just nodding, both knowing each other well, but still the ritual of holding up his identification card and a slight extending of his arms to show he was not carrying out any papers concealed under his light tropical-weight uniform.

Up the flight of stairs and a second door with yet another marine guard before finally stepping out into the foyer of the main administrative building of the base. He squinted for a moment, morning sunlight flooding in, disoriented, for inside his body was telling him it was five a.m. tomorrow. That always threw him, the whole dateline thing that it was a Sunday, November 9, and not Monday, November 10, 1941,

Japanese time, another bother when it came to duty assignments given holidays and weekends, both there and here.

"James?"

Still squinting a bit he turned, immediately recognizing the voice . . . it was Cecil!

"Damn me, when did you get in?" James cried, going over to his old friend and in a very un-Britishlike gesture slapping him with nearly a bear hug.

The traffic in and out of the building on this Sunday morning was light, it was, after all a Sunday at 9:30 a.m., but still there were enough passing back and forth to take a second, somewhat jaundiced glance at a very disheveled naval commander, with coffee-stained shirt, embracing a very proper-looking captain of the British navy, complete to, American eyes, the rather silly-looking tropical Bermuda shorts and knee-high white socks.

But the two didn't care and both looked at each other appraisingly as, a bit embarrassed, they stepped back from each other. Both, of course, had aged in each other's eyes since the last time they had seen each other.

"I'd suggest visiting the office," James said, nodding back to the door where at the mere mention of a visit, the normally friendly marine guard stiffened a bit, "but you understand."

"I took the liberty of picking up some sandwiches and coffee," Cecil said, gesturing to his leather attaché case which was bulging slightly, "my transportation was most kind in lending me a vacuum bottle, let's just go sit down by the waterfront and chat. I haven't much time."

"When are you leaving?"

"The Clipper takes off at thirteen hundred, your time here, a bit confusing I daresay, my watch is still set on San Francisco time, so how long does that give us?"

"Three hours or so," James replied, squinting at his own watch, doing a quick calculation since the watch was set to Tokyo time. He could see Cecil noting the difference as well, but nothing was said.

"I'll arrange a ride for you back to Pan Am, that should buy us a little more time together. Damn all, Margaret will tear my head off when she hears you were here and didn't visit."

Cecil smiled and shook his head, motioning to the door, the two stepping out into the warm humid heat of a Hawaiian autumn day.

"Do you still tell her everything?" Cecil asked.

James hesitated, then shook his head.

"No, I see. You aren't here," James said.

"Something like that?"

"Then why not mufti instead of that absurd getup you Brits call a uniform?" James asked with a smile.

"Do you think I'd have even gotten through the gate otherwise?" he asked, nodding back toward the main entrance.

The two wandered down to the waterfront, a small grassy area shaded by palms, a few benches set out for those who wished to take a lunch break outside. Across the loch was battleship row. The fleet, as usual for a Sunday, was in, Liberty Boats plying back and forth, a group of young sailors noisily disembarking wearing loud Hawaiian shirts, two of them toting a heavy wooden board, rounded at one end, TURRET ONE BOYS, OKLAHOMA stenciled on one side, a picture of the forward turret, all three guns firing with lurid flames stenciled on the other side. They assumed it would pass for a surfboard, the young men laughing, talking about the women they'd meet over at Waikiki, taxicabs lined up just outside the gate waiting for them . . . and he wondered how that group would get their homemade surfboard to the beach and if it would survive the day.

A lucky few had dates waiting by the gate, the girls drawing more than a few friendly wolf whistles as they waited for their boyfriends to come ashore.

He had all but forgotten days like this since coming back to duty. On Sunday morn, sometimes they'd go to mass, other times just sleep in then walk down to the beach or motor to the north end of the island up by Kano Point, and watch the local surfers trying the big waves and go for a dip themselves. Mornings like this in Hawaii were the closest he could imagine paradise to be, a warm tropical breeze drifting across the island, first clouds beginning to form along the high peaks, the air rich with the scent of flowers.

Cecil opened his attaché case and drew out what the Brits called a vacuum bottle, and two heavy cups, *Pacific Clipper* emblazoned on each. Unscrewing the lid he poured for both of them, black, no cream or sugar, the scent rich and inviting, not the oily slop that sludgelike would drip out of the ever-present pot down in the bowels of the cryptographer's lair.

The sandwiches were nicely wrapped in fresh linens, no wax paper here, still warm slices of roast beef and a small bowl of potato salad for each, even silverware, real silver from the feel of it.

"Damn, you are traveling in luxury!" James exclaimed.

Cecil grinned.

"Occasionally traveling at the expense of the Crown has its moments. Rare, but there are moments. Your clipper planes, good heavens, how the Huns boasted about their zeppelins, which do have an awful tendency to burn up. The appointments pale when compared to good old American catering to the rich, or agents bent on distant missions on the far side of the globe."

"So are you coming or going?"

"Going," Cecil replied, biting into his sandwich.

James looked at his, not sure. His inner clock telling him it was five in the morning, the outside telling him it was time for a breakfast of eggs and bacon, and Cecil feeling that this was an early dinner.

He decided to just sip the coffee.

"Back from England?"

"Yes."

There was a moment of silence and then both chuckled at the same time.

"Our business sure does teach us to be tight-lipped," James finally ventured. "I assume our visit is more than just a friendly stopover as you gallivant around the world.

Tell me what is going on out here."

And he gestured with a sweeping hand to the world around them.

"It's a madhouse, if you want the short answer. That Wells fellow, you know who I mean. Ever read any of his stuff?"

"You mean H.G.? Sure, *War of the Worlds, The Time Machine,* read them when I was a boy."

"How about *The Shape of Things to Come*?" James shook his head.

"Rather prophetic, I daresay. War comes, civilization finally collapses. New and terrible weapons using the atom as an explosive a million times more powerful than the guns over there," and he pointed to where the battleships were tied off.

"How is it in England?"

"They say the Blitz is nothing now, but I tell you, I don't like being under any kind of plane dropping bombs, be it five or five hundred. Rationing is tight; you can see it in the faces of the civilians. Gone is glamour, everything is khaki, even the women; though there is one small advantage."

"And that is?"

"Wartime rationing is so tight that hemlines have gone up quite a bit to conserve on cloth. For this old bachelor, rather a thrill."

471

James looked at him and forced a smile.

"My London, my old London, most of it is gone, there seems to be a perpetual grit in the air now, everything dusty, worn looking from the constant pounding. Perversely, the only bright spot is that at least the two dictators finally turned on each other. Reports coming out of Russia are horrific, but they still seem to be holding on."

"And do you think they will hold?"

"Hitler didn't snatch Moscow in August when he had the chance; last report is the freeze is on, the mud rock solid, they're moving again but I'll bet what was stationed in Siberia and Mongolia is now waiting for them."

Cecil was touching into 'their' territory now, and James found himself actually looking around. Even the most casual conversation about the war that in any way whatsoever might touch on Japan was forbidden outside "the dungeon" as they called it.

And yet he knew who this man really was, besides being a friend.

"It's all right," Cecil said, "If you want I can show you the letter of introduction signed by the PM himself, it's right here," and he pointed to his breast pocket.

"I know, but still, I don't have such a letter from our president; you know the old game."

"Even between allies and friends standing on the edge of the abyss," Cecil replied sadly.

James nodded and lowered his head.

"You stopped over here to talk with me officially, I mean actually officially in an unofficial way, is that it?"

"Nice play of words, James, but yes. The PM is eager for anything you chaps might have, anything. I can tell you that back in Washington and London they're building the same setup that you and I worked under in the last war. You've heard of Donovan?"

"Wild Bill?" James said, with a bit of a grin.

"He's setting some things up," Cecil announced. "It's not my place to say anything, but perhaps there might be something for you with his team."

James sighed and held up his left arm showing his "claw." "I doubt if they'd want a one-handed sailor," James said softly.

"Bastards," Cecil mumbled. "I'm sorry I couldn't get over to see you before you were shipped back." He reached over and patted James on the knee.

James said nothing. Strange, of late he felt a certain detachment from it all. The seething rage going into the background noise of life. The flying, introduced to him by Fuchida, soothed things a bit, and his work, so damn boring and numbing at times, was, in a boylike sort of way, a means of shoving it back under the table.

"You wrote me about Nanking," James said, "I read your reports, saw the pictures. What you went through makes *Panay* pale." He held the claw in front of Cecil. "I think I'd kind of stand out if you are talking about the old cloak-and-dagger stuff."

Cecil laughed. "They want your brains, James, not that hook of yours; though I daresay it'd be rather effective in tearing out the guts of some Jap."

"A bit bloodthirsty, aren't we?" James replied, surprised by the vehemence in his friend's voice.

"Thought you'd be too," Cecil replied coldly. "After what I saw at Nanking, the hell with all the bastards."

"Even your cadets, our friend Fuchida?"

"You still count him a friend? Hell, when I interviewed him a couple months after Nanking and *Panay,* I heard no apology there. I almost feel that was deliberate on his part."

He shook his head.

"No, that friendship is dead. I left him

with your address, have you heard from him?"

"No," James replied a bit wistfully. "I did try and reach him a few times, sent him a picture of me and my plane. No reply."

"Then that settles it as far as I'm concerned. But back to this other job. Are you interested?" James looked at him, incredulous.

"Well, would I? The answer is definitely a yes."

Cecil smiled. "Their efforts are primarily focused on Germany of course, but I think both you and I know that will change dramatically before the year is out, very dramatically. And when it does certain people are going to be head-hunting for chaps like us who don't just know the language, but know the people, the way they think, who they are, and that, old friend, defines you and me to a tee."

James looked around again, still a bit uncomfortable.

"Okay, as you Yanks say, I'll talk first. You can answer or not as you see fit."

James simply nodded.

"We both know that the Northern School, as they call it, is dead, though there are still a few in our services who think the Soviets are on the edge of a collapse and no matter what this Tojo is now planning, the army would rather jump northward and cut off a part of the dying corpse rather than fight a war where they will be highly dependent on the navy."

James again nodded.

"So south it is. I give it four weeks, six at most, perhaps two on the inside bet."

"Two is out," James said softly. "What little I can . . ."

He hesitated, even to say "decrypt" made him uncomfortable.

"What little I can see. The playing pieces are not in position yet. Too much open signal traffic. It's when they turn it all off, that to me is the countdown."

"I agree. I'm guessing around the twenty-fifth of next month. Christmas and all that; everyone will be on holiday."

"Dangerous though. We might just second-guess that as well and go to a higher alert. Besides, they know the sacredness of that day to us. They do want a war, but they do not want a vengeance match; and to attack on Christmas day, that's asking for vengeance in the name of the Prince of Peace."

"Nice turn of phrase there," Cecil replied.

"So it's somewhere in between, you'd guess."

Again he hesitated. "Strictly my own vision, of course," James said, and he could not resist the deliberate gesture of taking off his glasses and pulling out a dirty handkerchief to clean them.

"Of course, just your vision."

"Four to five weeks. They have taken to increasing the frequency of code changes. I tell you it is driving us to the point of insanity."

"I can see that," Cecil replied smiling, pointing to James's stained blouse and trousers, then with a friendly gesture ran the back of his hand across his stubbly face.

"Certainly a picture for a recruiting poster either for your navy or, as you say, an insane asylum."

"You've done the work, you know what I mean."

Cecil nodded. "At least last time it was a Western-based language, and we got some lucky breaks with their lax attitude about coding books in embassies. Not this time I take it."

James shook his head.

"Almost makes one wish we had some magic," Cecil said, this time looking closely at James.

James, glasses still off, was glad they were off. Not even to the closest of friends on the same team would he ever say that one word . . . Magic. It was the encrypting machine for Japanese diplomatic messages, one of the closest of all secrets. There was speculation that the Japanese Consulate Office had one, and there had been endless late-night discussions over coffee about bringing in some professional safecracker, maybe somebody even from the Mob on the mainland to pull a job off.

One of the team was from New Jersey, and he said he knew half a dozen who could pull it off for the right "consideration." The trick was to get it out, take it apart, photograph and measure everything, put it back together, and then do a second burglary job the same night to get it back in. Impossible, but fun to speculate about. If they were ever caught, the isolationist hotheads in Congress would skin all of them alive, CinCPac would deny he ever knew about it, the State Department would scream for a hanging . . . and the Japanese would junk the machine and go with something entirely different. As it was, they did have a handle on some of the messages thanks to the IBM calculating machines down in the dungeon, but having a real one would be better than anything a cryptologist could ever dream of holding.

He looked straight at Cecil and said nothing. The silence, though, was, he realized, answer enough, and his friend chuckled.

They sat in silence for several minutes, Cecil finishing his sandwich, poking around a bit at the potato salad, James just drinking his coffee, the idea of roast beef just not sitting right at this time of day.

"And your destination?" James finally asked.

"Flight leaves this afternoon at one. From here to Wake to refuel. Then across the long haul to Guam, then Manila, then Hong Kong. From Hong Kong I then head down to Singapore. A week or so if the weather cooperates."

"Amazing. Jump the entire ocean in a week. When we were kids it took a month or more, and that by fastest steamer."

"And for our old friends in Japan, they can see it the other way," Cecil replied. "Ever hear of a chap named Genda?"

James processed that. The name Genda was familiar. Something about their War College.

"He was naval attaché in London during the Blitz. Has us worried a bit. We know he's a smart one. At the height of the battle, he wasn't down in the basement cowering with the rest of their embassy staff. We had a report he used to go to one of the bridges and just stand out there, watch, and take notes. He might have drawn some conclusions from both sides. If he did, and he has someone like Fuchida testing them out, it could spell trouble for us some day."

"Sounds like you and your old friend had a falling out."

"War does that," Cecil said, a touch of anger now in his voice. "You only saw the photographs and newsreels of Nanking. Remember, I was there, and I will never forget it.

"Nor forgive it."

"Why bring him up?" James asked.

"Just the thought that he returned back to Japan the same way I'm now traveling by the Pan Am clipper planes. He had days to observe, to think. Writing up a little speculation on it for the PM along with my other notes. Imagine a Japan with five hundred such planes, based forward, say some of the islands up off Alaska for example."

"Absurd, Cecil," James replied, "the logistics of supporting that many aircraft up there; anyone who tried it would be insane."

"All right then, I'll grant that, but elsewhere, and the thought they could range the entire Pacific in a day."

"They have no such planes, nor the fuel

to feed them. Even the Germans must be feeling that pinch. Thank God it is we who hold nearly all the world's oil. The one who controls oil, until some other energy comes along, like those atoms that Wells fellow writes about, well we have the trump card."

"I agree," Cecil replied. "I guess I'm not making it clear enough. It is the thinking of the application of mass across a vast distance that was undreamed of in the last war. Move two, three, four thousand miles and then strike with five hundred, a thousand planes. The Germans had that number of planes, far more, actually, but they never quite grasped how to use them in mass, in one direct killing blow against the most important target. It was not our factories, at least in the short term, though in a long, protracted war that might be different. It was to kill the RAF itself by shooting them down and bombing them and bombing them until they smashed apart. That is where Herr Goering made his mistake, and I think this Genda must have seen that and reported it."

"How many carriers do you have out here now?" Cecil asked, completely shifting topics and pointing over to where the *Enterprise* and *Lexington* were docked.

James chuckled. "You know I can't tell

you that."

"I'm guessing three," Cecil replied. "Those two there, maybe *Saratoga* nearby. They have seven, will soon have nine if our scanty intelligence from inside Japan is accurate."

Again James did not reply, but the number was right. One of his listeners claimed he knew the "fist," the subtle nuances of different telegraphers, and could pick out the *Kaga* and *Akagi* in less than a minute, as distinct, he would say in his Texan drawl, as the way a Yankee from Boston sounded to him.

"They don't have the clipper planes and hell, for that matter nor do we. Your longest-range planes, your 17s and the new 24s can range, at best, a thousand miles, maybe fifteen hundred if stripped down. But the carriers now. At flank speed they can leap six hundred miles in a day, across the Pacific in a week if they pushed it. Seven carriers, five hundred planes or more for a killing strike."

Could it be here? All along from CinCPac on down the speculation had been on from day one it would be to take out MacArthur and the ragtag army he was ever so slowly, far too slowly, trying to organize in the Philippines, while constantly complaining about the need for yet more men, planes, and supplies and often blaming the navy for any delay. It was said that Kimmel had finally announced the only reason MacArthur had taken that post was because it was the only military position he could have where he could call himself a field marshal and get away with it, with enough gold lace on his hat to deck out a Paris streetwalker.

"What about Singapore?" James finally asked.

"What the PM thinks, and that, dear friend, is a confidence between friends and no further. Call it a sign of trust."

"Fine then."

"Why use carriers on Singapore when land-based planes out of Indochina can do the job. Once you have Singapore, the oilfields of Sarawak and the Celebes in the Dutch East Indies fall by default.

"I'd place my bet elsewhere."

"My God, you are talking about here," James whispered. Cecil did not reply. He carefully began to fold up the linen from his sandwich, motioned to where Cecil's sat on the park bench between them. James shook his head and several seconds later, a couple of gulls were happily tearing it apart, others swooping in to argue over the spoils.

He emptied out the rest of the coffee into

their cups and James took a gulp, his stomach rebelling slightly, all the caffeine and nothing down there to soak it up. He suddenly did feel hungry and looked a bit regretfully at the gulls who were now flying off, squabbling even as they flew away with the remnants of the meal.

His gaze went back to the harbor toward which the gulls were flying. Yet more Liberty Boats were coming in, boisterous sailors shouting and laughing. Over where the submarines were lined up, some of the crew, stuck with duty aboard, had spread out blankets and laid on the deck, soaking up the morning sun, a radio rigged up on the conning bridge of one of the subs playing the new Andrews Sisters hit "Boogie Woogie Bugle Boy."

Over on the north side of Ford Island, a PBY had just landed and was taxiing across the water and then up the ramp, the morning recon flight around the island completed for the day. A couple of Army P-40s cruised by at low altitude, skirting the edge of the naval base as their pilots put in an hour or two of flight time before knocking off for a secluded getaway up in the hills or on an isolated beach with a young wife or girlfriend.

Cecil looked at his watch.

"Think you can whistle up a ride for me?"
he asked. "I think it's time to go."

"Certainly."

The two stood up and stretched.

"I hope to see you again," James said.

Cecil smiled.

"Oh, we will. What we talked about earlier.
Who knows, I did bend the PM's ear a bit.
Our names are in the hat."

James nodded, it was an interesting speculation but at the moment all he could do
was look across the harbor which now
seemed to be bathed in a different light.

Hitokappu Bay, Japan
26 November 1941
6:00 a.m. Tokyo Time
25 November 1941
10:30 a.m. Hawaii Time

The two friends, Fuchida and Genda, stood
side by side on the bridge of the carrier
Akagi. The colors had just been raised, the
national anthem played by the ship's band,
and all had then turned to bow first to the
east and the sun which had yet to rise and
then south to the homeland and the Emperor.

They looked with excitement at Admiral
Yamamoto standing near them. He had

finally concluded that Genda was right and that he had to lead the fleet.

Furthermore, once Yamamoto had thought through the implications of the strategic gamble to which he was committing the navy he made a number of significant changes in the operational plan.

They were no longer on a smash-and-run raid. They were now committed to the destruction of the American Fleet and were planning for a cruise of decisive engagement. It was both exhilarating and awe inspiring. Once Yamamoto had thought through the logic of their position he had relentlessly and ruthlessly imposed changes to the plan to give Japan the greatest possible range of options in the opening weeks of the campaign.

Yamamoto's preparatory work was done, and he wasted no energy in anxiety or anticipation. He was now relaxed and beginning to build reserves of energy for the moment of engagement when his will, his creativity, and his nerve would matter. Until then he had competent subordinates to run the fleet and train the crews.

Fuchida found himself much more filled with adrenaline than Yamamoto. He was so intensely committed to success that he almost quivered with energy.

The deck was cleared of all but half a dozen planes, to be used for antisubmarine patrol as the fleet set out and *Akagi* built up to launch speed. But the harbor was already ringed by planes, skimming low and slow, back and forth beyond the opening to the bay. If but one American submarine should be present to see what was about to sortie out, the entire operation might be aborted, though orders were to attack any strange submarine without warning and hopefully to sink it before it could dispatch a message.

The flight deck was lined with all the ship's personnel, except for those absolutely needed in the engine room, the men most likely freezing in their formal uniforms in the near arctic cold.

The *Akagi*'s captain turned to his quartermaster and gave the slightest of nods. "Dismiss the crew to their regular stations," was all he said, "and take us out."

Yamamoto turned away, his back to those on the bridge, gaze fixed forward.

Seconds later Fuchida could feel the vibration run through *Akagi,* it was the engines beginning to rev up, in seconds water would start foaming under her stern, but it was more than that, an electriclike vibration coursing through the entire crew.

Down on the flight deck, boatswains' pipes shrilled, ordering the men below, but they did not break ranks at once, many just stood in place, sensing the moment. Though even now, only the pilots and a handful of officers knew their destination and mission, that secret would not be revealed to the crew until later in the day. Still even the lowest of enlisted personnel knew that this was no ordinary training mission. The pride of the Japanese Fleet, a force of nearly a hundred ships, were gathered in the harbor. Two fast battleships, six of her carriers, escort ships, cruisers, destroyers, mine sweepers, the crucial oilers, the destroyers already racing for the mouth of the harbor to form the forward screen.

One would have to be dead, very stupid Fuchida thought, not to realize they were sallying forth to war.

Morale had soared even higher when the evening before, Yamamoto had quietly arrived without fanfare. Fuchida suspected that Genda knew of this beforehand, but security had obviously been maintained. Once aboard *Akagi,* within minutes Nagumo had departed just as quietly, face drawn, tense, obviously enraged and humiliated. He had been beached at the very last minute, but few had complained for now everyone on board was drawing comparisons with Admiral Togo in 1905 sailing forth for Tsushima. Everyone saw it as a good omen.

Genda caught Fuchida's eyes, motioned for him to follow, and together they went back down the steps and back out onto the flight deck. The *Akagi* was rapidly gaining speed, an icy wind sweeping the ship, but hundreds now stood about the bridge, looking up, wondering, some started to approach Genda, but his gaze warned them off.

And then it happened. An overly enthusiastic young ensign leaned over the railing, cupping his hands to be heard above the gale of wind and the roar of the engine exhaust stakes.

"Admiral Yamamoto is leading us to victory!"

The response was electric.

One of the young lieutenants out on the open bridge did it first, throwing hands up high . . . Banzai . . . Banzai . . . Banzai.

The cry was picked up, reverberated, a thousand or more voices joining in as the wind begin to whip down the length of the ship as it turned majestically, gathering speed, heading toward the vast sea beyond.

"Did you do this?" Fuchida asked, looking at his friend.

"No, I think you did," Genda said softly.

"But you talked to him about what I said."

Genda nodded.

"But I thought he refused; he never said a word. This is the first I knew," and as he spoke his voice began to break.

That old man had kept his cards close, close indeed. He must have gone all the way to the Emperor though to discuss the change. Genda felt a twinge of pain for Nagumo now.

"Three cheers for Admiral Yamamoto sails with us!"

And again cheers swept the deck.

Fuchida could not contain himself, and he embraced his old friend.

"You just might have changed history," he said, voice choked.

"No, my friend. You are the strike leader. It will be you who will ultimately decide that."

Fuchida, broke, unable to hold back his tears. If ever there was a moment to be alive, to be a pilot for Japan, it was here, now, this moment.

The big E moved slowly but steadily toward the harbor mouth. Task Force 2 was on the way to Wake Island to deliver aircraft. Admiral Halsey was carefully disguising their destination. In fact, security was so tight the marine pilots had been told they were only going out to sea for two days of experimental flying off the carrier. They only had one change of clothes with them.

Admiral Halsey looked out at the three battleships and their accompanying cruisers and destroyers he would send off for training as soon as they got out of sight of land. He fully expected war to break out at any minute, hour, or day, and he did not want to run down to Wake Island encumbered by slow battleships. The *Enterprise* could make thirty knots and the cruisers and destroyers assigned to protect her could keep up. The old battleships were only capable of seventeen knots. As an airman, Halsey thought their guns were irrelevant to the kind of fight he might get into and their lack of speed could be fatal.

Halsey looked forward to this cruise

*Vice Admiral William F. Halsey, Jr.,
USN. Photographed circa 1941,
while he was serving as Commander, Aircraft, Battle Force. Cop-
ied from the USS* Enterprise
(CV-6) "War Album," Volume 1.
Naval Historical Center

toward Wake Island with confidence and
enthusiasm. They were out to sea and he
half expected that by the time he returned,
currently scheduled for the morning of
December 7, they would most likely be at
war.

■ ■ ■ ■

PART THREE: THE BATTLE OF PEARL HARBOR

■ ■ ■ ■

CHAPTER TWELVE

8 December 1941
7:30 a.m. Hawaiian Time
9 December 1941
3:00 a.m. Tokyo Time

"Haa, there it is!" Strike Commander Fuchida, shoulder harness loosened, half stood up, Zeiss binoculars raised, looking straight ahead. Kahuku Point was nearly straight ahead, perhaps five degrees off to port, about forty kilometers ahead.

He slapped his pilot on the shoulder, looking past him to their instrument panel. Speed 180 knots, some morning haze, a low scattering of clouds, ceiling about three thousand meters. Even as he watched intently, they went into a wisp of low-hanging mist, vision obscured, then broke back out, the slanting rays of the sun off his left shoulder illuminating all with a golden light.

The Zeroes, throttles back, weaved slowly back and forth, above, forward, and to the flanks of the strike column. No signals, no sudden throttling up to sweep forward to ward off interceptors. Nothing. Just the island ahead, the morning light, the steady reassuring roar of the 1,200-horsepower Mitsubishi radial engine pulling them toward their destiny.

In just a few minutes the peak at Kahuku Point resolved into a clearer view. After a week and a half at sea, most of it below decks as they pushed through forty-foot seas, even the most experienced of pilots wretched with seasickness, the lush inviting greenery of the peaks ahead were almost a soothing sight, a promise of warmth after cold, a promise of beauty . . . and a promise of a war so long contemplated, planned for, and now in but a few more minutes a war into which he would personally lead his nation into.

Thoughts raced through his head, a distraction. He had to focus, but still they were there. Boyhood dreams of samurai fantasies. The great legendary warriors, the famed duels of masters, the vast armies in the civil wars for the Shogunate. He was now the lead samurai, the one galloping forward, all eyes upon him. Fantasy he thought, even as he grinned and touched the ceremonial headband given to him by his crew chief.

The tension around him, the nearly two hundred pilots all looking toward his plane for the signal to attack, to charge forward.

He raised his binoculars again, scanning the peak, then the airspace to either side. Surely they would be up, the peak a rally point, surely two hundred of their fighters would now be airborne. Were they so asleep?

The airspace ahead was empty except for a tiny yellow speck. He focused on it, a Stearman biplane, a lone plane, civilian from the looks of it, most likely out to enjoy the sunrise. He smiled, it certainly was a beautiful sunrise and there was a fleeting thought to break radio silence, to tell his eager Zero pilots to leave it alone. But he knew they would, they were primed for bigger game.

The point was closer. He looked down at his wristwatch, strapped to the outside of his flight jacket. Zero: three zero seven Tokyo time, a quick mental calculation, 07:37 local time. The headphones still resonated with the soft gentle Hawaiian music of a station in Honolulu. Surely they would be off the air by now or broadcasting a warning, a general alert.

The music continued, so inviting . . . and he felt even a tinge of sadness, so naively American, the poor fools. For all hell was now bearing down upon them.

Zero: seven thirty-nine local time. He checked his watch again, as they raced toward the point at over three miles per minute. Already he could see clear into the middle of the island, the sugarcane fields along the north coast, the Waianae Range across the middle of the island, for the moment blocking the view of Wheeler Army Air Force Base and the harbor beyond.

Nearly to the critical point, he could sense the strike leaders gazing in his direction. It was still not sure if total surprise had been gained or not, but now was the moment. He slipped the canopy back, the wind stream buffeting him, cool air shrieking past, the cockpit had been getting warm, or was it his own tension that made him sweat.

It looked to be total surprise.

He unclipped the Very Flare Gun from its holster set into the back of the seat before him. Cocked it open and put in a red flare shell. Sticking his arm straight up into the slipstream roaring by overhead he fired the gun, red flare streaking up, the signal that total surprise had been gained. The two attack plans, either for surprise or against stiff resistance, required two fundamentally different attack formations. The former, the bombers would go straight in and hit before the enemy realized what was happening or were just beginning to prepare. A second flare meant frontal assault, with the Zeroes to streak ahead to clear enemy fighters before the attack commenced.

The bombers to either side began to peel off into their various directions, the main body breaking into waves that would sweep down the west coast of the island then turn in to hit Pearl Harbor from the west and south. The other strike force to come down from the north straight over the island, while secondary strikes went against the airfields, the Zeroes going in to strafe.

Within seconds the columns began to break off from the main stream . . . within minutes it would begin.

But the Zeroes did not seem to be responding, and after a couple more minutes, he loaded a second flare to signal, and instantly regretted it, for some now saw this as a second signal and not a repeat of the first. Confusion began to reign, and suddenly all planes just began to roar straight in, some thinking it was surprise, some not. There was nothing he could do about it now.

He turned aft to his rear gunner and radio operator.

"Send the signal for complete surprise,"

he shouted . . . "Tora . . . Tora . . . Tora!"

USN Carrier Enterprise
Two hundred and fifty miles west of Oahu
7:35 a.m.

Stunned, Halsey looked at the note just brought to him by signals. It came straight from the office of the Department of the Navy in Washington . . . a warning that war was imminent, perhaps as early as today.

He now thanked God for the storm that he had cursed but the night before. He had planned to arrive back at Pearl this morning, but the edge of the storm sweeping across the northcentral Pacific had sent towering seas southward, so rough that it had delayed the refueling of his escorting destroyers and nearly half a day of high-speed steaming had been lost. The slow movement had made him feel itchy, a perfect target if submarines were lurking about, but now . . . better to be out here than already in harbor.

"Did this come straight from Washington or was it relayed from Pearl?" he asked.

His signal officer shook his head. "Sir, we picked it up from the mainland; my boy on the radio receiver said it was nearly impossible to read but he got it. Given past

500

performances I'd venture no one at Pearl heard it. They'll most likely send it to them via cable."

He wondered for a second if he should relay the message back out, then shook his head. They were running under a self-imposed radio silence. He would not break that to second-guess whether this message had woken things up back on the island.

"What's our fix on *Lexington*?" He turned to look over at the chief petty officer on the plot board. He knew it'd be a guess; *Lexington* was under radio silence as well.

The petty officer shook his head. "Sir, it's only a guess on my part, but I'd say at least five hundred miles to our west, heading to Midway."

Halsey nodded, taking that in. Between them they could maybe muster a hundred and forty aircraft. He stood up and walked over to the plot table, the chief petty officer in charge already rolling out the large-scale map of the ocean between the Hawaiian chain, up to Midway, and the lower end of the roughly formed triangle that was Wake Island. A million square miles of ocean.

In eight hours they could be back into Pearl . . . but why? We still have enough fuel for several days of steaming, our strength in aircraft is down. If need be once things clarify a bit, I can order a squadron flown back out.

No, keep sea room away from the island for the moment, turn back westward and move toward *Lexington*. Maybe she's got the signal, maybe not. He'd assume not, always assume the worst, and then you aren't surprised.

Surprise, that's what those bastards would go for. It might be somewhere right out here, perhaps Midway and Wake, best to move to cover that.

He turned and looked at his expectant staff.

"Bring us about on a heading of 290, twenty knots, signal our escorts the same and sound general quarters. This is no drill."

Pearl Harbor
7:40 a.m. Local Time

James Watson, unable to contain himself, pushed back from his chair. He needed air, fresh air, not the steady hum of the air conditioner pumping its lifeless breath into the room. He had given up waiting for Kimmel and tried to return to his work, but it was impossible to concentrate.

He stood up, the others on duty looking at him with weary eyes. They were all half-crazed, he knew, but he knew as well that some thought him even more than half-crazed during these last few days. But no one said anything. You had to be crazy to be in this basement anyhow, a house of mad-men, a basement of Canutes raging against the impending storm.

He walked over to the door, pushed it open, held his ID card up for the marine guard. A new kid, he didn't know him, nor did he bother to even say good morning. The kid looked numbed, ready to doze off, kept awake only by the fact that he had to stay on his feet and would get a solid ream-ing if his sergeant found him slumped against the wall with lights out.

Back aching, James went up the long flight of stairs and out the second door, again the flash of his ID card and then into the foyer. The place was a ghost town. One officer hurried by, clutching a piece of paper. He didn't recognize him. There was some flurry of activity in the signals room and he looked in through the open door. Someone was talking about the "Ward." He wasn't sure, "Ward," a destroyer he thought, but some-one was certainly fired up over it. A petty officer, seeing him looking in, went over and closed the door. He felt the gesture a bit rude but then shrugged his shoulders and headed out the main door.

If Kimmel had arrived there would at least be some semblance of activity, at least some playacting that the weekend staff were doing their work and were not just dozing off behind desks or staring vacantly out windows.

He needed air, fresh air, and still clutching his coffee mug he went out the front door, yet another flash of an ID card, a mindless ritual he now thought, for who cared. He could show a Mongolian driver's license with a picture of Mussolini on it and chances were the nineteen-year-old marine guard would not even notice. It was Sunday morning in Hawaii, and if the guards were awake at all, they were contemplating when they'd get off duty and hit the beach, the surf, the girls, the cold beer, maybe even to catch the Army-Navy football game on a shortwave radio, which back stateside should be starting up by now.

He looked up toward the main gate as he stepped outside, hoping against hope that Kimmel might just be pulling in, but the parking spot marked for the admiral was empty. In fact, nearly all the parking slots were empty.

Oh well, he reasoned. Maybe for the best after all. His Cassandralike warnings had gone unheeded, it was well past sunup, if he tried to intercept Kimmel on the way in, waving a map with circles drawn on it, predicting the Japanese might very well be within three hundred miles of Pearl, he'd look like a complete and total fool, coffee mug in hand, shirt stained, unshaven. Kimmel was a good man, would smile and nod, most likely thank him for his concerns, then mark him off mentally as yet another reservist nutcase that perhaps needed a transfer for his own mental health.

He walked around the side of the building, yawning, covering his mouth as a couple of marines walked by and saluted smartly, he had to shift the mug to return the salute, and then realized he was completely out of uniform, no hat, shirt rumpled and, as usual, stained. Damn, he needed a cigarette and shifted the cup of coffee to his claw hand and with his good hand reached into his breast pocket and pulled out a pack. At least down here, he could keep them in that pocket, not having to hide them from Margaret. He fished one out, flicking the pack up, with his one hand, feeling slightly guilty at the taste of the tobacco, put the pack in his pants pocket, pulled out his Zippo and lit it, all while still balancing the half-full mug of coffee in his claw hand.

There, his image was complete, he thought with a wry smile. Coffee mug, stained shirt, no hat, cigarette dangling, a pirate-type look with his mechanical hand to finish the impression. But then again, as he looked over to one of the walkways, he was no worse looking than some of the last of the overnight Liberty boys coming back late for flag raising and morning roll. These last few were the really pathetic ones, drunk as lords, staggering down to the launches to take them back to their ships, if they had any sober thoughts in their minds, the fact that their chiefs would have them written up and liberty denied for a month to come and plenty of duty cleaning the heads. They were a sorry-looking lot, one of them sadly saluting him as his comrades pushed him along, two others with a passed-out comrade between them, his face puffy, obviously on the bad end of a barroom or back alley brawl.

A marine sergeant, sharp-looking, heading in the other direction, slowed at their approach, seemed ready to lay into the group, then just simply told them to move along and get back to their ships. He caught James's eye, saluted, and shrugged in a sort of "oh what the hell" way, as if to say there was no use in chewing out a bunch of drunk kids. James nodded in agreement and continued down to his favorite spot looking out over the harbor.

He settled down on one of the benches, mug balanced in his claw, cigarette still between his lips.

A beautiful morning. Forget about Kimmel, he thought. I've been here since Friday morning. Damn all, forget it for now. Margaret was most likely awake, God bless her. There wasn't one wife in a thousand who would tolerate this schedule of his. He had promised to be home by Saturday afternoon so they could go out for dinner and a movie. She had gone to bed alone, and woken up alone.

Go home, he thought. Sign out and go home. Grab a shower, try and stay awake, and listen as she talked, suggest skipping church and head to a secluded beach. She'd know that five minutes after they got there, he'd be fast asleep, but she had come to accept that. She'd most likely even pack along a small nip of scotch to lull him into an afternoon of quiet sleep under the palms, the sound of the surf gentle and soothing.

If I was still teaching he thought, I'd be home with her right now. Just waking up, her by my side, their old Sunday ritual of him making breakfast, habit started when young Davy was a boy and he would be home on leave, their boy tottering in to wake up "Pop" and he'd let Margaret get a few more minutes sleep while "her men" pampered her. He felt a stinging in his eyes. No, don't think of Davy, never think of that, at least not here, at least not during the daytime. Only when alone, when Margaret would not see the tears, during the middle of the night.

He took a deep drag on his cigarette, the smoke stinging his eyes now, causing him to blink. He watched the last of the kids piling into one of the launches. Davy would be their age now and he pushed that away, too many times, too many of those kids, most of them fresh-faced boys who had hurriedly joined the navy, with its promise of adventure rather than get swept into the draft for the army, reminded him of Davy, especially the tall, lanky ones, uniforms a bit too baggy on their narrow shoulders, but filled with a childlike pride and swagger after a night of being "a man," drinking beer with their buddies and making feeble attempts at picking up a girl.

He dropped his cigarette, took off his glasses, and wiped the mist from his eyes, then put his glasses back on. He lowered his head, a bit embarrassed by the sudden rush of sentiment, pulled out another cigarette and lit it, and raised his head.

He caught a flicker of movement and looked off to the northwest. Just a dot moving, more dots, dozens of them. A bird? Birds? Strange looking. What was it? Though the sun was to his back he shaded his eyes from the glare reflecting off the water. Another movement from the corner of his eye. The deck of the *Nevada,* bandsmen gathering on the stern for the Sunday morning flag raising, the designated band for the harbor this morning to play the National Anthem. On the submarines anchored nearby, several crew members were out, two young sailors, one of them carrying the flag under his arm as he came up out of the aft hatch. Eyes would turn to the signal tower atop the Navy Yard's water tank. In a few minutes the blue "prep" flag would go up, and then be lowered, signaling for all ships to have the national colors hoisted. The ritual, particularly on Sunday mornings, was done without much fanfare, the unlucky sailors assigned then quickly going back below decks, and if off duty, either grabbing breakfast or a little more sack time.

On the last of the returning Liberty Boats, the drunks and the half beat-up kid were loading aboard, the beat-up kid was now awake, looking around, exclaiming just where in the hell was he, and then he paused, looking to the north and, like James, shading his eyes and pointing.

A few more heads were up, turning, shading eyes, looking to the north, the west.

From the deck of the *Nevada* came the sound of a trumpeter tuning up, a few notes of a Glenn Miller piece, then back to a scale so the band master wouldn't chew him out for being disrespectful of the ceremony about to begin.

They would start the National Anthem in a moment, and he stood up.

He started to put his coffee mug down on the bench, ready to drop the cigarette, then looked back up again. It was 07:53 a.m., 7 December 1941 . . . and at that instant Lieutenant Commander James Watson felt a frightful chill.

Akagi
7:48 a.m.

The signal officer burst onto the bridge, holding a sheet of paper.

"Tora . . . Tora . . . Tora!" he shouted.

A cheer went up, men slapping each other on the back, Genda looking back at Yama-

510

moto who was sitting in a chair, silent, just staring out to sea.

"Anything else?" Genda asked.

"The report from the scout plane that flew over a half hour ago. Nine battleships, but no carriers."

"But complete surprise, though," Yamamoto finally said, breaking his long silence since after the report from the scout plane, launched from one of the cruisers escorting the fleet, had come in.

"Strange."

"How so, sir?"

"I assumed the carriers not being in meant that they had warning and they had made for sea. See if you can find out if any of the battleships are preparing to move. How many of their planes are up. I must know. Surely Washington must have warned them after our embassy handed over our note as planned."

And then he fell silent, looking back out to sea.

7:51 a.m.

Clearing the crest of the Waianae Range, Strike Leader Fuchida could see it now! It was the harbor, straight ahead. So intently studied on maps, the models, photographs, all of it so stark and clear now. He could see it!

At an approach average speed of just over three miles per minute he was closing at what seemed an amazing speed. What was shadowy, dulled by morning mist was now beginning to stand out clear, the "West Loch," Ford Island, the naval yard, and battleship row. Already he could see three clusters, two ships moored side by side, as studied in the maps and photographs, their high gunnery-control spotting towers indeed looking like pagodas. He looked to the east. The first of the Zeroes were now directly over Ford Island, winging up, breaking into the classic split S, the diving roll into a strafing attack to clear the way, behind them a formation of Vals preparing to do the same. Not a single burst of antiaircraft fire coming up, not a single American Air Corps green or navy blue aircraft in the sky. Not a single one!

Over the harbor, the same. In the final seconds he half expected to see a swarm of their planes diving down on them, concealed above the thin clouds overhead, or lurking, circling in the mountain canyons, ready to burst out. Not a single black burst of gunfire over the harbor, which was all so closer now.

They had done it!

The dots were turning, no longer dots, razor-thin silhouettes, reflected light glistening off canopies, no sound yet.

Around Watson only a few noticed, the beat-up sailor, a couple of the boys on the deck of the submarine.

A distant thump, more felt through the soles of his feet than heard. Turning to look north, it was up toward Schofield, Wheeler Army Air Corps base. Was that smoke? The first notes of the "Star Spangled Banner" drifted across the waters, white-clad band on the fantail of the *Nevada,* they were starting a few minutes early this morning, someone must have lowered the signal flag. He looked at his watch, calculating from Tokyo time, it was still nearly five minutes before eight. Ships' bells began to echo, flags started to go up, dozens of flags, from the smallest tug and submarine to the fantail of *Oklahoma* directly across the bay.

He came to attention, but still held his coffee mug, just letting the cigarette drop.

But some of the flag raisers were not watching to their duty, they were pausing, looking, pointing.

And then it struck. A multitude of sensations, all flooding into consciousness at once, each in itself near to overwhelming . . . together a nightmare.

Clearing the treetops lining the north end of the harbor, a dozen planes skimmed down low, full throttle, a whining hum, heading straight for Ford Island, a winking flash from their wing tips, the sight of it, an instant flash memory back to the strafing of the *Panay.*

PBY's clustered wingtip to wingtip began to burst into flames. One of the attacking planes, white with a red sun on its fuselage, banked sharply, sweeping toward *Nevada.*

the bombs bursting in air,
gave proof through the night . . .

The bandmaster started to swing his baton wildly, speeding up the anthem, as the plane banked over *Nevada.* Watson saw the red sunbursts on either wing.

A rising shriek, that corkscrew-down-the-spine sensation of plane engines at full throttle, half a dozen roaring in not from the west, nor north, but behind him, screaming past him, not a hundred feet away, the sound of their engines dopplering down as they raced past, dropping lower, leveling out.

He could hear the backfiring of the engines as the pilots throttled back, skimming lower. The details stood out so stark and clear. Dark green Kate torpedo bombers. The aft gunner of one looking straight at him, expressionless, red sun emblazoned on the fuselage, and strapped underneath, torpedoes.

More memories of the *Panay,* the plane soaring overhead as he floundered in the mud. My God, not again, not again.

An explosion, startling, slapping him hard, mud, water, fire rising in a column on the far side of Ford Island. A plane veering up and away from the exploding column, another plane coming directly across Ford Island, skimming across the bow of the old *California* anchored at the southern end of battleship row, a torpedo dropping free from that lone plane heading straight toward the huge number one dry dock which contained the *Pennsylvania.*

Suddenly dozens of planes were crisscrossing back and forth in every direction.

Strange, even in the mad confusion he could identify them, the low-flying Kates with torpedoes slung, Zeroes screaming by like bullets, almost a blur, guns beginning to fire. A plane turned toward *Nevada* opening fire on the formation of bandsmen.

Pearl Harbor attack, 7 December 1941, Japanese Navy Type-99 Carrier Bomber ("Val") in action during the attack. **Naval Historical Center**

"Over the land of the free . . . and the home of the brave . . ." The last notes trailing out, now the sound of gunfire, a Zero strafing the *Nevada*'s deck, bandsmen scrambling, even from that distance he could see the

large flag punching and shuddering, like the body of a boxer taking blows. And that struck him in that instant with a gut-searing intensity . . . they were actually shooting at the flag, the bastards!

Flags all across the harbor were hoisting up, a few fluttered back down, the men dropping lanyards and running, a few sticking to their ritual posts, the boys on the submarine nearest him tying off and then running, screaming . . .

"Japs, it's the Japs!"

Back to the Kates, it was all so overwhelming, so much to absorb.

And in those few seconds of trying to absorb so much, the formation of Kates swinging out from the narrow channel and into the loch, aiming straight for battleship row, began to release their loads. One torpedo, another, another . . . a dozen of them. He could see the splashes, but didn't someone say it was impossible to effectively drop torpedoes in a shallow harbor?

But they surfaced, he could see the trail of oxygen bubbles as they streaked across the narrow loch at over forty knots, the planes continuing to race straight toward their targets then pulling up, banking away.

The white bubbling streaks foamed across the muddy harbor.

The flash was startling. In an instant a column of water soared upward from the port side of the *Oklahoma,* impossibly high it seemed, higher than the tall pagodas of the gunnery control towers.

My God, not my ship! Not her. He remembered in that instant the flight with Fuchida, simulating what was now happening and looked upward, wondering. Are you up there? Are you up there, you bastard!

From a quarter mile away, the roar of the explosion hit him a second and a half later but already he was staggered by the impact, as the concussion raced across the channel, slamming into the soles of his feet as he stood at the water's edge. Another towering explosion amidships of the *Oklahoma* . . . he never knew a torpedo could fling such a column of water heavenward, a flash thought of that terrible force bursting through the armor plating, smashing lower decks, pulping any sailors below, most of the poor bastards still asleep, thousands of tons of water crushing interior bulkheads like a hammer blow shattering a fragile crystal.

West Virginia, another column soaring up. *Arizona,* though docked inward with a supply vessel anchored on its port side, two more explosions, the torpedoes passing under the shallow-draft ship beside it. Foaming waves raced outward in concentric circles from each of the blasts, hundreds of tons of water now beginning to cascade down like a hurricane blast.

The vast bulk of the *Oklahoma* seemed to actually lift clear of the water, hovered, then sagged back down . . . more Kates screamed past him. He felt a snap whip blow, as if someone had clapped a hand next to his head, and turning saw that one of the tail gunners was swinging his machine gun back and forth, firing wildly. James felt a strange shudder, almost a detachment. The bastard had been shooting at him. He could almost see the man's face as the plane raced away . . . there was no immediate reaction within. He still stood there numbed . . . another spread of torpedoes slapped into the water, more wakes. My God, more for the *Oklahoma* . . . hadn't she already taken enough?

Then four more explosions, four more columns of water, each several hundred feet high. The first blast had come as a total surprise to the men on that ship, few were on deck, but now the deck was swarming with men, racing to their battle stations.

How much time had passed he suddenly wondered, he started to look down at his watch, realizing that he had dropped his cof-

海軍省許可濟第三八七號　6

*See caption on next page.

fee mug, the brown liquid spilling down his trousers. A minute, five minutes?

The concussion of the four explosions hit him with near simultaneous blows and staggered him so that he was driven backward. Antlike figures seemed to be caught up in the rising columns of water, fire, smoke, torn metal, antlike; some intact, some just

---

*Photograph taken from a Japanese plane during the torpedo attack on ships moored on both sides of Ford Island. View looks about east, with the supply depot, submarine base, and fuel tank farms in the right center distance. A torpedo has just hit USS West Virginia on the far side of Ford Island (center). Other battleships moored nearby are (from left): Nevada, Arizona, Tennessee (inboard of West Virginia) Oklahoma (torpedoed and listing) alongside Maryland, and California. On the near side of Ford Island, to the left, are light cruisers Detroit and Raleigh, target and training ship Utah and seaplane tender Tangier. Raleigh and Utah have been torpedoed, and Utah is listing sharply to port. Japanese planes are visible in the right center (over Ford Island) and over the Navy Yard at right. Japanese writing in the lower right states that the photograph was reproduced by authorization of the Navy Ministry. Naval Historical Center.

parts of bodies, men who had raced up onto the deck, some in uniforms, some just in skivvies, blown clear off the ship, tumbling through the air.

The great ship lurched like a punch-drunk boxer taking the killing blow, seeming to stagger and then just slowly began to fall. The great ship was rolling. It was beyond any horror he had ever dreamed possible, such a ship, the pride of his navy, and it was dying, the great pagoda towers leaning now over the water, the entire port side of the battleship ripped open from bow to rudder, tens of thousands of tons of water actually blown back and away for an instant by the blasts, now filling the vacuum, punching inward, bulkheads within collapsing from the force.

Oklahoma was rolling over. Her deck was now visible, hundreds of men, so antlike in appearance, the image searing into his soul so that he knew, never again could he ever see an image of men falling without thinking of this moment as they tumbled down the length of the deck. The concussions of hundreds of explosions were now washing across the harbor, other ships exploding fireballs of dozens of PBYs caught on the ground on Ford Island were going up, dozens more at Hickman behind him exploding. A Zero, guns blazing, racing past him, strafing the subs, a boy valiantly struggling to get the sub's flag up, pitching backward off the deck.

But it was the *Oklahoma* that held him, as it continued to roll. The great pagodas, two hundred feet high, like skyscrapers twisted, groaned, and then tumbled over. Atop them he could see the horror of a half dozen men atop each, tangled up in the steel latticework beams, plummeting to their deaths.

The deck was now nearly vertical, men clinging to stanchions, splinter shields, gun barrels, ladders, some dropping, others hanging on, hundreds of heads bobbing in the water, upon which oil flames were beginning to spread.

She rolled, turning over, the three great gun turrets tearing free of their mountings, each turret weighing as much as an entire destroyer. He saw a brief instant of men in the water, holding hands up over heads as if to ward off the crushing blow . . . gone, foaming muddy waves spreading outward, the deck now nearly inverted, screaming men trying to swim out from underneath, sucked back in by the tidal-like surge of water rushing into the bowels of the ship.

A foaming wave, capped with flickering fire, black with oil, rolled out and away as the *Oklahoma* turtled and sank down to rest on the muddy bottom . . . hundreds of men, still alive, most of them dying, trapped inside. And in his feverish nightmares he could imagine the horror within. The ship in her death roll. It was his ship in a way, the way all men who love the navy feel about one ship in particular . . . when she was new and gleaming, smelling of fresh paint, the battle drills. He could remember the battle drills. We always knew they were drills, and the alarms would sound and those asleep would grumble awake to dog down the doors then practice emergency escape, climb one at a time up the narrow vertical ladders, unscrew the hatch in the false, or "splinter ceiling," then you had to jackknife yourself over because the escape routes were not lined up, but rather were offset one from the other, so that a plunging shot could not come straight down through them . . . but it meant that those getting out would have to know how to climb, jackknife, crawl along a narrow space between the "splinter shield" or false deck above, a space not much more than eighteen inches wide, then reach the next hatch, and open it, to gain the next deck. Then up another ladder, and repeat the process again. If down in the lower decks and engine room, it would take a dozen such climbs to reach topside.

And always it was a drill, and there was light, there was no being thrown from a bunk while still in deepest sleep into a nightmare of flame and darkness and cascading muddy water.

But there was no such warning this time, no whisper that the "old man" would pull an escape drill before breakfast today. There was no understanding of how, or why, of who had done this, and why it was happening to you now, as flames shot through open doors that were not "dogged down" and screams echoed, and a tidal wall of black, foaming water surged down the corridors, bearing with it burned men, screaming men, dead men.

Those still alive tried for the escape ladders, but now what had been topside in but a few minutes had pitched over to a forty-five-degree angle, and then a ninety-degree angle and he could imagine those boys within, clawing at the ladders, a petty officer trying to keep them calm, but then panicking as well, for what was up was now sideways . . . and then, merciful God, it was going upside down and the emergency lights snapped off, and water was racing upward at you, or was it downward, thousands of tons of water, and comrades were clawing at your legs, screaming for you to keep moving, but you couldn't move . . . you were trapped in a darkness as black as the lowest circle of hell . . . as the water crushed into your lungs and the only light, the blinding flashes within your mind as you died, trapped in the blackness.

James could not think, could not even begin to absorb the vision nightmares that were searing into him. He barely noticed *West Virginia* or *Maryland,* engulfed in flames. A pockmarking streak of machine-gun bullets stitched across the water in front of him, a round slashing the bench he had been sitting on but minutes before. Numbed, he looked, it appeared to be coming from *Arizona,* a gunner trying to track on a Zero streaking by, the gunner firing wildly. He didn't move.

And then, in that instant, the *Arizona* just disappeared. The flash of the explosion was so intense, so blinding, he shielded his face from the heat. The fireball bursting outward was as hot, as brilliant as the sun. Within its flame he could see glimpses of the entire ship, forward of the bridge lifting into the air, clear out of the water and then the shock wave hit, staggering him backward, for an instant he thought the flame of it would actually wash over him and for the first time . . . in how long now . . . three minutes . . . five . . . six or seven? . . . he realized his own mortal peril. He dove to the ground. Behind him he could hear hundreds of windows shattering, screams, the fireball climbing heavenward, or was it climbing into hell for it seemed as if the entire sky was awash with flame. Jagged hunks of metal soared out of the fireball, splashing into the water, there was a momentary glimpse of a plane, wing sheered off, perhaps caught in the blast, tumbling in a spiraling dive, slamming into the harbor, engine howling, propellers sheering off and spinning out and away . . . parts of bodies, entire bodies falling from the sky . . . damned souls descending into the fiery pit, for the harbor was now awash with flaming oil.

The top of a palm tree snapped off, crashing down beside him.

The fireball spread outward and then was gone, replaced by a plume of oily black smoke boiling up, the blown-out wreckage of the *Arizona* collapsing inward upon itself, the twisted pagoda tower leaning over drunkenly, boiling steam hissing as it settled to the bottom.

And then . . . they were gone. The tormen-

Sailors in a motor launch rescue a survivor from the water alongside the sunken USS West Virginia *(BB-48) during or shortly after the Japanese air raid on Pearl Harbor. USS* Tennessee *(BB-43) is inboard of the sunken battleship. Note extensive distortion of* West Virginia*'s lower midships superstructure, caused by torpedoes that exploded below that location. Also note 5-inch .25 caliber deck gun, still partially covered with canvas, boat crane swung outboard and empty boat cradles near the smoke-stacks, and base of radar antenna atop* West Virginia*'s foremast.* **Naval Historical Center**

tors were just gone. Already the Kates and the Vals were winging off, disappearing back into dots. Over the airfields the Zeroes still wheeled and turned like hawks, looking for some prey that had escaped their first pounce, as if offering a challenge to any that remained within the smoking wreckage to come up and offer a fight challenge . . . but the rest were just simply gone.

And the fleet before him was gone as well. Every battleship was aflame, settling into the mud, all except *Nevada,* though trailing a plume of smoke from a hit, there was smoke as well boiling up from her stacks, she was firing up, cutting anchor lines away.

But as for the rest, they were gone.

He came to his feet, the world a blur. He fumbled for his glasses, they were covered in mud and clumsily he took them off, wiping them clean on his mud- and grass-stained shirt. He put them back on.

There was a marine lying on the ground nearby, curled up by the tree whose top had been sheered off, lying face up. He wanted to speak to someone, anyone, and woodenly he started to walk over and then slowed.

The front of the man's shirt was a spreading pool of red, eyes wide, unfocused, mouth open in a silent scream. It was the marine sergeant who had saluted him but minutes before.

What do I do? He wanted to scream for help; he looked around. Out on the lawn scores of men were beginning to stand back up. Some were not moving at all, others were screaming, rolling back and forth in agony, one, sleeve torn off, arm torn off with it was just walking about in slow circles, blood coursing down his side.

He felt he should go to him, but what about the dead marine? Should I see to him?

I'm in shock, he realized. The moment came back, and he struggled to hold the tears. The moment when Davy had died, the last breath slipping out of him, and he could no longer react, think, even at that moment feel anything other than a black empty void.

Sound started to return to his consciousness. Sirens, ships' bells, a staccato barking of a machine gun, the heavier crump explosion of a gun firing from the deck of one of the destroyers anchored in the narrow loch. A ship's steam whistle shrieking, men shouting, a woman's screams, overarching all a roiling, hissing roar, the thunder of ships burning, explosions lighting off as ammunition stores detonated, the whine of a plane, a lone Zero streaking down the length of the harbor, machine guns blazing, strafing men struggling in the water, and now a growing fusillade of return fire, tracers crisscrossing the harbor, the wild firing causing him to momentarily duck again, some windows shattering in the main administration building.

That's where I should go, he realized. Get back to my post, find something there, that's where I should go.

He walked slowly, back aching from being knocked over by the explosion of *Arizona,* coming around the flank of the building and then to the front.

Now it was a madhouse. He caught a glimpse of Kimmel's car pulled up over the curb, more vehicles were piling in, horns blaring, men leaping out, some running about wildly, as if driven to a frenzied insanity, shouting wildly to no one, to everyone.

The marine guard he had walked past but a half hour ago was crouched against the side of the building, .45 drawn, looking heavenward, ready to fight his own war.

"Watson!"

It was Collingwood, standing in the doorway leading back down to the dungeon.

He looked at him, unable to reply.

"You all right?"

He couldn't reply and Collingwood came up, reaching out, motioning to his left arm, and James winced and looked down. His shirt sleeve was torn open, blood trickling down to his wrist and covering his claw.

"You're hit, man."

From what he couldn't tell. The Jap gunner, the wild firing, a fragment from the *Arizona*. He didn't know . . . other than the fact that it did indeed now hurt. He shook his head and almost chuckled. The claw was actually mangled, bent back, the leather socket holding it to his arm torn, blood oozing out.

Damn to be hit in the same place twice, how strange he thought. Both times in surprise attacks, and he looked back up at the sky, catching a glimpse of a Kate, flying high up, marked with distinctive yellow and red stripes . . . you goddamn bastards.

"My God, man, you were right. We were right. It was here," Collingwood gasped.

He stepped into the foyer, the clock on the wall . . . 8:15 a.m. He had walked out of here just 35 minutes ago.

"As if our being right matters now," James replied softly.

Over Pearl Harbor
8:22 a.m.

Orbiting at 3,500 meters, Strike Leader Fuchida trained his binoculars on the wreckage below. It was beyond all he had hoped for, two possibly three of the battle-ships were destroyed, one of them, he believed was the *Arizona;* it was hard to tell because of the smoke. It had just simply disappeared in the massive explosion that had buffeted his plane so hard that for a moment he thought he had been hit by flak.

Damage was far beyond the most optimistic estimates of what both he and Genda had made across all the long months of planning. They had assumed that 50 percent of the strike force might not make it to the target area or would be so harassed by enemy fighters and antiaircraft fire as to divert them away.

Nothing had stopped them, and only now were the antiaircraft bursts beginning to come up, nearly all of them ineffective.

He felt a strange mix of emotions. There was, of course, the sheer elation that a plan he had helped conceive had gone so flaw-lessly. And yet two things troubled him. Where were the carriers? Not one was in port, their usual mooring points empty. Even as he had his pilot orbit above the center of the harbor now, so he could scan out to sea, sweeping the horizon with his binoculars, hoping that either the carriers had fled upon some warning, but then if so, swarms of fighters would have been up to greet them, or were just now stumbling into the range and the incoming second-strike wave could still be diverted to deal with them.

That would finish the coup. The carriers sunk, not just in the harbor but out in the open sea, without any hope of recovery. But there was no sign of them, and he fixed his attention back below, for the second-strike wave would arrive in a few more minutes, and he was preparing a checklist of targets still to be hit.

Then he had a second thought. It had been almost too easy and as he surveyed the flaming wreckage of the battleships, the scores of planes burning on the ground at Ford Island, Hickam Field, he began to wonder, and to the north amid the rising plumes from Wheeler, he could see the dot-like figures in white and khaki running about, could imagine hundreds more burning in the flaming waters of the bay, watching even as the Zeroes that were still loitering over the target area, waiting for any challenging planes to come up, arcing down to strafe . . . and he did find the sensation chilling.

The target before had been an abstract, a map, a model, a test run on simulated targets. How many were dead down there?

. . . and though imbued with the firm belief that it was necessary for the survival of Japan, he felt as he had over China, that in fact there was no feeling, no hatred, no fierce desire to kill as some of his pilots had expressed so fervently, if for no other reason than to appear to have the spirit of bushido.

There was a moment of wonder, wondering what those below must now feel toward him.

"Sir! The second wave!"

His pilot was pointing forward as they continued to bank through a shallow turn, heading eastward. From over Diamond Head he could see the wave of Vals and Kates soaring in. A major part of the second strike had been detailed to come down on the east coast of the island, in part because in the interval of launching the first and second waves, the carriers had moved to the southeast, but also their planning assumed that any American defenses would swarm over the center of the island and to the north.

But still there was no opposition in the air. Had they truly caught all of them on the ground?

Zeroes leading the second strike raced in to assume covering positions, and as they did so, the last of the fighters from the first wave did one more dive to strafe, expending the last of their ammunition, then broke off, heading westward to depart the target area and once well clear, to turn northward to the rendezvous point twenty miles north of the island, where aircraft equipped with homing equipment would guide the fighters back to their ships. Switching his radio back on he began to detail off the targets. Kates armed with torpedoes were to now focus on docked cruisers and the one battleship, it looked like *Nevada,* which was beginning to make way, turning about to run for the open sea. If it could be caught and sunk at the mouth of the harbor, that would truly be a disaster for the Americans, perhaps shutting down the facility for weeks, even months, bottling up the entire fleet.

Many of the lighter vessels, destroyers and cruisers, were firing up their boilers, half a dozen of them beginning to make way. We must attack them as well.

And then the barrage started. This time, at least on the ground, the gunners were ready, sending up a blizzard of fire, little of it properly aimed but even as the first of the Kates dropped down for a run on the *Nevada,* it disintegrated into flames.

In less than a minute the second stage of the fight was on. Torpedo bombers and dive bombers were dropping in. Horizontal bombers at two thousand meters crossing over Ford Island and Hickam, aiming to take out the hangers. Another Val, trailing smoke, rolled over and went into a tight spiral, pilot regaining control at the last instant and guiding it into a hangar, dying as a samurai.

More explosions bracketed the battleships, though he was now ordering the remaining planes to stand off from there to seek other targets, but more than one pilot, drilled that the battleships were the primary target, dove in anyhow, unable to resist the claim that it was his bomb or torpedo that finished the deed.

Nevada was hit, and hit again, and he held his breath, waiting to see if it would begin to settle, or better yet, detonate, its wreckage blocking the entry. The ship began to swerve away from the channel, and he grunted with approval for her captain. He was making the right move, clearing the approach, moving to beach his mighty ship, which was all but fatally wounded. A cluster of bombs tore into the large dry dock, hitting the battleship and smaller destroyers contained within, but the great floodgates held. He tried to order a couple of the Kates to swing wide around the bay, line up, and drop their torpedoes for a straight-in run on the dry-dock gates, destroying that which would cripple their primary repair facility but in what was now a wild confusion of radio traffic, planes maneuvering in every direction, yet more explosions igniting, it was impossible to direct the fight any longer.

And as in the first attack, in little more than ten minutes it was over. The seventy Kates and Vals assigned to hit the main harbor in the second strike swinging clear of their targets, breaking to east and west, throttling up, skimming low and then climbing once well clear, but the price now was heavier, far heavier; he watched as three, then four more of his planes trailing smoke, plummeted down, or just simply disintegrated in midair.

It was hard to make any sense whatsoever of the action now. The entire harbor area was wreathed in a thick, black oily smoke, as the last of the Zeroes broke away from their covering positions.

It was over.

He tried to scan with his binoculars but that was useless, too much smoke. He ordered his pilot to break into a steep 60-degree bank, circling sharply, giving him a clear view straight down.

Battleship row was finished, both airfields

as well. Well over a score of other ships were damaged or destroyed to varying degrees . . . a victory in two strikes, each of little more than ten minutes' duration that made Tsushima pale in comparison.

And yet, in all the confusion of battle he saw so many more targets yet to be taken. The submarines, so feared and dreaded in all the planning for this strike. At least six were tied off, undamaged. In the narrow loch, a score of other ships, destroyers and cruisers, were untouched, their guns firing at the retreating planes.

The fuel storage tanks. That caught his attention now. There had been general talk that if the Zeroes and Vals ran out of targets to strike the oil tanks with strafing runs and those Vals ladened with 100-kilogram bombs to drop there as well. It appeared as if none had been touched even though the tank farms directly adjoined the navy base.

And yet again, the carriers. Where in hell were the carriers?

"Take us to the rendezvous, straight across the island!" he ordered, and his pilot, nodding, set a northerly course.

At 180 knots it would take little more than eight minutes to traverse Oahu, time to evaluate and radio in. In little more than three minutes what was left of Wheeler was clearly in view. Half a dozen Zeroes only now breaking away . . . and there, to the west he could see two of them weaving, dodging in and out of clouds, dark green planes in pursuit. At least two American fighters were finally up!

Two, that was all he could see. Two out of an estimated more than two hundred. Far off to the west he thought he could see a smudge of smoke darkening the horizon, the army air bases on the east end of the island, hit by both first and second waves.

But other than the distant dogfight there was nothing, no resistance! As his pilot edged around Wheeler, moving clear of the light scattering of antiaircraft fire coming up, he could see scores of aircraft burning on the ground, strangely they were parked wingtip to wingtip . . . what was left of them.

He picked up his radio mike and clicking the key, began to transmit the afterstrike report back to the flagship. Pushing to the north end of the island he kept a careful scan, the air, earlier so crowded with planes of the Empire, was now all but empty, and still no sight of American resistance other than the distant dogfight. Looking back he could see the blanket of smoke spreading out and upward from Pearl, from Wheeler, and Schofield, and even from the east end of the island at Kaneohe.

The island was all but defenseless. Crossing out over the surf he looked down and was diverted for a moment by the beauty of the place, the lush tropical green, the turquoise blue of the ocean, the foaming white surf pounding into shore. The final rendezvous point was twenty miles north of the island and he expected to pick up at least several of the fighters there, but the sky was empty. He ordered his pilot to circle tightly for several minutes, ignoring the news that their fuel was starting to run dangerously low. They had been one of the first of the strike wave to take off over four hours ago, all of that first wave should already be back and landed, preparing to turn around for the next mission.

He wanted to see, as well, if there was any organized pursuit or reconnaissance, for surely they'd send a scout plane up to loiter back, spotting the direction of the retiring aircraft and thus gain some bearing, but still the sky was empty.

"Time for home," he finally announced, and he could hear the sigh of relief as his pilot turned north, northeast, working on the calculation of where the fleet was predicted to be. But after a few minutes he felt a sudden concern and ordered a turn back to the rendezvous, those planes dogfighting, they were fighters, their navigational ability trying to pick out a fleet at sea minimal at best, and his effort was rewarded. Within a minute he spotted a lone Zero, flying slow, a fluttering of dark smoke from its exhaust. He swung in alongside the ailing Zero, the pilot recognizing the command markings on Fuchida's plane and saluting, obviously filled with relief as Fuchida smiled, saluted back, and signaled for him to follow . . . together the two planes, the last of the two strikes on Pearl Harbor, winged north, back to their carriers.

Malaya Near the Border with Siam
1:35 a.m. Local Time

"Sergeant Harris . . . come on now, come on!" Cecil shouted.

The first shell had hit near the side of the road leading into the airfield. The bastards had certainly marked out this target well. Through shelling the small airfield at night, they had already set several aircraft ablaze. He had hoped to get in, find a pilot, and commandeer a liaison plane to get him and Harris back to Singapore to report. It was a full-scale invasion, coming on hard and fast. They had left the beach a half hour ago when they saw the first of the Japanese landing craft coming in. This was no raid; it was a full-scale invasion, support shippings coming in closer to shore, ready to run into the small harbor once the troops aboard the landing craft had seized the position.

Two shells had bracketed the road, ridiculous thought, but he felt as if somehow they had spotted the small Bentley Harris was driving, a splinter blowing out a tire.

He had told Harris to just drive on the damn thing, but the marine sergeant refused.

"Have it changed in a jiffy, sir, can do this in me sleep."

And while jacking up the car, two more shells had winged in and blown fifty yards away, while yet more rained down on the airfield itself, heavy stuff, five- and eight-inchers from the looks of it.

"Harris?"

There was no answer. Cecil had sprawled out by his side when they heard the incoming.

In the darkness he reached out to shake him and then pulled his hand back.

He fumbled for the "torch" and flicked the switch on.

The man was dead, a fragment having sheered into his temple, side of his face shattered. It had been instant.

Damn all, he sighed. Poor bugger, survives Gallipoli, Palestine, Iraq in the 1920s, and then to die like this.

There was nothing he could do for him. It all seemed so senseless, so useless this death, focusing it all back down to one man, whom fate had decreed would find his end here, on a nameless road, halfway round the world from the East End slums of his boyhood to this final place.

More shells came in, and he crouched down, feeling guilty for using Harris's body as a shield.

He stood back up, felt guilty, but knew Harris had a pack of smokes in his pocket and half rolling him over he took them out along with his American lighter and lit one. The hell with light discipline, a burning hangar was lighting up the night sky, barrels of fuel blowing into the air like rockets.

Slinging his notebook bag over his shoulder, he walked toward the airport, hoping to find a ride to get the hell out of here.

Akagi
10:03 a.m. Local Time

"That's him!" Genda cried excitedly, and in a rare moment Yamamoto let his emotions

show, sighing with open relief. It was Fuchida's plane, flying low coming straight for
Akagi, a Zero, trailing smoke, by his side.

Fuchida shot past, wagging his wings and
snapping off a salute, canopy pulled back,
and then banked up high and away. Clearing the way for the damaged Zero to come
in.

The Zero banked in sharply, barely lining
up, drifting somewhat to port, correcting,
then coming down hard, bouncing, almost
losing control as it drifted a quarter of the
way down the deck of the carrier, then settling in, tail hook finally catching on the
fifth wire and screeching to a stop.

Deck crew worked feverishly, disconnect-
ing the hook, a crew chief up on the wing of
the plane, directing the pilot to throttle up,
rolling to the forward elevator to clear the
deck for the last of the planes to come in.

From four miles out Fuchida was taking
his time, letting the damaged Zero get clear
as he started in on his approach, lining up,
following in perfectly, wheels touching down
when only thirty feet past the fantail, tail
hook snagging, the Kate lurching to a stop.

It was the last plane in, and a wave of relief
seemed to sweep the deck of *Akagi,* the last
plane was in, the last plane bearing the hero
who had led the strike, and cheering

erupted, dozens of men breaking discipline, coming forward to swarm around the plane as Fuchida, with a flourish, stood up, saluted the flag of Japan, then the Z flag, and then finally the bridge where the admiral stood waiting.

Alighting onto the deck, grinning with delight, he was surrounded by admirers, his crew chief coming up a bit shyly to salute him. With a ceremonial flourish Fuchida removed the headband he had worn throughout the strike and handed it back.

"A keepsake to your family," he said. "Proof that you, too, were with me there."

The chief's eyes filled with tears, and he bowed low in thanks.

Pilots from both strikes swarmed around him, shouting, cheering but his eyes were on Genda, up on the open bridge, and he did not need to be told to report in. Gaining the stairs up he took them two at a time in spite of his heavy flying suit and boots, hot now in the late morning air at sea level.

Taking off his flight helmet he approached the open bridge and there was Yamamoto, standing rigid, but for once there was a flicker of a smile, an exchange of salutes, and then an open smile and handshake.

"I am pleased to see you safely back; you had us worried with your late return."

"I wanted to make sure all who could get back did," he replied modestly.

"May I ask about our losses?"

"We think thirty," Genda replied.

Thirty, he wondered who. To lose a comrade was always a shock, but still, just thirty. Only the day before, they had talked about a hundred, maybe a hundred and fifty. It was a miracle, a proof indeed of the support of the gods of Japan this day.

Yamamoto motioned for him to follow and with Genda, and chief of staff Kusaka, who had stayed on even though his "boss" Nagumo had been relieved, the four went to the small aft conference room, Genda closing the door.

"You must be thirsty," Genda offered, and Fuchida nodded, the mention of drink for the first time making him aware of just how thirsty he indeed was, his mouth as dry as a bone.

Genda motioned to a thermos, opened it and poured out a cup of tea into a mug and offered it over. Fuchida gladly took it and drained it in a few gulps.

"Your report now," Yamamoto asked, obviously impatient to begin.

"All battleships in the harbor have either been totally destroyed or rendered inoperative for months, sir."

"The carriers, though."

"As I reported by radio, no carriers were in the harbor."

"Your opinion?" Yamamoto asked, at the three gathered round him.

"Sir, even now their three carriers might be preparing a counterstrike," Kusaka offered heatedly. "We do not know where they are. We must assume there was some warning, and they were able to clear the harbor. They could be anywhere, even behind us, preparing to launch a surprise counterstrike. I strongly urge that we should clear these waters as was planned in the war games before we sailed."

Genda, standing almost on the balls of his feet, just behind Kusaka, was barely able to contain himself.

Yamamoto nodded to him to speak

"Respectfully, sir," Genda replied, "I must beg to disagree."

"Why so?" Yamamoto asked.

"Sir," and he turned to face Kusaka, "what was the purpose of this mission?"

"Is this the time for some didactic discussion of mission goals?" Kusaka replied sharply. "We have achieved what we set out to achieve, we have sunk the American fleet. To risk our precious carriers, which are needed elsewhere now, would be folly."

Fuchida, junior ranker in the room, was silent, and was grateful to all the gods that he had first ventured to speak to Genda two months ago about who should command this mission. For if not, perhaps it would be Nagumo they were having this meeting with rather than Yamamoto . . . and if that had been the case, he knew what the decision would have been.

"We have only sunk part of them," Genda interjected forcefully, "and might I add a part of their fleet that ultimately posed little direct threat to us."

"I would not call the guns of *Oklahoma,* of *Maryland,* and *Arizona* a minor threat," Kusaka snapped back.

"Those guns were destroyed in little more than ten minutes by the first strike wave. What happened this day changed naval warfare forever, sir. It is the carrier now that decides the day."

"In this most unusual of circumstances," Kusaka replied hotly, "ships anchored without warning of impending strike."

"A question, please," Yamamoto interjected, looking now at Fuchida.

"Anything, sir."

"There was absolutely no resistance, none as the first wave came in?"

"None, sir. No planes aloft, it was long

550

minutes before the first of their guns replied, and by then the damage was all but complete."

Yamamoto turned away from the group and went back out on the bridge for a moment, open doorway framing him. He finally turned and walked back in. "You are certain you had complete surprise?" And now he looked at Fuchida.

"Yes, sir. A few, maybe half a dozen of their planes sortied, to face the second strike. None for the first wave. For the first five minutes or so barely a gun was fired in reply. It was a complete and total surprise. My radio operator was tuned into their commercial station and they continued to broadcast music for at least ten minutes after the attack started before finally an announcer came on with a warning saying they were under a surprise attack and all personnel to report to their stations."

Yamamoto sighed and then wearily shook his head.

"How complete is the damage?"

"Sir, the battleships are burning hulks." He paused and looked over at Genda, who nodded for him to continue. "But there are still numerous targets."

"Such as?"

"Sir, their oil tank farms. You will recall

that in planning we talked about them. Enough fuel to keep their fleet in operation for half a year or more. The huge dry dock. Its gate is still intact. Shatter that and it can delay repairs of numerous ships. And besides that, sir, there are dozens of destroyers, cruisers, and, most importantly, submarines that are tied off in rows."

"Are you certain?" Yamamoto interjected. "The smoke, the confusion. Surely most of those ships were hit as well."

"Sir, I regret but I think too many of our pilots were intent on hitting the big targets, the battleships. More emphasis in the second strike should have been placed on these other ships and the oil supplies. I take responsibility for that fault."

"Heat of action," Yamamoto said quietly. "You did masterfully, Commander."

"Thank you, sir."

"Your recommendation?"

"Launch a third strike at once, sir. There will be little resistance now other than their antiaircraft fire, which did not prove to be too efficient. They were panicked. Gain complete air control. Expand the zone of damage. A third strike is essential now."

He gestured to the porthole where, barely visible, one of the fast battleships steamed as escort.

"Venture the battleships in, sir, at dusk and bombard the harbor during the night to sow even more confusion and damage. We have control of the target; exploit that control to the fullest while we can."

"To launch a third strike will mean our loitering here in these waters for the rest of the day," Kusaka replied sharply. "Surely they will acquire us and launch a counter-strike. Even now their carriers might be steaming this way, ready to launch. We have won. Let us not throw away our victory now with overconfidence."

Fuchida held his breath, looking from one to the other, and then, within seconds, the risk he had taken, the risk he knew Genda had taken, but would not admit to, became clear; they had indeed changed what might have been.

Yamamoto looked straight at Genda.

"Prepare for a third strike to be launched no later than 1400 hours."

Fuchida actually felt tears come to his eyes. He sensed that here, at this moment, some profound change had indeed occurred. Too many had spoken of this attack as "a raid." No, now it was a true fight, a true battle of annihilation, just as he and Genda had talked about for so many years.

"But what of their carriers?" Kusaka persisted.

"I think they are far away. We know they are used to ferry aircraft to other islands such as Midway and Wake. I think they are south of Oahu. But as a precaution we will send back but half our available bombers for the next strike. Some to be armed with light bombs to be scattered over the oil tank fields, others with heavier demolitions loads to smash the destroyers, submarines, and cruisers still at anchor, the precious torpedoes to be held back except for a special task group to torpedo the main dry-dock gate.

"The remaining planes will be divided into two groups. A strong air patrol of fighters to be maintained over our own fleet. A second strike force, armed with torpedoes and armor piercing if we should locate their carriers. Additional search planes to be sent out to seek them to the west and south of Oahu."

Kusaka stood rigid, unable to speak.

"Were you not followed back by any scout planes of theirs?" he asked, as if grasping for a final straw to hold back Yamamoto's decision.

"No, sir, not a one. It is why I lingered as long as I did and kept close watch on my return. No one followed us."

"Then prepare my orders. Commander Fuchida, your report has been decisive, now go and see to the next strike wave, I want you to lead it."

Fuchida sprinted from the room.

2:45 p.m. Local Time

"There it is!"

Though the air was cool at ten thousand feet, Fuchida had to lift his goggles up and wipe his eyes, which were stinging with sweat.

His pilot was pointing forward, slightly to port. He raised his binoculars, looking over the pilot's shoulder, and grunted approval.

Navigation was good. How could it not be, commercial radio stations in Honolulu were still broadcasting, some with announcements and news alerts, amazingly one still playing music. All the lead navigation planes of his strike force had to do was dial in the signal, set their directional antenna, and then ride the beam straight in to their target.

They were coming in at ten thousand feet, taking advantage of the high toppings of the midday clouds, a bumpy ride when going through them, dangerous as well for formations. He suspected that two of his Vals, which had disappeared, most likely had collided in one of the clouds, but it kept them concealed . . . and amazingly, they had yet to sight a single American plane!

Still, once near land, the Americans would be blind and deaf not to see and hear the strike force of 100 planes approaching Kahuku Point, a mix of Zeroes, dive bombers, and torpedo bombers. The admiral had decided that only fifteen of the planes would carry torpedoes this time, and both he and Genda agreed. When the enemy carrier force was finally spotted, those precious weapons would be of better use there. The mission of eight of the torpedo-laden planes was to blow open the gates of the massive dry dock and the smaller ones if possible. Its destruction would render Pearl Harbor useless as a major repair facility, forcing heavily damaged ships to retire all the way to the American West Coast. That would then set those wounded ships up for Japanese submarines who would be waiting off Hawaii to pick off slow-moving crippled ships. The other torpedo planes were to focus on any ships attempting to flee the harbor, ideally to sink them in the main channel, even a destroyer going to the channel bottom could very well bottle it up, and prevent ships from coming in for days, perhaps even weeks or months.

The other Kates and all the Vals were loaded with a variety of ordnance, a fair percentage carrying lighter 50- and 100-kilo bombs, to destroy repair shops, the headquarters for the American commander in the Pacific; the thin-skinned submarines, which the admiral had declared were now a highest priority target; and the oil tank farms that sprawled out to the northeast side of the harbor.

Kahuku was clearly visible through a hole in the clouds. Ten miles off, from there twenty-five more to Pearl. He could feel the sweat beading down his back. He wanted this attack; the rewards could be profound, but he knew as well that this time it was not going to be as easy. Surprise was gone and now the Americans would be trying to stop him.

"Over there!"

He looked to where his pilot pointed, a lone plane coming out of the clouds toward them, still about four or five miles off, but standing out stark and clear against the backdrop of a towering cumulus cloud.

They had been spotted, but so far no organized response.

Only one plane up, a lone scout. He made a quick decision. The primary plan would be followed. Half a dozen fighters to hover over the airbase at Kaneohe to keep any surviving planes on the ground, the rest of the strike force to push straight in, Zeroes in the lead in case there were any surprises ahead. He raised his flare gun up and fired it, one red shell, signal to proceed straight toward the target as planned. Seconds later, six of his Zeroes throttled up and banked to port, ready to close on the plane that had spotted them, then to push on to Kaneohe.

The lone fighter was closing in, its stubby form registering. Insane, an old P-36, only one, no formation, no squadrons. He could only shake his head at their stupidity or incompetence . . . and also he had to admit admiration for the spirit of bushido of that lone pilot, whoever he was.

Nine thousand feet over Kahuku
2:47 p.m. Local Time

"Repeat, eighty-plus Japs. Zeroes, Vals, looks like Kates. Bearing from Kahuku seven-five, at ten thousand, heading."

Lieutenant Junior Grade Jeremiah Sims, class of 1940, Purdue, who but a few months ago thought that being in the army air corps reserves was a grand deal, raised his goggles to wipe the sweat from his eyes then pulled them back down.

This wasn't supposed to be happening. It was supposed to be a posting to Hawaii; plenty of flying, weekends on the beach, just swarming with girls eager to date a pilot; not this. Seven hours ago he had actually been on a secluded beach below Diamond Head. A wonderful night with a girl named Dianne.

This wasn't supposed to be happening . . .

He caught a glimpse of the planes that disappeared into the clouds, only to surge out again seconds later. He tried to run the calculation, all the calculations, count them, their heading, his heading, a quick scan of instruments, throttle full open, manifold pressure nearing red line, carburetor deicer on, no switch it off, need more power . . . flick the cover off the machine-gun switch, slight fluctuation of the wings, unsteady on the stick . . . goddamn it, stop shaking!

"Their heading estimated 235 degrees," and his concentration broke. He caught the flash of a Jap, plane white, nearly invisible against the clouds except for that red meatball painted on the wing, breaking down toward him, two more following.

Turn in toward it. You won't make it to their bombers. Turn in on them. Head on!

Line it up in the sights. Jesus, it was coming on fast. They said the Zero was fast.

He remembered something, flicked the radio on.

"Repeat, eighty-plus Japs, eighty-plus, heading straight toward Pearl. I see them clearly! Closing to engage the bastards."

He dropped the mike, hand back on throttle, trying to push it just another inch forward, thumb poised on trigger. One Jap coming straight on. The other two now breaking, ready to circle.

Damn, they are fast.

He pushed down on the trigger, felt the recoil of the four thirty-calibers opening. Felt good, first time for real. Two of the Japs were breaking left and right as one came straight in.

What the hell do I do?

He kept his thumb down. Watched the tracers from his guns. They were plunging down, under the Jap. Pull back, raise your nose, drop them in on him!

When it hit, there was no sound, just the shattering of the forward canopy as a 20-millimeter shell from the Zero that had been turning to his port side slammed a 30-degree deflection shot straight into his engine, a dozen 7.7-millimeter machine-gun bullets stitching across his cockpit, severing rudder cables, one bullet slicing through his stomach. The Zero coming head-on opened up at nearly the same instant, the pilot shaking his head, the American firing far too soon, one of his 20-millimeter shells tearing into the guts of the Wright Cyclone engine, severing the gas line, the explosion of the shell and the heat of the engine igniting the hundred-octane fuel that sprayed out.

A second later the plane turned sharply into an accelerated stall, snap-rolled, and went into a spin, flame blowing into the cockpit.

Lieutenant Jeremiah Sims tried to struggle with the canopy release but already the Gs were building up from the spin, disorienting him, the explosion of flame searing into his lungs.

It was all happening too fast, dear God. The mountains, they're so green.

"Hail Mary, full of grace . . ."

Headquarters CinCPac
Pearl Harbor
2:47 p.m. Local Time

The phone rang, silencing the room. Admiral Kimmel picked it up, listened, features fixed.

"Sound the alert," was all he said, and he hung up. "It's a third attack coming in!"

Only seconds after he spoke the spine-chilling warble of an air-raid siren sounded, rising in pitch, all across the harbor more sirens began to echo, joined by the distant clarion call of a bugle aboard a cruiser sounding battle stations.

James stood in the far corner of the room. He had not said a word throughout the chaotic hour-long conference but felt throughout that he wanted to scream, to denounce, to scream a warning as the admiral, and vice admirals, captains, and commanders of all the various departments argued and recriminated and debated, with Kimmel silent, issuing few orders, his gaze at times drifting to the window with its shattered panes, the roar of ships burning along battleship row, a background symphony of disaster.

"Spotters along the northeast coast report an incoming wave of Japanese planes, fifty plus," Kimmel finally announced.

"Can we be sure?" a captain asked. "This is the fifth alarm since this morning."

"It was confirmed by a pilot in a P-36 out of Wheeler. He reported eighty-plus planes coming in."

Kimmel hesitated, looking back out the window.

"Said he was closing to engage, then contact was lost."

"Jesus Christ," someone whispered, "one of those antiques against a Zero."

James struggled against the nausea. He was enough of a pilot now to know what that lone pilot would accomplish.

"Gentlemen, go to your posts," Kimmel said quietly.

James looked over at Collingwood. What were their posts? During the infrequent drills for those on shore, they were told to simply put helmets on and stay in place down in the basement. They had men listening for any Japanese radio transmissions. There might be something for them to work on decoding. But now, with another attack coming in?

The room quickly emptied, men scattering, already there was gunfire. He looked out the window, a destroyer out in midharbor, racing past the burning battleships, with its forward and aft five-inch mounts pointed high, was already firing on something.

Kimmel remained motionless, and James realized that this man, at this moment, wished to be like the ship's captain of old, in fact was most likely praying for that fate. He would stay here, stand by the window, and pray that this time they hit him. A chief with hash marks halfway up his arm stood behind the admiral, and for a brief instant caught James's gaze of admiration, the flicker of his gaze indication for him to get the hell out and leave them.

He followed Collingwood out into the corridor. It was a flood of men rushing back and forth, some in panic, tin hats being put on, a few purposeful, grim-faced, it was like an ant nest stirred up into chaos.

"Let's get our people out," Collingwood shouted, "this place is a death trap."

James nodded in agreement and racing toward the door to their basement lair, he noticed that the marine guard was no longer there. Collingwood was far ahead of him, down the stairs, James unable to keep up. He had refused any morphine or treatment for his arm, sliced by something just above the stump of his hand. One of the female secretaries down in the basement had bandaged it with a torn-up piece of towel, blood soaking through, now dark, and by God it was hurting like hell now.

Collingwood, far ahead of him at the bottom of the stairs, again no guard there, fumbled for his keys, then pulled the door open.

"Everyone get the hell out!" he shouted. "Out now, we got another attack coming in!"

James felt absolutely useless and backed up against the wall as those who had worked for months trying to decipher warning of this moment began to race up the stairs. He wasn't sure what to do, some looking at him.

"Just get as far away from this building as you can," he offered. "Find some cover. We've got about ten minutes!"

The room emptied, Collingwood reappearing.

"Shouldn't we leave someone behind to guard," James offered.

After all, this was perhaps the most secured room of any room operated by the navy in the entire Pacific.

"It won't be here in ten more minutes," Collingwood said, almost grinning at the absurdity of James's offer. "Now let's get the hell out of here."

As they reached the top of the stairs and then out the main doors, they were greeted by a thunderous roar. The sound, the sight of it was spectacular. Of the eighty or so ships that had survived the first two attacks, only about a third of them had managed to round up crews, get a head of steam and start for sea, but every last one of them now had their guns manned. And most were firing, tracer shells arcing up, concussions from five-inchers, even some of the eight-inchers on the cruisers firing their heavy loads, hopefully fused to air-burst. James looked up at the blackening bursts of clouds dotting the skies over Pearl Harbor. He did not see a single plane, but by God, if an attack was coming in, it'd give them something to think about.

Six Miles Northeast of Pearl Harbor
2:55 Local Time

Canopy still open, Fuchida took the sight in, trying to stay calm, focused. So far only a scattering of American fighters had dared to intercept, their burning wreckage littering the landscape from Kahuku to the outskirts of Honolulu. His lead squadron of fighters were starting their dive on Hickam, ready to jump any opposition that was left and dared to come up.

But that was not his concern now. It was the wall of antiaircraft fire ahead. The sky was black with it. Panic firing, that was obvious, shells bursting at random altitudes from a thousand feet, all the way up to fifteen thousand feet or more. Below he could see several explosions igniting in the city, their gunners most likely forgetting to set for an altitude burst, the shells just arcing straight up and then coming down to kill on the ground. Indicator of their training, their panic . . . but still, the sight of it chilled him. This was not going to be like the first two attacks.

He slid the canopy closed, slapped his pilot on the shoulder, and leaning forward pointed straight ahead. Over Genda's objections, he had announced that this time he was going to personally lead the torpedo attack on the massive dry dock, rather than standing back. He wanted this, to add his own personal blow, and besides, his men needed this example now if they were going to brave what was ahead.

His plane banked over to the north, swinging wide, the other seven Kates of his attack group following, circling to the north of the harbor and then dropping down low, to race straight in and release at three hundred yards from the gates of the dock.

He felt his stomach surge up as his Kate nosed over and started to dive.

Planes and hangars burning at Wheeler Army Air Field, Oahu, soon after it was attacked in the morning of 7 December 1941, as seen from a Japanese navy plane. Donation of Theodore Hutton, 1942.
Naval Historical Center

Hickam Field
2:59 p.m. Local Time

Don Barber, moving awkwardly on what he called "his peg leg," stuck his head into the open cowling of a P-40, trying to help the crew chief trace back the wiring from the main solenoid, which must have been severed. It was one of the few surviving planes from the first attacks but had been hit by half a dozen rounds and some shrapnel. They had tried repeatedly to get the engine to turn over, but it refused to fire up.

He had no real business being here. It'd been nearly twenty-five years since he had flown for the army and had part of a leg blown away in the skies over France. But on Sunday mornings he liked to drop in, have coffee with "the boys," a couple of his old comrades from 1918 were still active on this base, with plenty of brass on their hats or hash marks on their sleeves and a pass on to the base was no problem.

He had arrived an hour before the first attack and since then had pitched in, helping with trying to get the few remaining planes airworthy in case the Japs came back.

The shriek of the air-raid siren had been background noise until someone came running toward them shouting that this was the real thing, not another false alarm.

"I think I got it!" the chief cried, pointing his flashlight up into the bowels of the Allison engine. Sure enough, several wires were clearly severed by what must have been a shell fragment not much bigger than a dime.

Without being prompted, Don pushed up a roll of black electrical tape. No time to replace the wires, splice, and tape. Hell, that's how it was done back in the last war.

The thought struck him hard. The last war. We're in another war.

"Goddamn it, chief! Fix it. I can see Japs!"

It was the pilot. The kid had missed the first two strikes but had finally made it into the base and had spent the last four hours strapped into the cockpit, ready to go up as soon as they figured out what the hell was wrong.

Don stuck his head out from under the cowling.

"We got it!" he said, trying to offer a reassuring grin. He could see the kid was scared, face pale, sweat soaked. He must be roasting in there, Don realized, remembering his own time, over twenty years ago, waiting to go up, ready to vomit with fear, and then trembling with anticipation when the engine of his Sopwith fired over, plane shaking, coming alive. Now he was reduced to just hanging around the base, watching with envy, offering flying lessons to civilians like his friend Watson, who had the luck of being called back in. The army had not seen fit to call him up, but damn it, he could still do something this day, even if it was just to hand up some tape to repair a plane and get back at the bastards.

"Shit, I need some more wire!"

The chief was halfway up inside the engine cowling, hand reaching back. Don looked around, a corporal tearing into a toolbox, pulling out a strand of medium gauge, a foot-long section.

"Strip the ends," Don shouted, the corporal using a pocketknife, blood suddenly spluttering from his thumb as he severed off the end of the wire rather than strip it.

Don grabbed the wire and the knife, worked to strip both ends clean.

"Give me the damn wire!" the chief shouted.

"It's coming," Don replied, trying to sound calm, he had to stay calm.

"Jesus Christ, they're coming in!"

Don looked up, saw several men were pointed toward the east end of the runway, razor-sharp silhouettes banking out of a diving turn, lining up, coming in. Men working on the few surviving planes began to scatter, running in every direction, a cacophony roar of gunfire. Hundreds of guns opening up, machine guns, but mostly handheld weapons, Springfields, a sergeant with perfect poise leveling a .45, a corporal with a tommy gun.

From one of the two Zeroes, he could see flame bursting from a wing, it started into a roll . . . it was coming straight toward them.

Goddamn, it was coming straight at them.

"The wire, give me the damn wire!" The chief mechanic was still up inside the guts

Sailors stand amid wrecked planes at the Ford Island seaplane base, watching as USS Shaw *(DD-373) explodes in the center background, 7 December 1941. USS* Nevada *(BB-36) is also visible in the middle background, with her bow headed toward the left. Planes present include PBY, OS2U and SOC types. Wrecked wing in the foreground is from a PBY.*
Naval Historical Center

of the engine, oblivious to what was about to happen.

The pilot in the cockpit, Don turned and caught his gaze, the boy was wide-eyed with impotent rage.

"Get me up there!" he screamed. "Get me up there!"

Feeling a strange detachment Don turned back and handed the wire up to the mechanic who did not see death winging in. The Zero, a hundred yards off, just another second . . . its starboard wing on fire, dug into the runway, the plane cartwheeling over, tumbling, tail section detaching in a fireball, coming straight at him.

Survive France, he thought. Die here . . . what the hell . . .

The disintegrating Zero plowed into the line of P-40s, in another second all, Japanese Zero, four American P-40s, twenty-three men, were consumed inside the fireball explosion.

He felt absolutely useless, yet again. He couldn't fire a gun, and many around him were, most of them firing wildly; all he could do was stand and watch as it started to unfold, yet again.

A fireball erupted off toward Hickam; it was hard to see since the battleships that were still afloat were burning fiercely, their oily black smoke drifting across the harbor, commingled with the continuing fires over on Ford Island.

The noise, an insane mix. Air-raid sirens, which had been silent during the first attack, now continued to howl, but were

Scene on the southeastern part of Ford Island, looking northeasterly, with USS California *(BB-44) in right center, listing to port after being hit by Japanese aerial torpedoes and bombs.* **Naval Historical Center**

nearly drowned out now by every gun in the harbor and beyond firing. A cruiser swinging to the north of Ford Island, what the hell was he doing going that way? was sending up a firestorm as 20-mm, 40-mm, five-inch mounts, and even the 8-inch mounts blazed away, concussion ripples racing across the harbor. Ships still tied off simply pointed their guns straight up, impromptu machine-gun nests, set up by marines to guard the approaches on to the base, fitted out with light .30-cals, water-jacketed .50-cals, or just Lewis guns and Springfield rifles, were pouring it upward as well. Though he felt guilty for feeling it, there was almost a thrill to it, as if he were a boy overawed by a long-anticipated Fourth of July show. Tracers, red, green, orange, crisscrossed the sky, puffs of smoke bursts, some at frightfully low levels, as the cruisers let loose. He swore for an instant that he could see the heavy shells soaring upward to detonate in crimson and black blasts of fire.

Collingwood tugged his sleeve and pointed. Coming in from the east, low . . . Kates, torpedoes slung beneath, eight of them. They were already west of Honolulu, some tracers snapping around them, from the north, two P-40s were zooming downward as if hugging the mountain slope north of the city.

"Get the sons of bitches!" Collingwood shouted.

James looked over at him. He had worked with this gentle, mildly spoken man for nearly a year . . . it was the first time he had heard him swear.

"Sir!"

It was his tail gunner, reaching around

with one hand to slap him on the shoulder and then point to the north. Two enemy fighters.

He turned back to his task, the two Zeroes assigned to escort this group would contend with them.

At far lower altitude it was harder to distinguish landmarks. He felt a flash of regret, he should have taken the more difficult responsibility of command, stayed up at ten thousand feet as he had in the first strikes, to observe, direct. But no, he was in it now, and there was a fierce joy to it.

They were straight on course as planned, approaching from the east toward the north end of the base. Almost directly ahead was the largest of the oil tank farms; that is where he would turn, to start swinging around to line up on his target.

They were skimming low, less than a hundred feet off the ground now, buildings racing past, glimpses of people running, some tracers snaking up, rattlelike hailstones striking the plane, their starboard wing, a few holes, nothing serious.

Half a mile . . . quarter mile. Just a few more seconds.

Flash of movement, he looked up. The first of the Vals were coming down, diving on the oil tanks. His plane lurched, his pilot banking hard over now, turning to the north, fifteen seconds to swing around the reserve oil farm then turn out to the harbor and line up for the run in.

He tracked the movement of the Val, more were coming down, the first plane released, bombs dropping away, he pulled out, skimming low, behind him, seconds later, detonations. He half expected huge fireballs, the explosions seemed muffled . . . no this was bunker oil, it would not flash and explode, but it would still burn, several tanks rupturing from the bomb blasts. The second plane . . . an instant later it was nothing but a fiery comet, wings folding back, plummeting straight down into the oil field, its bombs detonating, the same fate for the third, wing sheering off, corkscrewing down, crashing into the edge of the harbor, exploding.

Looking across at the tank farms, Fuchida felt a wave of envy. Every liter of aviation gas, of fuel oil for the navy was doled out like a miser parting with his gold. Below was enough fuel to match the entire reserve of his Imperial Majesty's Fleet for a year. And he knew that for the Americans it was nothing; they had a thousand times more . . . but they would not have it here, where needed most, in a few more minutes. Still it

Aerial view of the Submarine Base, with part of the fuel farm in the foreground, looking southwest on 13 October 1941. Note the artfully camouflaged fuel tank in center, painted to resemble a building. Also camouflaged as a building is the most distant fuel tank in the upper left. The building beside the submarine ascent tower (in right center, shaped like a backward "C") housed the U.S. Fleet Headquarters at the time of the Japanese attack on 7 December 1941. Alongside the wharf in right center are USS Niagara *(PG-52) with several PT boats alongside (nearest to camera), and USS* Holland *(AS-3) with seven submarines alongside. About six more submarines are at the piers at the head of the Submarine Base peninsula. USS* Wharton *(AP-7) is the large ship at left.* **Naval Historical Center**

seemed such a horrid waste.

Another sharp banking turn then the startling rattle of the 7.7-millimeter gun behind him, his tail gunner shouting, opening up. He spared a quick glance aft, a P-40 was swinging in behind him. The seven planes of his flight, as briefed, were turning in a tighter arc. He would lead them to the final turn for the run-in to target but would then swing wide, to come in last, saving his torpedo if the others failed. The third plane in line simply blew apart, a P-40 nearly colliding with the wreckage as it shot through the formation, pursued by one of his escorting Zeroes. Damn all! The fighter should have hit first!

"He's on us!"

Tracers flicked past the portside wing, his pilot ruddering to starboard, skidding, dodging, long continual burst from the tail gunner. Fuchida looked aft, the view frightful. The P-40 was not more than fifty yards back, guns winking, his pilot skidding again, trying to throw off aim.

A stream of tracers converged, he felt a shudder, saw part of the vertical stabilizer buckle and sheer off, another shuddering thump, his tail gunner grunting, gun now swinging wide as the boy doubled over in pain.

Damn . . . to die like this . . .

A hoselike stream of tracers tore into the tail of the P-40, shells detonating, splitting the plane in half, forward half with the doomed pilot, visible for a brief instant, tumbling over, smashing into the ground, tail section spiraling up, then twisting over in flames to go down.

One of the Zeroes? He followed the smoking trail of tracers back. It was from the cruiser out in the harbor, now just a half mile away. Damn, saved by the panicked firing of the enemy.

But now that garden hoselike stream of tracers was swinging toward him.

The surviving six planes of his section had completed their banking turn around the oil farm, dropped down to just above the harbor in formation line astern, and were closing on the dock's massive gate. He and Genda had debated if they could indeed shatter it. The largest dry dock in the Pacific Ocean between San Francisco and Tokyo.

As the six planes ahead of him closed in, it seemed as if every gunner in that harbor knew what they were aiming for, and in an instant every gun was turned on the six Kates, geysers of water foaming a hundred feet up as an eight-inch shell fired to hit the middle of the harbor blew, the fountain of water catching the lead Kate, spinning it onto its back, plane plunging in, torpedo exploding, explosion taking out the second plane in the attack.

Fuchida spared a quick glance aft as they turned across the north end of the harbor, just east of Pearl City, his pilot working hard, he could feel the imbalance, from the hits to the rudder and elevators, an unsteady vibration bucking the plane. Now he knew why that cruiser was up here, to lay down fire and it was all aimed at him as they dodged and weaved.

He saw the third plane of his strike team disappear into the smoke, water tumbling down from the heavens, hundreds of shells and bullets crisscrossing the harbor every second.

They'd have to go in.

He slapped his pilot, Matsuo, on the shoulder, pointing directly forward, there was a nod of understanding, down lower. They lined up and started their run in. Without warning there was a sharp flash of light and then, a second later, a concussive blast that he thought for an instant would slam them down into the harbor, his pilot barely recovering. He ignored the erupting flash of light to left and concentrated on what was ahead.

■ ■ ■ ■

"Jesus Christ!"

James was on the ground, he needed no urging this time, Collingwood at his side, both of them hugging the earth as machine gun bullets danced across the lawn, tossing up tufts of grass, a shell, a large one blowing against the guard hut, where only hours before he had helped the drunk sailors, the hut disappearing. Shells were screaming overhead, bullets zinging past, a high-pitched howl of a racing engine, he glanced up and saw just that, a plane engine, no plane behind it, just the engine, propeller still spinning madly, tumbling from the sky, tumbling end over end into the oil tank farm.

Fires were igniting there. The bastards had indeed figured out it was worth the effort. So far half a dozen dive bombers had made their runs on it, three of them getting nailed, the other three dropping squarely on target, a dozen or more tanks were already burst open, rich black oil cascading out, some fires beginning to ignite and then a huge fireball, whether from a bomb, crashing plane, or the insanity of antiaircraft fire hit an aviation gas storage tank. A hundred thousand gallons of hundred-octane fuel blowing. The expanding fireball soared heavenward, expanding out, he could feel the heat, the same as when the *Arizona* blew, raised his hand for a moment to shield his eyes from it, as if looking into the morning sun. Streamers of fire poured down from the skies, now setting flame to the hundreds of thousands of barrels of oil spilling out of ruptured tanks. The tank farm to the north was burning as well.

"Another!" Collingwood shouted.

James looked back to where his friend was pointing. The fourth Kate had emerged out of the wall of water kicked up by the exploding eight-inch shells, torpedo dropping away, and barely an instant later it was into the harbor, bouncing back up, cartwheeling end over end and exploding.

He could hear guttural cheers from those around him. It was but one plane, but somehow it seemed like payback, an ironic payback since the attacking Kates were not more than a hundred yards out from the *Arizona,* still burning fiercely.

"They're going for number one dry dock!" James cried.

Admiral Kimmel stood by the window, silent, unmoving, watching as the fourth

Kate tumbled end over end in a fireball explosion.

"Burn, you bastard."

It was his chief who had remained silent till now.

Kimmel looked over at him. The chief was holding a flask and motioned toward it. Kimmel nodded, unscrewed the cap, admiring the handwork of the silver flask, USN insignia on one side, Marine on the other, he took a long sip, handed it back.

He did not even hear the brace of two 250-kilo bombs plummeting down, crashing through the roof of the headquarters of CinCPac, "Commander in Chief, Pacific," the first bomb detonating as it struck a steel support beam between the second and third floors, the second one crashing through floor after floor, clear down to the basement, striking but a few feet from where Commander James Watson's now empty desk rested, hitting the concrete floor, plunger striking detonator, both bombs igniting less than a second apart, the first lifting the roof off the building, the second, explosive force contained by the basement blowing upward and out, bursting the frame walls, the entire building seeming to lift and then collapse in on itself, with more than a hundred men and women, who had stayed at their posts, dead, including Kimmel and his chief who was just about to take a drink himself when the two bombs hit, a hundred more, most of them fatally injured, staggering, crawling out of the flaming wreckage.

James gave a sidelong glance toward the collapsing headquarters building, Collingwood catching his gaze, both sharing that glance that only survivors of disaster could ever understand, that they had, by the grace of God, made the right choice together, otherwise they would now both be dead.

Bombs were falling around them now, striking into repair shops, down at the harbor's edge four submarines, incredibly, still tied off together burst asunder from three hits by hundred-kilo general-purpose demolition bombs, no need for armor piercing on their thin skins. One sub, trying to back out into the harbor to make good its escape, was bracketed by two more bombs, rocking it like a toy boat in a child's tub, the Val that had dropped them trailing black smoke, pulling up slightly then adding itself to the spread conflagration of the oil farm. The sub quickly listed to port, men pouring up from hatchways and bridge, billowing black smoke engulfing them and then something lit off, the submarine exploding, splitting asunder and settling to the harbor floor.

Too much was happening all at once to possibly take in. An explosion. James caught a glimpse of it, flash memory of the torpedoes slamming into his beloved *Oklahoma.* It was the dry-dock gate, column of water soaring several hundred feet heavenward. Another Kate raced past, dropped, then jinking madly, banked over sharply and skimmed directly over the turtled hull of *Oklahoma,* disappearing into the smoke boiling out of the burning battleships. Yet another Kate, but this one disintegrated before dropping, a hundred machine guns from all around the harbor shredding it, the tens of thousands of rounds that missed screaming overhead, kicking up turf, hitting sailors, marines, civilians scrambling to get away, some rounds arcing so high that half a minute later they'd crash into a window of a building, a car, or kill someone standing on a street corner in downtown Honolulu . . . a death of course to be blamed on the ruthless Japs, strafing innocent bystanders.

"She's holding," Collingwood shouted.

James said nothing. Somehow this moment of the fight seemed to focus everything. He had enough of a sense of the battle this day to know that the first two strikes, though a shock unlike any suffered by this nation since Shiloh or Gettysburg, had not been a killing blow. The carriers were at sea, the vast reserves of the Atlantic Fleet would soon be steaming to the Pacific, the ships lost, even those he loved, were as obsolete as the Buffalo and P-36 fighters matched against Zeroes.

But now they were going for the jugular. The burning oil farm, four and a half million barrels, enough oil there to fuel the entire Pacific Fleet, ships and planes, be they Japanese or American, for a year or more. Without the largest dry dock, any serious repairs below the waterline, for battleship or carrier, impossible. They were back, and this time, if successful, they could very well knock Pearl Harbor out of the war for months, perhaps a year or more to come.

The torpedo dropped by the second surviving Kate struck, another column of water, this one by the east end hinge of the dock, column of water subsiding, antlike figures scrambling along the dockside . . . still it held.

"Another!"

Collingwood pointed as yet another Kate, this one marked with stripes on its tail, the upper half of the vertical stabilizer shot away, raced past them. Obviously some sort of command plane, oblivious to the firestorm that now focused on it. Whoever was in that plane, he hated the bastard, and yet he could not help but feel some admiration as well . . . the son of a bitch, if he survived the next few seconds . . . would decide it.

"Steady . . . steady!" Fuchida shouted the command, looking over the shoulder of his pilot. Another spray of shot hit them, stitching across the canopy, glass shattering, plane lurching to port. He had kept his right hand lightly on the stick, ready to take over, feet barely touched the rudder pedals, left hand on throttle. His pilot was hit, he could feel it, stick swinging to port, he braced it hard, steadied it.

"I'm fine. I can do it!" The pilot's voice gasped through the speaking tube that connected them.

It was nearly impossible to see, tracers flicking past the forward windscreen, another blow, where on the plane he couldn't tell. Water foaming up, shots fired low to blind them, to knock them over as they skimmed in at thirty feet, now throttled back to 120 knots for release in the shallow harbor.

"Steady . . . steady!"

Fuchida caught a glimpse of a wingtip,

red rising sun on it, sticking out of the water, aviation gas burning on the surface. Another explosion, huge, geyser to starboard. He turned for a second . . . a ship burning. *Arizona*? Hard to tell with the smoke. Another ship, red hull inverted, glimpse of men standing atop the overturned ship, some with guns, shooting.

"Steady!"

Now he saw it. Column of water from who, Tomida or Usaka, dropping? He thought he saw Usaka banking away. Hoped so. A friend, comrade from China.

"Steady!"

He was within range. Drop now. No. Risk it, a few more seconds. He pushed in a little left rudder, a touch of aileron, righten, line up at the centerline of the gate, hit it there.

"Steady . . ."

Another thump, more thumps. Smoke, us or a shell burst? Blinding for an instant. Shoot through it. Yes! Now!

"Launch!"

Fuchida pulled the manual release at the same instant letting go of the stick long enough to strike the electrical release button. He felt the plane instantly surge up as the one-ton mass of the torpedo dropped away.

His pilot was hurt, badly hurt, no reaction.

Keep it down low, the loss of the one-ton torpedo had lifted them higher, straight into the overarcing storm of antiaircraft fire. He took over, pushing his stick down, for an instant fearing he had overreacted and would hit the water, leveling out, propwash churning the harbor surface. Dodging now, gaining a few feet in order to bank to starboard, then weave back to port. Don't go over Ford or Hickam, race straight for the channel opening and out to sea.

Ahead he saw a ship, back broken, destroyer . . . light cruiser? It was sinking in midchannel, settling to the bottom. Flash of tracers coming from overhead, hitting the water ahead. Glimpse of a wing, looking up, American . . . trailing smoke, caught in the maelstrom of fire from every direction, breaking away. He aimed straight at the sinking ship, skimming over its deck, already awash, turned, felt another hard thump, blow on the port wing, heart-stopping moment, stream of fuel venting . . . but no fire. He headed for the open sea beyond.

"Oh God, oh God, no," James cried.

The last torpedo, he could see its wake, streaked unerringly toward the dry-dock gate. Another hammer blow, the third one now. Another column of water rising up, wreathed in smoke and flame, and even before it began to settle he could see the surface of the harbor swirling and then become a tidal cascade, a wall of water thirty feet high bursting into the dry dock as the great gate buckled and gave way. Horrifying, a launch busy plucking men out of the harbor was caught, upended and swept in, wooden hull splintering, millions of tons of water flooding over the shattered hulk of the old battleship *Pennsylvania,* which had been inside the dry dock for overhaul and shattered in the first two attacks. Now its broken mass shifted and pivoted as the wall of water poured in, the wreckage of the broken ship upending. The surge of water reached the far wall of the thousand-foot-long dock, a tsunamilike wave splashing up over the far end, sucking some men into its swirling mass, then recoiling back, the flood now racing back in the opposite direction, the force of the surge tearing one of the dry-dock doors completely free of its hinges, sending it to the bottom of the harbor.

There was nothing he could do now but just stand there and watch. Already the attack was subsiding, though the antiaircraft was still nearly as intense, gunners firing blindly into the smoke engulfing the harbor, now killing far more of their comrades than enemies. Explosions were igniting from Pearl City, across Honolulu, and as far north as Schofield as antiaircraft shells rained down.

In spite of the continuing fusillade he stood back up and looked over at Collingwood. The oil tank farms were ablaze now, a conflagration with a plume of smoke that already was soaring ten thousand feet to the heavens, surely a beacon that could be seen from a hundred miles away. A dozen more

Battleships West Virginia *(BB-48) (sunken at left) and* Tennessee *(BB-43) shrouded in smoke following the Japanese air raid. Courtesy of the U.S. Naval Institute Photograph Collection.* **Naval Historical Center**

ships were burning or sunk, several of them out in the main channel, one looked to be a heavy cruiser, down at the bow, propellers sticking out of the water, amazingly still turning. The submarine pen was a shambles, they had hammered that good, three of the four boats that had been tied off were either blown apart or settling to the bottom, a fifth boat sunk out in the harbor, bridge sticking out of the water, men clinging to it. Repair yards were a sea of flames, his own building gone, collapsed in on itself, burning fiercely.

Collingwood was as silent as he.

"I'm going home," James said quietly.

"What?"

"Margaret. She'll be frantic with worry. I'm going home."

"James?"

"What in hell am I supposed to do?" James snapped, and he held up the twisted claw of what had once been his hand, the steel "hook" covered with dried blood. "Did anybody listen to us, goddamn it? So what the hell are we to do now?"

Collingwood could not reply.

"I'm going home. I'll be back tonight, if there is anything to come back to," he said again, and without waiting for a reply he turned and walked away.

He walked past the flaming ruins of headquarters, pushing around a fire crew that stood impotent, cursing, hoses hooked up to a hydrant but there was no water pressure. In the parking lot a dozen or more cars were wrecks, several burning, one with what looked like an airplane propeller speared through its roof. His own car, '39 Plymouth, untouched except for a neat hole through the passenger side windshield, drilled by a spent bullet, rest of the window cracked.

It felt almost surreal fishing the keys out of his pocket with his good hand, sliding them in, hitting the starter with his foot, engine turning over.

He backed out of his slot, weaved around the side of an abandoned car, blackened, still smoking, he gave it a sidelong glance fearful of what he might see inside, and then wished he hadn't looked.

He hit the gas, heading for the gate. There was a guard, but he was checking the line of cars that amazingly, were still trying to get into this madhouse and pulling out, he had, for the first few blocks, an open road ahead. A concussion blow, distant. He looked in his rearview mirror, saw a ship, anchored, bursting asunder, magazine most likely touching off.

Honolulu. Chaos. Several blocks in flames,

partially collapsed apartment, dozen or more bodies out front, covered in blood-soaked sheets, pulled over several times to let ambulances pass, a convoy of half a dozen army trucks, a crazed civilian with a shotgun, pointing it straight up, just firing at nothing, a cop suddenly stepped out of nowhere, motioning for him to stop, an instinct telling him that they were commandeering cars, or he'd have to put up with some damn stupid interrogation, he floored it and weaved around him. Then the sight of several dozen civilians, all of them Japanese, hands resting on the tops of their heads, standing in front of a police station, a lone cop with a shotgun watching them.

He looked away, hit the gas, kept on going, heading up into the pass over the mountains via the Pali highway. The air was a bit cooler, clean, afternoon clouds breaking over the top of the pass, it'd rain in another hour or so. He cleared the pass, weaving through the tunnel, coming out the other side, plumes of smoke rising on the trade winds from fires at Kaneohe Naval Air Station. He weaved down the mountain, shifting gears, damn the stump really hurt now, he spared a glance, fresh blood oozing through the rough bandage.

Coming into Kailua people were out in

the streets, a few buildings burning. From a turn in the road he caught a glimpse of the small army air base at Bellows, smoke from there, another fire up on the slope, most likely a plane down. And then, amazingly, puffs of smoke out to sea, more tracers arcing out from shore, a glimpse of a Jap plane, my God, was it the one with the yellow tail? It was limping north, a mile or so out from the coast, skimming the waves.

North. No one, absolutely no one prior to this third attack had figured out where the Jap carriers were located. Well, that answer was obvious now and for a few seconds he thought of pulling over, finding a phone, calling it in. Call who? He drove on.

He watched the plane disappear. If you lived through that, you bastard, you are one lucky son of a bitch . . . till next time.

And as he turned the corner, there in the street he saw Margaret. Somehow that instinct of hers, or maybe her "secret telescope," had told her, she was running toward him. He pulled over to the curb below their house and frantically she was tearing at the door, opening it, sobbing, pulling him out of the car, hugging him fiercely.

He was afraid to put his injured arm around her, she was wearing her favorite

Sunday dress, ivory colored, close fitting.

"Oh, my God, James!" and she drew back, sensing his pain, gently touching his arm.

"I'm all right. All right."

And she was in his arms again, oblivious to the blood soaking her.

He looked up toward the lanai of his house, his beloved mother-in-law carefully coming down the steps, leaning on her cane, face filled with relief.

She was, of course . . . Japanese . . . and as she came to his side to embrace him, he did not know what to say.

4:45 p.m. Local Time

He struggled to line up onto the glide slope. Their carriers had the most advanced landing system in the world, angled lights that when you were aligned center, at the right glide slope, you'd see the green shaded lights to either side of the center line of the deck. It worked fairly well, except in rough seas with deck pitching.

It was rough seas, the deck was indeed pitching, and he was bringing in a dead plane. He knew his tail gunner was dead, the stench was present, the boy's body having voided its contents after long minutes of a painful death rattle. He suspected his pilot was dead as well, slumped to one side of the cockpit, right foot jammed against the rudder pedal, making it all but impossible to counter the dead weight as he struggled to fly the plane from the midseat position. Instruments were impossible to see from where he sat, no way to adjust anything other than throttle, stick, and rudder. He had almost crashed when after clearing the island, he struggled up for altitude, unbuckled, and leaned over Matsuo, who was unconscious and managed to flip over the fuel tank lever, but every liter in the port wing was long gone. All the tanks were dry now. Engine was sputtering in and out, something hit in there as well . . . it wasn't as bad as back in China when he was blinded by oil, but then again, he wasn't trying to bring a crippled plane in onto a rolling deck at sea.

Nose down, trying to keep up air speed, he leaned to one side, canopy open, horrified to see that the Zero that had cut into the pattern in front of him had pancaked, wheels up, skewing sideways, and burst into flames. The deck was not clear!

The aft-deck fire crew was spraying the wreckage down with foam, deck crew trying to close in, to push the wreckage aside, a couple of men in white asbestos suits clawing at the canopy, pulling the pilot out of the flame-engulfed cockpit.

He was lined up, quarter mile out. Ditch? No. Might still save this plane. If Matsuo is still alive, and they ditch, he'll drown.

Try to angle to the starboard side a few more feet. More right rudder, left stick, crab in. Engine sputtered again, seized, propeller stopped. He couldn't reach the control to feather them, they were now drag, the Kate started to fall like a rock.

Damn!

Straighten out. Edge of the landing deck coming up. He could see men scrambling, jumping away, fire crew dropping hoses, running.

The Kate slammed in barely a dozen feet forward of the aft end of the landing deck. There was no way for him to know that the support struts for the left wheel had been shot away, and it sheered off under the blow of the hard landing, the Kate collapsed onto its portside wing which snapped at the wing root into the fuselage, plane pivoting, wooden deck splintering, his vision blurred by the impact. Barely enough time to try and brace as the Kate skidded into the wreckage of the burning Zero, the impact spraying gas from the rupture tanks of the fighter, coating the Kate in flames.

Panic. He saw the fire splashing in through the shattered canopy, Matsuo now coated in fire. Frantically he tried to slap the flames down with his gloved hands.

Blindness . . . white foam spraying in. Smashing glass, someone up by his side with a crowbar, prying the canopy back. He started to choke on the smoke and foam. Hands reaching in, unbuckling his harness.

"Matsuo first!" he gasped, trying to grab the shoulders of his pilot, but his rescuer ignored his pleas, pulling him bodily out of the plane, a blanket, asbestos, thrown over him, blocking the heat as he was dragged clear.

He stumbled trying to regain footing, cursing, unsure for a second where he was, disoriented. My plane, my crew!

"Fuchida!"

He felt arms around his shoulders, blanket falling away, as if returning to the world again. It was Genda.

Genda was holding him by the shoulders, tears streaming down his face.

"You're alive!" and he unashamedly grasped him in a bear hug.

"Of course I'm alive," Fuchida gasped, startled as Genda actually began to visibly shake, sobbing.

Even as they spoke the fire crew were

pushing the two back and away from the fire on the deck, a blizzard of foam washing over the wreckage of the two planes. Fuchida looked back. They were pulling the bodies out of what was left of his Kate. Matsuo and the boy. They were both dead.

He looked aft, the sky was empty, no one else in the pattern even as a small tractor pushed up against the side of his Kate and edged it over the port side, trailing torn fabric, aluminum, a bent propeller digging into the wooden deck, tearing a furrow. The wreckage upended and went over the side.

Somehow, the sight of that horrified him. It had been his plane, a damn good plane. It had carried him back to safety. He felt as if he had betrayed it somehow, that a prayer should be said as she floated for a moment, inverted, and then disappeared beneath the wake of *Akagi.*

He looked forward. Where were the rest of the planes, and it was as if Genda sensed his question.

"For *Akagi,* only you and one other Kate returned. Four Zeroes, six Vals, ten Kates, now counting yours, eleven out of twelve gone."

That was nearly half the strike force launched from here little more than two and a half hours ago.

"Oh god," Fuchida sighed.

"Later," Genda said. "He's waiting for you."

Genda helped him as they skirted around the smoldering wreckage of the Zero, which was now receiving the same treatment as his Kate, bulldozed over the side. Her pilot . . . he didn't look. The man was dying, terribly burned, unable even to scream his lungs so badly seared by the fire, several of the deck crew kneeling by his side as a corpsman held him. He wanted to go over, fearful to find out who it was, unable to recognize him; but Genda, clutching him tightly, steered him toward the bridge.

By the doorway he was waiting, Yamamoto, breaking with protocol, coming to meet his returning samurai, rather than waiting for him to approach.

Fuchida could not reply when, to his amazement, Yamamoto stepped forward and embraced him, tears in his eyes, the sight of it causing the strain of the last few days, the last ten hours, the terrifying seconds before release to finally take hold at last. Fuchida lowered his head, ashamed of his own tears, the sob that wracked his body.

"My son, we thought you were dead," Yamamoto gasped.

Fuchida could not reply.

"You are the last plane in," and then the admiral, aware of all who were watching the role he must play, braced himself, chuckled softly in spite of his tears of emotion, "you keep coming in last, making us worry, we have to talk about that."

"I'm sorry to have caused you concern," Fuchida said, and realized his words were somehow hollow, wooden.

"It was reported you disappeared after destroying their dry dock. I hoped against hope . . ." and his voice trailed off for a moment.

"We did it?" Fuchida asked.

"You didn't know?" Genda interjected.

He could only shake his head.

"Three torpedoes hit. Yours was the last, it shattered the gate. We're sending a scout plane over now to photograph the results."

He thought of that firestorm of gunnery, he pitied the pilot who had to face that just for a damn photograph.

"It is reported the oil farms are totally destroyed," Genda continued. "At least three more ships sunk while trying to flee, one of them in midchannel, a dozen more damaged or destroyed along with numerous buildings, including their headquarters. Six or more of their submarines destroyed."

He tried to take it in. He remembered the oil tanks burning.

"Rest now," Yamamoto said, and he stepped back from the entry to the bridge, gesturing for Fuchida to be led below.

"How many?" Fuchida asked.

"What?"

"How many lost?"

There was a momentary pause.

"A price to be paid," Yamamoto said, and now his voice was cold, distant.

"How many, sir?"

"A third of the strike force has not returned. Thirty-one planes lost, including seven like yours that crashed on landing. Another third damaged."

"By the gods," Fuchida whispered.

"Victory is never cheap," Yamamoto replied, and now his voice was sharp, clear, emotion gone, so that those around them, listening, would hear every word and let it spread.

"I'd have sacrificed this carrier, two carriers this day to inflict the damage we have achieved. Achieved thanks to your leadership and the bravery of our pilots and crews."

Fuchida could not reply. Of himself, he did not care. But he thought of the curled-up body of the dying fighter pilot, not a hundred feet away, of the Kates that went in ahead of him and disappeared, and even of the insane bravery of the lone American pilot who in a futile gesture had come up to meet their attack.

"Their carriers?" Fuchida asked.

Yamamoto smiled.

Fuchida could feel the wind shifting and looking past the admiral he saw that the *Akagi* was beginning to turn, to come about now that the last of her surviving planes had been recovered. Out across the white-capped seas, destroyers, cruisers, the other carriers were beginning to turn as well.

"Rest tonight, Commander. We're moving west to rendezvous with our oilers before dawn. Then south. Our two battleships with their escorts will detach come dark, race due south, and by midnight will begin to bombard what is left of Pearl Harbor."

He took that in. It was a plan never discussed. The battleships had been assigned to the task force by surprise, when Yamamoto had taken direct command, with the claim they were support in case the American battleships escaped the air attack and attempted to close.

"With that bombardment the American carriers, wherever they are hidden, must come out, they cannot lurk in cowardice.

605

And when they do, we will be southwest of Oahu, ready to strike them."

He could not reply.

Yamamoto looked into his eyes and again there was a momentary softening.

"I am thankful you are alive, my son," he said, and then there was a sharpness to his voice. "I'll have need of you tomorrow."

His friend led him below to his bunk and helped him to remove his flight suit and like a loving brother, left for a moment and returned with a small tray, upon which were several rice balls, some strips of tuna and a cup of saki. He had no stomach for the food, but drained the saki in two gulps and it went straight to his head, so that he did not protest when Genda helped him to crawl into his bunk and switched off the light.

But sleep would not come. In the darkness he stared at the ceiling . . . remembering . . . wondering . . . what would tomorrow, 9 December 1941, bring.

Admiral Yamamoto looked up as Genda stepped into the small conference room.

"How is our hero?"

"The saki knocked him out, he'll sleep," Genda replied.

"Good, he was pushed to the edge today."

"He did his duty for the Emperor, as expected of all of us," Genda replied, and then could not resist, "as you did as well, sir."

Genda looked over at his commander and never had he felt such love for a man, but Yamamoto looked far from pleased, brows furrowed, head lowered, and finally he spoke, not to anyone in particular, but just in general to the staff gathered around him.

"We have achieved much, but I also fear we have achieved the wrong thing," he finally said, and his comments stilled the room. No one dared to reply as to what he meant.

"How so, sir?" Genda asked.

Yamamoto was silent for a moment. "The report of our young hero Fuchida on the surface reads as a victory," he was silent again, "but it might be a report of a tragedy."

Genda and Kusaka were silent, saying nothing.

"If you have misgivings," Genda interjected, almost fearful now of what he was saying, "withdraw and our victory is complete. The third strike did fearsome damage."

Yamamoto shook his head.

"Long before this attack took final form, I had insisted upon one key element, which would not be the responsibility of our navy, but instead, the government and foreign minister.

"You know how many years I spent in America, the close friends I have there, my admiration for so much of what they are, who they are, what they can achieve. They have a different sense of war than we do. We see war as a continuum. Peace can change to war, and from war back into peace without moral qualms, if by so doing the position of one is assured, and yes, the position of the other is not pushed beyond a certain breaking point where they would then choose death rather than dishonor. In our own history we are replete with stories of warlords who contended, fought with honor, but did not push too far, so that in the end peace could again be achieved and perhaps even a day of alliance.

"Americans see war differently. They see it as an aberration, a disruption of the norm. But if forced to war, it must always for them be a moral war, a moral crusade. Though any sensible man knew the absurdity of it, their war with Spain was whipped up with false reports of Spanish atrocities. They entered the last war with the idealism that it would end war. Even the detestable Washington Treaty was dreamed up by them as a means of preventing war."

He sighed again. "Months ago, when I appeared before the Emperor to discuss the plans for action, I had been assured, the Emperor had been assured by our Foreign Office, that the Americans would be informed, at least one hour prior to the attack that negotiations would cease and all diplomatic efforts broken off, as near as possible to an open declaration of war.

"I was assured that this would be done in the clearest most unambiguous of terms, making it clear, prior to the start of hostilities, that a state of war would therefore exist. From that, I then felt assured that a warning would immediately be sent from Washington to all bases."

Genda could not help but shake his head.

"What? To give our enemy time to prepare to receive us. It would have doubled, perhaps tripled our losses."

"Why is this a concern now?" Kusaka asked, his hostility of earlier dropping away, so troubled was the admiral's features, the sound of his voice.

"If you knew America as I did," Yamamoto replied softly, "yes, you would understand.

"I have always believed in the old code of the samurai. That if sent to kill a man and he is asleep, the only honorable action to take is to awaken him first, to let him dress to face death and take up his blade and step outside where family will not witness the fight. To kill without warning is the act of a ninja, an assassin, a coward, not of an honorable man. I fear that is now how America will see this day, and the result will be a whirlwind of rage.

"We have perhaps focused too much on the plan of the strike itself rather than the intent of the mission of this strike. May I ask of you, what was the mission this day?"

And he looked at Genda.

"To render inoperative the American Fleet in the Pacific."

Yamamoto nodded in reply.

"I fear that a most significant part of the plan, to at least give to the Americans a warning by the rules that they observe to apply to war, has failed. I had hoped that in a fair and honorable fight, we would best the Americans.

"Instead, yes, we have sunk their battleships, which according to the theories of some of our own doctrines are obsolete anyhow, and their carriers are still at sea. But far worse, far, far worse, we have enraged them."

"War brings about rage," Kusaka interjected. "It is the essence of war and helpful when directed."

"You have not lived there," Yamamoto snapped. "I have."

"This American sense of fair play seems ludicrous at times. But there is a core of honor to it. From what Commander Fuchida said, it is obvious no warning was delivered prior to our attack, otherwise, at least on the ground, their defenses in response to the first wave would have been as intense as this last attack.

"To Americans that is, as they say, 'a cheap shot,' a sneak attack. To them despicable. If anything it will serve only to arouse them to a fighting fury. They will not see that this is a limited war, as we do, to settle the balance of power in the Western Pacific, but instead as a war now of revenge, and they will unleash their full fury upon us. It is what I had feared; it is what I had hoped would never happen. But it has now happened and we must face that reality."

Genda was silent for a moment then finally ventured to speak.

"Sir, you say our attack has enraged the Americans and now they will fight it as total war. Then I must ask, why venture to stay in these waters?" To his own surprise he found himself looking over at Kusaka.

"Perhaps we should withdraw after all."

Yamamoto shook his head violently.

"No, you do not see it as I do," he replied sharply, almost angrily. "Now we must fight all the harder, with all the more fury at the start. The primary target is no longer Pearl Harbor," Yamamoto snapped, "though the targets to be hit are worthy."

He looked over at Genda.

"By hitting again, and in so doing, threaten to hit again tomorrow morning, we will sow fear. They will assume we will invade as a followup. Their carriers will be forced to stand by, hoping to jump us. The carriers are now my immediate operational goal beyond the destruction we can still rain down on Pearl Harbor.

"Their carriers are somewhere at sea. I am willing to bet all that they are nearby. Perhaps not a hundred miles south or west of Pearl Harbor on maneuvers, perhaps toward Midway or Wake Island, maneuvering there or delivering additional aircraft. I plan to seek them out tomorrow . . . and I plan to destroy them. I plan to take this war to the Americans with a ferocity they have yet to imagine. That is why I ordered the tankers to stay close to us instead of sailing off to a northeastern rendezvous point as the original plan provided. I wanted the flexibility to respond to reality, and I did not want to be trapped by assumptions that might fail."

"But our plan to strike, then fall back, to lure them into the Marshalls, to form a defensive barrier to weaken them till they seek a peace?"

Yamamoto shook his head forcefully.

"I fear that our plan for a negotiated peace once we had destroyed their fleet is no longer possible. Beneath our brave Commander Fuchida's report there is a message concealed. The Foreign Ministry has failed to deliver what was promised."

He sighed and looked off.

"I know America. There will be no negotiations as there were with the Russians in our last war. This will now be bitter and a fight to the death, until they realize the futility of a fight against us.

"That leaves me with but one option. To so thoroughly cripple their fleet, to so completely destroy their carriers, their docks, their ships at Pearl, that it will not be six months, but a year, two years before they can even hope to respond.

"If need be we must now take this war clear to their West Coast to sow panic, and in that panic irresolve. We must sweep the ocean clean of their shipping. Let Hawaii be the bait now. Cripple it beyond repair but do not take it. Force them to try and keep the shipping lanes open and now their navy will be stretched on two fronts, here and in the Atlantic.

"I believe some thought that after this, after what too many considered to be a raid merely to cripple, we could run riot for six months and seize what we need, dig in, then let the Americans come and defeat them till they grow weary. I can tell you. They will not grow weary. They will be filled with a terrible resolve and that will be to prosecute this war until Japan is destroyed.

"Our only chance now? We must carry the war, instead, to them. That is our only hope."

He fell silent, eyes again closed as if looking off to some distant, dark land.

"Commander Genda, we shall find their carriers and sink them.

"And this time, when we do sink them, they will not merely settle into the mud of the harbor to be restored, their trained crews taken off to be used on other ships. No, we must sink them in a thousand fathoms of water, all hands aboard, and thus destroy every carrier in the Pacific before the year is finished.

"It will be a different war now, a more terrible one," Yamamoto said, his features fixed, cool, as if another hand of poker had just been drawn.

Two Hundred Fifty Miles West of Pearl Harbor
The Enterprise
5:00 p.m. Local Time

Admiral William "Bull" Halsey crumpled the note that had just been handed to him by his signal officer.

The news was horrifying. Every battleship, sunk or seriously damaged by two waves of Jap attackers. Thousands feared dead, the once proud fleet a shambles, oil tank farms, dry dock, repair facilities, and more ships destroyed in a third strike. And damn all, still no one thought to track which direction they had departed to after the strike was over. For all he knew the Japs were fifty miles away, or five hundred miles away. He had been running his scout squadron ragged all day looking for something, anything.

He stood up, walked out onto the flying bridge and looked down as a Grumman Wildcat prepared to lift off, to maintain patrol over the fleet.

Where were the damn Japs? Not a single fool back on Oahu had bothered to take the time to just watch for a few minutes, to see which way the Japs had departed, where did

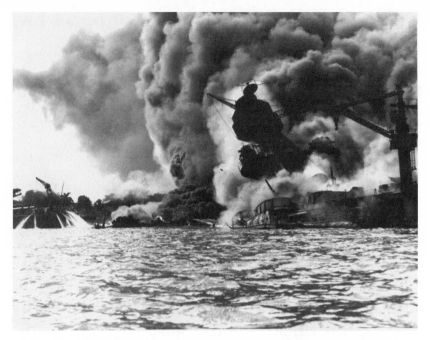

USS Arizona *(BB-39) sunk and burning furiously, 7 December 1941. Her forward magazines had exploded when she was hit by a Japanese bomb. At left, men on the stern of USS* Tennessee *(BB-43) are playing fire hoses on the water to force burning oil away from their ship.* **Naval Historical Center**

they rendezvous after the strike, did they run north, west, east, south? They could be anywhere within two hundred miles of Oahu in any direction . . . more than one hundred thousand square miles of ocean to hide in . . . but by God he would find the bastards.

Turning, he looked back at his staff.

"By the time we are done with them," he

snarled, "Japanese will only be spoken in hell. Now let's go find their carriers."

FREEDOM ALLIANCE

SCHOLARSHIP FUND — *Supporting the Children of America's Military Heroes*

The Freedom Alliance Scholarship Fund honors the bravery and dedication of Americans in our armed forces who have sacrificed life or limb by providing college scholarships to their children. Through the generosity of the American public, the Scholarship Fund has awarded more than $1 million to the sons and daughters of American heroes.

Many of freedom's brave defenders, who have lost their lives fighting terrorism, have left behind young children. We believe it is our duty to help their children meet the rising costs of a college education, but more importantly to remind them that their parents' sacrifice will never be forgotten by a grateful nation.

SUPPORT OUR TROOPS — *Honoring America's Armed Forces*

The Freedom Alliance Support Our Troops program honors and supports our servicemen and women and their families — especially those that are serving on the front lines, or who have been wounded and are recuperating at our military hospitals.

Freedom Alliance provides financial assistance and gift packages to these troops. The program also includes events such as Military Appreciation Dinners and special holiday activities. Freedom Alliance sponsors these activities to say "thank you" to our service members and their families.

Freedom Alliance, which was founded in 1990 by Lieutenant Colonel Oliver North, USMC (Ret.), is a nonprofit 501(c)(3) charitable and educational organization dedicated to advancing the American heritage of freedom by honoring and encouraging military service, defending the sovereignty of the United States and promoting a strong national defense.

For more information or to donate, contact:
Freedom Alliance
22570 Markey Court, Suite 240
Dulles, Virginia 20166-6919
1(800) 475-6620
www.freedomalliance.org
"Lest We Forget"

The employees of Thorndike Press hope you have enjoyed this Large Print book. All our Thorndike and Wheeler Large Print titles are designed for easy reading, and all our books are made to last. Other Thorndike Press Large Print books are available at your library, through selected bookstores, or directly from us.

For information about titles, please call:
(800) 223-1244

or visit our Web site at:
www.gale.com/thorndike
www.gale.com/wheeler

To share your comments, please write:
Publisher
Thorndike Press
295 Kennedy Memorial Drive
Waterville, ME 04901